STORM OF IRON

'CULLAIN, DAEKIAN, DID either of you see that?'

'See what, princeps?' asked Cullain.

'I saw nothing through the smoke,' affirmed Daekian. 'What did you see?'

'I'm not sure, but for a second it looked like—'

The words died in his throat as the wind lifted the concealing smoke and Fierach saw a towering nightmare lurch from the traitor lines like a daemon from the warp. Its red and brass structure towered over him, its guns and towers horrifying in their size. The monstrous Titan stepped towards him and its blazing green eyes seemed to lock with his own, promising nothing but death. Fierach's heart pounded and the *Imperator Bellum* faltered in its stride, the mind impulse link attempting to match its princeps' reaction.

More Warhammer 40,000 from the Black Library

• GAUNT'S GHOSTS •

FIRST & ONLY by Dan Abnett
GHOSTMAKER by Dan Abnett
NECROPOLIS by Dan Abnett
HONOUR GUARD by Dan Abnett
THE GUNS OF TANITH by Dan Abnett

• THE EISENHORN TRILOGY •

XENOS by Dan Abnett
MALLEUS by Dan Abnett
HERETICUS by Dan Abnett

• SPACE WOLF •

SPACE WOLF by William King
RAGNAR'S CLAW by William King
GREY HUNTER by William King

• LAST CHANCERS •

13TH LEGION by Gav Thorpe
KILL TEAM by Gav Thorpe

• OTHER WARHAMMER 40,000 TITLES •

NIGHTBRINGER by Graham McNeill
EXECUTION HOUR by Gordon Rennie
PAWNS OF CHAOS by Brian Craig
EYE OF TERROR by Barrington J. Bayley

A WARHAMMER 40,000 NOVEL

STORM OF IRON

Graham McNeill

To all the Guardsman Hawkes out there and the idea of getting a second chance. Don't waste it.

A BLACK LIBRARY PUBLICATION

The Black Library,
An imprint of Games Workshop Ltd.,
Willow Road, Lenton,
Nottingham, NG7 2WS, UK

First US edition, August 2002

10 9 8 7 6 5 4 3 2 1

Distributed by Simon & Schuster
1230 Avenue of the Americas
New York, NY 10020

Cover illustration by Clint Langley
Map by Ralph Horsley

ISBN 0-7434-4316-0

Set in ITC Giovanni

Printed and bound in Great Britain by
Cox & Wyman Ltd, Cardiff Rd, Reading, Berkshire RG1 8EX, UK

See the Black Library on the Internet at
www.blacklibrary.co.uk

Find out more about Games Workshop
and the world of Warhammer 40,000 at
www.games-workshop.com

STORM OF IRON

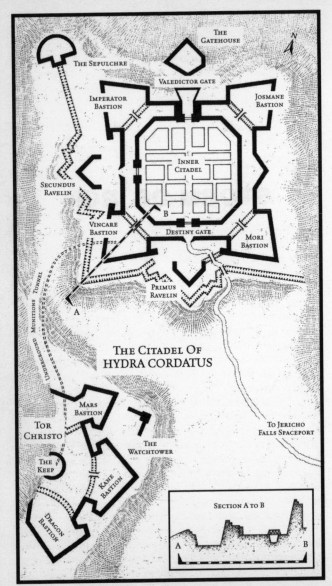

THE
GATEHOUSE

THE SEPULCHRE

VALEDICTOR GATE

IMPERATOR
BASTION

JOSMANE
BASTION

SECUNDUS
RAVELIN

INNER
CITADEL

B

VINCARE
BASTION

DESTINY GATE

MORI
BASTION

A

PRIMUS
RAVELIN

THE CITADEL OF
HYDRA CORDATUS

TO JERICHO
FALLS SPACEPORT

MARS
BASTION

TOR
CHRISTO

THE
WATCHTOWER

THE
KEEP

KANE
BASTION

DRAGON
BASTION

SECTION A TO B

A   B

Imperial cartography ref: GC43/b [Index Expurgatoris]

PROLOGUE

THE ELECTRO-CANDLES in the astropaths' chamber were kept dim, though its occupants neither cared nor were aware of their surroundings, their eyes long since burned from their sockets. The aroma of sacred incense filled the chamber, the quiet hum of machinery and the scratching of a score of tonsured quill-servitors the only sounds.

The servitors sat facing each other in two rows, hunched over gnarled lecterns, their ink-stained fingers darting across parchments as information poured into what remained of their minds and out through their calloused hands. Behind each servitor stood an angled, brass capsule, sparkling like a gleaming coffin. Golden wires trailed from each one's frosted surface and ribbed cabling snaked from their sides, running in long lines along the chamber's edge.

A hunched figure, swathed in the red robes of the Adeptus Mechanicus with gold lettering stitched along the hem made his way slowly along the stone-flagged nave towards the chamber's end, pausing every now and then to peruse the elegant scriptwork of a servitor. Shadows hid the adept's face, the telltale gleam of bronze all that was visible beneath his thick hood. He stopped beside the furthest servitor, examining the expressionless features of the lobotomised slave. Its quill hand was making quick, angular patterns over the page.

He moved past the servitor, coming to stand before the golden coffin device behind it. A coiled bundle of fine wires trailed from the top of the coffin to a series of plug-in sockets drilled in the back of the servitor's skull.

The adept wiped a black-gloved hand across the glistening surface of the golden coffin and stared through a misted glass panel. Inside, a young female astrotelepath lay recumbent, her emaciated body fitted with transparent cables that fed her nutrients and chemical stimms, and removed her bodily waste. Like the quill-servitor, she was eyeless, her lips moving in a soundless whisper. The telepathic message she was receiving from half a galaxy away passed from her to the quill-servitor along psychically-warded cables and thence to its wiry fingers, where the message finally became tangible on the blessed parchment.

The adept removed a small vial of amber liquid from beneath his robes, easing past the girl's prison and kneeling beside the massed rows of pulsing cables attached to its rear. He picked through a handful of tubing and sorted through it, at last finding the one he sought. He disconnected the nutrient tube from the back of the girl's capsule and broke the seal of the vial, careful not to allow any of the liquid to touch him.

The adept held up the disconnected pipe, gruel-like nutrients oozing from its end, and emptied out a portion onto the floor. He carefully poured the vial's contents into the pipe, allowing it to seep into the colourless jelly before reconnecting the pipe to the capsule. Satisfied, he stood and returned to the nave as the amber liquid began working its way around the chamber, flowing through the nutrient pipes to each of the astropaths' capsules.

Swiftly he made his way to the chamber's door, pausing as he opened it to listen.

He smiled beneath his hood as, one by one, the scratching of quills was silenced.

BRIDGEHEAD

One

THE EMPEROR DAMN Major Tedeski's soul to the warp, thought Guardsman Hawke bitterly as he huddled closer to the plasma wave generator that provided what little heat there was in the cramped surveyor station. With no small measure of glee, he imagined putting a las-bolt into the back of his company commander's head as he stalked up and down the ash-coated esplanades of Tor Christo.

One thing! Just one little thing and Tedeski had busted them from a cushy little number up on Tor Christo, free from interfering officers, to this damn place!

He glanced without interest at the sensor display before him, noting with boredom that – surprise, surprise! – there was nothing happening outside.

As if anyone in their right mind would want to try and attack Hydra Cordatus. A single crumbling citadel on a damned dusty rock, bleaker than a killer's heart, with nothing of remote interest to anyone. Least of all, Guardsman Hawke.

People didn't come to Hydra Cordatus voluntarily; they ended up here.

He sat inside the cold, cramped confines of one of the sixteen mountain surveyor stations that ringed Jericho Falls spaceport, the one lifeline this place had with the outside world. The machines housed here constantly swept for the approach of any would-be attackers. Not that there ever would be, even if they knew about the citadel.

It was a nightmare detail to be posted here and everyone knew it. The heaters barely worked, the deafening roar of the scouring wind as it howled down from the high peaks was maddening, there was nothing to do and the sheer boredom could drive even the strongest willed to despair. The only thing there was to do was watch the machines and report the odd spike on the display slate.

He cursed his foul luck and went back to imagining new and inventive ways of busting Tedeski's head.

Sure, so they had turned up for duty pretty badly hungover. Well, probably still drunk from the night before, truth be told. But it wasn't as though there was anything else to do on this Emperor-damned rock. It wasn't as if they'd been entrusted with some kind of top-secret, highly important mission. They were just on the early watch before changeover. By the Throne, they'd turned up for duty drunk before and had never had any problems.

It was just bad luck that Tedeski had pulled an alert drill that morning and the three of them had been caught sound asleep on the Christo's walls. Bad luck as it was, they counted themselves lucky they hadn't been caught by Castellan Vauban.

They'd received a roasting from Major Tedeski, and here they were: stuck in the mountains in a rockcrete can, looking for enemies who would never come.

He sat alone for now. His two companions in misery were out in the dust-stained rocks, some hundred metres in front of the post. He rose from beside the ineffective heater, stamping his feet and slapping his arms around himself in a futile effort to warm up, then stepped closer to the rockcrete walls of the miniature bunker. He peered through what were – laughably – named vision blocks, over the stubby firing grip of the rear assault cannon, to see if he could spot either of his two fellow victims of Tedeski's wrath.

After a few minutes he gave up in disgust. He couldn't see a fragging thing through the swirling dust. They'd be lucky if they found anything in that grey soup. One tiny spike had registered on the display and they'd drawn straws to see which lucky pair would venture outside and check it out.

Thank the Emperor he'd cheated and didn't have to leave the meagre warmth of the post. The others had been gone for nearly half an hour and he realised it was about time he checked in with them. He thumbed the dial on the vox-panel, 'Hitch, Charedo? You two find anything out there?'

He turned the dial to 'receive' and waited for a response.

The white hiss of static poured from the battered vox, filling the surveyor station with a haunting, empty noise. He turned the dial again, staring through the vision blocks and fingering the trigger guard on the assault cannon.

'Hey, you two. If you're okay, answer me. Do you copy?'

Static came again and he anxiously flicked the external cannon's safety off. He was ready to call again when the vox barked into life and he laughed with relief.

'You gotta be kidding, Hawke. There ain't a damned thing out here except us!' said a voice that, despite the roaring of the wind, he recognised as belonging to Guardsman Hitch. The distortion on the soldier's voice was thickening so he adjusted the controls, relieved to hear a friendly voice.

'Yeah, I figured that,' he replied. 'Miserable out there, I bet!' he laughed.

'Frag you, man!' snapped Hitch. 'We're freezing our backsides off out here. Sod this, huh?'

Hawke chuckled to himself as Hitch swore again.

'There's nothing here. It must be a surveyor fault or something. We're right where we're supposed to be and there ain't a damn thing alive for kilometres around us.'

'You're sure you're in the right place?' asked Hawke.

'Of course I'm fragging sure!' shouted Hitch. 'I can read a map, you know. We're not all as stupid as you.'

'Don't bet on it, Hitchy-boy!' said Hawke, enjoying his comrade's annoyance.

'There's nothing out here,' cursed Hitch, 'we're coming back in.'

'Okay, see you in a while then.'

'Just get the caffeine on, huh? And make sure it's hotter than hell, okay?'

'Sure thing,' answered Hawke, flicking off the vox-unit.

He'd already drunk the last of the caffeine, so he took a belt of amasec from his silver hip flask, savouring the heat as it snaked its way down his neck to his gut. It was the only thing that gave him any real warmth here. He tucked it away deep in his pocket, not wanting to share any with Hitch and Charedo, and knowing that they'd be back any minute.

The storm continued to howl around the small listening bunker as he stomped around, his foul mood worsening with each step. He'd just made his routine two-hourly check-in with the command post back at the spaceport and had been told by a smug vox-flunkey that their relief would be a couple of hours late. The ash storm was playing hell with the ornithopter's engines again, so they were stuck here until the Emperor knew when.

It was just one thing after another!

He supposed he should be used to it by now. He'd been in the Imperial Guard for almost ten of his twenty-five years now. Picked from a clutch of the best PDF troopers on Jouran III to serve in the 383rd Jouran Dragoons, he'd looked forward to seeing new worlds and strange creatures. A life of adventure surely beckoned.

But, no, he'd been stuck on this damned rock for nearly all ten of those years with nothing but demerits and black marks against his name. There was nothing here but the citadel, and nothing inside that worth fighting for as far as he knew. Why they felt it was worth stationing over twenty thousand soldiers of the Emperor, a demi legion of Battle Titans and all those batteries of artillery here was beyond him.

Used to a life of boredom in the PDF, it had been a wake-up call to him when he joined the regiment. Constant drilling, weapons training and tactics had been drummed into him like there was no tomorrow.

And for what?

He hadn't fired a shot in anger in ten years!

In truth, he was bored.

Hawke was a hellraiser. He wanted some action, a chance to show his stuff. He picked up his rifle and shouldered it, imagining some alien raider in his sights.

'Bang bang, you're dead,' he whispered, spinning and squeezing off more imaginary shots at his imaginary enemies.

He should be so lucky. He chuckled to himself and put down the rifle, having won the battle.

Yeah, right, he thought.

THE HUNTER WHO was about to kill Guardsmen Hitch and Charedo had been stealthily approaching the surveyor station in the darkness for the last hour, his enhanced vision turning night into day.

His name was Honsou and in the last hour he had advanced two hundred metres on his belly, centimetre by centimetre, the auto-senses in his helmet alerting him to the surveyor sweeps of the armoured bunker. Each time his earpiece growled a warning he would freeze as the questing spirits of the ancient machinery sought him out.

The other members of his squad were invisible to him, but he knew that they too were slowly approaching the station. Two of their targets had left the bunker. Were they hunting? Was it just a regular patrol or had someone inside the bunker caught something suspicious on their surveyors? Briefly, he wondered if the soldier within had reported yet.

Probably not, he thought, as he watched the two morons blunder about in the dust storm. They'd passed within a metre of his position as they headed to where they thought their quarry was, making enough noise to stampede a herd of grox.

Hopefully the third soldier in the surveyor station was as pathetic as these two. He had waited, watching them wander aimlessly for nearly half an hour before seeming to come to the conclusion that their hunt was fruitless, and beginning the trek back.

They stumbled away and Honsou wondered again how the Imperium had lasted for the last ten thousand years with men like these defending it. Would that all the False Emperor's soldiers were like them.

Slowly, he followed them, making better time on his belly than his prey did on foot until he was practically on top of them. He was now less than seven metres from the bunker's rear, and only, door.

He shivered as he saw the stubby, multiple barrels of the rear-mounted assault cannon and took a deep breath.

Patience. He had to wait until they entered the code and opened the door.

Still flat on his stomach, he pulled his bolt pistol from its insulated holster and worked the action, chambering a round. The storm easily swallowed the noise. He flicked off the safety and waited.

His targets entered the sheltered lee of the bunker and the tallest of the pair began punching the entry code into the keypad. Honsou sighted on the soldier nearest him, lining the fore and back sight precisely on the gap between the man's helmet and flak jacket. He exhaled slowly, calming his breathing, preparing to shoot.

Everything faded from his perceptions. Everything except the shot.

The code was almost entered. His finger tightened on the trigger. His vision narrowed to a tunnel, following the path his bolt would take.

HAWKE GRIMACED AS the door to the bunker slid jerkily open, draining away the little heat left in the listening post. Why the hell didn't they put a two-door approach system on these places? Not just for the security, but to keep the warmth in.

He glanced at the external pict-display as the door slid further open and did a slow double-take as the wind dropped and the swirling dust abated. Behind Charedo he saw a huge armoured figure with a raised pistol.

Without a second thought he leapt for the emergency door override and slammed it down.

The roaring of the wind drowned the first shot.

Hawke heard a second, followed by two dull thuds. He swore, seeing Hitch and Charedo slump to the ground, gaping craters where their faces had been.

He grabbed the handle of the rear cannon and yanked the trigger hard. He swung the gun from side to side, not aiming, just shooting. The roar of the cannon was deafening, the rattling of spent shells ringing from the grey walls.

The supersonic shells blew up a storm, churning the mud and earth outside to atoms as thousands of rounds turned the area before him into a death-trap, shredding anything within its arc of fire.

He screamed as he fired. He didn't know whether he was hitting anything and didn't much care.

'You just messed with the wrong guy!' he yelled.

Dust blew in his face, filling his mouth and he angrily spat it clear. Then he–

Dust? He glanced quickly at the door.

Oh no...

Hitch's body was blocking it, preventing it from closing.

Indecision tore at him. Door or cannon?

'Damn you, Hitch!' he shouted and jumped down from the cannon's firing step. He grabbed Hitch's headless corpse and pulled, hauling his former squadmate inside, out of the door's path.

A shape loomed up out of the dust. He fell back as a bullet tore across his shoulder.

Hawke screamed and snatched up Hitch's fallen rifle as a giant shape loomed in the doorway.

He fired the rifle, laughing as his shot punched into the figure's chest. The massive silhouette reeled, but didn't fall. Hawke unloaded the remainder of the power cell through the door, shot after shot. He laughed as he finally managed to pull Hitch's body inside the bunker and slammed himself against the door-closing handle.

'Ha! Get in now, you fraggers!' he shouted at the closing door, whooping with excitement.

Something clattered on the ground as the door finally shut and the laughter died in his throat as he saw the two gently spinning grenades at his feet.

'Oh no...' he whispered.

Instinctively he kicked out, sending them skittering across the sloping floor to the grenade sump, a deep and narrow trench cut into the floor at the wall of the listening post for just such an emergency. The first grenade dropped into the sump, but the second bounced clear, rolling back towards him.

Dropping everything, he sprinted for cover behind the vox-panel.

The grenade exploded.

Fire and shrapnel, blinding light and ringing eardrums. Blood and noise as the bunker became a raging inferno.

Guardsman Hawke screamed as fire and whickering fragments lashed his body. The force of the explosion picked him up and slammed him against the wall of the listening post.

Bright lights sunburst before his eyes and pain swallowed him whole. He had time to scream once before the pressure wave snatched the breath from his lungs, slamming his head into the wall and taking the pain away.

As THE DUST settled, Honsou stepped across the shattered threshold and surveyed the devastated remains of the bunker. Blood clotted on his chest where the Guardsman had shot him.

But that was the least of his concerns. The Imperial lackey had turned his carefully planned assault into a bloodbath.

Two of his men were dead, blown away in the first roar of the assault cannon.

A couple of grenades into the bunker had silenced the cannon, however. Frags weren't the most powerful grenades, but contained within the cramped confines of this bunker they had been devastating.

He kicked the blackened, smouldering corpse of the Guardsman, venting his frustration on the dead body. He ducked below the lintel of the bunker, black smoke pouring from its interior, and stood erect. Almost as tall as the bunker, Honsou was a giant of a warrior. He was clad in power armour the colour of burnished iron, its surfaces pitted and scored by three months of living in the hostile environment of Hydra Cordatus. He wiped the dust clogging his visor and engaged the illuminator on his shoulder. The powerful glow cast a stark light across his armour, shadowing his moulded breastplate and the symbol of the Iron Warriors on his right shoulder guard.

He crunched through the dust and trained his gaze further down the mountains towards the spaceport. He could barely make it out through the dust clouds, and knew the storm was beginning to blow itself out. They must move quickly.

He had lost two men, but, in the end, he supposed it did not matter. With two listening posts down, they now had a narrow blind-spot running towards the spaceport and he had more than enough men to successfully complete his mission.

He voxed the remainder of his warriors.

'We are clear now. All teams close on me and move out.'

Two

JERICHO FALLS SPACEPORT squatted at the foot of the mountains, a glowing beacon of light in the greyness of the dust storm. Such storms were not uncommon on Hydra Cordatus, and were just one of the unpleasant phenomenon that simply had to be endured. A typical Imperial military establishment, it boasted a collection of three dozen buildings, ranging from armoured hangars for Marauder and Lightning aircraft, fuel stations and mess halls to barracks and maintenance sheds. The landing strips and hardened runways covered over eighty per cent of the ground enclosed by the three metre high perimeter walls, enough to land or launch an entire attack wing of aircraft in under five minutes. Vast supply shuttles, each capable of landing a Battle Titan, could be handled by the base, though it had been many years since anything larger than a Thunderhawk gunship had availed itself of the facilities.

The command post of the spaceport was housed in what was known by the soldiers as 'The Hope', due to an oft-repeated mantra amongst the Guardsmen stationed on Hydra Cordatus that they *hoped* not to pull duty at Jericho Falls. A thick, armoured tower with a flattened disc on top, set on the northern edge of the landing fields, the Hope was protected by reinforced rockcrete walls, which in turn were plated in sheets of adamantium specially commissioned from the shipyards of Calth. Howling winds swept across the open ground of the base, whipping the abrasive dust into every fold and crease of a soldier's uniform, getting into mouths and behind goggles to choke and blind.

The only way in or out of the Hope was through an adamantium door that required four gigantic pistons to open.

Five companies of the Jouran Dragoons were stationed here, housed in reinforced barracks and a hardened hangar. Green and red lights winked on the numerous landing platforms and runways, and powerful arc lights fought to penetrate the swirling dust and illuminate the outer perimeter of the base. Patrol vehicles, their engines modified to resist the intake of dust, circled the base, their headlights feebly piercing the gloom.

THE ATMOSPHERE WITHIN the Hope was subdued. This close to dawn was always slow, no different from any other time of the day. An hour before the shift change, the staff were tired and restless. The soft ticking of logic engines and hushed conversations with patrolling vehicles and soldiers were the only sounds.

Operator Three, Koval Peronus, rubbed his grainy eyes and took a hit of caffeine. It was cold, but did the job. Once again he leaned towards the vox-panel.

'Listening post Sigma IV, come in please,' he said. A burst of static was his only answer. He checked the time. It had been two hours and ten minutes since Hawke's last check-in. He was late. Again.

'Listening post Sigma IV, come in. Hawke, I know you're there, so pick up the damn vox!'

Disgusted, Koval dropped the vox-handset and took another gulp of caffeine. Trust bloody Hawke to put a spanner in the works.

He'd try once more and if he couldn't get an answer then he'd have to kick it higher and tough luck to Hawke.

He called again. Nothing.

'Okay, Hawke. It's your butt if you want to sleep on the job again,' he whispered and thumbed the vox-link connecting his panel to the adept's station.

'Yes, Operator Three?' answered Adept Cycerin.

'Sorry to disturb you, adept, but we may have a problem. One of the surveyor stations has not checked in and I can't raise them.'

'Very well, I shall be there directly.'

'Yes, adept,' replied Koval, lounging back and waiting for his superior.

Hawke was for it this time. He'd already been busted onto report, ending up in the mountains and if this was another of his classic screw-ups, then he was finished as a Guardsman.

Adept Cycerin appeared at his shoulder and leaned over the panel, the rasping static of his vox-amp in his throat hissing in displeasure. He smelt of incense and oil.

'Who is stationed at Sigma IV?' he asked.

'Hawke, Charedo and Hitch.'

The adept's vox-amp crackled in what Koval took to be a sigh of frustration; apparently Hawke's reputation had spread even to the priests of the Machine God.

'I've tried them three times, adept. I can't even get the standby signal.'

'Very well. Keep trying, but if you still can't raise them after another ten minutes, send a flight of ornithopters to investigate. Keep me informed.'

'Yes, adept.'

There would be no saving Hawke this time.

HONSOU COULD SEE the hazy glow of the spaceport just ahead. The bobbing lights of a vehicle wove their way through the gloom, a pair of sweeping beams swinging in their direction. He dropped to his knees and raised his fist. Behind him, thirty armoured figures dropped to their knees, bolters at the ready. It was unlikely that the vehicle's beams could penetrate the thick, dusty air as far as their position, but there was no sense in being reckless.

The lights moved on and Honsou relaxed a fraction. Routine had made the Imperial troops careless. These last few months had allowed him to study the circuits made by the patrol vehicles and plot their routes and timings. The warp alone knew how long these particular soldiers had been stationed on this planet, but it must have been a long time. It was only natural that their alertness would drop and patrol patterns would become predictable. It was an inevitable price for long tours of duty and it would soon see them dead.

Satisfied the patrol vehicle had moved on, he extended his fist once again, opening and shutting it three times in rapid succession. They were too close to the spaceport to risk any form of vox communication. Honsou heard muffled footfalls behind him and turned as a figure in steeldust armour, chevroned with yellow and black, crept towards him. Goran Delau, his second-in-command, knelt beside him and nodded. The newcomer's power armour was heavily modified and ornamented with skull-faced rivets and brass mouldings of writhing faces cunningly worked into the edging of his shoulder guards. A whining servo limb, like a clawed digger arm, lolled over Delau's right shoulder, the ribbed grip sighing open and closed as though with breath of its own.

Honsou pointed to the sky then clenched his gauntleted fist again, hammering it into his palm. Delau nodded and removed a crude looking slate from the side of his bulky backpack, adjusting a brass dial on its front. A red light flashed on the otherwise featureless front panel, flickering for a second before becoming a steady, blood-red glow.

Delau raised his hands to the sky, the servo arm mimicking his movements. Honsou could not hear his words, but knew that Delau was offering his thanks that the Dark Gods had again given them a chance to strike back against the ancient enemy.

Honsou watched the red light on Goran's slate and marked this moment in his memory. The targeting beacons they had spent the last three months planting around the spaceport on this barren rock were all now active, shrieking their locations into space.

This was the most dangerous part of their mission. The Imperials within the spaceport would now know that there were enemies close.

If the favour of their Lords deserted them then they would all be dead soon. He shrugged, the servo muscles in his armour whining as they tried to match the gesture. If it was the will of the gods that he should die here, then so be it. He had asked nothing of them and expected nothing in return.

He just hoped that if he was to die on this barren world it would be by the will of the gods, and not because of that madman Kroeger.

PIERCING SHRIEKS FILLED the command centre of the Hope as Honsou's signal locators screamed into the sky. Technicians wrenched headsets from their ears at the din, and alarm sirens began wailing.

Adept Cycerin stared, ashen faced, at the runic display. Bright dots of light pulsed on the map projected before him. Each dot indicated one of the orbital torpedo silos or air defence batteries, and operators hurriedly tried to contact the men stationed there to ascertain what was happening.

Were they broadcasting? Were they under attack? What in the name of the Emperor was going on?

Cycerin returned to his monitoring station, placing his hands on the ridged, metal fixtures of the armrests. Thin, wiry tendrils of silver metal slithered from beneath his fingernails like gleaming worms and clicked into brass sockets on the ridges. The adept sighed, and his organic eye flickered behind a pale lid as information relayed from the multitude of surveyors and augurs positioned around the spaceport flooded his senses through the technology of his mechadendrites.

Awareness flooded him, his mind-sense perceiving space and distance as vectors, ranges and coverage of ground. His senses reached into space, following the sweeps of the orbital augurs. Information flowed through him, processed and compartmentalised in the synthetic logic stacks of his augmented brain. Even with his machine affinity, he could barely keep pace with the barrage of sensory data.

There had to be something, this couldn't be happening without reason. Logic dictated that there was a cause for this effect. Something must be out of place…

There, in the north sector! He narrowed his perceptions, shutting off areas of sensory retrieval that were extraneous to his search and closing in on the anomaly. Where there should have been washes of energy sweeping down from the mountains, there was only black emptiness. The surveyor stations on the northern slopes were silent, their auguries no longer active. He immediately saw that this left an open corridor, through which an enemy could approach undetected to the very perimeter of the base.

How had this not been seen? Why had the operators here not reported such an unforgivable lapse in security? The identity of the surveyor station flashed up.

Sigma IV.

He cursed as he realised that the anomaly had been seen, but that the surveyor station's failure to report had been put down to human error on the part of those within. He swore again, uncharacteristically letting slip his emotionless demeanour, as yet more sirens screeched around the control room.

Startled, Cycerin reopened his mind to other portions of his awareness and his breath caught in his throat as he felt the presence of dozens of starships in orbit above Hydra Cordatus. Inconceivable! Where had these ships come from and why had they not been detected before now? Nothing should be able to enter even the outer edges of the system without them being aware of it… could it? Or was this another example of human error? No, the logic engines would have screamed the place down many days ago if it had detected this size of fleet approaching. Somehow these starships had avoided detection by some of the rarest and most precious equipment available to the Adeptus Mechanicus.

Briefly he wondered what technologies these ships had and how it worked, but shook his head at such irrelevance. He had more important things to worry about. The defenders at the citadel must be warned that an invasion was imminent. He opened the mind-link to Arch Magos Amaethon's Machine Temple in the citadel and sent the psychic alert code. The astropaths stationed there would detect it and send a more powerful psychic distress call for aid to Hydra Cordatus.

Hurriedly he closed off his mind-link and withdrew his digital mechadendrites from the monitoring station, opening his eyes on a scene of controlled efficiency. System operators called to the torpedo outstations, authenticating launch codes and feeding their operators firing solutions towards the collection of starships in orbit. Time was of the essence now and they had to get the torpedoes in the air.

Alert sirens would be ringing out in the pilots' barracks by now and soon there would be a swarm of aircraft in the air, ready to meet whatever threat was approaching, and soldiers from the Jouran Dragoons were mustering even now to repel the attackers.

He had drilled the operators here for this eventuality time and time again, and now that it was happening for real, he was pleased to note the calmness evinced by his staff.

'Adept Cycerin!' shouted one of the orbital monitoring operators. 'We have multiple signals detaching from several contacts in orbit.'

'Identify them!' barked Cycerin.

The operator nodded, bowing his head to his station, running his finger down the slate beside his display.

'They're too fast for landing craft, I believe they are inbound orbital munitions.'

'Plot their vectors! Quickly, man!' hissed Cycerin, though he feared he knew the answer already.

The man's hands danced across his slate, and green lines extended from the rapidly moving blips, reaching out to the representation of the planet's surface. Cycerin's vox-amp crackled in sudden fear as he saw the approach vectors of the incoming bombs matched almost exactly the locator signals being broadcast from the torpedo launch silos.

'How…?' whispered the operator, his face ashen.

Cycerin lifted his eyes to the armoured glass windows of the Hope.

'There's someone out there…'

NEARLY A THOUSAND men died in the first seconds of the Iron Warriors' initial bombardment of Jericho Falls spaceport. The battle barge *Stonebreaker* fired three salvoes of magma bombs into the desolate rocky slopes surrounding the spaceport, blasting vast chunks of rock hundreds of metres into the air and flattening almost all the torpedo silos in the mountains with unerring accuracy.

Alarm sirens screamed and the spaceport's weapon batteries rumbled into firing positions as their gunners desperately sought to acquire targets before being annihilated. A few hastily blessed torpedoes roared upwards through the orange sky on pillars of fiery smoke and powerful beams of laser energy stabbed through the perpetually cloudless heavens.

More bombs fell, this time within the perimeter of Jericho Falls, demolishing buildings, gouging great craters and hurling enormous clouds of umber ash into the atmosphere. Flames from burning structures lit the smoke from within and bodies lay aflame in the wreckage of the shattered spaceport. Smashed aircraft littered the ground and more exploded as the heat from the fires cooked off their weapons and fuel tanks.

Bombs slammed into the rockcrete, scything lethal fragments everywhere. Others smashed into the runways, cratering them and melting the honeycombed adamantium with the heat of a star.

The Marauders and Lightnings out in the open took the worst of the barrage, pulverised by the force of the explosions.

The noise and confusion were unbelievable; the sky was red with flames and black with smoke. Heavy las-fire blasted upwards.

A number of shells impacted on the main hangar's roof. Its armoured structure had absorbed the damage so far, though vast cracks now zigzagged across the reinforced walls and roof.

The main runway was engulfed in flames, burning pools of jet fuel spewing thick black smoke that turned day into night.

Hell had come to Hydra Cordatus.

Three

THE FIRST WAVE of drop-pods fired from the *Stonebreaker* landed in clouds of fire and smoke as their boosters slowed them after their screaming journey through the atmosphere. As each pod hit the ground, the release bolt on its base slammed home and the sides unfolded to reveal their interiors.

Each pod in this wave was Deathwind class, equipped with an auto-firing heavy gun platform. As they opened, the weapons began to pour their lethal fire in a spinning, circular arc. Fresh explosions erupted across the ready line as the bolts found their marks in the exposed attack craft and pilots. The volleys from the battle barge in orbit ceased as more streaking lines of fire followed the first wave. Gun turrets mounted on armoured bunkers engaged the weapon pods, methodically targeting them one at a time and destroying them with well-aimed gunfire. But the Deathwinds had done their job, keeping the gunners occupied as the second wave of drop-pods slashed downwards, unmolested, through the atmosphere towards the base.

KROEGER GRIPPED HIS chainsword tight and repeated the Iron Warriors' Litany of Hate for the ninth time since his Dreadclaw drop-pod had fired from the belly of the *Stonebreaker*. The pod shook with the fury of its fiery journey through the atmosphere and, as their passage became smoother, he knew that the curses and offerings to the Powers of Chaos had appeased their monstrous hunger. He grinned beneath his helmet as he watched the bone-rimmed altimeter unravel, counting the seconds to their landing.

They would now be within the lethal range of the spaceport's guns, but if the half-breed, Honsou, had successfully completed his mission, then there should be little or no incoming fire to meet them. His lip curled in contempt as he thought of that mongrel leading one of the Warsmith's grand companies. It was unseemly for a half-breed to attain such responsibility, and Kroeger despised Honsou with every fibre of his being.

He cast his gaze over the armoured warriors who sat around the steel-panelled walls of the drop-pod's interior. Their dented power armour was the colour of dark iron, heavy and baroque, none less than ten thousand years old. Each man's weapon had been anointed with the blood of a score of captives, and the stench of death filled the pod's interior. The men strained at the harnesses that held them in place, eyes fixed on the iris hatch on the pod's floor, every thought slaved to the slaughter of their foes.

Kroeger had picked these killers personally; they were the most blood-soaked berserkers of his grand company of the Iron Warriors, those who had trodden the path of Khorne for longer than most. The Blood God's hunger for death and skulls had become the driving imperative for these warriors, and it was doubtful that they would ever break from the cycle of murder and killing that had swallowed them. Kroeger himself had revelled many times in the fierce joy of slaughter that so pleased Khorne, but had not yet fully surrendered to the frenzy of the Blood God.

Once a warrior lost himself in that red mist, he was unlikely to survive and Kroeger had agendas yet to follow, paths yet to tread. For Khorne was no sanguineous epicure. He cared not from whence the blood came and as the worshippers of the Blood God often discovered, their own vital fluid was as welcome as that of the enemy's.

The drop-pod's retros fired, filling the cramped vessel with a howling shriek like a banshee's wail. Kroeger took the hateful screaming as a good omen.

He raised his sword in the salute of the warrior and roared, 'Let blood be your watchword, death your companion and hate your strength.'

Barely a handful of the warriors acknowledged him, most too immersed in thoughts of the blood they would shed to even register that he had spoken. It was immaterial; the hated Imperial followers of the corpse-god would die screaming as he ripped their souls from their torn flesh. His blood sang at the prospect of killing yet more of their ancient foes and he prayed to the Majesty of the Warp that the honour of the first kill would be his.

He felt the bone-jarring impact of the Dreadclaw drop-pod through the thick ceramite plates of his power armour as it slammed into the ground. Scarcely had the bottom hatch irised open than he dropped through it, bending his knees and rolling aside as the next warrior followed him down. Thick, grey smoke from the retros obscured his vision, and the flames burning across the spaceport rendered the heat augurs in his helmet useless.

He drew his pistol, offering his thanks to the power of Chaos for giving him such a chance to bring death to his enemies.

ADEPT CYCERIN WAS close to panic. He had had no response to his pleas for aid from the citadel, though they must surely be aware of their plight. The thought that there were enemies with the power to circumvent their surveyors and approach their fastness, unseen and unknown, had all but unmanned him. He cursed the weak, organic part of him that felt such bowel-loosening terror and wished again for the emotional detachment of his superiors.

The data-slate on the wall indicated a breach in the outer wall and garbled contact reports howling across the vox circuits told of giants in armour of burnished iron slaughtering all those who stood before them. He could not co-ordinate a defence without better reports and the chaos of battle was…

Chaos.

The very word sent a hot jolt of fear down Cycerin's spine and suddenly he knew how their enemies had managed to elude their auguries. Accursed, warp-spawned sorcery must have confounded the spirits of the machines and rendered them blind to the monstrous evil that approached Hydra Cordatus. As soon as this first thought had struck, a second followed.

There could only be one reason the followers of the Ruinous Powers would come to this place and the thought made him shake with fear. Confused icons flashed on the holomap of the base, representing friendly forces deploying from barracks and attempting to engage the invaders. Cycerin could see that it would not be enough; there had simply been too much devastation in the opening moments of the attack.

But he consoled himself that he and his staff were safe enough in the Hope. Protected high within its armoured structure, there was no way an enemy could penetrate its security. No way at all.

HONSOU HACKED HIS sword through a weeping soldier's torso, separating his upper and lower halves with a single blow. Their attack through the breach in the wall had caught the mustering Imperial soldiers completely by surprise. Most were already dead, crushed by masonry blasted from the wall by his heavy weapon teams.

An enemy officer attempted to rally his men from the hatch of his command Chimera, screaming at them to stand firm. Honsou shot him in the face and vaulted a rebar-laced chunk of rockcrete, swinging his mighty sword amongst the horrified soldiers. Gunfire raked the ground beside him, explosions of ash kicked up in red spurts by the Chimera's hull-mounted heavy bolter. Honsou rolled aside as the turret began traversing in his direction.

'Take that vehicle out!' he yelled.

Positioned on the walls, two iron giants carrying long-barrelled cannons on their shoulders swung their heavy weapons to bear. Twin streaks of incandescent energy blasted into the vehicle. Seconds later, it vanished in an orange fireball, raining yet more debris down upon the battlefield. Honsou picked himself up as another Chimera attempted to back away from the breach, firing its weapons as it retreated. His gunners on the wall methodically swept their weapons around and destroyed it with contemptuous ease.

The base was in flames, but Honsou's practiced eye could see that the vital runways and landing platforms had escaped most of the violence of the bombardment. As his men gathered at the foot of the wall, he aligned himself with the map projected on the inside face of his visor. Through the smoke and billowing flames, he could see the faint outline of a tall tower with a flattened circular top. This must be the control tower and it was his next target. Wreckage and bodies littered the battlefield: drop-pods, aircraft and burning vehicles, their crews either dead or battling for their lives.

The sky was streaked with lines of fire as more Iron Warriors descended to the planet. His fellow company commanders, Kroeger and Forrix, would even now be bringing death to this world. He could not be seen to be doing less in the eyes of the Warsmith.

'We have them now, brothers, and there is death yet to be done. Follow me and I will give you victory!'

Honsou raised his sword and set off at a sprint towards the control tower, knowing that its capture would earn him great reward. He wove a zigzag course towards the tower, pools of burning fuel and wrecked machines forcing him into frustrating detours. After three months of creeping through the mountains, it was a cathartic release of his fury to be amidst such brutality. The air was thick with death, and though he was no sorcerer, even he could feel the actinic tang of slaughter that they had brought to Hydra Cordatus.

Here and there, they met pockets of resistance, but the sight of his thirty blood-soaked warriors charging towards them broke the courage of all but the most stalwart. Honsou's blade was dripping with gore as he and his men finally reached the tower.

Grudgingly he was forced to admit that its construction and defences were formidable. Soldiers in prepared positions surrounded it in well-constructed, angled redoubts, laying down a hail of bright las-bolts. Behind four linked and high-walled berms, Honsou could see the aerials of tanks, but what pattern they were he could not yet tell.

Armoured bunkers at each of the compass points sprayed the area in front of the tower with deadly bullets, turning the open ground into a killing zone.

Honsou and his men moved into concealed positions behind the twisted wreckage of a Marauder bomber, as the thunderous crack of a tank's main gun activated the dampers on his armour's auto-senses. Clouds of dust and rubble rained down and Honsou could hear the cries of those wounded by the blast. They had to move fast or the citadel's defenders would be able to counterattack before the Iron Warriors were able to consolidate their position here.

He peered through a ragged hole torn in the side of the aircraft, wrenching the pilot's bloody corpse out of the way and pondered the situation. The corner bunkers were the key: take them and they could roll up the Imperial line with ease. The gunfire sawing from the bunkers was murderous; anyone who attempted to charge through it would pay the price for such stupidity. He grinned wryly as he saw several of Kroeger's men, berserkers by the look of them, lying torn open, their blood leeching into the dusty ground. He wondered if perhaps Kroeger himself might be numbered amongst the dead, but knew that, despite his recklessness, Kroeger was no fool and would not risk his own neck if he did not have to.

Even as he formed the thought, he caught sight of his nemesis some two hundred metres away, firing his pistol ineffectually at the Imperial defenders. Kroeger's attack on the tower had failed and Honsou knew that this was his chance.

He crawled along to his heavy weapon gunners and hammered his fist on the shoulder guards of the warriors with the lascannons, slung across their shoulders as easily as a human soldier might carry a walking cane.

The gunners turned, acknowledging their leader with curt nods.

Another rain of debris fell around them as a tank shell exploded nearby. Honsou pointed towards the tower, shouting, 'When I give the order, aim for the salient angle of the near bunker, and keep firing until you break it open.'

The gunners nodded and Honsou moved further down the line. He knew he was condemning those men to death, but didn't care. Another of his heavy gunners carried a hissing weapon with a wide, flaring barrel etched with elaborate traceries of flame. The gunner's armour was dented and scorched in places, but the weapon was pristine, as though freshly pressed from a weapon forge.

'When the lascannons blow open the bunker, I want you to put enough melta fire into that bunker to make the rock run like liquid.'

Without waiting for a response, Honsou rolled over towards the lascannons and jabbed his fist towards the bunker, voxing the order to stand to throughout his squads. He scrambled to the edge of the wrecked Marauder, watching as the two warriors carrying the lascannons moved into firing positions and aimed their weapons. Bolt after bolt of powerful las-blasts slammed into the protruding salient angle of the bunker, blasting away huge chunks of armaplas and rockcrete. Realising the danger, Imperial gunners switched their fire to the two heavy gunners, tearing up the ground in a storm of las-blasts and bolter fire.

The two Iron Warriors paid no attention to the incoming fire, sending shot after shot of unimaginably powerful energy into their target. Honsou watched as the angled corner of the bunker cracked wide open, the rockcrete burning orange in the heat. For a moment it appeared that the gunners might survive the hail of shots directed at them.

But the thunder of Imperial battle cannons settled the matter, obliterating both gunners in an explosive storm of ordnance. Before the echoes had died, the Iron Warrior with the multi-melta rose from his concealment and charged forwards to fire. The gun's discharge built to a deafening screech before erupting from the barrels in a searing hiss. The warrior's aim was true and the air within the bunker ignited with atomic fury, spurts of vaporised flesh and superheated oxygen blasting from the weapon slits.

A huge hole had been blown in the tower's line of defence. Honsou rose up from his cover and screamed, 'Death to the False Emperor!'

He leapt over the Marauder's fuselage and sprinted towards the molten hell of the wrecked bunker, its walls now flowing like wax across the ground. His men followed him unquestioningly. To his left, he could see Kroeger gathering his men for the charge, obviously realising that Honsou would beat him to the tower.

Honsou leapt onto the remains of the bunker, his iron-shod boot sinking into the molten rock. The heat scorched his leg armour, but it held firm as he pushed off and dropped into the heart of the defence.

He caught a glimpse of the carnage his men had inflicted and rejoiced to see that his labours had borne such bloody fruit. Scorched and blackened limbs lay strewn about, all that remained of those stationed too close to the bunker; the backwash of the melta impact had burnt flesh and bone to cinders in an instant. An open mouthed head lay perched bizarrely atop a pile of rubble as if placed there by some macabre prankster. Honsou punched it aside as he passed.

Imperial soldiers were frantically reorganising their battle line as the Iron Warriors poured in through the gap in their defences. Honsou could see a tank – a Leman Russ Demolisher – reversing from its revetment and bringing its ponderous turret to bear on the attackers. Honsou dropped as the sponson-mounted weapons sprayed shells overhead, the ricochets tearing up the blasted rubble around him. Another white-hot blast of melta fire flashed and the Demolisher's turret was engulfed in the inferno of the impact. Steam and smoke obscured the tank for brief seconds, but, unbelievably, it continued onwards through the boiling cloud.

Time slowed as Honsou watched the barrel of its main gun depress and knew that any second it would blast him to atoms. Then, with a terrific explosion, the turret lifted clean off, the tank detonating spectacularly from within as the shell exploded inside the main gun. Deadly shrapnel whickered through the Imperial ranks, scything men down by the dozen and ripping them to bloody rags. Honsou roared in release as he realised the heat of the melta blast must have warped the barrel enough to cause the weapon to misfire and the shell to detonate prematurely.

He rose to one knee and opened up with his bolt pistol, raking his fire over those fortunate enough to survive the destruction of the Demolisher, killing everything he saw in his battle rage.

Kroeger's blood-maddened berserkers clambered across the shattered walls of the redoubt, ignoring wounds that would have felled a normal human a dozen times over. Not for them the elegance of precisely orchestrated attacks using sound principles of military engineering. Bodies were hurled aside, ripped apart with their bare hands when there was no weapon to wield.

Honsou spotted Kroeger amongst his men, wading through a press of bodies, hacking left and right with his chainsword. He raised his own sword in acknowledgement towards his fellow commander, but Kroeger ignored him, as Honsou knew he would. He smiled beneath his helm and sprinted through the blazing wreck of the Demolisher towards the tower.

ADEPT CYCERIN WATCHED the battle raging below with analytical detachment. His moment of panic had passed. Now, secure within the Hope, he watched the dance of attackers and defenders as coloured icons moving across a topographical representation of the base. Red icons surrounded the tower, periodically closing in, but each time fading as the fire of the defenders below saw them off.

He felt mildly ashamed at the panic he had displayed earlier and resolved again to request ascension to the next level of symbiosis with the holy machine. He would seek permission once these impudent creatures had been defeated. Despite his failures in the past, surely Arch Magos Amaethon would not deny him again after his masterful defence of Jericho Falls? He smiled to himself as he watched yet more red icons fade from the slate.

The smile fell from his face as the icon representing the southern bunker faded from a steady blue to an ominous black.

'Operator Three, what's happened?' he asked.

'It's gone, destroyed,' replied Koval Peronus. 'One second it was there, now it's not!'

Cycerin watched, horrified as the red icons suddenly spilled over the location that had, only moments before, been one of the lynchpins of his defence. As the defences were breached, the entire line fell apart with horrifying rapidity. The blue icons vanished as they were systematically eliminated. Cycerin could not even begin to imagine the carnage occurring less than twenty metres from where he stood.

Eerie orange glows from the fires flickered through the armoured glass windows, but no sound penetrated the control room, making it appear remote and detached. Just below him, countless lives had been lost and there would be many more before this day's slaughter was over.

He consoled himself with the knowledge that the tower itself was totally secure and that there was nothing more he could have done to prevent this disaster.

A deathly hush fell upon the operators and staff within the tower as a massive thudding boom suddenly echoed up from the main entrance.

'What in the name of the Machine was that?' Cycerin whispered in terror.

FORRIX WATCHED THE adamantium door shudder under the impact of the Dreadnought's siege hammer, the metres-thick door buckling under the repeated blows. It was only a matter of moments until the door would be ripped from its frame by the screaming war machine. Thick chains, looped through bolted rings, ran from its legs and shoulder mounts, where two dozen of the strongest Iron Warriors stood ready to restrain the machine once it had broken down the door to the control tower.

He could well imagine the torment the damned soul bound within the armoured sarcophagus must be undergoing. To be cut off from the sensation of bloodletting, never to feel the beat of blood in your veins at the moment of the kill. To be denied the thrill of bare flesh against flesh as you took another being's life. Such a fate was indeed misery and suffering. It was small wonder that, once confined to the shell of a Dreadnought, the scraps of flesh that awoke to find themselves confined within the cold, metal walls of such an eternal prison could not escape the clutches of madness.

At least for those lunatic war machines, madness was some sort of release. For killing held no joy for Forrix any longer. Ten thousand years of butchery and murder had allowed him to explore the deepest, most wretched corners of the human capacity for cruelty and death. He had shot, cut, tortured, strangled, snapped, choked, bludgeoned and dismembered uncounted souls in his long life, yet he could remember none of them. Each blended into a seamless segue of banal horror that had long since dulled his senses and vicarious enjoyment of such slaughter.

Gunfire sounded sporadically, the last pockets of resistance being mopped up even now. The half-breed's warriors were clearing out the Imperial soldiers from the ruins of their barrack complex, and despite Forrix's contempt for Honsou's flawed heritage, he had to admit that his rival was a competent commander. Furthermore, he still believed in the dream of Horus, and the unification of Humanity under the terrible Powers of Chaos.

Forrix watched Kroeger pace like a caged animal, straining to be let loose within the confines of the tower. Kroeger's impatience had long ceased to anger Forrix; now it simply irritated him. The man was a proficient killer, and he had fought the Warsmith's enemies for ten thousand years, admittedly, but he lacked the perspective that such an eternity of war and despair should bring. Unlike Honsou, Kroeger had long since cast off any notions of the good of humanity. He fought for greed, for slaughter and the chance to exact a measure of revenge upon those who had bested them so long ago.

As for himself? Forrix no longer knew what he fought for, only that there was nothing else he could do. He had been damned the instant he had spat upon his oaths of loyalty to the Emperor. Now he could walk no other path.

His own warriors waited behind him, drawn up in serried ranks, ready to begin the massive logistical operation of landing tens of thousands of slaves, workers, soldiers and war machines from orbit. In the centuries since the betrayal on Terra, Forrix had organised hundreds of such operations and could land ten thousand men and have them ready to march off in battle order in under five hours.

Until they landed the Titans, the sheer mass of the tower was proof against their available weapons, and the Warsmith himself had impressed upon Forrix the need for swiftness in this campaign. He could not risk bringing the massive bulk carriers, essentially vast barrack ships, down into low orbit until the control tower was theirs. It was entirely likely that there were torpedo silos or orbital batteries concealed within the mountains just waiting for the chance to down such valuable targets.

Once Kroeger had taken the tower he would begin the landings.

And then this world would burn.

KROEGER WATCHED THE Dreadnought rip the bludgeoned door from its frame and hurl the massive piece of metal through the air. The mad howl of the machine echoed across the spaceport as its keepers dragged its massive bulk away from the low-ceilinged interior of the tower.

He snarled and leapt through the shattered remains of the door, blood pounding through his veins in hot excitement. His bloodlust was up, stoked by the infuriating delays in achieving entry to the tower. Screams and roars followed him, as a tide of armoured killers poured inside the last bastion of the Imperial defenders.

Las-bolts burst around him and ricocheted from his armour, but nothing could stop his powerful form. Around fifty men defended the internal space of the tower, cowardly wretches who had allowed their comrades to be butchered while they had prayed for a deliverance that would never come.

Kroeger charged straight for the heart of the defence as Iron Warriors armed with gargoyle-mouthed heavy bolters took up position either side of the tower's door, spraying the defenders' barricades with shells.

Five powerful strides and Kroeger was amongst the Imperial soldiers, chopping and hacking with his sword. Blood fountained and cries of terror echoed from the gore-spattered walls as the Iron Warriors slew every man that stood before them. It was an uneven struggle and as Kroeger wrenched his sword from the belly of the last man, it was with a snarl of displeasure. Where was the sport to be had in slaughtering such weaklings? The Imperium had grown soft.

Not one of these soldiers could have stood on the walls of Terra in the last days and held their head high. Kroeger shook his head, clearing his mind of ancient memories. There was battle still to be had.

ADEPT CYCERIN SAT at his monitoring station and awaited death. He listened to the shrieks of the dying echoing from the vox-speakers, and felt his terror rise once more, suffocating in its intensity. His hands shook uncontrollably and he had not been able to move his legs for the last few minutes. He was going to die. The logic stacks in his engineered brain could offer no other probable outcome, no matter how often he pleaded and prayed.

The staff of the command centre huddled, shaking, at the far end of the room, holding one another as death approached. Koval Peronus stood alone, holding a pair of laspistols pointed at the door. Cycerin was under no illusion now as to how flimsy a barrier it truly was and was impressed by the determination that shone from his underling's features.

Suddenly the awful shrieks and clamour of battle ceased from below and Cycerin knew that the soldiers were all dead. Strange how inviolable he had felt here, and how quickly that security had been stripped from him. Watching Peronus, he saw beads of sweat gathering on his forehead, muscles bunching along his jaw-line and noticed the barely perceptible tremor to his arms. The man was terrified, yet stood his ground in the face of insurmountable odds. Cycerin was no soldier, but recognised true courage when he saw it.

Stiffly, he rose from his seat, forcing his trembling body to stand beside Koval Peronus. He may be about to die, but as an adept of the Machine God, he would die standing before the enemy with chin held high. Koval turned his head as the adept stood alongside him and smiled weakly, nodding briefly in gratitude for his superior's support.

He reversed the grip on one of his pistols and offered it to Cycerin.

'Have you ever fired a weapon in anger?' he asked.

Cycerin shook his head. 'I monitored the production of them in a weapons forge on Gryphonne IV for fifty years, but never managed to actually fire one.'

He swallowed hard. It was the longest sentence he had ever uttered to one of his staff.

'It's easy. Just point and pull the trigger,' explained Peronus. 'I've set the power to maximum to give us a chance of actually hurting one of these heretics, so you'll only get three, maybe four shots at the most. Make them count.'

Cycerin nodded, too scared to even reply. The pistol felt heavy in his hands, but reassuringly lethal. Let the enemy come, he thought. Let them come, and they will find Adept Etolph Cycerin ready for them.

KROEGER CROUCHED AT the end of the corridor leading to the control room and watched as two Iron Warriors planted shaped melta charges across the door's centre. They turned to him and nodded, retreating and taking cover as the timers activated, detonating the charges in a ball of incandescent light.

Kroeger was momentarily blinded as his auto-senses darkened his receptors to compensate, but when they reactivated, he snarled in satisfaction as he saw the door and half the wall had been obliterated.

Nothing came through the door, not a single shot, grenade, or warrior intent on dying with some measure of honour. Angry now at having been cheated of the chance for glory, Kroeger smashed his way through the smouldering remains of the door, his bulk taking a portion of the wall with him and wreathing him in smoke.

Two figures stood before him, pistols held wavering before them. Perhaps here he would find a foe worthy of his blade. He grinned as he smelled their fear.

The smile faded as he saw that neither man was a warrior. One was a tonsured technician, while the other was one of the deluded priests of the machine.

What then could they offer him that he had not already ripped from five score men already? The robed machine priest shouted and fired his pistol, the blast punching a hole in the wall beside Kroeger. The technician fired a heartbeat later and Kroeger rocked back on his heels as the impact blasted a crater in his power armour. Before the Imperial could shoot again, Kroeger was upon him, backhanding his fist across his face and decapitating him in an explosion of blood and bone.

The adept fired again, the blast scoring across Kroeger's back. He spun, plucking the pistol from the man and tearing the hand from his wrist. The adept dropped to his knees, open mouthed in horror as blood jetted from the ragged stump.

Kroeger drew his pistol, ready to finish off the fool, when a sibilant, velvet voice hissed from the blasted doorway.

'You would cost me my victory, Kroeger? That would be unwise of you.'

Kroeger spun, the blood surging to his head as he lowered his weapon.

'No, my lord,' he stammered, dropping to his knees, awed and humbled at the unexpected presence of the Warsmith.

The darkness within the room swelled as one of the mightiest leaders of the Iron Warriors entered to claim his victory. Kroeger had a barely perceived vision of armour of darkest iron, almost black, and a ravaged face glowing with pale light. Horrible vitality pulsed from that face. Kroeger fought to keep from vomiting inside his helmet, such was the force of his leader's presence.

The Warsmith's burnished armour was magnificent and, eyes cast down, Kroeger could see writhing shapes and leering faces swimming up from its translucent depths. Their agonised wails clawed at the edge of his hearing, bound forever within the blasted stuff of the Warsmith's body. His footfalls fell with the weight of ages, imbued with the authority of one who had fought alongside the Legion's Primarch, the great Perturabo, on the accursed soil of Terra.

Wisps of ghostly smoke smouldered where he walked, each twisting like a tormented soul before fading into nothing. Kroeger dared not look at the Warsmith without first being commanded, for fear of instant death at the hands of one of his infernal Terminator bodyguards. They stood a respectful distance from their lord as he slowly circled Kroeger.

The Warsmith brushed his gauntleted fingers along his scarred armour and Kroeger felt intense clamps of nausea seize him in a burning grip. Every cell in his body seemed to recoil at the Warsmith's touch and only through a mantra of hate did Kroeger remain conscious. Though the pain was intense, he felt a powerful yearning for such power. What must it be like to command the power of the empyrean, to have its unimaginable power pump through your veins like blood itself?

'You are reckless, Kroeger. Have ten thousand years of battle taught you nothing?'

'I desire only to serve and to kill those who would deny us our destiny.'

The Warsmith chuckled, the sound like earth falling on a coffin. 'Do not talk to me of destiny, Kroeger. I know why you fight and it is not for anything so lofty as that.'

Kroeger felt blinding waves of pain lance through his skull as the Warsmith leaned in close to the back of his head.

'That you kill the lackeys of the corpse-emperor is enough for me, but have a care that your own needs do not interfere with mine.'

Kroeger nodded, unable to speak, again feeling the roiling sensation of the Warsmith's impending change wash over him. He fought to retain consciousness.

The Warsmith turned from him and Kroeger sighed in relief. The master of the Iron Warriors stood over the still-twitching form of the adept who'd shot at him. From the corner of his eye, he saw the blurry outline of the Warsmith bend and scrutinise the howling adept with the bleeding stump.

'My sorcerer, Jharek Kelmaur, spoke of this man. The servant of the machine with only one hand. He is important to me, Kroeger. And you almost killed him.'

'I... I beg your forgiveness, my lord,' gasped Kroeger.

'See to it that he does not die and you shall have it.'

'He will not die.'

'If he does, you will follow him screaming into hell,' promised the Warsmith, stalking from the room.

As his master departed Kroeger felt the nauseous contractions in his gut subside and pushed himself to his feet. He turned to the mewling form of the bloodstained adept.

He lifted the whimpering man roughly by his robes and dragged him from the room.

Why the Warsmith should want this one saved was beyond him, but if it was his lord's will that the enemy be spared, then so be it.

Four

THE LAST SOUNDS of battle had faded as the commanders of the three grand companies of the Iron Warriors that had come to Hydra Cordatus gathered at the behest of their lord and master.

The Warsmith stood, resplendent in his monstrous suit of power armour, pleased with the bloodletting wreaked in his name. His three champions knelt before him, each man's armour spattered with blood, hued orange by the high midday sun. The Warsmith ignored them, casting his gaze out over the blasted wasteland that had once been a spaceport. The devastated appearance was deceptive, however.

Lumbering, earth-moving machines, brought down from orbit less than an hour ago, were already bulldozing wrecked aircraft and drop-pods from the runways and landing platforms. Bodies were crushed under their grinding tracks or gathered up in vast dozer blades and dumped unceremoniously in giant craters. He cast his eyes to the fiery sky, remembering the first time he had set eyes on this world. Both he and the planet had been very different back then, and he wondered if those who called this place home even knew how it had come to resemble such a pleasing vision of hell.

Far above him he saw a bloated shape, blurred and indistinct, but visible to his enhanced and changing eyes, floating in the fiery haze of the upper atmosphere. The massive starship strained against the oppressive attraction of gravity, disgorging hundreds of landing craft from its belly like some vast sow giving birth to her litter.

Each of this craft's spawn was hundreds of metres in length and crammed with a mixture of slaves, soldiers, ammunition, weapons, siege engines, tools and all manner of materiel required for a besieging army. Forrix knew his trade and the Warsmith was confident that this complex and demanding operation would proceed without problem.

He knew that time was his greatest enemy. Abaddon the Despoiler had bidden them complete this task before his great machination unfolded in return for settling the debt of the Iron Warriors' withdrawal from his designs. To the Warsmith, the Despoiler's plans reeked of the same betrayal that had forced their hand so long ago and driven them to the fold of the dark gods. Perturabo had made the mistake of trusting one he thought was his friend and lord. The Warsmith would not make that mistake himself.

Abaddon may have his plans, but the Warsmith had his own as well.

There was a pleasing synchronicity to his return to Hydra Cordatus. Just now, as he stood on the brink of greatness, he had returned to the world where he had first put into practice the skills he had learned as a novitiate on Olympia.

What he had once helped create, he would now tear asunder.

He returned his gaze to his war leaders, scrutinising each in turn.

Forrix, captain of the foremost of his grand companies, with whom he had held the last gate of the Jarelphi Palace, who had led the retreat from Terra and whose oath of loyalty had been sworn above the clone body of Horus himself.

His experience was second to none and the Warsmith valued his counsel above all others. The fires of glory had long since burned out in his one-time brother, but ten thousand years of war had not dimmed his strength, the saturation of Chaos imbuing his ancient frame with incredible power. His crafted suit of Terminator armour had been struck in the forges of Olympia itself, each greave, vambrace and cuissart hand-tooled by artificers whose skill was now all but a whispered myth.

Beside Forrix: Kroeger, the young-blood, though such a term seemed laughable now, given that Kroeger had fought the long war almost as long as Forrix. But he had always been the young firebrand, with a physical need to plunge into the crucible of combat. His armour was dented and burned in a dozen places – testimony to his ferocity in battle – yet the Warsmith knew that Kroeger possessed a cunning beyond that of a simple butcher. No Khârn of the World Eaters this one, but a killer possessed of single minded drive. Had he simply been another one of those who succumbed to the hunger of the Blood God he would never have lived this long.

Even though they dared not look at each other in his presence, the Warsmith could feel the hatred between Kroeger and the half-breed Honsou. The blood of Olympia flowed in his veins, but he had also been implanted with gene-seed ripped from the bodies of their ancient foes, the Imperial Fists. His blood was tainted with the seed of the corpse-emperor's lapdog, Rogal Dorn, and for that Kroeger would never forgive him. No matter that he had proven himself time and time again, some hatreds were carved on the heart. No matter that his dark deeds were at least the equal of Kroeger's. Honsou had led the Forlorn Hope through the breach in the Cadian bastion of Magnot Four-Zero after a volley of Basilisk fire had obliterated his captain. He had personally broken the siege of Sevastavork and led the Lorgamar Rebellion to ultimate victory. Yet nothing could atone for the hated blood that flowed in his veins and for this, and other reasons, the Warsmith had not named Honsou as captain of the grand company, despite his utter suitability.

The Warsmith could smell the stench of belief and ambition on Honsou, and its sickly aroma pleased him greatly. This one would risk much for the honour of his captaincy. The rivalry he had carefully cultivated between his commanders was a pungent sweetmeat that nourished his senses.

The Warsmith no longer saw as other men did: his gaze was increasingly drawn into the realm of the immaterium, perceiving things beyond the ken of mortal men, things that would drive them to insanity. In every twisting weave of air he saw hints, suggestions and lies of the future. Every dancing particle of matter whispered tales of things to come and things that might never be. He saw a myriad of futures emanating from his champions, the roar of toxin-ridden filth flashing through nightmare darkness, a terrible explosion like a new born sun, and a mighty battle with a one-armed giant whose eyes burned with icy fire. What they were he did not know, but the promise of death they imparted made him smile.

'You have done well, my sons,' began the Warsmith, lowering his eyes to his champions. None answered; none dared to utter a word unless so bidden by their master.

Pleased at their awe, the Warsmith continued. 'We come to this world at the behest of the Despoiler, but it is for my purposes that we do what we must. There is a fortress here that contains something precious to me, and I would see it in my possession soon. You, my sons, shall be my instruments in its obtaining. Great reward and patronage awaits the man who brings me what I desire. Defeat and death await us all should we fail.'

The Warsmith raised his head to the rocky slopes that stretched upwards to the west of the smouldering spaceport. A well-maintained road wove its way towards their goal, the reason for the coming battle. At the road's end, the Warsmith knew that the culmination of everything he had striven for lay secreted below the world – a prize so valuable and so secret that not even the highest and mightiest within the corrupt Imperium knew of its existence.

Without waiting for his champions, the Warsmith set off towards a chevroned Land Raider with thick armour plating bolted to its side and bronzed tracks. The adamantium door slid open with a grating hiss, and the Warsmith turned to address his champions.

'Come, we shall gaze upon the enemy we must destroy.'

HONSOU STEADIED HIMSELF on the cupola of his command Rhino, scanning the skies for any airborne threats to their column of vehicles. He did not really expect anything, the spaceport was in their hands and the skies above it were filled with craft launched from the orbital landers. But Honsou's natural caution made him wary.

Dust gathered in his throat and he hawked a morsel of phlegm over the side of his vehicle, the neuroglottis implanted in his throat assessing the chemical content of the air.

The organ no longer functioned as effectively as it once had, and many of the faint echoes of toxins he could taste were unknown to him. But he tasted enough foulness in the air to know that this planet had once been poison to any living thing that set foot on its blighted surface.

He craned his neck around to look back over the route they had taken, over the dusty, arid rocks of the mountains he had called home these last three months. A haze hung over the rocks where centuries of accumulated sands had been blasted free by the orbital bombardment. Under normal circumstances, an orbital barrage was a risky venture, and surgical strikes almost unheard of. But Honsou's covert mission in the mountains had given the gun creatures on the *Stonebreaker* something to aim for, and allowed them to bring the fearsome power of a battle barge to bear upon this planet's defences.

It felt good to have the armoured might of a Rhino beneath him as he rode into battle at the head of his warriors. The foe awaited and Honsou craved the excitement of battle as it pounded, hot and thrilling, through his veins. The battle at the spaceport had been a huge release, but now he looked forward to the destruction of an Imperial fortress, the logical methodology, the precise cause and effect initiated by careful planning and organisation.

Dust filled the air and he spat again, wondering what had happened to this world to make it so barren. He dismissed the question as irrelevant, turning his gaze towards the top of the ridge ahead where the transports of Kroeger, Forrix and the Warsmith had halted, their engines idling, plumes of black smoke belching from their gargoyle-topped exhausts. It was galling to be forced to travel behind the company captains, like some kind of lap-dog. He had fought and killed for almost as long as Kroeger and Forrix; he too had committed heinous acts in pursuit of their goals, had led men through the fire and proved his worth time and time again. Why then was he denied his captaincy; why must he constantly fight to prove his worth?

The answer came easily enough as he glanced at the pattern of dried blood on his gauntlet. His polluted blood was his curse. To be created from the seed of the enemy was an insult to both himself and that enemy, and a constant reminder that he was not pure, not of true Iron Warrior stock, despite those fragments of gene-seed that had come from the chosen of Olympia.

Bitterness rose in him and he let it come, revelling in the ashen taste in his mouth. Bitterness was easier than the stench of desperation and frustration he smelled on himself, the knowledge that no matter how hard he strove, he would never be accepted.

The driver of his Rhino, once an Iron Warrior, now so mutated that he and the vehicle were virtual symbiotes, pulled onto the top of the ridge, halting the vehicle beside that of Forrix. The gnarled veteran acknowledged his arrival with the briefest nod of his head, while beyond Kroeger ignored him.

Honsou allowed himself a tight grin. No matter how bitter he felt towards his master, he could always take solace in the fact that he was warrior enough to threaten Kroeger. He knew that the Warsmith valued Kroeger, and if the headstrong captain of the second company felt that Honsou was a threat, so much the better.

The Warsmith stood at the edge of the ridge, lost in thought, and Honsou shuddered in unreasoning fear as his eyes followed the writhing of the damned souls that undulated within the substance of his lord's armour. His eyes stung if he stared too long, but his attention was claimed by something far, far greater than the Warsmith's armour.

Ahead, cupped within the red-brown rocks of the valley, sat the fortress complex of Hydra Cordatus.

Honsou could scarcely believe his eyes. The perfection of the citadel before him was breathtaking. Never before had he laid eyes upon such a wondrous example of the military architect's art.

Ahead, hunched on a rocky promontory high above the plateau sat a small, three-bastioned fort, with sloped walls of featureless rockcrete. Before the centre bastion stood a tall, crenellated tower, with sweeping walls protecting the narrow gorge between the left and centre bastions. The tower commanded the plateau, though in a protracted siege, Honsou saw that it would be the first location to be destroyed. The height and steepness of the slopes leading up to the fortress presented a formidable barrier in itself, and Honsou knew well enough that any assault on its walls would be bloody work indeed. Every centimetre of the plateau before the fort was sure to be covered by guns and there could be no approach to the main citadel while this outwork remained in Imperial hands.

But as his gaze travelled further north from the high fortress, Honsou forgot the impressiveness of the fastness atop the promontory. It was but the smaller cousin to the main citadel itself, and Honsou felt the blood thunder in his veins at the prospect of attacking this mighty edifice. Its proportions were so perfect that he wondered whether even he or any of the Iron Warriors alive could have designed such a majestic creation.

Two vast bastions, each large enough to contain thousands of warriors, squatted threateningly on each side of the valley, the majority of their armoured structure concealed below the slope of the ground as it angled downwards towards Honsou. The geometry of their construction was flawless, the precision of their construction a marvel. A long curtain wall connected them and, between the two massive bastions, Honsou could see the top of what looked like a forward ravelin, an angled structure shaped, in plan, like a flattened 'V'. The ravelin protected the curtain wall and gate behind from attack, and could sweep attackers from the faces of the two bastions with murderous flanking fire. Both fronts of the ravelin were in turn covered by the faces of the bastions, so there could be no refuge from the storm of gunfire and artillery.

Though the slope of the ground concealed the foot of the bastions and ravelin, Honsou knew that each would have a lethal mix of ditches, fire traps, killing zones, minefields and other defensive traps.

Hundreds of metres of razor wire stretched out from the lip of the glacis, the slope built up at the forward edge of the ditch before the walls to prevent them from being targeted with direct-fire artillery weapons, the wire forming a barbed carpet across the entire floor of the valley.

Much of the remainder of the fortress was concealed from his vision by the angle of the ground and the cunning of its builders, but in the centre of the northernmost face of the valley, Honsou could see a diamond-shaped blockhouse built high on the slopes, its upper walkways bristling with guns. Its positioning could only mean one thing: that it was protecting something below and out of sight, possibly an entrance to the underground defences within the mountainside.

Positioned on higher ground, nearly a kilometre to the west of this blockhouse sat an ornate tower, crowned with winged angels and carved from a smooth black stone. Even from here, Honsou could see that it was not constructed from local materials, but ones brought from off-world. A statue lined walkway sloped down from this tower, vanishing from sight as it travelled below the horizon of the bastion tops.

What its purpose was, or how such an exquisite piece of delicate architecture had come to be built in such a desolate place, was a mystery, but Honsou paid it no heed. Its strategic importance in any plan to attack this fortress was negligible, and thus it was irrelevant to him.

Whoever had designed this citadel was a master of the art indeed and Honsou felt a fierce stirring in his belly as he imagined this place churning with men and machines, blood and death, the thunder of artillery rumbling from the valleysides, blinding clouds of choking, acrid smoke and the screams of men as they drowned in thick, sucking mud, crushed underfoot by the tread of mighty Titans.

What secrets did this citadel hold? What mighty weapon or unknown treasure was concealed within its walls? In truth, Honsou did not care, the chance to assault a place of such majesty would be honour enough. That the Warsmith desired to unlock its mysteries was sufficient for Honsou, and he vowed that whatever it took, whatever acts he had to commit, he would be the first across the shattered rubble of this citadel's walls.

A hollow boom echoed from the sides of the valley and Honsou saw a puff of dirty smoke blossom from behind the walls of the promontory fort. Even as the shell arced through the orange sky, Honsou could see it would land short. Sure enough, the shell impacted over half a kilometre before their position on the ridge, throwing up great chunks of earth and a long plume of smoke.

The Warsmith stared in the direction the shot had come from and said, 'The battle has begun and it is time we learned more of our foes' capabilities.'

He turned to his champions, nodding to Kroeger.

'Bring up the prisoners…'

Five

THE COMMANDER OF the 383rd Jouran Dragoons regiment, Prestre Vauban, took a lungful of tobacco from his cigar and closed his eyes, allowing the acrid blue smoke to swirl in his mouth before exhaling slowly. The thick cigar was a gift from Adept Naicin and, while he normally preferred a milder cheroot, there was something strangely satisfying about the powerful taste of this monstrous, hand-rolled cigar.

Naicin smoked them constantly and swore blind that a day would come when the Imperial apothecaries would finally admit that cigars were a healthy pastime for a man to indulge in.

Vauban somehow doubted it, but it was hard to put a dent in Naicin's conviction once he had an idea in his head. Vauban rested his arms on the iron guard-rail and surveyed the landscape before him.

The view from the briefing chamber's south balcony was spectacular, to say the least. The blazing orange sky had awed him with its primal fire when he had first come to this world, but now its radiance simply nauseated him. Much like everything else on this Emperor-forsaken rock. Ash covered mountaintops stretched as far as the eye could see, and were it not for his cold fury and the thick pillars of black smoke burning far to the south-east, he might have been able to enjoy the rugged beauty of the scene.

Vauban would never forget the horror of the images of Jericho Falls he'd seen on the remote pict-viewers for as long as he lived: the spaceport had burned red with the blood of his regiment. That he could not have prevented it did nothing to ease the burden of his soldiers' deaths. They were his men and had a right to expect their commanding officer not to put them into harm's way without good reason. He had failed in his duty to his men and the pain of that failure was a splinter in his heart.

Jericho Falls in enemy hands, and so many dead it was inconceivable to the soldier in him.

Vauban caught himself staring at the magnificent panorama of steep-sided mountains before him, thinking about the battles to come.

What would it matter if they lived or died here, he wondered? Would the mountains crumble to dust, the wind blow any less fiercely or the sun grow dimmer? Of course not, but then he thought of the vile images he'd seen at Jericho Falls. The evil they promised was unlike anything Vauban had experienced before, and every nerve in his body recoiled at the thought of such forces. They had no right to exist in the universe.

Beings who would wreak such carnage were, by their very nature evil and must be opposed.

It might not matter to the rocks and the sun whether they died here, but Vauban knew that such evil had to be opposed wherever it appeared.

'Sir?' said a voice, rousing him from his grim thoughts.

A staff officer stood at the armoured door that led to the briefing chamber, coughing in the stagnant air. He held a thick sheaf of folders and papers clutched close to his chest.

'Are they all here?' asked Vauban.

'Yes, sir. Everyone has arrived,' replied the officer.

Vauban nodded his acknowledgement as the staff officer gratefully retreated within. He took a last look at the soaring peaks and breathed deeply, drawing his sky blue uniform jacket tighter and buttoning his collar.

They might be at war, but appearances had to be maintained.

Vauban shivered, telling himself it was the crisp mountain air, but he only half believed it. An enemy more evil that he could possibly have imagined had come to this world.

Now they would plan how to fight it.

THE BRIEFING CHAMBER felt uncomfortably warm to Vauban, but he ignored the sweat prickling on his brow and made his way to his chair at the head of the meeting table. Regimental colours and plaques of all the regiments that had garrisoned this citadel over the centuries lined the walls and Vauban nodded respectfully to the ghosts of his predecessors.

Every seat was taken. The senior commanders from his battalions and heads of station were gathered around the long, oval table. The commanders of his regiment sat along one side: Mikhail Leonid, his second-in-command, and the three battalion commanders Piet Anders, Gunnar Tedeski and Morgan Kristan. Along the other side of the table sat the representatives of the Adeptus Mechanicus. Adept Naicin sat with his gloved hands laced before him, smoking a long cigar, his artificial lungs purging the smoke from exhaust ports along his flexing, silver spine. A retinue of blind scriveners and auto-recorders stood behind him, meticulously noting down their master's every movement and utterance.

Beside Adept Naicin, a brass-rimmed, holo-slate displayed a flickering image of an ashen face, haloed by wires and gurgling tubing. The face twitched as half-remembered muscle memories flickered across its features, their organic nature now subservient to the pulse of the machines around them. Arch Magos Caer Amaethon, Master of the Citadel of Hydra Cordatus, frowned from the depths of his machine-temple where he was forever linked to the beating, mechanical heart of the citadel, interfaced with every facet of its operation. So immersed in the internal matrix of the citadel, the scant remnants of Amaethon's body could never leave his mechanised womb buried deep in the heart of the fortress.

Junior officers circled the table pouring caffeine and handing out briefing notes packed with columns of numbers listing operational strengths of units and supply readiness.

Vauban grunted with distaste. 'There's three kinds of lies,' he said, quickly scanning the document, 'lies, damn lies and statistics!'

Behind the table, tonsured technicians prepared the view-slate for the graphics Vauban had ordered and a gunmetal grey lectern was set up slightly to the side.

As the last of the techs and aides left the room, Vauban rose from his seat and moved to stand behind the lectern. The brusque commander exhaled a prodigious cloud of smoke and addressed the council of war.

'Well, gentlemen, we've been hit badly and the situation's probably only going to get worse before it gets better.'

A few scowls crossed the faces of his junior officers at this apparently defeatist statement. Vauban ignored them and continued.

'We don't have a lot of time, so I want to keep this as brief as possible. Then we can start getting even. We've taken a hit, and a damn bad one at that, but if we act now, I think we've got a good chance of kicking the enemy right in the teeth.

'First, I'm going to give you all a rundown on what we've been seeing from here. Now, I'll be fast, so keep up, and if I ask a question you'd better answer me quickly. But if you want to ask any questions, wait until I'm done.'

Taking the officers' silence as assent, Vauban turned to a large scale map of the citadel and its surrounding environs that had appeared on the slate behind him. Jericho Falls was highlighted in red, while the citadel, Tor Christo and the underground tunnel between the two were picked out in green.

'As you can see, the enemy have taken Jericho Falls and has denied us any hope of utilising the facilities there. This also precludes us from expecting any air cover or superiority.'

Vauban turned to face Gunnar Tedeski. 'How many aircraft were based there, Major Tedeski?'

The stocky major was a small man, an ex-Marauder pilot with one arm and a crudely cauterised right eye socket of burnt flesh. Shot down whilst strafing an ork convoy, he had been taken prisoner and tortured by the greenskins before being rescued by warriors from the Ultramarines Fourth company.

Tedeski answered without consulting his notes. 'Five squadrons of Lightnings and four of Marauders. A total of one hundred and twelve aircraft, mostly air interceptors and, we suspect, mostly destroyed.'

'Very well, so at least we can be fairly sure that the enemy won't be using our own craft against us. Anyway, putting that to one side for now, we still have the logistical and strategic advantage. How long that con–'

'Excuse me, Colonel Vauban,' interrupted Magos Naicin, 'but can you explain how you arrived at such a conclusion? It is my understanding that we have lost the one lifeline we had to the outside world and now the enemy is using our own facilities to land yet more troops and war machines. I fail to see how this is to our advantage.'

Vauban didn't bother to hide his annoyance, leaning on the lectern and speaking as though to a particularly stupid junior officer.

'Magos Naicin, you are a man of science, not war, so you cannot be expected to understand, but it is plain to me that this attack on our citadel cannot succeed. We have over 20,000 soldiers, a brigade of armoured vehicles and a demi-legion of the Legio Ignatum at our disposal. I know this fortress and have read the journals of its former castellans. The kill ratio for the citadel's bastions is, at worst, four to one and I am sure that even you will admit that such numbers are beyond the pale of what we can expect from any opposition.'

Naicin bristled at such a dismissive answer, and Vauban returned to the view-slate. Troop dispositions flashed up onto the screen, and Vauban pointed to each glowing icon in turn. 'Our forces are dispersed throughout the main commands. Battalion C is based here along with Battalion B, altogether some 12,000 soldiers and 900 armoured vehicles. Battalion A was split between Jericho Falls and Tor Christo, and, taking into account the losses suffered at Jericho Falls, the battalion now stands at a little under 7,000 men, all currently based in Tor Christo.'

The viewscreen changed again as enemy troop positions and strengths were overlaid on the map.

'As to the enemy, we know that since the battle at the Falls, very little has moved out of the spaceport. As to their numbers we can only guess, but we're assuming they can't have more than 30 to 40,000 soldiers, well armed and, right now, well motivated and led.'

Vauban paused to let the hugeness of the number sink in, pleased to note the absence of any fear in his audience.

'Right then, so that's the situation, as far as we can understand it. Now I want each of you to give the rest of us a quick update on your commands. Nothing fancy, and be honest. If your unit's a mess, short of supplies or otherwise below par then I need to know about it. Understood?'

Vauban addressed the flickering, holographic figure of Magos Amaethon at the end of the table. 'Arch Magos Amaethon, you are closer to the workings of this fort than most men, is there anything I need to know?'

The image of the arch magos fluttered on the holo and Vauban was about to repeat his question when Amaethon answered, his voice wavering and unsure.

'I believe we must hit hard and hit quickly... yes. This citadel is strong... but any fortress will ultimately fall unless it is assured of relief, you see. We are on borrowed time unless we know that reinforcements are on their way to us. We must strive to hold out until reinforcements can arrive.'

'Very well, you all heard the magos. I want full ammo inventories by tomorrow morning from every station. Now normally I don't like reacting to an enemy's moves, it gives him the initiative and keeps us on our back foot. However, in this instance, I don't think we've got much choice.'

Vauban turned to his battalion commanders. 'Gunnar, Piet, Morgan? What's the status of your units?'

Piet Anders was the first to answer. 'Sir, we'll teach those curs a thing or two about fighting, 'pon my soul we shall! Battalion C will send those heretic dogs packing with their tails between their legs before they even get to see the walls of the citadel.'

'As will Battalion A,' snapped Tedeski.

Vauban smiled, pleased at the aggressive spirit of his officers.

'Very well. Good work.'

The officers saluted, eager to please their commanding officer and anxious to see some action.

The castellan of the citadel continued his briefing, emphasising each point with a jab of his fist as he circled the table.

'Major Tedeski will continue to hold Tor Christo, reinforced by two artillery platoons from each of the other battalions. I want to lay as much ordnance on these fraggers as we can before they even get near the citadel. Major Kristan, you will hold the Vincare bastion while Major Anders holds the Mori bastion. Elements from both your battalions will take rotations in the Primus Ravelin, falling under the command of Lieutenant Colonel Leonid.'

Vauban's officers nodded as he outlined more of his plans.

'We are in for a hard fight, gentlemen, and we won't do ourselves any favours by giving the enemy any respite. Assuming I can get Princeps Fierach of the Legio Ignatum to agree to my proposals, I intend to use his Titans and our armoured companies to take the fight to the enemy when a suitable opportunity arises and allow them neither time nor peace to complete their works. The longer we can delay the enemy's advance and keep him from reaching the walls of the citadel, the more time we give reinforcements to arrive.'

Leonid leaned forwards, resting his elbows on the table and said, 'How soon before we can reasonably expect reinforcements to arrive?'

'I can answer that,' replied Magos Naicin. 'With your permission, Castellan Vauban?'

Vauban nodded his assent and the magos continued.

'Before the capture of Jericho Falls, the Adeptus Magos stationed there was able to despatch a coded communiqué with the highest priority prefix. This will be received by all nearby Adeptus Mechanicus outposts very soon. The security prefix I detected on the message should engender the swiftest response.'

'And how soon will that be?' pressed Leonid.

'It is impossible to say with any degree of certainty. Travel over such distances is fraught with all manner of variables and there are many factors that could adversely affect the arrival of our reinforcements.'

'Your best guess then.'

Naicin shrugged and sighed, the sound like a burst of static from his vox-amp.

'Perhaps seventy days, no more than one hundred.'

Leonid nodded, though he was clearly unhappy with the answer he'd received.

'Have we despatched another message from the Star Chamber here? In case the first message does not get through.'

Magos Naicin shuffled uncomfortably, glancing over at the holographic form of his master before continuing. 'Unfortunately we have been having some problems with encoding messages for transit recently and the Star Chamber is… currently unavailable to us at this time.'

Regaining his composure, Naicin said, 'Do not let this concern you, major. It may be that our foes can defeat us by sheer weight of numbers, but that will take them time. Time they do not have if we have reinforcements on the way. They will be reckless with the knowledge that time presses upon them, making them careless. This works to our advantage.'

Naicin sat back as Vauban returned to his seat.

'Alright, gentlemen, are we clear on what we're all doing? We're going to have to be sharp and quick. And we can't afford any mistakes, so keep your rifle close and your sword sharp. Any questions?'

There were none, and Vauban continued. 'Make no mistake, the threat we face here is very real. The coming conflict will demand the best of you and your men. The price of victory will be high, damnably high, and it is a sacrifice we must all be willing to make.

'Now let's go. We have a battle to fight.'

THE FIRST PARALLEL

One

BLOODY, BROKEN AND dejected, the column of men and women shuffled up the road that led from Jericho Falls spaceport to the plateau above. Their heads were cast down; many were grievously wounded and would soon be dead without medical attention.

The Iron Warriors that herded them to their deaths cared not for the condition of their charges. That they could walk was enough.

The column was a mix of thousands of emaciated and malnourished slaves, brought to Hydra Cordatus to work and die, and prisoners taken captive during the attack on the spaceport, spared from death only because it suited the purposes of the Warsmith.

Kroeger marched alongside the wretched column, feeling his contempt for these pathetic so-called humans as a disgusted knot in his belly. How could these snivelling excuses for a species ever hope to rule the galaxy? They were weak and followed the teachings of a rotted corpse on a planet few of them even knew the name of and none would ever have set foot upon.

It galled him to have to use these beasts as fodder, but what choice did they have? The Warsmith had decreed that they be the first into battle and the honour he did them in this manner stuck in Kroeger's throat.

Kroeger felt his rage building and swallowed hard, fighting it down. He was slipping more and more into the frenzied lusts of the Blood God and knew that he must restrain himself.

To satiate his sudden anger he lashed out with his fist, smashing a nearby prisoner's ribs to splinters. The man dropped to the ground, wheezing and wide-eyed in agony. A few nearby captives stooped to help the dying man, but a warning growl from Kroeger soon dissuaded them. The prisoner was unceremoniously kicked aside, and rolled out of the path of the thousands who followed.

'You march to your deaths and know not the honour you are being accorded!' shouted Kroeger as the top of the ridge came into sight. He swung his arms wide, walking backwards up the hillside, lifting his voice so that more could hear him.

'I make you a solemn promise: if any of you survive the task that you have been given, you shall live. You have my word as an Iron Warrior.'

Kroeger turned his back on the column with a hollow laugh before a woman's voice called out, 'And what is that worth, traitor?'

A frozen moment stretched for long seconds as Kroeger drew his chainsword and marched back to the column of people, his face twisted in fury.

'Who dares address me?' he bellowed. 'Which of you weakling scum thinks to question me?'

Terrified men and women desperately pushed themselves from Kroeger's rampage as he swung his sword about him like a butcher, hacking limbs and heads from bodies in his rage.

Kroeger's chainsword rose and fell a dozen times more before the same voice, stronger now, spoke again.

'I do, traitor. Lieutenant Larana Utorian, 383rd Jouran Dragoons. I question what the word of a heretic such as you is worth.'

Kroeger felt the red mist descend upon him, his vision narrowing to a point where all he could see was the woman who had dared speak to him, the pulsing artery in her neck, the arc his sword would take before it hacked her head from her shoulders. But he held the rage in check and forced himself to lower the chainsword. He towered over the prisoner, a lean, insolent-faced woman in a tattered sky blue uniform of the Imperial Guard. The woman was bloody, her arm held in a crude sling, but she stared at him with a fierce hatred.

A strange, unnatural sense of familiarity struck him, though he could not say why. Strangely, Kroeger felt his rage dissipate. What could she hope to achieve by this show of defiance but a swift death? Kroeger leaned down to meet Larana Utorian's gaze, gripping the woman's wounded arm in his gauntlet and squeezing.

Her face contorted in agony, but Kroeger kept pressing until he felt the splintered ends of bone grinding beneath the skin.

'What is your word worth?' repeated Larana Utorian through gritted teeth.

'Not much,' admitted Kroeger, twisting his grip and drawing a fresh cry of pain from Utorian, 'but you are possessed of a modicum of courage, prisoner, and you shall bear the fruits of that courage.'

Laughing, Kroeger released the woman's arm and said, 'This one shall be in the first wave.'

Two

THE FIRST THOUGHT that penetrated the fog of Guardsman Hawke's semiconsciousness was that he had taken it too far this time, that he had drunk something that had finally got the better of him. In all his notorious drinking sessions, he'd never felt such all over pain before, as though his body was one enormous bruise being pounded on by an angry carnosaur.

Darkness and dust surrounded him and he coughed as his lungs heaved, wondering what the hell was going on. He slowly opened his eyes, taking a moment to focus on the view before him. The rockcrete of what looked like the floor of the listening post was right in front of his face, but he could see nothing beyond that. Orange light and swirls of dust ghosted before him.

He tried to shift his position and hot pain stabbed in his left shoulder, drawing a colourful oath and a sticky wetness that ran down his arm.

Hawke turned his head slowly, trying to make sense out of the scorched, acrid-smelling place he was lying in. A blackened, lumpen mass lay against one wall, though he could not make out its nature in the gloom. Hawke's ears rang and every sound his movements made seemed tinny and far away. He shifted position once more, twisting onto his back and gritting his teeth as pain lanced through his shoulder again. But this time he was able to gain more of a sense of his situation. Something heavy lay across his legs and as he twisted around he could see it was the shattered carcass of the vox-unit.

Hawke dragged himself from under the bulky unit as the events of – how long ago now? – came trickling back into his consciousness. He propped himself up against one wall, exploring his injuries with his good arm and remembering the clatter of the grenades as they landed inside. He'd gotten one into the sump, but the other had detonated before he could reach. Thank the Emperor that the decrepit equipment installed in this wretched place was so clunky that it had shielded him from the force of its blast.

He rubbed his arm, feeling the pain from the gash at his shoulder flare anew then glanced over at the blackened shape across the bunker from him. The gleam of bone and the hand burned into a claw told him that it had once been his fellow squadmate, Hitch.

Hawke couldn't feel sorry for Hitch, he had his own problems to deal with – like what the hell was he supposed to do now? The equipment here was smashed and he was sure that there was no way he could fix it. He was stuck near the top of a fragging mountain with no sure way down, and his arm hurt like a cast-iron bitch.

With a groan Hawke pushed himself onto wobbling legs and leaned back against the wall of the listening post. His breath hurt in his chest and he wondered if any of his ribs had been broken. He lurched drunkenly towards a gunmetal footlocker, partly concealed beneath the remains of the assault cannon and vox-console. He kicked the debris clear and hauled open the locker lid, lifting out a canvas rucksack and rummaging around inside. He lifted out a small medi-pack and ripped it open, painfully shrugging off his uniform jacket and undershirt.

As he doused his wound in analgesic fluid and applied a pressure swab to his arm, he wondered who the hell had attacked him. The question only occurred to him as his thoughts became less disjointed and confused. He hadn't had much of a look at them, but whoever they were they were enormous. He'd had a fleeting impression of iron-grey vastness, too bulky to be anything but a Space Marine.

Hawke paused in his ministrations as the breath caught in his throat.

Space Marines…

He'd seen Space Marines a few times – when he'd been unlucky enough to pull a tour at the Hope and had watched them march from their armoured gunships. At first he'd been in awe of their stature, longing to ask one of them about his life, the battles he'd fought and the places he'd seen. But their stoic demeanour, martial bearing and enormous guns had made it clear that to do so would probably be the gravest and last mistake he'd ever make.

Still, there was something about the glimpse he'd had of the anonymous warrior that caused him to shiver in sudden fear. He was like no Space Marine Hawke had ever seen before. For all their arrogant superiority, none of them had, even when they deigned to glance his way, chilled him with such ancient malevolence. This was something else entirely.

A wry smile creased Hawke's ash-streaked features as he suddenly realised that his desire for action had been granted in the most concrete way possible. He had come eye-to-eye with the enemy and was still alive. The puzzle of why his attackers had let him live was solved when his gaze fell once more on the body against the wall. They'd seen Hitch's corpse and figured it for his. He laughed, the pitch a little too high.

'Well, Hitchy boy,' giggled Hawke, 'looks like you managed to do something useful with your life after all.'

Like most people had throughout Hawke's life, the enemy had underestimated him and he felt a sudden anger rise up in him. He was a soldier, damn it, and he'd make sure these bastards knew it.

Cradling his arm close to his chest, he fashioned a crude sling with bandages from the medi-pack and dumped the contents of the rucksack onto the floor, tossing aside items that were just extra weight and loading up with anything that looked useful, not that much had survived the explosion. He stuffed as many ration packs as he could find into his pack as well as a couple of plastic bottles of hydration capsules. He checked his uniform jacket for detox pills, sighing in relief as he felt the container in his inside pocket. Without them, he might as well put a bullet through his brains right now as the poisons within the atmosphere would cause him to sicken within the day unless he took the purgatives and cleansing chemicals the Adeptus Mechanicus Biologis distilled and manufactured for the soldiers. They were perhaps the foulest things Hawke had ever tasted, but if they kept him alive, then he guessed he could bear it. He didn't have too many left, though...

He rummaged around the locker, pulling out a battered respirator kit and stuffing it in the rucksack. The oxygen level inside was just over half-full, but it would come in handy if he got caught in one of the frequent dust storms that lashed the mountains.

Hawke grinned as he pulled out a portable vox-unit from the bottom of the locker, though calling it portable was a joke. The bulky battery packs weighed a kilo each and the vox itself would take up over half the space in his pack. Still, he'd heard it said that there was nothing more dangerous on the battlefield than a man with a means of communication.

Personally, he would rather have a lascannon, but such was life.

He emptied Hitch's and Charedo's packs, searching for anything useful amongst his former friends' gear.

A direction finder and a set of magnoculars once belonging to Charedo went into one pocket, as well as six energy packs for a lasgun. A gleaming knife and tooled leather scabbard, once the pride and joy of Guardsman Hitch, was buckled around his waist with a quick nod to the blackened corpse.

'You don't mind if I take this, do you? No, thought not. Cheers, Hitch.'

Satisfied that he had salvaged all he could from the listening post's meagre supplies, Hawke turned to search for his lasgun, overturning twisted debris and kicking aside drifts of amber dust that had drifted in through the door.

There. He reached down and gripped the stock, pulling the weapon clear of the dust. Seeing that the barrel was twisted and buckled he dropped the useless weapon with a growl of disgust, and turned towards the buckled doorway.

Hawke stepped outside, squinting in the sudden brightness and staring in open-mouthed surprise at the pillars of smoke rising in the distance from Jericho Falls.

'Emperor's holy blood!' hissed Hawke as he gazed up at the packed sky, clustered with enormous craft that surely should not have been able to stay aloft such was their vast bulk. The Falls was busier than he had ever seen it. Tens of thousands of men and machines filled the environs of the spaceport, even more than when the entire regiment had been gathered for embarkation at the Great Muster on Joura.

His knees sagged and Hawke felt the hotness of the mountain ash through his combat fatigues as he sank to the ground. Who could believe that anyone could organise such vast numbers of men? He put his hand out to steady himself, his fingers meeting cold metal and closing around the barrel of a gun.

Hawke looked down, seeing a Jouran pattern lasgun on the ground, its stock smeared with dark blood. Smiling, he picked it up and saw that the charge indicator read a healthy green.

Fresh resolve filled him, and he pushed himself to his feet.

He had to do something, but what?

He couldn't fight that many men. Even the fireside legends of the Space Marine primarchs balked at such odds, yet the Emperor had seen fit to grant him this chance to prove himself worthy. How he would do that he wasn't sure, but he was pretty resourceful, he would think of something.

He couldn't see the citadel from here, but the knifeback ridge that ran north-west from the listening post climbed another thousand metres or so, and should provide him with a fine view down onto both the valley of the citadel and Jericho Falls spaceport.

He slung the lasgun and picked his way over the rocks to where the ground became steeper and more rugged. He sucked in a deep breath, coughing as the dusty air caught in the back of his throat, and took stock of his situation.

Stranded on the mountains with nothing but a portable vox, a rifle with six clips and a combat knife to his name.

Enemies of the Emperor beware, he thought grimly, and began to climb.

Three

FORRIX WATCHED AS yet another column of flatbed trucks carrying sallow-faced troopers roared across the runway towards the gateway in the outer wall of the spaceport. All manner of conveyances rumbled in an endless line from the vast bellies of scores of transports as they touched down and disgorged convoy after convoy of tanks, trucks, supply wagons, armoured carriers and mobile artillery pieces. Thousands of vehicles passed him, directed at each stage of their journey by an Iron Warrior from Forrix's grand company. Nothing was left to chance; every aspect of this logistical nightmare had been foreseen by Forrix and planned for.

Each craft descended in a precise pattern, landing in blinding clouds of ash and retros, disgorging their cargoes before lifting off in a carefully ordered sequence. Forrix knew exactly which ship captains were cautious and which were reckless in their approaches, how long each would take to land and how efficient each one's ground crew were. The noise was deafening and most of the humans landing on this planet today would never hear again.

To the uninformed observer's eye, the spaceport was a heaving mass of bodies and machinery, but had that observer looked closer, they would have seen an underlying structure to the movements. No random Brownian motion this, but a carefully orchestrated manoeuvre whose complex patterns could only be perceived by those with centuries of experience in moving such gargantuan volumes of men and machines.

The sheer scale of the operation and the speed with which it was being undertaken would have amazed Imperial logisticians. Were it not for the Iron Warriors' damnable purpose, those same logisticians would have willingly prostrated themselves before Forrix and begged him to teach them his skills.

As well as overseeing operations from within the spaceport, Forrix had his warriors directing operations from without. The pitiful excuse for defence that had been broken open during the initial attack was even now being repaired and lines of contravallation were being erected to defend the spaceport from any external threat. Not that Forrix particularly expected any, but it was procedure and thus was done. If history and his long years of war had taught him anything, it was that the minute you thought yourself safe from attack was when you were at your most vulnerable.

With a speed that would have put the finest Imperial engineers to shame, a nightmarish assembly of trench lines, razor wire fields and armoured pillboxes were being constructed in defensive formations around the spaceport's perimeter. By nightfall, Forrix expected the lines of contravallation to be complete and Jericho Falls to be as secure as it had ever been in its long existence.

The spaceport was his responsibility and he would not allow it to remain unprotected, no matter how much the Warsmith had assured them that there was no way the

Imperial forces could summon aid, that their psychic link to the rest of the galaxy had been terminated.

Forrix was not so sure. Jharek Kelmaur, the Warsmith's cabal sorcerer, had looked uneasy as the Warsmith glibly dismissed the Imperial telepaths and Forrix wondered what guilty secret the sorcerer might be keeping. Had the Imperial forces been able to make some communication with the outside world that the sorcerer's machinations had been unable to prevent? It was an interesting notion and Forrix would store that nugget away lest it prove a valuable bargaining tool at some later date. The passion for intrigue had long since left Forrix, but he was astute enough to realise that knowledge was power, and it never hurt to have some potential advantage over your rivals. For now he would assume that there was at least the remote possibility of the citadel being relieved and he would plan his defences accordingly.

A rune flashed on his data-slate and Forrix put aside the paranoid intrigues that were the meat and gravy of the Iron Warriors and watched as the main runway was smoothly cleared of soldiers and vehicles as yet another vast ship hauled its bulk through the deep amber sky in shrieking clouds of engine fire. No sooner had the vessel cleared the outer markers of the landing field than a ponderous shadow slipped slowly across the spaceport, its inky blackness spreading across the entire facility like an obscene oil slick.

Forrix knew without looking which craft had entered the approach pattern, and while more easily impressed heads craned skyward to gawp at the leviathan descending towards Jericho Falls, he was merely irritated that it was almost thirty-six seconds behind its schedule. A groaning like the sound of the world cracking open split the air, the grinding screech of massive organic pistons and gears overcoming the bass thrumming of the mechanisms that kept the bloated craft aloft. These ancient and arcane devices, a hideous mix of what had once been organic components and ancient technology, had been created specifically for this craft and there was nothing in the galaxy like it. Their construction owed as much to the power of hyper-evolution and sorcery as engineering, and the physics of their operation should have been impossible. Forrix knew for a fact that their manufacture had only been possible within the Eye of Terror, that region of space where the warp spewed into realspace and all laws of reality ceased to have meaning. That region of space called home by the Legions of Chaos.

As the ominous shadow stopped moving and the deafening grinding noise continued, Forrix glanced up to check that the ship was maintaining the correct altitude.

The cargo now being delivered here was vital to the success of the campaign.

The massive vessel resembled a vast spire of rock pitched on its side and left to lie for millennia at the bottom of some depthless ocean. Its ancient surface was a loathsome, glossy black, like the carapace of some vile insect, pitted and encrusted with lesions and fluid-leaking orifices. Its underside was studded with sphincter-like caverns that shimmered in a monstrous heat haze.

Once, long ago, this vessel had plied the icy depths of space in the unutterable vastness between galaxies, home and locus to billions of creatures linked together in a gestalt consciousness, enslaved to the imperative to consume biological matter and reproduce. It had drifted from world to world, stripping each bare of life, each creature within its shared mind acting in perfect concert with the vast overmind. That had come to an end when the Warsmith had caused its neural pathways to become infected with the same techno-virus that infested the insane Obliterators, severing the vital link between the massive parent vessel and its offspring, stripping away the smothering blanket of belonging from the swarm.

No one knew how long the leviathan had fought the infection before the Warsmith's sorcerers had defeated its defences and dragged the barely sentient carcass to the Eye of Terror. Perhaps the creature-ship had thought it was to be granted succour, but in that regard it was to be sorely mistaken.

Defiled and perverted to serve instead of rule, it had been enslaved to the Warsmith's desires and became yet another cog in his grand design.

Like some bloated sea monster from legend, the gargantuan vessel's vast belly hung open, geysers of putrescent gases venting from its interior. Over two thousand metres in length, it hovered impossibly above Jericho Falls.

From the sweating darkness of its ribbed interior, two shapes slowly descended from the vessel, cries of terror and welcome rising in equal measure as the human soldiers pressed into the service of the Iron Warriors screamed a welcome to their gods of war.

Their upper reaches swathed in metres-thick cable-like tentacles, two vast Battle Titans of the Legio Mortis descended to Hydra Cordatus. First came their massive legs, each like the tower of a castle, their surfaces studded with gun ports and scarred by millennia of war, followed by wide torsos and armoured chests.

Shaped in the image of Man, their resemblance to their creators ended there. Powerful arms, bearing guns larger than buildings, hung inert from wide, turret-like shoulders. Then came the heads, and Forrix, for all his weariness of battle, could not help but be struck by the terrible power inherent in these glorious creations. Whether they had been carved, moulded or shaped by the will of the dark gods themselves none could say, but their daemonic visages shone with the very power of Chaos, as though a fragment of that raw energy might be contained within their hellish features.

The ground shook with thunderous vibration as the feet of these glorious machines slammed down like the tread of an angry god. The glistening cable-tentacles, slipped free of their charges, coiled back into the belly of their host and vanished from sight as the next two Battle Titans were readied for landing.

Forrix watched as the two Titans stood motionless on the landing field, their power and majesty palpable even in their stillness. A sinuous tail, bearing a spiked wrecking ball larger than the greatest super heavy tank, twitched at the back of the largest Titan and a massive cheer burst from the assembled warriors.

A powerful whine burst suddenly from the Titans as the mighty weapon-arms began to move, a fierce and monstrous anime enlivening each of the war machines with vigour. The first war machine, once an Emperor-class Titan in the service of the corpse-god, now known and feared as the *Dies Irae*, took a ponderous step forward, its mighty foot crashing down on the ground with teeth-loosening force, its daemonic princeps eager to plunge into battle lest his monstrous war machine turn its fury upon its allies.

Its companion in death, the *Pater Mortis*, raised its guns to the heavens, as though saluting the gods for delivering it to war once more and roared its battle lust across the world. Smaller than the *Dies Irae*, it followed its massive sibling like a devoted acolyte.

Forrix allowed himself a tight smile as he watched the two mighty engines of destruction stride from the spaceport towards the mountains. Tanks and infantry swarmed around their legs. Those who had fought alongside these lethal machines before kept a sensible distance from them while those unused to seeing the power of their masters so physically manifested clustered around to pay homage. Many of their foolish human soldiers paid the price for their unwise devotion, as whole swathes of men were crushed underfoot with each step of the gigantic machines.

Two more Titans were even now descending to the planet's surface and there would be many more before this day's operation was complete. Forrix had much yet to do, but was content that everything was proceeding on schedule.

Within another two hours there would be an army of conquest ready to take this world apart in a storm of iron.

Four

LARANA UTORIAN FOUGHT to keep the pain of her ruined arm at bay just a little longer. Even if she lived through this nightmare, which she acknowledged was unlikely, she knew she would lose it. The giant who had brought them here had seen to that, crushing every bone and ripping every tendon in her arm. Each step sent bolts of pain shooting through her and it took a supreme effort of will not to drop to her knees and just give up.

She had seen what happened to those who had done that, and had no wish to end her days as a screaming, eyeless wreck, nailed to the chassis of a traitor's tank. She would face death on her feet like a true soldier of the Emperor.

Painfully, she shuffled uphill, keeping her eyes focussed on the neck of the man in front, concentrating on putting one foot before the other. She glanced up as he suddenly stopped and felt a hot, roiling sensation of fear work its way through her gut as she saw the formidable, rocky slopes of Tor Christo before her. The grey bastions on the rocks above were over a kilometre away, but Utorian fancied she could make out the faces of the gunners and soldiers on the firing steps. What must they be thinking, she wondered? Were they afraid, or were they full of bravado, confident that nothing could breach their high walls? Larana hoped they were afraid.

Their column began moving forwards as smoke-belching trucks roared alongside them. The trucks skidded to a halt at the head of the columns and sudden hope flared in Larana's heart as she saw men in crimson overalls with crude eight-pointed stars stitched over their left breast on the back of the trucks handing battered, but serviceable looking rifles to the startled prisoners. If these traitorous curs thought that the men and women of the Jouran Dragoons would fight for them, then they were even more deluded than she had thought. As soon as she was given a weapon, she would turn it on their captors and damn the consequences.

But any hope of a swift death in a glorious last stand were dashed as Larana took hold of one of the rifles and discovered it was nothing more than a hollow framework, the internal workings missing. She felt tears of frustration well up inside, but suppressed them viciously. Hands pulled at her, dragging her and the others forward and lifting them onto the backs of the trucks. Too numb to resist, she allowed herself to be packed into the vehicle, biting her lip to avoid screaming as more and more prisoners were pressed inside the truck. The stench of fear was overpowering. Soldiers vomited and soiled themselves in terror as their reserves of courage finally reached their limit.

Larana, pressed at the side of the truck, caught only glimpses of what was happening outside. The revving of engines built to a deafening crescendo and she could see hundreds of trucks, all as crammed as this one, lined at the edge of the plateau. Interspersed between the trucks, Larana could see boxy, armoured personnel carriers, similar to the ones she had seen Space Marines using. She knew they were called Rhinos, but these bore little resemblance to the noble vehicles she had seen members of the Adeptus Astartes employ. Their armoured sides had a disgusting, oily texture, as though somehow alive, their every surface festooned with spikes, chains and skulls. The roar of their exhausts was like the bellowing of some impatient predator, and each bucked madly, as though chafing at the delay enforced upon them.

Larana bit her lip hard enough to draw blood as the truck lurched forward, its wheels churning the dusty ground as its wheels fought for purchase. Her vision spun crazily and she gripped the stock of her useless lasgun trying not to imagine the next horror that awaited her.

GUNNER FIRST CLASS Dervlan Chu watched the approaching line of vehicles through the gunsight of his Basilisk artillery piece mounted behind the walls of Tor Christo's Kane bastion with undisguised relish. The image was grainy and static interference washed through the sight, but its beauty was unmistakable. It was an artilleryman's dream. He tried to get a count on the number of targets approaching the fortress, dividing the approaching line in two and then halving it again. He made out roughly three hundred trucks, no doubt laden with traitorous scum eager to dash themselves against the bulwark of Tor Christo, and perhaps two dozen APCs.

These fools hadn't even bothered to commence their attack with an artillery barrage or under cover of smoke. If this was the calibre of their opposition, then the warnings of their company commanders had been largely unnecessary. They would send these incompetent idiots home in pieces.

Chu already had his zones of fire mapped out, he knew the precise ranges of his gun, and his loading team already had one of the metre-long shells loaded in the breech of the massive artillery piece. He allowed himself a quick glance along the line of emplaced artillery, pleased to note that every other gun appeared to be locked and loaded. Jephen, the commander of the next Basilisk in line, gave him a smiling thumbs-up.

Chu laughed and shouted, 'Good hunting, Mr Jephen! A bottle of amasec says I tally more than you and your boys!'

Jephen sketched a casual salute and replied, 'I'll take that wager, Mr Chu. Nothing tastes as fine as amasec another man has paid for.'

'A fact I shall no doubt rejoice in later, Mr Jephen.'

Chu returned to his gunsight as the line of vehicles rumbled closer, the roar of their engines little more than a distant growl from his elevated position. Smoke and dust billowed behind the attacking vehicles and soon they would be in range.

Chu swivelled on his gun-chair to watch the senior officers of the Christo, together with the omnipresent priests of the Machine God, gathered far behind the guns, consulting an attack logister that was no doubt wired into the gunsights of their artillery pieces.

A liveried aide passed round crystal glasses of amasec to the senior officers from a silver tray as another handed out ear protectors. The officers laughed at some private joke and toasted the success of the venture, downing their drinks in a single gulp.

The officers removed their peaked caps and donned their ear protectors. One officer, who Chu recognised as Major Tedeski, stepped towards the guns and raised a portable vox to his mouth.

The oil-stained speaker beside Chu hissed and Tedeski's harsh, clipped tones announced, 'My compliments to you, gentlemen, you may fire when ready.'

Chu smiled and returned to his gunsight, watching the range counter unwind as the enemy approached.

HONSOU DUCKED INSIDE the crew compartment of his Rhino and spun the locking wheel of the hatch behind him. There was little point in manning the bolters now, and he would only expose himself to unnecessary risk by riding with the hatch open.

He returned to his commander's seat as the Rhino bucked over the undulating ground, the driver easing back on its speed and allowing the trucks carrying the prisoners to take the lead. There were sure to be minefields before the hill fort, and it was the trucks' job to find them first.

The warriors accompanying him chanted a monotonous dirge – a prayer to the Dark Gods, memorised and unchanged these last ten millennia. Honsou closed his eyes and allowed it to wash over him, his lips moving in time with the words. He clutched his bolter tight, though he knew that it was not yet time to sate its battle hunger with the blood of traitors. The only deaths likely this day were those of worthless prisoners, men who deserved to die anyway for their stubborn refusal to follow the only true path that could save mankind from the multifarious horrors of this universe.

Where else but in Chaos could humanity find the strength to resist the implacable advance of the tyranids, the barbarity of the orks or the nascent peril of the ancient star-gods that were even now awakening from their aeons-long slumbers? Only Chaos had the power to unite a fragmented race and defeat that which sought to destroy it. The soldiers of the corpse-god only speeded the ruination of that which they purported to defend by resisting Chaos.

Well, the great work they undertook here would bring the ultimate victory of Chaos one step closer, and the Warsmith would surely reward all those who aided in his victory with the patronage of the gods. Such a prize was worth any price and Honsou knew he would risk anything to win such reward.

The roar of the Rhino's engine deepened, startling Honsou from his reverie and he knew that the time had come to implement the next stage of the attack.

THE TRUCK BOUNCED over the uneven ground and Larana Utorian felt her legs sag as pain washed over her. She fell against the side of the truck, sinking to her knees and slamming her face against its timber panelled sides. She tasted blood and felt a tooth snap from her gums.

Larana tried to push herself upright, but the press of bodies was too great and she couldn't move. She was trapped by jostling legs, her trousers soaking up the human waste swilling around the truck's floor.

Through a splintered plank, she watched the truck alongside them, the crimson overalled driver heedless of the human cattle in his vehicle. She locked eyes with a young soldier across from her, his eyes wide in terror, tears streaking tracks down his dirty face. The boy's eyes were full of mute pleading, but Larana could do nothing for him. As though in a race, the boy's truck began pulling ahead and she watched as it bounced across a rugged patch of scrub.

A huge explosion lifted the vehicle into the air, spinning it onto its front section, the chassis breaking in midsection. Bright flames and afterimages danced across Larana's eyes as she saw bodies flung in all directions. The buried mine threw out secondary munitions – anti-personnel charges that exploded seconds later to shred anyone fortunate enough to survive the initial blast. She lost sight of the boy as the wrecked truck was swallowed in the dust behind them, knowing there was no way he could have survived.

She was thrown forward, the cries of terror growing louder as she heard more explosions. The truck skidded to a halt in a billowing cloud of obscuring red dust. What was happening? She heard desperate shouting and screams as the tailgate of the truck was wrenched down and fiery light flooded the rear of the truck. Snarling voices and barbed clubs hammered into the prisoners, their captors were dragging them from the illusory safety of the trucks.

Larana was propelled to her feet by the mass of men debarking from the truck and fell to the hard-packed ground. Black smoke billowed upwards from scores of wrecked vehicles, their twisted hulks broken by the detonation of mines. Bodies lay strewn about and the screams of the wounded were ignored as the prisoners were clubbed forward. The spike adorned Rhinos ground to a halt behind the smoking wrecks and, with practiced ease, the iron giants who had brought them to this slaughter emerged, weapons at the ready.

A terrified man, his eyes wild, stumbled past her, heading in the opposite direction. Larana watched as one of the giant warriors casually gunned him down, a single bolt from his weapon blasting the man's entire torso away. Larana rose to her feet, dazed and blinded by dust and pain. Smoke stung her eyes and she could no longer feel her arm. She stumbled in the direction everyone else was running. Was it to safety? She couldn't tell.

Howls of pain and confusion tore at her ears and she gripped the barrel of her impotent lasgun, vowing that she would use it to crush an enemy's skull before the day was out. More gunfire sounded behind her. A body, gory holes torn in its flesh, fell into her and streaks of bullets whipped by her head.

She pushed the body away and ran into the smoke.

DERVLAN CHU PRESSED the firing stud on the armament panel and closed his eyes as the Basilisk fired. The massive barrel's recoil pushed almost its entire length into the track unit, the crack of the shell's discharge easily penetrating the ear protectors he wore. Despite the bolted locking clamps, the track unit rocked under the force of the recoil. Even as the first shell arced through the air, his loading team was ejecting the spent casing and unlimbering a fresh shell from the gurney beside the gun.

He pressed his eye to the gunsight, checking to see how much the recoil had caused the barrel to drift from its aiming position. Not much, he saw, spinning the correction wheel, bringing the aiming reticle back to centre, and adjusting fire for the next shot.

'Loader alpha ready!' came the shout from below.

'Up!' answered the breechman.

Chu smiled. Their first shell hadn't even impacted yet and they were ready to fire again. He and his crew had trained hard for just this kind of fight and now that training was paying off.

He centred the aiming reticle on a smoking truck with scores of men milling in confusion around it and pressed the firing stud again.

EVEN OVER THE screaming and confusion, Larana Utorian could hear the shriek of the incoming shell and recognised it for what it was. She hurled herself flat, screaming as her arms jarred on the hard earth. The ground whipped upwards, tossing her through the air as the first Basilisk shell impacted, blasting a crater fifteen metres across and obliterating a dozen men in an instant. Shrieks sounded as further shells struck the ground with thunderous hammer blows. Huge chunks of rock and dust were blasted skyward as the first volley hit. Larana slammed back to the ground, the impact driving the breath from her lungs. She rolled over, across the lip of a crater, and flopped to its smoking base.

Scraps of flesh and bone spattered the interior surface of the crater, the stench of scorched human meat and burning propellant filling her nostrils. Another prisoner sheltered in the crater. His mouth was open, stretched wide as he screamed in terror, but Larana could not hear him, her skull filled with an all-encompassing ringing.

She felt wetness seep from her ears.

The man sheltering in the crater stumbled over to her, his mouth working soundlessly up and down, but Larana ignored him, crawling to the lip of the crater, clutching her lasgun like some kind of protective talisman. The man was insistent though and clawed at her uniform. Larana pushed him away, shouting something incoherent over the whoosh of displaced air as another volley of shells screamed in. The man rolled into a foetal ball, rocking back and forth in terror.

Larana buried her head in the ground as she felt the awful vibrations of the shell impacts hammer the ground. With her good arm she clutched the soil. Dust filled her mouth and the shockwaves from the explosions threatened to pulp her bones to jelly.

She knew she couldn't stay here. She had to get back. But which direction to go? One place was as likely to take a hit as another and the smoke and disorientation had made a mockery of her sense of direction.

She scrambled to the weeping man at the crater's base, and dragged him by the collar towards the rear edge of the crater.

'Come on! We have to get back!' she yelled.

The man shook his head, fighting Larana's grip with the strength of a madman and pulling free of her grasp.

'You'll die if you stay here!' she shouted. The man shook his head and Larana was unsure whether he'd even heard her or she'd made any kind of sense. She'd tried her best, but if the idiot didn't want to move, there was nothing she could do to make him. She dropped flat as another thunderous detonation rocked the ground, the impact throwing her from the crater.

She landed on something soft and yielding, and rolled clear with a terrified cry as she saw that she was lying on shredded flesh and mangled limbs. Shapes ran through the smoke, but where they were going or who they were, she couldn't tell. She could see nothing more than a few metres away, the drifting smoke and dust rendering everything beyond invisible.

A smoking wreck lay on its side, belching black clouds just at the edge of her vision and she began crawling towards it over torn-open corpses and crying men with no legs or arms. One man was on his knees, vainly trying to gather up his looped entrails and push them back into his ruptured belly. Another stuffed his severed arm into his jacket, beside a man vomiting thick ropes of red gore. Each few paces brought fresh horrors and Larana wept as the ground continued to shake as though in the grip of the most violent of earthquakes.

She reached the blazing truck, weeping and laughing hysterically at this small victory. A blackened corpse lay under the shattered cab of the vehicle, severed through the torso by the truck's fall. Larana could see the corpse wore the crimson overalls of their captors and felt a burning hatred light in her belly. She snarled in fear and anger, pounding her rifle butt against the corpse's skull, smashing it to destruction, fresh sobs bursting from her lips with every blow. She threw aside the bloody weapon and took what shelter she could from the burning truck. Tyre tracks from the vehicle led back through the smoke towards the place where – presumably – this insane venture had begun. Taking a deep breath she waited until another barrage of shells landed.

Knowing that there was no way she could survive, but unwilling to give up, Larana Utorian set off to find a way out of this hell.

ACRID PROPELLANT FILLED Kane bastion, but Dervlan Chu was exultant despite the sting in his eyes and the ringing in his ears. The attack had been stopped in its tracks before it had covered even half the distance to the Christo. They had comprehensively bracketed the enemy force within their fire zones and put their entire load on target. He knew for a fact that his crew had laid more shells on target and in a faster time than Jephen, and looked forward to receiving his bottle of amasec in the mess hall tonight.

Night was drawing in and drifting smoke obscured much of the shattered battle line of what had once been hundreds of vehicles. Major Tedeski had called a halt to the barrage until the smoke cleared, unwilling to waste ordnance on a foe that was already destroyed.

He sat back on the railings of the gun platform and pulled out a silver case of cheroots, lighting one and tossing the case down to his loader and breechman.

'Well done, men, I think we managed to put a sizeable dent in the foe this time.'

His crew smiled, teeth gleaming in their soot-stained faces as he said, 'When I get that bottle of amasec from Jephen, I'll be sure to share it with you.'

He took a satisfied draw on his cheroot, and took another look through the gunsight of the Basilisk. The smoke was clearing and his professional eye was pleased with the utter destruction he saw. Hundreds of burning wrecks littered the ground, flames licking skyward as they and their traitorous passengers burned. Their fire zones were cratered wastelands, the ground churned unrecognisably by the sheer power and fury of the barrage.

As he swivelled the gunsight around, he saw that the guns mounted in Mars bastion had been equally thorough. The guns of the Dragon bastion covered the southern approaches to the Christo, and Chu could well imagine the frustration of its commander that the gunners in the Kane and Mars bastions had got the glory of the first kills.

Chu returned the gunsight to his own fire zone. The wind was beginning to clear the smoke more rapidly and he could make out shapes moving in the dusk. Chu was surprised there was anything left alive down there. He switched up a level of magnification as the smoke cleared still further and saw more vehicles through the haze: the armoured personnel carriers that he had briefly glimpsed just prior to the commencement of the barrage.

He pressed the range finder button on the armament panel and cursed as he realised the APCs and the warriors standing before them were some hundred metres beyond the maximum range of his gun. A handful of stumbling shapes crawled or walked towards the warriors. As he increased the magnification another level, Chu was suddenly sick to the pit of his stomach as he saw the stained uniforms their targets were wearing.

Dust covered and bloodstained, but unmistakably the sky blue of the 383rd Jouran Dragoons. Horrified, he spun the gunsight back to the cratered desolation his gun had helped to create, moaning as he saw more and more familiar uniforms scattered across the ground, lifeless and broken.

Chu felt his gorge rise as he realised what they had just done. The thought of winning a bottle of amasec from this slaughter made him want to weep.

HONSOU WAS PLEASED. He had watched the barrage from the hilltop fort with calm detachment, noting how far the shells reached, how long they had taken to travel to their targets and how wide each bastion's arc of fire was. The southernmost bastion had not fired, but Honsou knew that, at this range, its big guns were irrelevant. Its artillery pieces could only cover the far southern approaches, but the close-in guns and soldiers on the wall could sweep the face of the centre bastion with murderous crossfire.

His armour's auto-senses had easily penetrated the smoke of the barrage and, despite his hatred for the men in the fort, he grudgingly admitted to himself that they were competent gunners. Competent, but not intelligent. Honsou now had an exact plan of the fort's fire zones mapped out in his head. Normally an attacker would pay a fearsome butcher's bill to obtain such information, but where was the cost when you could use prisoners?

Honsou watched the survivors of the artillery barrage stagger back from the killing ground and drew back the hammer on his bolter. Looking at the sorry state of the men that emerged from the rolling banks of smoke, he realised that there was little point in letting them live. Most would be no use as slaves, for how could a deafened man understand orders or obey them? What use was a man with one arm? How could he dig a trench? And if they could fulfil no useful function then they were of no interest to Honsou.

He nodded to his men and in perfect concert, the Iron Warriors raised their bolters and opened fire.

They worked their weapons left and right, shredding the pitiful survivors in a hail of mass-reactive bolts. Pleading faces screamed for mercy, but the Iron Warriors had none to give.

Within seconds almost every last one of the five thousand prisoners who had advanced into the teeth of Tor Christo's guns was dead.

Honsou watched a swaying figure emerge from the smoke, cradling her arm close to her chest, and levelled his bolter at the woman's head.

Before he could pull the trigger, a gauntleted hand reached up and slapped aside his weapon. Snarling, Honsou reached for his sword.

Kroeger whipped his own sword up to swipe Honsou's hand from the scabbard.

Honsou stepped back, his pale features twisted in fury.

'Damn you, Kroeger! You go too far.'

Kroeger chuckled and turned his back on Honsou, gripping the tunic of the sole survivor of the attack and hauling her level with his face.

'Do you see this woman, half-breed? She has courage. She may be a lapdog of the False Emperor, but she has courage. Tell this mongrel scum your name, human.'

Honsou watched the woman's features twist in incomprehension until Kroeger repeated his order. He saw the woman's eyes focus on Kroeger's lips and realised she was probably deafened by the violence of the shelling.

At last she seemed to understand Kroeger's words and croaked, 'Lieutenant Larana Utorian, 383rd Jouran Dragoons. And you gave your word–'

Kroeger laughed and nodded. 'Yes, I did, but did you really expect me to keep it?'

The woman shook her head and Honsou was surprised when Kroeger threw her towards one of his squad leaders and said, 'Take her to the Chirumeks and have the wounded arm removed. Replace it and bring her to me.'

'You are sparing her life, Kroeger? Why? Mercy does not become you.'

'My reasons are my own, half-breed,' snapped Kroeger, though Honsou could see that he seemed just as surprised himself. 'You would do well to remember that, but I am wasting my breath on you. The Warsmith demands you lead your men forward and obtain information regarding the defences closer in. Now that I have the guns mapped I can begin the first parallel.'

'Before we know the sites of any close-in redoubts or traps?'

'Aye, we are to proceed with all speed. Or did you think that the Warsmith's orders did not apply to you?'

'You are unwise to begin the trenches before we know more,' pointed out Honsou.

'And you are a mongrel whelp, not fit to lead a company of the Iron Warriors. I can smell the stench of the ancient enemy upon you. You and your disgusting bastard company. It is an affront that you wear the symbol of the Iron Warriors upon your shoulder guard and I weep for the future of our

Legion to know that unclean hybrids like you are counted amongst our number.'

Honsou fought to keep his bitter rage in check, clenching his knuckles white on the hilt of his sword. How easy it would be to rip it from its scabbard and attempt to strike Kroeger down, but that was just what his rival wanted, for him to prove that he was not worthy of the Iron Warriors. With difficulty, he forced down his anger, seeing the disappointment in Kroeger's eyes as he realised Honsou was not about to rise to his challenge.

'It shall be as the Warsmith commands,' replied Honsou and turned away.

Five

NIGHT HAD CLOSED in completely as Honsou crept through the cratered wasteland before the walls of Tor Christo. The sky was a dull, lustreless orange, streaked with scarlet bands drifting in the upper atmosphere. But to Honsou, the ground before him was as clear as though he walked in the brightest sunlight, the augmented senses of his armour turning night into day.

Far behind him, the warriors of Forrix's company pegged out the arc of the first trench to be dug before the walls of the hilltop fortress. Called a parallel, it was dug in line with the curtain wall of the fortress to be attacked. Deep, but narrow, it was just outside the range of the fort's guns, and would form the first line of attack. From this first parallel would be dug the attack trenches, known as saps. These would be driven towards the fortress on a line which, if extended, would miss the fortress, thus preventing the garrison from firing down the length of them.

When the sap had reached a point where the Iron Warriors' artillery pieces had the range to the hilltop fortress, a second parallel would be dug and breaching batteries placed to batter the walls to rubble in preparation for an escalade. Should it prove necessary, more saps could be dug forward and a third parallel established to place yet more batteries that would lob high explosive shells over the walls and into the heart of the garrison.

Honsou doubted that such a thorough siege would be required to take Tor Christo. The garrison would clearly be able to see the progress the attackers were making and would, in all likelihood, abandon the fortress and pull their men back to the main citadel.

Taking Tor Christo was a necessary precursor to any assault on the citadel, but it was sure to be thankless, bloody work and there would be little glory to be had in such a venture.

This current mission was a prime example of the gritty necessities of a siege. From a distance it was all too easy to rely only on what you could see, trusting to distant observations to prepare a plan of attack on a fortress. Honsou had seen dozens of attacks on fortifications founder due to lack of proper reconnaissance when attackers had run into previously unseen traps or redoubts that rendered their plans obsolete.

Honsou kept one eye on the watchtower that commanded the plateau and one on the ground before him, careful to avoid any fragments of shell casings or discarded weapons and battle gear. Sound carried further at night and the last thing he needed was to be caught out in the open with no immediate support in the vicinity. He and forty warriors from his company crept through the killing zone that had seen thousands of men die that very day, and by stealth, managed to get closer than any of the prisoners had by direct assault.

Carefully, he stepped around a mine his auto-senses detected and dropped a marker for the following troops to avoid. The minefield they traversed presented no significant threat to the Iron Warriors, but it would slow the digging if the prisoners and slaves were afraid of unexploded munitions every step of the way. The crack of metal sounded and Honsou cursed silently as he saw the ponderous form of Brakar Polonas, one of Forrix's senior engineers, step around the mine, marking its position on a light-proofed data-slate. The venerable warrior walked with an awkward, limping gait, his left leg a bionic replacement. It seemed this augmentation also made him incapable of moving quietly. It was a calculated insult by Forrix to send Polonas, letting Honsou know that his information was only trustworthy if accompanied by verification. It was just another entry in a catalogue of carefully measured insults to his prowess. He just hoped Forrix's clumsy insult didn't get them all killed.

He pushed the interloper from his mind as they continued forward, making good time despite their caution and Polonas's lack of stealth.

Honsou was now less than two hundred metres from the base of the rocky promontory that Tor Christo sat upon. Already this reconnaissance was bearing fruit. Ahead he could see three concealed artillery pits carved into the base of the hill. Rock-sheathed doors led within and, were it not for the rails that would carry the guns forward into position, he might never have spotted them.

Again he was forced to admire the cunning of the architects of Hydra Cordatus. These artillery pits were designed to remain silent and hidden until the Christo's attackers believed they had knocked out the fort's guns. Once attackers had established their breaching batteries, these guns would unleash deadly salvoes of ordnance to destroy their artillery pieces.

They were dug at an angle into the rock face, making it difficult, if not impossible, to target with counter-battery fire and Honsou realised that with this information he had a chance to prove his worth to the Warsmith.

He waved over his second-in-command, Goran Delau, and indicated the artillery positions.

'Clever,' observed Delau.

'Aye,' agreed Honsou darkly. 'It will be a devil of a job to destroy them.'

'Indeed.'

Honsou glanced round as the scrape of metal on rock sounded again, and he stifled a curse as Brakar Polonas noisily joined them.

'Why do we stop?' he asked.

Honsou didn't answer, he simply pointed towards the concealed artillery positions.

Polonas nodded, studying the positions with his practiced eye.

'We can mark their positions and shell them once the first parallel's batteries are in place,' suggested Delau. 'We can bring enough rock down to block the guns.'

Polonas shook his head. 'I do not believe it can be done with guns. Look, there is a rock canopy built across the top of the door and a ditch before them to catch any rubble that may be blasted loose.'

Honsou was impressed. He had not noticed those defences and his respect for the old man rose a fraction.

'Then we take the fight to them, and capture the guns now.'

Once again, Polonas shook his head.

'Keep your impatience in check, half-breed. We must not act in haste. Think about it. These doors lead within the rock of the fortress, most likely just to this outwork, but possibly even to the main citadel. Were we to attack now, the enemy would simply seal the tunnels beyond our means to breach and defend them with great vigour.'

'Then what do you suggest, Polonas?' snapped Honsou.

Polonas turned his gaze on Honsou and snarled, 'You must learn to respect your betters, half-breed. The first lesson of intelligence gathering is knowing how to use the information you accumulate. To act precipitously would be to alert the enemy of what we know.'

'Then what? We just ignore the fact that we have discovered these positions?'

'No, far from it. We continue as though we are unaware of their existence. Await their deployment and take the positions by storm by previously infiltrated troops. In conjunction with a frontal escalade, this will allow us to take Tor Christo in a matter of hours.'

Honsou bit back a retort as he saw the sense in what Brakar Polonas was suggesting. It was a salutary lesson and Honsou bowed his head, accepting the words of Forrix's engineer.

'Very well, we will do as you direct, Brakar Polonas,' said Honsou formally.

Swiftly, Honsou contacted the remainder of his warriors and issued the command to return to the rally point. He deactivated the vox-link and was preparing to move out when Brakar Polonas turned and slipped on a loose patch of shale, the metal of his bionic leg scraping noisily between the faces of two boulders.

The Iron Warriors froze.

Tense seconds passed in the stagnant darkness as Honsou held his breath. He scrambled across to the veteran warrior as quietly as he was able and saw that his leg was wedged tight between two rocks. He cursed silently to himself and pressed his gauntlets flat against Polonas's shoulder guards.

'Be still,' he warned.

Just as he had begun to think they had not been detected, a spear of phosphorescent light streaked skyward, closely followed by a second. Both burst within seconds of one another and the plateau was suddenly illuminated by twin suns burning brightly as they slowly descended on small grav-chutes.

A cry of alarm was raised high above them and Honsou cursed aloud this time, uncaring of who heard him.

'Damn you, Polonas!' snarled Honsou, wrenching the ancient warrior from the ground. The metal of the bionic leg was wedged tightly and it was the organic components of the limb that failed first, tearing free in a wash of blood as Honsou ripped Polonas from the ground.

Polonas grunted in pain, the accelerated healing mechanism of his body stemming the flow of blood from his severed leg in seconds. Honsou shucked the man onto his shoulders and shouted, 'Iron Warriors, go! As fast as you can!' He heard the unmistakable cough of mortar fire.

Honsou knew that the first rounds would be for ranging purposes, but there would be spotters on the wall to direct subsequent volleys. They had to make as much use of this time as they could. The strobing light of the two sunflares cast lunatic shadows across the cracked ground and it took all Honsou's skill not to lose his footing as he raced from the base of the mountain. The ground rocked as mortar shells burst ahead of them, scything deadly fragments in all directions, but they were landing too long. The height of the mortars was working against the Imperial gunners now. Their elevation gave them longer reach, but also meant that it was impossible to engage targets within a certain range.

Perversely, Honsou knew they had been safest where they were, but also knew it was only a matter of time until troops were sent to flush them out. It was unlikely the Basilisks would join the fight, as it would be a waste of ordnance to engage so few targets with so remote a chance of hitting.

Another volley slammed into the ground, closer this time, and Honsou stumbled to his knees, just barely keeping his balance with the weight of Polonas on his shoulder. More sunflares exploded overhead and now small arms fire began bursting around them. Las-bolts vitrified the dust and heavy bolters churned the ground. He felt an impact graze his shoulder and another clip his thigh, but these were little but annoyances; his armour was proof against such weaponry.

Heavier impacts blasted into the ground beside him and he swore again as he realised that the defenders had managed to bring some heavy weaponry up to the firing step. A bolt from a lascannon hammered into the ground beside him, cracking the earth and flashing the dust to vapour.

More shells landed and this time Honsou was thrown to the ground as a mortar shell burst less than five metres directly above him, spraying him with razor sharp shrapnel. Red runes winked into life across his visor as the spirit within his armour registered breaches in its structure. Honsou could feel the stickiness of blood briefly run down his leg and back before his enhanced metabolism clotted the wounds.

He offered a brief prayer of thanks to the gods for sparing him. Power armour was amongst the best protection a warrior could have, but even it had its limitations. He reached over to grab Polonas and realised why he had been spared.

The veteran's back was laid open to the bone, his thick ribs and spine glistening and red. His head was a mass of gristle and bloody flesh, pulped grey matter pouring in a glutinous flood from his shattered skull. Honsou shrugged and tapped

Polonas's Iron Warriors' icon on his shoulder plate in thanks for saving his life, then picked himself up from the ground.

Honsou pushed himself forward and, freed from the weight of Polonas, was quickly able to outdistance the mortars, pounding across the cratered ground in a lumbering sprint.

Shells continued to land behind him, but the gunners on the walls were firing at phantoms now, their targets having escaped their wrath. Honsou slowed to a jog and counted in his men, coming up one short. Aside from Polonas, only one other warrior had fallen. Honsou considered they had been lucky.

More sunflares continued to turn the valley's night into day, but the Imperials were simply wasting shells now.

Honsou strode through the picket lines protecting the digging parties, satisfied at the progress the slaves were making. The ground was dusty and hard-packed, but given the right threats and impetus, the slaves were working fast enough.

Over two thousand men dug the barren soil of Hydra Cordatus, creating a trench that ran from the eastern edge of the valley wall to a point mapped out by today's foray of the prisoners at the extreme range of Tor Christo's guns. Here the trench bent southwards, following the curve of Tor Christo's curtain wall.

The earth excavated from the trench was piled on its outer edge, on the side facing the fortress, providing a ready-made fire step and protection for the diggers. Once the trench had been completed, the Iron Warriors would build more permanent fortifications along its length, adding linked bunkers every fifty metres and laying minefields of their own.

Honsou jumped across the trench, nodding in acknowledgement to men from his company as they supervised the labouring slaves, ensuring everything was constructed to their satisfaction. The work was progressing at speed and, barring interference from the Imperials, the trench was sure to be complete before morning.

He moved easily through the swarming throng of bodies engaged in digging and stockpiling supplies ready for the push towards Tor Christo. Slaves either dragged enormous flatbeds of shells and explosives forward or sweated under the load of adamantium sheets to form roadways for heavy artillery and tanks. Others were arranged into chanting groups gathered around hastily emplaced shrines to the Dark Gods, their mutterings overseen by one of Jharek Kelmaur's sorcerers.

Bright arc lights were erected on baroque towers of iron, each placed at points decreed by the sorcerers to create some form of cabalistic arrangement. Quite what this would achieve, Honsou was unsure, but he reasoned that it couldn't hurt to appease the gods, whatever measures were used. Honsou honoured the Dark Powers of Chaos, but preferred to rely on the strength in his sword arm and the explosives in his artillery to win campaigns. To rely on Chaos was to invite disaster at the capriciousness of the gods. Had Angron himself not failed on Armageddon by doing just that?

He saw the Warsmith's pavilion set upon the rocks on the eastern flank of the mountains. Its bronze poles supported billowing steeldust fabric patterned with twisting, chaotic designs that enraptured the eye and held its fascination until reason itself became lost forever within the swirling significance that remained forever elusive. Honsou had learned never to allow his gaze to be lured into the foul pattern and kept his eyes firmly fixed on the figures that reclined beneath its treacherous design.

The Warsmith sat on an enormous throne, carried from lost Olympia and said to have been crafted by the holy Perturabo himself. The Warsmith claimed it was a gift from the primarch after the fighting on Tallarn, though Honsou doubted that their monstrous, daemonic progenitor would have been so generous after that particular campaign. Beside the hulking, sickening presence of the Warsmith stood the dead-faced Forrix, reading out lists of numbers and displacements of troops from a bone-rimmed data-slate.

Behind the throne stood Jharek Kelmaur, the sorcerer whose pronouncements had led them to this world. The sorcerer's armour was embossed with gold and silver, the traceries and patterning bewilderingly complex. Skulls decorated his greaves and cuissart, and his breastplate was moulded in the shape of Adonis-like musculature. He wore no helmet and his features spoke of a sly cunning: a lipless mouth and sewn-up eyes, set within a swept-forward brow. His pale skull was hairless and tattooed with bizarre symbols that seemed to writhe with a life of their own.

Honsou disliked Kelmaur, and did not trust his magicks and subtle manipulations. Kelmaur's head turned in Honsou's direction, as though sensing his thoughts, and a hidden smile creased his papery skin.

Crouched at Kelmaur's feet was a robed figure, its face hooded and unseen. A monochrome cogwheel symbol stitched on its back identified it as a member of the Cult of the Machine, and briefly Honsou wondered what purpose the creature served.

He dismissed the thought as he halted at the entrance to the pavilion, awaiting his lord's permission to enter his presence. Forrix looked up from his lists and his eyes narrowed as he saw that Honsou was alone. The Warsmith glanced up, his face shrouded in flitting shadows, and said, 'Honsou. Enter and tell us of your mission.'

'My lord,' whispered Honsou as he stepped into the pavilion. He felt the queasy sensation build in his stomach at the Warsmith's presence, fighting down his nausea as he gave his report.

'We were able to approach to within two hundred metres of the promontory and I have to report that there are concealed artillery positions at its base. They will be almost impossible to target with gunnery and it is my belief that–'

'Where is Brakar Polonas?' interrupted Forrix.

'He is dead,' stated Honsou with no small measure of satisfaction.

'Dead? How?' asked Forrix, his tone emotionless.

'He took a hit from a mortar shell at close range and was killed instantly.'

Forrix glanced over to Jharek Kelmaur, who nodded imperceptibly.

'The half-breed speaks the truth, Brother Forrix, and the information he brings will aid us greatly.'

Surprised at the unexpected support of the sorcerer, Honsou continued, wondering what price the magicker would later expect.

'We can infiltrate warriors into a position whereby the guns can be seized as they prepare to fire. If we combine this attack with an escalade on the main walls, we should be able to take Tor Christo within hours. The tunnels are sure to lead within its walls, and perhaps even run to the main citadel.'

'You presume too much, Honsou,' stated the Warsmith, his voice like the scraping of iron nails on slate.

'My lord?'

'You seek to plan this campaign for me? Is it your belief that I do not understand the proper workings of siegecraft?'

'No, my lord,' said Honsou quickly, 'I merely thought to offer a suggestion as to–'

'You are young and have much to learn, Honsou. Your inferior mixed blood holds much sway over your thinking and it saddens me to see that you have not learned from your betters. You think like an Imperial.'

Honsou flinched as though slapped. His anger arose, but he clamped bands of iron will around it, holding it and letting it smoulder dangerously within him.

'When I desire your "suggestions" I will ask for them, Honsou. You are not yet worthy to make such offerings to my table. Understand that it is not your place to suggest anything to me. You must spend another thousand years as my servant before even daring to think you are qualified to do so. I shall permit you this one indiscretion, but I will not again. You are dismissed.'

Honsou bit back an angry retort, seeing the satisfaction Forrix took in yet another of his public humiliations. He should be used to the insults and slaps in the face his polluted blood brought him, but it was almost too much to bear when he knew in his gut that he was right.

Stiffly, he bowed and withdrew from the Warsmith's pavilion, his heart burning with controlled fury.

He would prove them wrong. All of them.

* * *

Six

DAWN BROKE ITS first light over the mountain peaks in sickly red streams, bathing the mountains in the colour of blood. As the echoing boom of distant artillery fire roused him from a fitful sleep, Guardsman Hawke rolled over and grunted as his shoulder grazed an outcrop of black rock. Groggily, he opened his eyes and stared into the lacerated sky.

His limbs ached, his throat was raw and his eyes felt like someone had been rubbing them with sandpaper all night.

He sat up and rummaged through the pouches on the side of his pack, pulling out his hydration pills. He swallowed a pair of blue capsules with a mouthful of water from his canteen. He had water and tablets enough to last for maybe three weeks and meal packs for two – depending on how he was able to ration himself.

But food and water weren't his main worries.

No, his main concern was his lack of detox pills. He pulled the plastic pill container from his pocket and counted out the capsules inside. Without this medicine, the Adeptus Mechanicus claimed, anyone stationed on this planet would become unbearably sick. It had never happened to him yet, but he was in no rush to put the theory to the test.

Glumly he realised that he had enough for another six days, but, Emperor willing, he hoped to be back in the citadel by then. He had a vox-unit and though he had been unable to raise anyone last night, he fervently hoped he'd be able to make contact today.

He yawned and stretched, pushing himself to his feet with a groan of stiffness. He had climbed a thousand metres over steep, rocky terrain and, though he hated to admit it, he realised he was badly out of shape. It had been early evening by the time he'd reached this perch overlooking the valley of the citadel and Jericho Falls, his legs burning and his lungs afire. He'd needed ten minutes on the respirator just to get his breath back.

Just in time for a grandstand view of the horror of watching thousands of his comrades in arms herded forward like cattle to be butchered in the storm of shelling from Tor

Christo. He'd screamed himself hoarse with frustration. Couldn't they see they were shelling their own men? He'd burned out a whole battery pack trying to raise the gunners on the Christo and tell them of their error.

The smoke had obscured the worst of the horror, but when it cleared, he'd been shocked rigid at the carnage he saw below him through the unflinching lenses of the magnoculars. What manner of foe had come to Hydra Cordatus? Death in battle he could understand, but this senseless slaughter was beyond his comprehension.

Though he'd tried to get some rest, sleep constantly eluded him. The rumble of artillery, heavy vehicles and ultra-rapid construction had echoed constantly from below. When the sky had lit up with sunflares, he'd used the magnoculars to try and see what was happening, but all he could see were tiny explosions bursting on the plain before the Christo as the gunners lobbed shells over their walls.

Hawke pulled his jacket tighter about himself and shouldered his pack, tossing aside the burnt out vox-battery and ration pack he'd consumed last night and limped towards the edge of the ridge. He pulled out the magnoculars, training them on the base of the mountains to see what this morning's light brought.

The pace of operations at Jericho Falls had slowed, but not by much. The huge cargo ships that had been descending in a more or less constant stream were still arriving, but there were noticeably fewer than yesterday.

'Great balls of the saints!' swore Hawke as he shifted his gaze from the spaceport to the gap in the mountains that led from Jericho Falls to the citadel.

Enormous numbers of vehicles, artillery and siege engines rumbled along the road in ordered ranks, though there was a strange, shimmering haze obscuring some of the larger machines, and what seemed like an unnecessarily large number of guards stationed around them. Hawke noticed that these guards were all facing inwards as though the machines themselves were the threat.

Shocked by the sheer amount of hardware on its way to the citadel, he turned and clambered across the jagged rocks

to the other side of the knifeback ridge and trained the magnoculars on the valley below.

He gasped as he saw the vast scale of the engineering
works carried out during the night. A vast trench, at least a
kilometre long, stretched due west, its outer edges piled high
with earth, before bending in a sloping, concave arc to the
south-west. The curving arm of the trench exactly followed
the sweep of the walls of Tor Christo and its outer face was
likewise strengthened with earthen walls.

Further trenches, like snaking roots, wound their way back
to enormous supply depots, huge stockpiles of artillery
shells and construction materials where long trains of men
dragged supplies throughout the sprawling campsite.

Already Hawke could see working parties digging forward
from the main trench parallel to the walls. A constant thunder of distant artillery boomed from the high walls of the
Christo, powerful explosions slamming into the earth
around the working parties, but the high, earthen berms
thrown up on the exterior faces of the trench protected the
workers from the worst of the blasts.

And the saps continued inexorably towards Tor Christo.

Behind the trenches sprawling bunkers and massive
artillery positions had been built. Though nothing occupied
the latter at present, Hawke wondered what manner of gun
might fill such a site. The stone of their structures appeared
to have been quarried from the mountainside during the
night by vast, tracked drilling machines. Hawke could see
these were even now boring into the rock for more building
materials. Everything suggested a monstrous controlling
influence that knew every last detail of every operation. The
sheer mechanical, unfeeling nature of what he saw chilled
Hawke to the bone.

A swelling roar of affirmation rose from the valley floor
and Hawke saw that almost the entire population of the
camp had ceased its labours, parting before something as yet
hidden from Hawke's sight.

The echoes of ponderous footsteps reached him and
Hawke's blood slowed as he watched a legion of enormous
dark gods tread the earth.

He shucked the pack from his shoulders and desperately fumbled for the vox-unit.

HONSOU WATCHED IN rapt adoration as the Battle Titans of the Legio Mortis strode the earth, the thunder of their footsteps threatening to break apart this planet's fragile crust. The majority of the hellish war machines stood over twenty metres in height, their fearsome physiques cast in the form of mighty daemons from the depths of the warp. Each growled with a primal ferocity, their hunger for destruction only barely kept in check by that which controlled them.

The largest of these monstrous leviathans, the *Dies Irae*, led the Battle Titans, its barbed tail sweeping back and forth in anticipation of the slaughter. Vast spires, like perverted and defiled cathedrals, rested upon its gargantuan shoulders, gun platforms and massed batteries of artillery clustered on each twisted steeple.

To witness the gathering of creations which were so close to Chaotic divinity was a privilege Honsou had experienced only a handful of times, and he felt humbled by such a potent display of the power of the gods of Chaos. The shadows of the Titans swallowed the camp, swathing the acres of men and materials in darkness as they passed.

Honsou watched as hundreds of chained prisoners were herded forward to be crushed underfoot as an offering to the daemonic powers that dwelt within the Titans' unholy bodies. Their lumbering stride continued, giving no sign that they even noticed the carnage they caused with every step. The *Dies Irae* paused in its thunderous march and its upper body ground towards the fortress of Tor Christo, as though taking the measure of its foe. Honsou watched as it raised the enormous bulk of its hellstorm cannon and plasma annihilator towards the fortress in mocking salute.

Honsou knew the commanding officers in Tor Christo would be watching the arrival of these magnificent war machines, and the message they delivered was sure to be clear.

Your time has come.

* * *

Seven

MAGOS FERIAN CORSIL adjusted the dials on the communi-
cations panel again, tweaking the broadcast bandwidth in
an attempt to increase the capacity of the long range vox-
casters. Beside him, the row of servitors plugged into the
long vox-console sat in lobotomised silence, each attuned
to one of the various Imperial Guard frequencies. Their
shaven heads and cable-plugged eye sockets nodded
monotonously in time with the cycling bands of static that
filled their skulls.

Since the unexplained quarantining of the Star Chamber
by Magos Naicin, they had been forced to try and adapt the
vox-casters to provide them with some sort of link to the
outside world. Much as it went against everything Corsil
had learned on Mars, he had spent the last day and a half
working on a dozen disassembled vox-panels attempting to
alter the divinely decreed circuitry within each blessed
device.

A burst of static spat from the speakers indicating the
machine spirit's displeasure and Corsil hastily made his
obeisance to it.

'Blessed machine, a thousand pardons for my unworthy
hands. Deus in Machina.'

Mechadendrites waved from his spine plugs like dreaming
snakes, each ribbed, copper prosthetic terminating in mechanised digits or some form of power-driven tool. Two
mechadendrites worked deep inside an open access panel
on the side of the console, adjusting the power couplings in
attempt to reroute some of the power to the broadcast
amplifier.

If he could isolate some of the more redundant systems –
perish the thought that such a term could exist in relation to
a machine – then he might be able to increase the range of
the vox-casters by up to four per cent. His mechadendrites
continued working away inside the panel as he cycled
through the various vox-nets.

As he hit upon the squad-level net, a servitor suddenly
stopped its repetitive bobbing and sat upright, its mouth
jerking into life.

'–dy hear me? What the hell's the point of a vox if no frag-ger ever answers?'

Corsil jumped at the sound of the voice, knocking the dial on the panel and glancing in puzzlement at the servitor as it returned to its previous static-filled life. The squad-level vox-net? That was normally reserved for small unit actions; for platoon and squad leaders to issue tactical orders. It was not supposed to be in use now.

Hurriedly he returned the dial to its previous setting and disengaged his mechadendrites from beneath the console.

Once again, the servitor sat upright, its expressionless face relaying the message from this unknown source.

'...come in. This is Guardsman Julius Hawke, serial num-ber 25031971, lately of listening post Sigma IV; I repeat this is Guardsman Julius Hawke attempting to raise Imperial forces in either Tor Christo or the citadel. Enemy Titans are inbound on your position together with brigade strength armour and infantry support.'

Corsil stared, open mouthed, at the console and the servi-tor relaying Hawke's message for long seconds before bolting from the room.

WORD OF HAWKE'S survival spread quickly through the upper command echelons of the citadel with mixed reactions. Many believed it was a trick of the invaders to feed them dis-information, while others felt that the Emperor had spared this man for some divine purpose. The irony of the idea that a man like Hawke could be an instrument of divine purpose was not lost on the officers that knew him.

Castellan Vauban paced his chambers, sipping a glass of amasec and pondering the Hawke dilemma. Lieutenant Colonel Leonid sat behind a desk reviewing Major Tedeski's file on the Guardsman, preparing a selection of questions they could use to verify that they were indeed talking to Hawke, and that he was not speaking under duress. Men from Hawke's platoon were even now being questioned for additional information that could verify his identity.

Should the voice on the end of the vox genuinely prove to be Hawke, then they would have a first-rate source of intelligence regarding the enemy's disposition, strength and movements, but Vauban wanted to be absolutely certain before he made any kind of decision. Magos Naicin was at this very moment researching the logic stacks within Arch-Magos Amaethon's Machine Temple for some way of detecting whether the words spoken over the vox-caster were genuine, though he hadn't sounded hopeful. Naicin had balked at Vauban's idea of employing an empathic scryer to gauge the truth, citing the unreliability of such a procedure without the subject actually being present.

For now, at least, it looked as though they were going to have to do this on their own.

Vauban knew of Hawke, having seen his name appear on more disciplinary reviews than he cared to remember, but had never met the man. Drunkenness, disorderly conduct, brawling and theft were but a taster of the trouble Hawke had been involved in and Vauban was reminded of the story of the Hero of Chiros, Jan van Yastobaal. Lionised by the people of the Segmentum Pacificus as a true hero of the people, Yastobaal had fought in the wars against the Apostate Cardinal Bucharis during the Plague of Unbelief. History told that he had been a noble, selfless man who had sacrificed all he had to free his people.

Vauban had been inspired by Yastobaal as a youth and had made a study of the man while a captain in the Jouran Planetary Defence Force. The deeper he researched and the more he had become acquainted with the real Yastobaal, the more he had found him to be a reckless, unorthodox man, prone to taking unnecessary gambles with his mens' lives. Everything he read of the man spoke of a rampant ego and colossal vanity that bordered on psychosis, and yet there was still much to admire about him.

But read any Imperially approved historical text and the story of Yastobaal would be told as a noble battle of courage over tyranny.

In years to come, what would the history books say of Guardsman Julius Hawke?

TOR CHRISTO

One

THE VAST, SOUTHERN gate of the citadel measured exactly forty-four metres high, thirty metres wide and was known as the Destiny Gate. Each layered half of the bronze gate was four metres thick and weighed hundreds of tonnes. No one knew exactly how they had been constructed, when they had been brought to Hydra Cordatus, or even how such massive portals could be opened with such ease.

Both gates were covered with battle scenes etched into their surfaces, the detail obscured by the ravages of time and green trails of oxidation, but they were impressive nonetheless. Flanked by the threatening forms of Mori and Vincare bastions, they were set within the sixty-metre high curtain wall of the citadel, surrounded by carven statuary.

Morning sunlight gleamed gold on the surface as the gates smoothly swung outwards, the battles immortalised on their faces seeming to twist with life as the light caught them. At last they were opened fully and massive shapes began to move through the gateway with thunderous footsteps.

Like giants from legend, the Battle Titans of the Legio Ignatum marched to war, their armoured hides painted in vivid reds and yellows, the power in their mighty steps shaking the ground. Huge honour banners hung between their massive legs and enormous kill banners fluttered from their weapon mounts, a litany of battle and victory stretching back to the days of the Great Crusade, unmatched by any other Titan Legion.

Princeps Fierach commanded the Warlord Titan *Imperator Bellum*, marching at the head of eleven more god-machines. Another two Warlords flanked Fierach, the *Honoris Causa* and the *Clavis Regni*, their princeps similarly eager to take the fight to the enemy. Fierach brought the *Imperator Bellum* to a halt at the open rear of the Primus Ravelin, the soldiers inside cheering as his thirty-metre high war machine raised its weapons high in salute.

Yet more Titans of the Legio Ignatum joined their Warlords. Five Reaver Titans, smaller cousins to their leader's war machine, took up rear positions and four Warhound Scout Titans loped alongside the Battle Titans. The Warhounds split into pairs, each taking position on the flanks of the larger machines. The Titans waited in the shadow of the counterguard wall as the armoured units of the Jouran Dragoons rumbled from the citadel and swarmed around the massive feet of the Battle Titans.

From his elevated position in the head of the *Imperator Bellum*, Princeps Fierach watched the mustering of the tanks and infantry carriers with mixed emotions. He was glad of their support, but knew that, with enemy Titans in the field, they could be unreliable allies. Fierach knew how easy it could be to break the courage of an enemy with the unstoppable power of a Titan. Like many princeps who had commanded a Titan for a considerable time, Fierach had a scornful disregard for those not able to take to the field of battle as he did. To have such destructive power at his fingertips bred arrogance and a withering contempt for the insignificant weapons and machines employed by those armed forces without the heritage of the Titan Legions.

Fierach sat within the head of the *Imperator Bellum*, wired into its every system via the ancient technologies of a mind impulse unit. Only by becoming part of the god-machine's consciousness was it possible to take command of these awesome machines, to feel each motion of its limbs and surge of power along its fibre bundle muscles as though they were his own.

To have such power to command was an intoxicating sensation and, when not joined with the god-machine, Fierach felt weak, shackled to the limitations of his mortal body.

Fierach shifted in his seat and meshed his senses with those of the Titan, allowing the barrage of information the sensorium of the *Imperator Bellum* was receiving to wash over him. He closed his eyes, feeling the sudden vertigo as his mind's eye shifted into a top-down view, depicting the battlefield as a series of bright contours and pulsing blips. Icons representing his own forces and those of the Jourans continued to mass in the ditch before the counterscarp that protected the base of the walls and bastions. Concealed tunnels sloped upwards through the ground, emerging on the plains before the citadel, allowing the armoured units of the Guard to rapidly deploy and support the Titans. Five hundred vehicles, a mix of battle tanks and armoured fighting vehicles, formed up in lines along the length of the ditch, smoke belching in blue clouds from their throbbing exhausts.

Fierach was unhappy with this attack and had voiced his concerns to Castellan Vauban in the strongest terms, but he was a senior princeps of the Legio Ignatum and pledges of servitude had been sworn many millennia ago between the Legio and the commanders of this citadel, and Fierach would not be known as an oath breaker.

It reeked of desperation to Fierach to gamble so much on the word of a poor soldier, but if this Hawke was correct, then they had an opportunity to take the fight to the enemy before they were able to properly deploy their Battle Titans. Despite his reservations, Fierach was elated at the prospect of taking his warriors into battle. While their duty to protect this citadel was sacrosanct, it was not the most satisfying of postings for a warrior who had forged his reputation on countless battlefields throughout the galaxy. The honour and kill banners hanging from the *Imperator Bellum* were the latest in a long line. Many that had previously been carried into battle were now hanging in the Chapel of Victory on the Legion's homeworld of Mars, their roll of honour scarcely able to contain the sheer number of battles won and enemies slain.

Fierach removed his senses from the tactical plot, grunting in satisfaction as Moderati Yousen reported, 'Lieutenant Colonel Leonid reports that Force Anvil is in position and ready to move out on your order.'

Fierach acknowledged the information with a raised finger, impressed at the efficiency of Leonid. He had always liked Vauban's second-in-command more than the castellan himself, feeling that Leonid was far more a natural warrior than Vauban.

'Very good, Moderati. Open a channel to all Titans.'

Yousen's finger danced across the panel before him. He nodded towards his princeps.

'All princeps, this is Fierach. You all know what to do, so carry out your orders. I wish you joy of the day and good hunting. May the Emperor guide your aim.'

He closed the channel without waiting for a response and trained his eyes on the red expanse of plain that stretched before his Titan, noting the distant plumes of smoke that marked the locations of the enemy camp.

Fierach whispered a mantra of salute to the spirit of the *Imperator Bellum* and said, 'Engineer Ulandro, give me striding speed. We go to battle.'

PRINCEPS CARLSEN RELISHED the sense of speed that coursed through his body as his Warhound Titan, the *Defensor Fidei*, sprinted ahead of the Legio's Battle Titans. Less than half the size of a Reaver Titan, the Warhound was an agile Scout Titan, the forward eyes and ears of the Legio. Less well armed and protected, it was no match for larger Titans, but could tear apart infantry formations with a combination of its deadly assault weaponry and speed.

His wingman, the *Jure Divinu*, thundered alongside him, keeping pace with his evasive manoeuvres to throw off any incoming fire that might be directed at them. There was none at the moment, but it never paid to be too complacent when your void shields could be taken out with one good volley.

Carlsen turned to Moderati Arkian and said, 'Anything?'

Arkian shook his head. 'No, not yet. But it won't be long now.'

Carlsen nodded and returned his attention to the ground before him. A spur of rock from the valley sides some five hundred metres away offered some protection should it prove necessary to take shelter from incoming fire. The enemy line was a kilometre away and he knew their speed would protect them from all but a desperately lucky shot.

Behind him, advancing abreast, came a portion of the armoured might of the 383rd Jouran Dragoons, and unlike the princeps of the larger Titans, Carlsen had a healthy respect for infantry and armoured vehicles. Friendly support was vital for a Titan of his size. Enemy infantry and vehicles could pose a serious threat to a Warhound.

'Have they even seen us yet?' he wondered aloud.

'Maybe we caught them at meal time,' offered Moderati Arkian with a grin.

'That would be handy indeed, but I think we've just disturbed them,' replied Carlsen as he spotted tongues of flame belch skyward from artillery behind the monstrous earthworks thrown up before the enemy camp.

He jinked the *Defensor Fidei* sideways, keeping close to the valley walls.

LIEUTENANT COLONEL LEONID rode in the top of his command Chimera, the wind whipping past his face. His goggles and bandana kept the worst of the dust from his mouth and eyes, and, riding at the head of his tanks, he had a magnificent view of the battlefield. His bronze breastplate shone gold in the red afternoon sun and as he rode to battle he was filled with a fierce pride in his regiment.

Like Fierach, he too had reservations about this attack, but seeing so many tanks roaring forward at speed with the ground shaking to the tread of the Legio Ignatum, he was swept up in the glory of this charge. Ahead he could see the traitor lines, their dark fortifications raised high in an impossibly short time. Whoever was organising this operation must be working his men to death.

Leonid watched the two Warhounds tasked to his storming force race ahead, their speed incongruous for such large machines. Slower moving Reavers strode alongside his formation while the majority of the Legio advanced on the salient angle of the attackers' trench line – the point where it bent towards the south-west and could bring the least amount of fire to bear. The Titans were to smash through the salient with the guns on Tor Christo covering their exposed right flank with the tanks and men of the Jouran Dragoons covering their left.

At the same time, the Jouran armoured thrust would hit the east/west trench line, storming the trenches with four thousand warriors hell-bent on revenge. Leonid had allowed the true identity of those soldiers killed in the initial attack on Tor Christo to become known and the Dragoons were hungry to avenge them.

Once the Titans had established their breakthrough, they would link with the fighting in the trenches, allowing them to sweep forwards into the invaders' camp, wreaking whatever havoc they could before falling back in good order to the citadel and avoiding the inevitable counterattack.

On paper it was sound strategy, but Leonid was enough of a warrior to know that few plans survived contact with the enemy, and was prepared to exercise his own initiative if the situation turned sour. But looking at the armoured might at his command and the gargantuan god-machines that marched beside them filled him with supreme confidence.

Distant booms of artillery roared from behind him as the citadel's guns fired, supporting the attack with carefully arranged fire plans that would hopefully keep the invaders' heads down until the charge was right on top of them and the men and women of the Jouran 383rd smashed home.

Beneath the bandana covering his mouth, Leonid smiled to himself.

FORRIX WATCHED THE charging Imperial forces approaching their lines with disinterest, knowing that their circumvallations were as secure as they could be. He stood at the salient angle of the lines, watching the Imperial Titans march towards them. The transparency of their plan was obvious even from here.

The guns of Tor Christo opened fire, sending screaming projectiles towards their lines, but Forrix had been building fortifications for thousands of years and was a true master of siegecraft. The high, earthen ramparts of his trenches absorbed the worst of the blasts and the damage inflicted was minimal. A few parties of slaves fled their work, but as soon as they broke cover they were shredded by the storm of explosions.

The guns from the citadel were also firing, wreathing the plateau in smoke, but Forrix had situated the first parallel beyond their range so the Imperial defenders were simply wasting ammunition. Thick grey smoke wreathed the plateau, obscuring the Imperial tanks, but the Iron Warriors in the bunkers were able to penetrate such petty obstacles as smoke with their gunsights.

The Titans of the Legio Mortis stood behind the main lines, ready to be unleashed at the foe once the Warsmith decreed where they should attack. The *Dies Irae* stood motionless just behind him, its mighty guns awaiting the coming conflict. Its form shimmered as the void shield generators powered up, sheathing the machine in layers of protective energy fields.

Diesel smoke and the choking stench of exhaust fumes filled the air as hundreds of armoured tanks rolled through the campsite, heading for the gateways in the defensive lines, ready to sally forth and engage the enemy. Gunners in artillery positions cranked their guns around to face the plain before the citadel, Tor Christo no longer their target for now.

Forrix could see Honsou and Kroeger marshalling their warriors for the coming battle, bellowing orders to the indentured soldiery and thrusting them into the trenches. He could practically feel their lust for battle and wished he shared it. But this conflict promised to be yet another that would eventually blur into a seamless life of slaughter for him.

Glancing round at the Warsmith's pavilion, he was again struck by the sense of impending change that saturated the Iron Warriors' great leader. There was always a feeling of barely contained power around the Warsmith, and Forrix's gut told him that his master was on the brink of some monumental change, but what?

The gods of Chaos were fickle beings, capable of raising their servants to the highest pinnacles of daemonhood or dashing them to a life of mindless savagery as a spawn. It was for them to decide which and no one could predict what choice they would make.

Could this explain the urgency of the Hydra Cordatus campaign?

Was daemonhood to be the Warsmith's reward for its successful completion?

If so, might it not be possible for those who had accompanied him and aided him on that journey to follow in his wake, to ride his ascension to newer and greater things, where the time spent since the defeat on Terra was just the blink of an eye and a universe of potentiality might be opened up?

Forrix felt an unfamiliar sensation stir in his belly and was mildly surprised to find that the fires of ambition, which he had thought extinguished forever, had merely been smouldering unnoticed in the farthest corners of his mind.

He returned his gaze to the Warsmith and a cold smile touched his lips.

PRINCEPS FIERACH STRAINED to see the enemy battle lines through the clouds of smoke thrown up by the barrage from the citadel and Tor Christo. Billowing banks of red dust hung in the air, rendering him virtually blind and he quickly voxed the senior gunnery officers, shouting, 'All guns, cease fire! I repeat cease fire!'

A few explosions erupted before the traitor lines from shells already in the air, but Fierach could see that his order had been obeyed with alacrity, the smoke that drifted from those impacts was not followed by fresh detonations. He swung the ponderous head of his Warlord to the left, looking to see what damage the citadel's guns had inflicted on the main trench line, but the slow-drifting smoke frustrated his efforts.

He linked his consciousness to the Titan's sensorium, noting that his battle group was moving a little too fast, outpacing the slower tanks of the Guard in their haste for battle. Briefly he considered ordering Engineer Ulandro to reduce speed, but immediately discarded the idea. It did well to reinforce their superiority over the Guard now and again, and a little rivalry between the different arms of the citadel's defenders never hurt either.

The smoke ahead parted momentarily and his breath caught in his throat as he caught a glimpse of something vast and obscene moving through the haze. Surely it could not be... it was too large.

But if it was...

He opened a channel to Princeps Cullain and Princeps Daekian, commanders of the Warlords on either side of him.

'Cullain, Daekian, did either of you see that?'

'See what, princeps?' asked Cullain.

'I saw nothing through the smoke,' affirmed Daekian. 'What did you see?'

'I'm not sure, but for a second it looked like–'

The words died in his throat as the wind lifted the concealing smoke and Fierach saw a towering nightmare lurch from the traitor lines like a daemon from the warp. Its red and brass structure towered over him, its guns and towers horrifying in their size. The monstrous Titan stepped towards him and its blazing green eyes seemed to lock with his own, promising nothing but death. Fierach's heart pounded and the *Imperator Bellum* faltered in its stride, the mind impulse link attempting to match its princeps' reaction.

'Blood of the Machine!' swore Cullain, the vox-link between the princeps still open.

'Legio Mortis!' snarled Daekian, recognising the skull icon on the massive enemy Titan's upper bastions.

Fierach saw the kill banner hanging between the gargantuan towers of the Titan's legs and the host of blasphemous symbols that writhed there. Hot anger flooded him as he knew that some of those markings must represent Titans and princeps from the Legio Ignatum. The beast's head was plucked from his worst nightmares, a hellish fusion of machine and daemon, the very image of death.

Legio Mortis, the ancient foe! And not only that…

If he was not mistaken, this diabolical machine was none other than the dreaded *Dies Irae*, that infernal blasphemy that had breached the walls of the Emperor's Palace at the dawn of the Imperium. Here on Hydra Cordatus. Could a warrior of the Legio Ignatum ask for anything more? Fierach's lip curled in hatred, and burning excitement coursed through his veins at the thought of combating this monster from the dawn of time. A primal battle fought between two ancient foes. The honour that would be his at having finally brought down the Legio's most ancient nemesis was immeasurable. Fierach roared in battle fury.

'*Clavis Regni*, *Honoris Causa* and Battle Group Sword with me! Ignatum!'

'Princeps?' queried Cullain, 'Are you sure? Such a manoeuvre will leave the Jourans dangerously exposed.'

'Damn the Jourans!' bellowed Fierach, 'I want that Titan! Now be silent and follow me!'

Fierach bellowed to Engineer Ulandro for more speed and activated the *Imperator Bellum's* massive chain fist as he charged into battle.

Two

AS THE ARTILLERY ceased its deafening barrage, the battle tanks of Leonid's charge spread into a line formation, firing everything they had. The traitor lines vanished in explosions as the Imperial weaponry struck. The smoke was quick to disperse though, blown clear by the day's breeze.

As the distance between the two forces closed, the wedges of troop carriers unfolded into line formation. Several of the heavier tanks halted and assumed firing positions, their mighty battle cannons pounding the trench line. The noise was deafening as laser fire, shell fire and artillery mingled with the bass rumble of straining tank engines. Leonid was dismayed to see how little an effect their guns were having.

The gap between the two enemies closed still further.

Leonid watched the manoeuvres of his battalion with a fierce admiration. He had seen his share of combat, but there was nothing quite so inspiring as watching an armoured cavalry charge across open ground. They were almost there and hundreds of tanks belched smoke from their dispensers to confound the targeting spirits in their enemy's weapons.

He wondered why their Titan support hadn't opened fire yet as planned. He reached for the vox handset to request a fire mission when a shot streaked from a bunker in the centre of the traitor line, covering the distance to its target in less than a second. A Leman Russ was slammed sideways as the missile punched through its frontal armour. The superheated core of the missile ignited the vehicle's fuel and cooked off its ammunition, blowing it apart in a greasy black fireball.

The shot was the signal for the rest of the Iron Warriors to engage and the line erupted in a flurry of lascannon shots and missile contrails as the massed firepower of the traitor legion was unleashed.

The closest vehicles had no chance.

The gunners of the Iron Warriors picked off tanks with ease and huge explosions blossomed along the Imperial lines as lascannon shots and missiles found their targets.

The screaming of soldiers was audible even over the continuous thump of explosions and the hiss of flashing lasers. Then the heavier blasts of enemy Titan weapons joined the fray, blasting tanks to atoms with the unimaginable power of their weapons.

Trapped by the burning wreckage, tank drivers attempted to ram their vehicles to safety, the crash of buckling metal adding to the din. A Leman Russ smashed into the remains of a blackened Chimera, attempting to clear a path, but a keen-eyed gunner spotted the breakout and despatched the battle tank with a well-placed missile to the vehicle's rear.

The doors of the Leman Russ opened, spewing black smoke and burning Guardsmen from the crew compartment. They rolled desperately in the dust while screaming in agony as the flames consumed them.

Leonid held on for dear life as bright spears of lascannon fire ripped through the armoured hulls of his Chimeras with ease. Vehicles exploded in quick succession, slewing from the line and belching thick plumes of smoke.

He was flung sideways as his driver threw the Chimera into a series of screeching turns in an effort to throw off the enemy gunners' aim. The Chimera crashed into the rear quarter of the burning tank and the roaring of its engine intensified as the frantic driver gunned the engine and attempted to barge the heavier tank out of his way. But the Leman Russ was wedged tight and immovable.

Leonid dropped into the Chimera's crew compartment and slammed the rear ramp release lever, yelling, 'Everybody out! Go! Go! Go!'

His command squad needed no prompting. To stay in the Chimera was to die. Leonid hustled his men down the ramp before following them into the confusion of the battle. He had barely cleared the ramp when a missile ripped through the side of the Chimera. With the rear ramp open, much of the force of the explosion was vented outwards, but still the tank was lifted into the air by the blast. Leonid staggered, feeling as though a giant fist had swatted him to the ground. He spat dirt, a terrific ringing in his ears. He turned to see Ellard, his sergeant, yelling at him, but he couldn't make out the words. The sergeant pointed towards the enemy trench line and Leonid nodded, hauling himself to his feet.

He saw Trooper Corde dragging a body, its sky blue jacket splattered red. He shouted, but realised he stood little chance of being heard over the roar of explosions and gunfire.

Confusion reigned supreme as he saw scores of tanks and Chimeras belching noxious black smoke. A hand grabbed his shoulder and he turned as Sergeant Ellard handed him his rifle. The sergeant had already fixed the bayonet for him and Leonid nodded his thanks.

Bodies lay everywhere. On tanks. On the ground. Blood, fire, noise and screams.

All he could smell was smoke, burning oil and flesh.

Another vehicle exploded and he dropped to the ground, losing his grip on his rifle as red hot fragments scythed overhead, pinging on the side of another tank.

Dim snatches of desperate shouts came to him. Shouted questions that made no sense. Calls for support, medics and extraction. Soldiers lay all around in the oil-slick dust firing their rifles at the trench line. Without conscious thought, he grabbed his rifle from the ground, shouldered it and began firing until the charge counter read empty.

He removed the empty power cell and slammed in a fresh one. It took him two attempts; his hands were shaking so much.

All around him, surviving tanks fired their main guns whilst their drivers desperately zigzagged in an attempt to evade the enemy fire. Some succeeded and began returning fire against the traitors. Those that did not were quickly isolated and blown apart.

Leonid slithered across to Sergeant Ellard, who handed him a vox-unit as he ripped off his helmet and put the handset to his mouth.

'Princeps Fierach? We need a fire mission now! Come in please! Where are you?'

The vox hissed and spat static at Leonid as he continued to call for help. 'Princeps Fierach, anybody, come in, damn it! Acknowledge please!'

Garbled voices and more static were his only reply, and he threw down the handset in disgust.

'Colonel!' screamed Ellard, 'What's happening? Where the hell's our Titan support?'

Leonid scooped up his helmet, pushed it on and said, 'Damned if I know, sergeant.'

Another explosion rocked the earth close by. 'Sound off!' Leonid shouted, 'Who's missing?'

Corde yelled, 'Commissar Pasken and Lieutenant Ballis are dead and Lonov is wounded. I doubt he'll make it.'

Leonid nodded stoically and flinched as another vehicle exploded nearby. The squad was in bad shape, their faces blackened and terrified. For many of them, it was their first real taste of hard combat and he knew that one of two emotions would win out here: fear or courage.

In the first heat of battle an infantryman would be plunged into a flash flood of emotions. Terror, anger, guilt and hate. All the feelings that boiled to the surface when confronted with the prospect of dying or killing another human being. In the right combination they would carry a man forwards to the enemy, as a fearsome, merciless killer. But equally they could send him fleeing in terror back to his own lines. Some men were born with the right combination; others needed it hammered into them.

It was his job to make sure he got the best out of his men and he knew that they were close to going either way. He'd have to push them to get the fires of anger burning in their hearts. To stay here would drain their courage to the point that not even the threat of a commissar would get them moving.

He scrambled to the edge of their shelter and ducked his head around the gutted Chimera, trying to get a feel for the situation.

By the Emperor, it was bad! The sky blazed red and black as scores of tanks burned fiercely and countless bodies littered the bloody ground. Heavy weapons fire was sporadic now as the drivers whose vehicles had escaped the initial slaughter took refuge behind their wrecked comrades. They were trapped, realised Leonid.

What the hell had happened to the Titans?

'CYCLE THE AUTO LOADERS!' yelled Princeps Fierach, 'and get those void shields back up!'

The *Imperator Bellum* was closing the gap between it and the *Dies Irae*, but it had taken a punishing barrage from the leviathan's hellstorm cannon. From a distance the massive barrels appeared to be turning at a leisurely tempo, but the rate of fire was deceptive and explosive shells had almost stripped them of their protective void shields in a single volley.

'Moderati Setanto, charge the plasma generators! Prepare to fire plasma cannon!'

'Yes, princeps!' replied the weapons officer.

Fierach knew that if they were to defeat this monster they had to quickly knock down the *Dies Irae's* shields or close with it and take it down in close quarter battle. Neither prospect promised to be easy.

Fierach saw the *Honoris Causa* rock under a volley of gunfire from the enemy Titan, the enormous machine reeling under the ferocious impacts. The Warlord staggered, one massive foot slamming down on the salient of the enemy trench system, crushing two bunkers and a score of men. One of the Titan's arms slammed into the ground, sending up a tall plume of dust, the other flailing wildly as Princeps Daekian fought for balance.

Fierach stepped forward to shield the *Honoris Causa* and raised his weapon arms as Moderati Setanto shouted, 'Plasma cannon fully charged, princeps!'

'I have you now!' snarled Fierach as he unleashed a torrent of white-hot plasma at the devil machine before him. The viewscreen darkened as the bolts struck the *Dies Irae*, its void shields flaring as they overloaded under the onslaught of the *Imperator Bellum's* guns. It was still shielded, but the range was closing.

The Reavers of Battle Group Sword circled to Fierach's right, using their superior speed to flank the enemy Titan. A flurry of powerful laser blasts overloaded the void shields of the lead Reaver and even as its crew realised their danger, an incandescent pulse of energy slashed from the *Dies Irae's* plasma annihilator and hammered into the command bridge in the head section.

Fierach shouted a denial as he saw a huge explosion rip the head from the Reaver and topple the machine. Gracefully, the Reaver collapsed, its artificially generated muscle movements dying with its princeps. The machine's knees buckled and it smashed into the ground in a vast cloud of red ash. The remaining four Reavers scattered as Fierach shouted for more speed.

As though sensing that the *Imperator Bellum* was the leader of this force, the *Dies Irae* turned its ponderous upper body to face Fierach.

This was how it was meant to be. Man against daemon, flesh, bone and steel against whatever horror animated the daemonic machine.

The *Clavis Regni* charged before him, its void shields flaring as enemy heavy tanks and weapon teams added their fire to that of the *Dies Irae*. Impacts hit his own Titan, knocking down another shield, and, as he saw another battle group of enemy Titans emerge from the smoke with hundreds of tanks following them, Princeps Fierach knew doubt for the first time in many years.

It was not for nothing that this foe had stalked the galaxy with impunity these last ten thousand years. It was a deadly enemy and many a vaunted princeps had met his end by its guns.

A volley of cannon fire from the enemy reinforcements slammed into the *Clavis Regni* and Fierach watched, horrified, as his brother princeps struggled to hold his Titan upright. Flames roared from the inferno gun mounted on its arm and suddenly the weapon exploded, showering the *Clavis Regni* with superheated fuel.

Moderati Yousen shouted, 'Princeps! Colonel Leonid requests immediate support. He reports they are taking heavy casualties!'

Fierach nodded, too busy to respond as he sidestepped a powerful blast from the *Dies Irae's* defence laser. He felt, rather than saw, another of the Reavers go down, the war machine toppled by the horrendous firepower arrayed against them.

One of the enemy Titans lurched towards the *Imperator Bellum*, shielding it from the fire of the *Dies Irae*, its monstrous head swinging ponderously from side to side as it charged.

Fierach stepped forward to meet this new foe, swinging his chainfist at the Titan's head. The vast motorised saw-blade grazed the armoured carapace of the enemy machine, sliding clear in a shower of fat orange sparks. In reply, the monster thrust its own roaring chainblade at the *Imperator Bellum's* midsection. Fierach felt the thunderous impact, the shriek of tearing metal as the energised blade ripped through the thick armour of his Titan like paper.

Screams filled the internal vox as men below died and Fierach heard Engineer Ulandro yell, 'Princeps! We have a reactor breach on level secundus!'

Fierach didn't reply, desperately fending off another blow from the enemy Titan and stepping inside its guard to deliver a mighty stroke across its neck. Orange fire blasted from the enemy war machine as the *Imperator Bellum's* blade sheared through its armour and tore its head from its body. Fierach roared in triumph as massive secondary explosions ripped through the falling Titan.

Smoke boiled throughout the command bridge and furious red warning symbols flashed urgently before Fierach. The reactor was going critical, but he knew that Ulandro was the best there was, and if he couldn't prevent an overload, then no one could.

He swung the *Imperator Bellum* around in time to see the death of the *Clavis Regni*, its void shields finally collapsing in a spectacular pyrotechnic display as its generators overloaded and massive explosions whiplashed inside the machine. The Titan convulsed as the internal detonations ripped it apart from within and Fierach bellowed in anger to see such a heroic Titan die in such a manner.

A thunderous impact shocked him from his fury and he turned to see the *Dies Irae* in all its hellish glory, its leg bastions wreathed in flames. He snarled, pushing the *Imperator Bellum* forwards as he saw yet more warning runes wink into life on the reactor panel.

Engineer Ulandro was fighting a losing battle to contain the reactor breach, and as Fierach heard the desperate, pleading screams of the Imperial Guard soldiers over the vox, he knew he had made an unforgivable tactical decision.

By indulging his lust for vengeance on the Legio Mortis, he had deserted his brother soldiers, and Fierach was filled with shame.

The Reavers of Battle Group Sword had defeated the supporting enemy Titans, but only two remained standing, flames billowing from their weapon mounts and twisted carapaces.

He had doomed them all.

The *Clavis Regni* was gone, but the *Honoris Causa* still stood, trading shots with the *Dies Irae* in an unequal battle that could have but one outcome.

Fierach opened a channel to Princeps Daekian as he marched resolutely towards the firefight.

'Daekian! Pull back eastwards, reinforce the Jouran units.'

'Princeps?' queried a breathless Daekian.

'Do it, damn your eyes! Take what's left of Sword and try and salvage something from this disaster!'

'Yes, princeps,' acknowledged Daekian.

Fierach saw the reactor breach was getting steadily worse and felt a fatal sluggishness to the *Imperator Bellum's* movements. The god-machine was dying, but he would not allow such a mighty warrior to walk the road to hell alone and turned his Titan to face the towering form of the *Dies Irae*.

Death awaited him and he welcomed it.

Suddenly calm, Fierach said, 'Daekian, I ask only one thing of you. Avenge us.'

LEONID'S SQUAD HUDDLED in the dust, glittering with the sheen of spilt engine fuel, and kept their heads down as the constant thump of heavy weapon fire blasted from the enemy trenches.

Despite shouted promises over the vox-net, their Titan support had yet to materialise. The Chimera rocked with the shockwaves of nearby explosions and Leonid had to shout to be heard over the noise of battle.

'Corde! Any news on those Titans?'

Guardsman Corde shook his head furiously as another blast shook their refuge and Leonid knew that it was only a matter of time before the Chimera was blown to bits.

The entire squad, or at least what was left of it, was filled with the same indignant fury as Leonid, and even the normally placid Guardsman Corde was hell-bent on getting to grips with the enemy.

But, courageous as they were, it would be almost impossible for them to charge across such open ground. They would be heroes, but not even heroes could take a missile and survive, no matter how brave they were. Leonid knew that they had to do something and realised that this was a time when he had to earn the rank badge on his shoulder boards. This was the time when, as a leader, he had to do just that. Lead.

His mind made up Leonid turned to face Ellard and shouted, 'Sergeant, gather the men. We're going forward!'

The sergeant looked for a moment as though he hadn't heard Leonid, then nodded sharply and started shouting at the men, gathering them into position. Leonid snatched the handset of the vox unit carried on Corde's back and opened a channel to the units under his command.

'All units, this is Lieutenant Colonel Leonid. We are attacking the traitor trench line. Be ready and remember, the Emperor expects every man to do his best! Leonid out.'

He dropped the vox and locked eyes with Ellard.

'Ready, sergeant?'

Ellard nodded. 'As I'll ever be, sir. You?'

Leonid grinned. 'I guess we're about to find out.'

He reached out to shake Ellard's hand, saying, 'Good luck, sergeant.'

'You too, sir.'

Leonid hefted his rifle and, after taking a deep breath to slow his pounding heart, burst from cover with a roar of hatred. His command squad rose and followed their leader's example, charging forwards with a howling battle cry.

Gunfire reached out to them, instantly cutting a swathe of Guardsmen down and scattering the rest.

'Spread out! Spread out!' yelled Leonid.

They fired their lasguns and grenade launchers, but the range was too great.

Despite the tiny impact Leonid's command squad had on the traitor line, the effect on the Imperial troops was electric.

The embers of a fierce, wounded pride and a towering sense of outrage were stoked amongst his soldiers. The men of the Jouran Dragoons rose and followed their courageous commanding officer.

Leonid and Ellard charged forwards together, their boots throwing up great clouds of ash behind them. The squad followed at their heels, incoherent yells of anger and fear carrying them through the fire.

Hot adrenaline dumped into Leonid's system. As he fired his rifle, he was engulfed by a wash of emotions. Mad exuberance gripped him, a wild sense of danger and excitement. His fear was swept away and he laughed with the sheer vitality he possessed. The sky above had never seemed quite so red, nor his eyes so preternaturally sharp. He could make out the faces of the enemy before him in graphic detail.

He felt like he was charging in slow motion, bullets and lasfire flashing past him like bright streamers, and he turned to yell encouragement at the men behind him. Explosions burst around him, but he ran on, invincible.

New strength filled his limbs and he surged ahead of the others.

Firing from the hip, the noise was incredible. He heard wild howling. His own?

Something jerked his sleeve. Sharp red pain blossomed up his arm, but he didn't care.

He was riding a wave of courage and insanity.

A terrible roaring, ripping sound dopplered in and out and he saw the dirt kicked up in spurts before him. The line of fire kinked right and tore amongst the squad beside him. Four men were pitched backwards, bright blood spraying from their shattered chests.

That couldn't be right. This was a charge to glory! Their faith in the Emperor and the justice of their cause was their shield against harm. They were supposed to be invincible.

His step faltered and his vision suddenly expanded to encompass the carnage around him. Bodies littered the ground. Hundreds? Thousands? There were so many, who could tell?

Brave and glorious though their charge had been, the rational part of Leonid's brain suddenly realised its folly. Frantic charges against fortified positions without fire support were the stuff of legend until you actually had to do it yourself. Though he didn't appreciate it on a conscious level, Leonid had reached the point that all infantrymen must at some point face.

The point where the initial surge of adrenaline had worn off and the body's innate sense of self preservation kicked in. This was when true courage was required to carry a soldier the last few metres towards the enemy.

Leonid screamed and continued forwards, side by side with his soldiers, his blood pounding and his heart racing.

They were going to make it!

The traitor line was barely ten metres away.

Then it vanished in a series of bright flashes, smoke and thunderous noise.

A giant fist smashed him in the chest.

He fell, fighting for breath, his vision cartwheeling.

The ground rushed up to meet him and slammed into his face, hot and solid.

Someone screamed his name.

Pain, bright red, razor stabs of pain in his chest.

He rolled onto his back as noise swelled around him; screams and gunfire. He lifted his head and moaned as he saw scarlet blood on his breastplate. Was it his?

He dropped his head and closed his eyes as an immense weariness settled over him.

Then screamed as he was hauled violently up and thrown over someone's shoulder, his chest spasming in pain. He saw broken, blood stained earth bouncing below him and a bloodstained Jouran uniform jacket.

He was being carried away from the trenches, he realised, bouncing around on his rescuer's shoulder, the world spinning around him. Nothing made sense. He tried to find his voice, but all that he managed was a hoarse croak.

The man carrying him suddenly stopped and shucked Leonid from his shoulder, propping him up against the side of a wrecked tank.

Leonid's eyes swam into focus.

Sergeant Ellard knelt beside him, checking the wound in his chest.

'What happened?' Leonid asked thickly.

'You got yourself shot, sir,' answered Ellard.

Leonid looked at his chest. 'Did I?'

'Aye, sir. You were ahead of everyone else and took a round to the chest. Good thing you had your flak jacket on underneath your breastplate, eh? Still, you're going to have a hell of a bruise, sir.'

'Yes, I suppose,' said Leonid, relief flowing through him. 'The last thing I remember, we were just about to jump those bastards.'

'Well, I guess our charge wasn't meant to hit home. Anyway we've got to keep our heads down, because Corde tells me that our vaunted Titans are inbound any minute and we sure as hell don't want to be anywhere near those trenches when they open fire.'

Leonid tried to stand, but pain flooded through him and he slumped back. 'Imperator, this hurts!'

'Yes, I think you caught it in the solar plexus, so just lay still for a while, sir. You're going to be alright.'

'Sure.' said Leonid. 'By the way, thank you, sergeant. For carrying me out.'

'Not to worry, sir, but if you don't mind me asking, what the hell were you doing? With all due respect, sir, you took off like a bloody madman.'

'I don't know, sergeant. I couldn't think straight,' said Leonid, shaking his head. 'All I could see was the line of trenches and how I had to get there. It was insane, I know, but, by the Emperor, it felt amazing! It was as though I could hear and see everything so clearly and there was nothing I couldn't do... And then I got shot,' he finished lamely.

More bodies began to join them as the distant thunder of Titan footsteps carried through the afternoon air. Leonid had never heard a more welcome sound in his entire life.

He pushed himself painfully to his feet and shouted to everyone in earshot, his parade-ground voice cutting through the bark of sporadic gunfire and the thump of explosions.

'Right, listen up, everybody! We have Titans coming in, so everyone on your feet! As soon as they hit I want everyone back to the citadel in double time or better. Make sure we don't leave anybody behind and we'll get out of this in one piece, okay?'

A few muted affirmations greeted Leonid's words, but the survivors of the attack were too weary and shell-shocked to respond with much enthusiasm.

Leonid turned his gaze to the north-west, seeing the lumbering shapes of Titans approaching through the smoke. Despite the pain in his chest, he grinned to himself.

The god-machines would surely turn the traitor line into a maelstrom of death and shredded bodies.

KROEGER WATCHED THE slaughter before the trenches with fierce longing, his fist thumping against the side of his Rhino in time with the crack of explosions. The carnage was pleasing to him, though he was disappointed the Imperials had not had the courage to even reach their lines. His sword was unsheathed and was yet to draw blood. Its spirit would be angered if it was to be scabbarded unwetted. It took all Kroeger's willpower not to climb aboard the Rhino and order a full advance, but he could not do so unless decreed by the Warsmith.

Kroeger stood resplendent in his freshly polished armour, the burnished iron gleaming like new. The female prisoner he had spared from the initial massacre had restored his armour's lustre, and though he still couldn't say why he had not killed her, it was pleasing to him to have a lackey of the Emperor serve him. There was more to it than that, but he did not know what, and the feeling that the decision had not been his would not leave him. Kroeger dismissed the woman from his thoughts; he would probably kill her within a day or two.

The din of battle echoed from the valley sides and the discordant clash of steel on steel was music to Kroeger's ears. For thousands of years, Kroeger had lived with this sound and he wished he could make out the huge shapes battling through the smoke to the west, where the Legio

Mortis grappled with the enemy Titans. There was a battle indeed! To fight in the shadow of such creations was to fight in the realm of true death, where a warrior's life hung by the threads of chance as well as skill.

Kroeger impatiently stalked to the edge of the trench's firing step, watching the wall of smoke and flames with hunger. He cast his gaze over the troops that waited either side of him, pitiful humans who thought that by their service to the Iron Warriors they would be honoured in the sight of Chaos. He despised them.

Further west, Kroeger could see Honsou and his company of mongrels. Honsou also looked impatient to enter the fray, and in this at least, Kroeger knew they shared a common bond.

He heard the rumbling of powerful engines behind him and turned to see three massive Land Raiders moving into position at the main gateway. The frontal ramp of the mighty vehicle in the lead dropped with a heavy clang and a powerful figure, clad in ornate Terminator armour stepped out into the red, afternoon sun.

Forrix marched across the steel decking that bridged the trench and joined Kroeger on the firing step, an ancient and heavily ornamented combi-bolter clutched in his right hand, while the left was a monstrous, crackling power fist.

'The Warsmith has decreed that we are to attack,' said Forrix.

'We?' asked a bemused Kroeger. Forrix had not taken to the field of battle in nearly three millennia.

'Yes, we. I am an Iron Warrior, am I not?'

'You are that, Forrix,' nodded Kroeger as Honsou strode across to join them.

'Forrix?' said Honsou. 'You fight with us this day?'

'Aye, half-breed, I do. You have something to say?'

'No… brother. You do us honour with your presence.'

'I do,' nodded Forrix.

Kroeger and Honsou shared a glance, both equally puzzled and a little unsettled by this latest development. Kroeger laughed and slapped a gauntlet across Forrix's shoulder guards.

'Welcome back, Forrix. It has been too long since you shed the blood of the enemy. I'll wager that power fist comes back with more blood on it than even the half-breed or I can shed today.'

Forrix nodded, clearly uncomfortable with Kroeger's bon-homie. He shook off Kroeger's hand and snapped, 'Stay away from me, Kroeger. You are nothing to me.'

Kroeger removed his hand with exaggerated care and took a step back.

'As you wish.'

Honsou stepped away from Forrix and returned to his position in the line just as Kroeger left the firing step to rejoin his company. He cast furtive glances back towards the giant figure of Forrix, silhouetted in the deep red of the sky. Something had happened to Forrix and Kroeger was instantly suspicious. There had been a fire in the ancient vet-eran's voice that Kroeger had not heard for many centuries.

Something had rekindled Forrix's spirit and Kroeger sus-pected that the old general was privy to some secret that both he and Honsou were ignorant of. What that might be or how he came by it, Kroeger could not guess, but he would make it his business to find out.

Further speculation was ended when a deafening roar sawed through the front ranks, blasting dozens of men on the firing step to shreds. Heavy calibre shells ripped apart the lip of the trench in a hail of fire, sending earth and bod-ies flying in all directions and a fierce grin broke on Kroeger's face.

Through the billowing smoke he could make out the blurred outline of what looked like a Scout Titan. He jogged quickly to his Rhino, jumping onto the running boards and hammering his fist upon its roof.

The Rhino's engine roared as it powered forwards, follow-ing Forrix's Land Raiders through the gateway and into the smoke of battle.

Kroeger stood tall and raised his chainsword for all his warriors to see.

'Death to the followers of the False Emperor!'

* * *

Three

LEONID WATCHED THE loping forms of the Warhounds as they circled his position, pouring fire from their Vulcan bolters onto the traitor lines. The men under his command cheered and punched the air at this show of defiance, though Leonid knew that was all it was. The Warhounds would buy them time to regroup, but nothing more.

'All units, this is Colonel Leonid. Regroup and fall back to the rally point immediately. Do it quickly, we don't have much time,' ordered Leonid as the deep throated roar of vehicles swelled from the traitor lines.

PRINCEPS CARLSEN JINKED his agile Warhound Titan from side to side, frantically evading enemy shots while attempting to manoeuvre into a favourable firing position for his weapons moderati. He and Princeps Jancer in the *Jure Divinu* took it in turns to dart forwards and hose the trenches with their Vulcan bolters and turbo lasers, shredding anything that dared show its face, before rapidly withdrawing to safety in the smoke. Their height made a mockery of the protection offered by the firing step, killing scores of men with each volley, but he knew that the casualties they were inflicting were largely irrelevant.

Without the heavier guns of Battle Group Sword, their efforts here were purely a delaying tactic. Carlsen had not believed his ears when he heard Princeps Fierach give the order to abandon the Jourans in favour of going head to head with an Emperor class Titan, and had listened with growing horror to the vox traffic flashing between the Battle Titans as they fought for their lives.

He and his brother Warhound were too far east to go to the aid of their brethren, and had had to content themselves with following the Jouran armoured attack, though without the Reavers they had been forced to wait until the Imperial Guard either broke through or were repulsed.

Las-bolts and bolter fire flared against his void shields, but he ignored them as irrelevant. It was the enemy tanks that gave Carlsen cause for concern. Each time he'd gone forward, he had seen more and more of them lurking behind the trenches and knew it was only a matter of time until the enemy commander counterattacked.

Three Land Raiders burst from the smoke, followed by a wide line of Rhinos and transports that looked like some bizarre cross between a Chimera and a flatbed truck. The troops crammed into them screamed as they bounced along the ground towards the retreating Guard.

'Princeps Jancer, with me!' shouted Carlsen as he turned his Vulcan bolter on the lighter vehicles following the Land Raiders. Shells tore up the ground, stitching a path towards them and sawing three apart in a burst of flames and blood. All three exploded, the shells ringing from the side of a Land Raider. The heavier vehicle lurched sideways, smashing into one of the Chimera trucks and flattening it with a shriek of tortured metal.

The *Jure Divinu* appeared at his side, its guns bellowing with thunder and raking the enemy attack with deadly shells. Two Land Raiders skidded away from the Titans, attempting to evade their guns, but Carlsen was quicker, lashing out with his Titan's foot and catching the closest vehicle square in the side panels, buckling its armoured hull with ease and hurling the wreck through the air.

The second slewed around, bringing its sponson mounted lascannon to bear and Carlsen felt the painful sensation of his void shields collapsing as the Land Raider's gunners found their mark.

'Damn you!' yelled Carlsen, hauling backwards as the tank's guns fired again, the deadly beams flashing overhead.

'Moderati Arkian, get those shields back up! Now!'

Carlsen walked his Titan backwards, spraying the traitor vehicles with fire, careful to try and avoid the running soldiers of the Imperial Guard. Sweat ran in runnels from his face as the strain of such precise piloting took its toll.

The *Defensor Fidei* stumbled as Carlsen brought one of its feet down upon the smashed hulk of a Leman Russ, the pilot's compartment swaying dangerously close to the ground. The *Jure Divinu* stood sentinel over its brother Titan, firing and moving as the enemy advanced more cautiously now.

'Arkian!' bellowed Carlsen, 'Where are my damn shields?'

'Working on it, princeps!'

'Work faster!' demanded Carlsen as he saw the two surviving Land Raiders emerge from the smoke on a direct course for him.

THE IMPERATOR BELLUM was dying, but Princeps Fierach was not about to give up just yet. Blood and sweat coated his features and he was sure Moderati Yousen was dead. The Emperor alone knew what was going on in the engineering decks; he had not been able to raise anyone down there. The *Dies Irae* was taking him apart piece by piece, but Fierach was not going down without a fight, and it was taking terrible damage. The tanks that had accompanied the other enemy Titans had swept past him, content to allow their war god to destroy him.

Fierach just hoped that the survivors of Battle Group Sword were able to protect the Jourans and allow them to escape.

Another hammer blow fell upon him and shooting bolts of fire lanced through his skull in sympathetic pain. What the *Imperator Bellum* felt, he felt.

He brought up his chainblade, the now dulled edge scoring across the barrel of the *Dies Irae's* plasma annihilator. Gouts of searing plasma energy spurted from the enormous gun, hissing clouds of superheated vapour geysering downwards and vaporising a hundred men in its fury.

The *Dies Irae* stepped in and smashed its leg against Fierach's, buckling the knee joint and destroying it in an explosion of sparks. Warning klaxons blared and thick ropes of blood ran from Fierach's mouth as he bit down hard on his tongue, the pain almost unbearable. He vainly tried to step away from the enemy Titan, but the *Imperator Bellum's* left leg was fused solid and he could not escape.

The *Dies Irae* advanced again and hammered one of its weapon arms against the *Imperator Bellum's* torso. Fierach's Titan was slammed sideways by the thunderous blow and yet more warning lights flared into life as systems failed all over his war machine. He fought for balance, but the external gyros were smashed and he was forced to rely on his own reeling senses rather than those of the Titan.

Amazingly, he was able to recover his balance and faced the *Dies Irae* once more, swinging his chainfist, the one system he knew he could rely on.

The blade shrieked across the *Dies Irae's* midsection, tearing away great chunks from the beast's armour. Fierach knew an Emperor class Titan's reactor was buried deep within its belly and if he could but hack through enough of its armour, then others might later have a chance to slay the monster. The *Dies Irae* stepped aside and batted away the chainblade with the barrels of its hellstorm cannon, planting the muzzle of its weapon flat against the top of his hissing leg joint.

Incandescent fire erupted from the weapon, explosive shells bursting at point blank range against his already damaged leg. The joint exploded, the metal running molten like mercurial blood down the war machine's leg. Fierach screamed as he felt his Titan's pain as his own, the feedback along the mind impulse unit frying much of his cerebral cortex.

The mighty war machine slumped sideways, the Titan's groin hammering into the severed leg, wedging the *Imperator Bellum* there at an angle.

Fierach laughed hysterically as his fall was arrested.

'Thank you, old friend!' he screamed, and with one last herculean effort, forced his dying brain to command the Titan in one last act of defiance.

The *Imperator Bellum* pushed off with its one good leg, lurching forward to smash its bridge section against the *Dies Irae's* head with terrifying force.

The impact smashed the armoured front of the Imperial Titan's cockpit and Fierach's last sight before the *Imperator Bellum's* reactor went critical was of a single, burning green eye as he was crushed against its surface.

FORRIX WATCHED THE Warhound in front of them back off through the smoke, realising its shields must have been knocked down.

'Follow it! Go after it!' he bellowed. The Titan was not just an enemy war machine to him now, it was a beast from the Olympian legends and he felt a burning, primal desire to slay it. He almost laughed aloud at the passions seething within him. Emotions and desires once thought lost forever rushed to the surface of his mind like a drowning man clawing for oxygen. He felt hate, bright and keen, battle-lust hot and urgent, and desire as fervent as anything he had ever felt in his long life.

His new-found purpose was reawakening in all its visceral glory.

Forrix fixed his eyes on the viewing holo, watching the chaos of the battle before him. Another Land Raider roared alongside his own, its lascannon stabbing into the smoke. He could see enemy infantry falling back towards the citadel, some carried on vehicles or grabbing onto their running boards. Here and there, pockets of resistance fired on their attackers, buying time for their comrades to escape.

A ringing impact slammed into the Land Raider, throwing Forrix sideways and he knew they had been hit badly. Smoke and flames spewed into the crew compartment and as he looked back, Forrix saw a great hole torn in the side of the vehicle's side armour. Through the ragged tear, he could see the red sky and the looming form of another Warhound Titan coming for them. Its snarling face was carved in an expression of fury and Forrix was again seized by the desire to slay one of these beasts.

'Disembark now!' bellowed Forrix, as the frontal ramp dropped and four giant warriors, similarly clad in Terminator armour, debarked from the Land Raider after their leader.

KROEGER CHARGED THROUGH the smoke, screaming a blood-curdling battle cry as he scythed the head from an Imperial Guardsman with a single stroke of his chainsword. He kicked another soldier in the gut, rupturing his belly and shattering his spine. Terrified faces surrounded him, some screaming, some begging for mercy. Kroeger laughed at them all, killing anything that came within reach with equal impartiality.

Kroeger's warriors hacked a bloody path through the men of the Jouran Dragoons, their blades soaked in gore. This was no battle any more, it was simple butchery and Kroeger revelled in the slaughter, feeling the surge of satisfaction hammer in his blood as he slew. His senses contracted until he could see nothing beyond the arterial spray and hear nothing beyond the screams of the dying.

A man fell to his knees before him, weeping and screaming, but Kroeger spun low, slashing his sword across the man's neck. He dropped his sword and reached down to pluck the dying man from the ground. Kroeger tore off his helmet, raising his victim up and allowing the spray of the man's lifeblood to spatter his face. Blood streamed down his face in thick rivulets and Kroeger tipped his head back to allow the life-giving fluid to fill his throat.

The hot blood tasted sublime, infused with terror and pain.

Kroeger roared with a monstrous lust, ripping the corpse in two then raising his sword high. His senses screamed at him, every nerve alive with hunger for more.

Always more. There could never be enough blood.

The red mist dropped over his eyes and Kroeger set off once more into battle.

HONSOU FIRED AS he ran, leading his warriors forward. He dived forward as a disciplined volley of las-fire blasted overhead, rolling to his knees and firing bursts at the source of the shots. Distorted screams echoed through the smoke as his bolts found homes in human flesh. His warriors darted forwards in groups, each covering the other's advance with carefully placed fire.

Men and tanks roared through the smoke, swirling banks of white clouds belching from the vehicles' smoke dispensers.

Honsou cursed as one of Forrix's Land Raiders rumbled past him, its sponson-mounted lascannon missing him by less than a metre. His auto-senses kicked in as the powerful weapon fired, flaring the smoke to vapour as it speared into the distance.

A massive burst of light from ahead told Honsou that there was a Titan there, one of its void shields now stripped away. He grinned as he imagined the desperate crew within, frantically trying to raise that shield as the Iron Warriors continued their attack. The soldiers pressed into their service sprinted alongside Honsou, the Warsmith deeming his company in need of support from such rabble. It angered Honsou that these scum fought beside his men, but he would not lower himself to voicing his outrage at this latest insult.

He worked the fire of his bolter left and right, deliberately catching a few of the red-clad soldiers in his volley, and rose to his feet. He sprinted forward, joining a firing squad of Iron Warriors. They had a large number of Imperial Guardsmen pinned in a dusty crater, its lip wreathed in barbed razorwire. A missile slashed from the crater, slamming into a rumbling transport vehicle behind him and blasting it open with a ringing clang.

Seconds later another missile streaked from the crater, but foolishly, the weapon team had not displaced before firing again and an answering volley of gunfire ripped the two-man team apart in a hail of bullets.

Keeping low, Honsou ran over to where a rabble of men in crimson overalls squatted behind shattered rockcrete tank traps. They fired crude, bolt-action rifles over their tops towards the crater. Honsou gripped the back of the nearest man's overalls and hauled him level with his helm.

'You are wasting ammunition, fool! Dig them out with your blades.'

The man nodded frantically, too terrified of Honsou to reply. Honsou hurled the wretch aside, wiping his gauntlet against his thigh armour and returned to his squad.

LIEUTENANT COLONEL LEONID lay on the slopes of a cratered ridge, firing his lasgun as the first platoon sprinted back to the next rally point. His face was blackened and lined with fear-induced fatigue, but he was still alive and fighting, which was something given the confused nature of this battle. Sergeant Ellard lay beside him, pumping shot after shot into the indistinct shadows running through the smoke. The terror and threat of being surrounded, cut off and over-whelmed was a physical thing, and Leonid had to consciously fight to remain calm.

He had to lead by example, and though his chest was a knotted mass of pain, he fought it to set a good one to his men.

'Front rank fire! Rear rank withdraw!' he shouted as Ellard pushed himself to his feet and began chivvying the rear rank back towards the next rally point. Volley after volley of las-gun fire hammered through the ranks of the red-coated troopers charging through the madness of the battle, who were dropping by the dozen. So far he was holding the retreat together, but it was balancing on a knife-edge. The men were stretched to the limits of their courage and they had performed as well as he could ever have asked. But they were nearing the end of their reserves and could not hold forever.

It was a race against time as much as anything as to whether they could get back within the cover of the citadel's guns before that courage was exhausted.

Guardsman Corde crawled over to him, yelling over the crack of gunfire and rumble of tanks and explosions. The vox slithered around on his back as he crawled and he car-ried a hissing plasma gun, steam drifting from the coolant coils on its barrel.

'Sergeant Ellard reports they're at the rally point, sir!'

'Very good, Corde,' said Leonid, slinging his rifle and shouting, 'Front rank, let's get the hell out of here!'

The Jourans did not need to be told twice. They scrambled back down the slope as covering volleys of lasgun fire from Ellard's section stabbed into the smoke. Leonid waited until the last of his men had withdrawn before he and Corde moved to join the rest of the platoon.

A roar, like that of a Jouran carnosaur, came from the slope behind him and Leonid turned to see a legion of hor-rifying iron behemoths lurch over the ridge, slamming down with teeth-loosening force. The tanks were huge, per-verted Leman Russ variants, their armoured flanks daubed with obscene symbols and their turrets grinding with the squeal of ancient gears. A wide-barrelled gun mounted on the nearest tank's forward hull chattered, spewing high velocity shells down the slope and ripping across the blasted ground. Leonid grabbed Corde and dropped, bullets sawing through the air above them.

He raised his head and terror flooded him as the tank rumbled forwards, ready to crush him under its bronze tracks. More bullets filled the air and the main gun fired with an ear-splitting crack, followed seconds later by a distant explosion. The track rumbled towards Leonid and he rolled in the only direction he could.

He rolled beneath the hull of the tank, its roaring metal underside passing a whisper from his head. Hot gasses and stinking exhaust fumes belched and he gagged. Something splashed him and he felt warm wetness cover his face and arms. He covered his ears and pressed his face into the dust, flattening his body as much as he could.

'Emperor protect me...' he whispered as the monstrous tank rumbled overhead. A protruding hook of metal caught on a fold of his uniform jacket and Leonid grunted in pain as he was dragged along the rough ground beneath the tank for several metres before he was able to work himself free.

Suddenly he was clear and the tank rumbled onwards, leaving him shaking with fear and relief. He took a deep breath and crawled back to Corde, who lay unmoving behind him.

Leonid felt his stomach rise and vomited explosively at the sight of Corde's mangled corpse. Corde had not been as lucky as he had, his lower body crushed to an unrecognisable pulp by the tank's mass. Blood still flooded from his mouth and Leonid dry-heaved, realising what the wetness that had splashed him under the tank had been.

The vox was crushed, but Corde's weapon was still intact and Leonid snatched it from the dead trooper's hands. A towering rage filled him at the thought that Corde's murderers probably didn't even know that they had killed someone. Leonid pushed himself to his feet and staggered drunkenly after the iron monster.

The thing wasn't hard to find; it was rumbling slowly after his men, slaughtering them with bursts of gunfire and shells from its main gun. Leonid screamed himself hoarse at the traitors within, skidding to a halt less than ten metres from the rear of the tank and raising Corde's plasma gun.

He squeezed the trigger twice in quick succession, sending bolts of white-hot plasma energy towards the tank. The shots impacted squarely on the thin rear armour and punched through it easily, instantaneously igniting the tank's fuel and ammo. The tank exploded in a red fireball, the turret buckling from the pressure of internal detonations. The shockwave swatted Leonid down, his chest searing in pain as he fell.

Black smoke plumed from the ruptured tank and Leonid screamed in fury as another shape came running towards him through the battle. He swung the plasma gun up, but it was still recharging. Angrily, he tossed the weapon aside and reached for his lasgun as Sergeant Ellard emerged from the smoke.

The sergeant didn't waste any time, hauling his commanding officer to his feet and dragging him away from the blazing wreck.

CARLSEN CRUSHED ANOTHER vehicle beneath his heavy tread and sidestepped as another tried to ram him. He groaned with effort as he spun the agile Warhound on its central axis and unleashed a short volley into the tank's rear. The ammo requirements for his main guns were eating into the reserve hoppers and he knew that, at this current level of engagement, his guns would be empty in minutes.

And then this battle would be all over. Moderati Arkian had worked miracles, coaxing the Machine Spirit to invest their shields once more, and without a second to spare as that damned Land Raider had come at them again. Once again it had stripped him of his protective shields before the *Jure Divinu* had flanked it and blown it back to the warp. Some warriors had gotten out, but before he could bring his weapons to bear and finish them off, they were swallowed up in the smoke and confusion.

If they could just hold on a little longer, then they would be back within the visual range of the citadel and its guns. Then they would be safe.

FORRIX CHARGED ACROSS a crater, a loop of razor wire trailing from his leg, and worked the fire of his storm bolter across the backs of some cowering Guardsmen sheltering in its base. Across the battlefield he could see Kroeger slaughtering a clutch of soldiers unlucky enough to have been outpaced and cut off.

Forrix paused in his charge and his eyes narrowed as he watched the slaughter-maddened frenzy with which the young-blood butchered the enemy soldiers. His silver armour, gleaming and pristine before the battle, was now soaked in gore, its iconography obscured by glistening blood. Kroeger was going too far now, the call of the Blood God too strong for him to resist.

Honsou appeared on his right flank, leading his men forward in good order, firing and moving, firing and moving. Much as he hated to admit it, the half-breed was an adept commander, despite his mixed blood.

The battle had devolved into a series of smaller engagements now that the main Imperial offensive had been routed. There was little point in continuing the pursuit, those units that had escaped were so badly mauled that they were unlikely ever to regain field readiness.

All that remained was to slay the Titan.

With blissful synchronicity, the smoke parted and there it was before him, its red and yellow carapace blazing in the sunlight. Its snarling face challenged him to fight it.

'You task me…' he whispered, 'You task me,' and set off to meet this armoured monster, but as suddenly as it had appeared, it turned and set off at speed into the smoke.

Cheated of his prey, Forrix halted and whispered, 'Another time, beast…'

LEONID STUMBLED AND lurched across the wasteland before the citadel, each breath hot in his chest. Were it not for Sergeant Ellard's support, he would surely have collapsed.

He could hear the cries of the enemy close behind, and the screams of those they had caught.

Suddenly he caught sight of three massive forms standing just at the edge of sight before him and, as Ellard continued pushing him forward, he almost laughed with relief as the shapes resolved themselves into the welcome form of two Reaver Battle Titans and a Warlord.

But as he drew nearer he saw, with a mounting sense of horror, that the Titans were horrendously damaged. Their carapaces were buckled and scorched by repeated weapon impacts. What had happened to these war machines? As he took in the scale of the damage he realised again the terrible nature of the foe they faced here and the folly of underestimating them. How many lives had been lost today because of such a mistake?

Two Warhounds lurched backwards through the smoke and dust, their weapons firing controlled bursts into the ranks of the enemy. Both were damaged, their armoured flanks scored and burned, but both were still fighting.

He watched as the Reavers and the Warlord opened fire and the air exploded with the shocking noise. The Warhounds gratefully took shelter in the shadow of their larger cousins, adding their own gunfire to the barrage.

Leonid stumbled forward, past the Titans and into the cover of the guns of the Primus Ravelin, relieved beyond words that he had made it back alive. Fresh troops manned the firing step at the edge of the forward ditch and Ellard passed him off to a frightened-looking soldier before returning to the battlefield to see to his men. Leonid leant against the wall of the parapet, cradling his head in his hands as the full horror of the battle crashed down upon him.

With those Dragoons who could escape now under the protection of the Titans of the Legio Ignatum and the citadel's gunners, the majority of the enemy did not appear too keen to continue the massacre, turning back to their own lines with raucous cries and taunts on their lips. Some could not contain their lust for killing and tried in vain to catch their victims, only to be mown down by close range fire from the Titans and the columns of fire from the ravelin and bastions.

Leonid felt an unbelievable exhaustion smother him. He put a hand out to steady himself, but the world spun crazily and he slid down the wall and collapsed before the soldiers next to him could catch him.

Four

DESPITE THE WARM wind that gusted across the mountain peaks, a shiver passed down Major Gunnar Tedeski's spine as he watched the activities below the fortress of Tor Christo. The stocky major leant over the parapet of Kane bastion, steadying himself with his one arm, and tried to guess at the number of men working below on the plains. At a conservative estimate, he guessed there were perhaps eight or nine thousand workers digging or otherwise engaged in the siege-works below. The enemy was not short of men to dig, that was for sure, but how many actual warriors faced him was impossible to say.

'Uh, Major Tedeski, I'm not sure that's such a good idea,' ventured his aide-de-camp Captain Poulsen, who followed behind him clutching a data-slate.

'Nonsense, Poulsen, these Chaos scum aren't the sort to go in for snipers.'

'Even so, sir,' reiterated Poulsen as the boom of artillery echoed from the sides of the valley.

Tedeski shook his head, saying, 'It's too short to matter.'

Sure enough the shell landed in the ruins of the watch-tower, sending up a plume of dust and rock fragments. The watchtower had been demolished after less than a day's shelling, but it had never been designed to withstand such a comprehensive bombardment in the first place.

Tedeski pulled back from the parapet and continued his walk around the perimeter of the bastion's walls. Soldiers sat, playing dice or sleeping below the level of the parapet. A few scanned the ground before them, their faces lined in exhaustion and lack of sleep. The more or less constant shelling had denied everyone sleep, and nerves were stretched taut.

In the week since the abortive attack on the traitors' trench system by the Legio Ignatum and the armoured units of the Dragoons, the plateau had changed beyond all recognition. Enemy artillery had pounded the plains day and night with high explosives, obliterating razor wire and detonating mines. Zigzag trenches covered the ground, reaching out towards the promontory that Tor Christo sat upon, their sides heavily reinforced with earthen ramparts. Tedeski's gunners had done their best, but the trenches had been constructed with mathematical precision and they were impossible to enfilade. Only once, when a portion of the trench had overreached, were they able to cause some real damage, killing the diggers and obliterating their machinery.

But since then, as each trench approached a point where the guns would be able to fire down their length, giant figures in grey-steel armour would direct the workers to alter the angle of digging.

A spider web of communication trenches and redoubts spread back to the main campsite and, though the Christo's guns shelled them daily, his observers could see no appreciable damage. It was maddeningly frustrating to see the foe advance with such impunity. The enemy had thrown out a second parallel at the termination of the saps, its sharp curve matching the sweep of his walls exactly. In two sections of this new parallel, high walls had been built. No doubt the trench behind them was being deepened and widened to allow the placement of large-bore howitzers.

Though the men in the Christo had been under fire for over a week, the range was too great for the enemy guns to do more than chip away at the walls. However, the range was ideal for delivering ricochet fire, which had dismounted a great many of Tor Christo's wall-mounted guns. Tedeski had ordered the remaining guns to be pulled back into the fort, and though casualties had been light – fifty-two men dead so far – that would all change when the batteries of the second parallel were completed.

But Tedeski had a surprise in store for Tor Christo's attackers.

Guns situated at the base of the rocky promontory, kept in reserve thus far, would soon make their presence felt when the enemy moved their heavy artillery forward into those newly constructed batteries.

'It won't be long now, Poulsen,' mused Tedeski.

'What won't, sir?'

'The attack, Poulsen, the attack,' replied Tedeski, unable to mask his irritation. 'If we can't stop them from completing those batteries, they will bring up their big guns and lob high explosive shells right over our walls. Then they won't need to batter our walls down, they'll be able to walk right up to the main gate and come in, because there will be no one left alive to stop them.'

'But the guns below will stop them, surely?'

'Possibly,' allowed Tedeski, 'but we'll only be able to pull that trick once. And that's assuming they don't know about them already. Remember that reconnaissance party we fired on at the beginning of all this?'

'Yes, sir.'

'Well there's every chance our enemies know of the guns down there, and have planned accordingly.'

'Surely not, sir. If the enemy had discovered them, they would have attempted to shell them before now, would they not?'

Tedeski nodded thoughtfully, resting his elbow on the stonework of the parapet, its sharply angled construction allowing a soldier to fire at attackers almost directly below.

'There is that, Poulsen, and that's the only reason I haven't had the passages below ground blocked. I can't risk not having those guns firing when the time comes.'

Emboldened by his superior officer's cavalier attitude to the potential danger of snipers, Captain Poulsen stood at the edge of the parapet and watched the bustling activity on the plains.

'I never thought to see such a thing,' he whispered.

'What?'

Poulsen pointed towards the towering form of the *Dies Irae*, standing immobile where the death of the *Imperator Bellum* had crippled it. Its lower legs were blackened and still smoking where the meltdown of the Imperial Titan had scorched it. Vast swathes of scaffolding and buttresses had been erected around its legs as hundreds of men worked to try and repair the grievous damage done to it. The Titan's upper body had escaped the worst of the blast and each day its guns would fire upon the citadel, wreathing its walls in tremendous explosions, daring its enemy to come out and face it once more.

Tedeski nodded, 'Nor I. It was an honour to watch so brave a warrior fight such a diabolical monster. His brother Titans will avenge him though.'

'And who will avenge us?' pondered Poulsen.

Tedeski rounded on his aide-de-camp and snapped, 'We shall not need avenging, Captain Poulsen, and I will have words with any man who publicly voices such an opinion. Do you understand me?'

'Yes, sir,' replied Poulsen hurriedly. 'I only meant–'

'I know what you meant, Poulsen, but do not say these things aloud,' cautioned Tedeski, waving his arm at the soldiers who manned the parapet and the gunners who tended their artillery pieces.

'What do you think is the single most important element of a fortress, Poulsen? Its walls? Its guns? Its position? No. It is the men who stand behind its walls and say to the enemy, "No, you shall not take this place". The fighting spirit of these men is all that keeps the enemy beyond these walls and only by standing together, with faith in the Emperor and an utter belief in our ability to hold, will we prevail. Regardless of the facts, the men need to believe that *we* believe the Christo can hold. Otherwise we are lost.'

Poulsen nodded thoughtfully before saying, 'Do you believe we can hold, sir?'

Tedeski returned his gaze to the plains below. 'Ultimately, no, we cannot hold. Tor Christo will fall, but we will hold it for as long as we can. When I decide that the day is lost, I will order the withdrawal along the tunnels and overload our reactor to blow this place apart before I allow these bastards to make use of the Christo.'

* * *

HONSOU PUSHED ASIDE an emaciated slave worker and followed Forrix along the twisting trench that led to the forward parallel. As the two Iron Warriors passed, slaves hurriedly dropped their shovels and picks and abased themselves before their masters. Neither Forrix nor Honsou paid the wretched creatures any heed, too intent on the looming shape of Tor Christo above them. Honsou felt the familiar anticipation as they stepped into the main parallel and he saw the thoroughness with which it had been constructed.

It had been dug to a depth of three metres, the wall nearest Tor Christo angled inwards to minimise the effect of airbursting shells. Propped dugouts were cut into the trench sides where slaves slept, ate and died. Too bone-weary to dispose of their dead in any other way, corpses were pushed to the side of the trench, the rotted remains filling the air with the stench of decay. Timber boards on iron sleepers were laid across the base of the trench and Honsou was impressed with the speed with which Forrix had driven the trench forward.

'The first battery will be here,' said Forrix, pointing to a portion of the trench Honsou estimated was some six hundred metres from the base of the mountain. He could see that work had already begun on widening the trench. Thick sheets of steel were piled at the entrance to the new battery, ready to be laid across the ground to enable the big guns to fire without their recoil burying them in the ground.

Honsou nodded, looking up towards Tor Christo, picturing the angle of fire this guns placed in this battery would have.

The most vulnerable point of any fortification was its salient angles, the projecting points of its bastions where the ground in front was not covered by direct fire from the parapet. Forrix had dug the main sap directly towards the central bastion, with this forward parallel constructed well within the range of the fort's guns, but protected by their depth and earthen ramparts.

Honsou could see that batteries were being dug to either side of the bastion's salient, angled inwards so that the guns placed there would fire perpendicular to the face of the bastion and break it open efficiently. Once the walls had been breached with direct firing guns, howitzers would send screaming shells into the gap to sweep it clear of enemy infantry before the main attack went in. Even so, it was sure to be a bloody enterprise.

There was a pleasing inevitability to the mechanics of a siege thought Honsou, as he watched dying slaves digging the gun battery. He had heard tales that in ages past there was a prescribed series of stages an attacker would be forced to go through before it was deemed that he had done enough to earn the surrender of a garrison. Once it had been decreed that both forces had done all that honour demanded, the defenders would surrender and be allowed to quit the fortress carrying their weapons with their colours raised high. Such a notion was clearly ludicrous, and Honsou could not imagine a time when he would accept an enemy's surrender.

Once the Iron Warriors began a siege, there was no way to stop it.

When the great Perturabo had still led his warriors in battle, he offered his foes one chance to surrender before he had even planted a single shovel in the ground. Should that offer be refused, there would be no others, and such a siege could end only one way: in blood and death.

'You have sited your batteries well, Forrix,' noted Honsou.

Forrix nodded briefly, accepting the compliment. 'I do not believe we need to dig any further. To do so is pointless – we would expose ourselves needlessly to airbursting shells and the slope of the promontory will obscure the walls of the fortress should we press forward.'

Honsou saw that Forrix was correct. 'What about the batteries at the foot of the mountain? This will be well within their ideal range and the guns here will undoubtedly be targeted.'

'I realise that, Honsou, but when our guns are in place I will lead warriors from my company to take the enemy gun positions by storm.'

Honsou narrowed his eyes, aware that Forrix had called him by his name for the first time. Then the notion that he would be denied the chance to capture the guns he had discovered hit him and he snarled, 'You will capture the lower guns? I discovered them, the honour of their capture should be mine!'

'No, Honsou, I have another task for you.'

'Oh, and what would that be? Keeping the guns fed with shells? Guarding slaves?'

Forrix said nothing and pointed to a gap in the trench wall that was filled with sandbags and defended by a full squad of Iron Warriors.

'When the time is right, you will lead the storming parties from this point and take the breach. You will hold it until the human soldiers are able to scale the rock face and escalade the walls with ladders and grapples.'

Honsou opened his mouth to retort, then snapped it shut as he realised the honour of the task he was being given. His chest swelled with pride before his natural cynicism and suspicion came to the fore.

'Why, Forrix? Why do you do me this honour? You have done nothing before now but deride me and keep me in my place as a mongrel, a half-breed.'

Forrix was silent for long seconds, as though he himself did not know exactly why he had made such an offer. He turned from the mountain and faced Honsou.

'There was a time I thought like you do, Honsou. A time when I believed we fought for something more important than simple revenge, but as the millennia of battle ground on, I came to realise that there was no point to what we did. Nothing ever changed and nothing brought us closer to victory. I have been too long from the field of battle, Honsou, and as I watched you fight the Imperials, I knew that in your heart, you are an Iron Warrior. You still believe in the dream of Horus; I lost my hold on it many centuries ago.'

Forrix grinned suddenly. 'And the fact that it will send Kroeger into a towering rage.'

Honsou laughed, feeling uncharacteristically charitable towards the venerable Forrix.

'That it will, Forrix, but he will be shamed by your decision. Are you sure you are wise to antagonise Kroeger in this way? He descends further into the grasp of the Blood God with each passing day.'

'The young-blood is nothing to me. I see nothing for him beyond mindless slaughter, but you... for you I see great things. The Warsmith does too, I see it every time he speaks to you.'

Honsou said, 'In that I think you are mistaken. He hates me.'

'True, and yet you lead one of his grand companies,' pointed out Forrix.

'Only because Borak died at Magnot Four-Zero and the Warsmith has not yet named his successor.'

'Again true, but ask yourself this: how long ago was the Battle at Magnot Four-Zero?'

'Nearly two hundred years.'

'Aye, and do you think that in all that time the Warsmith could not have found someone to lead the company?'

'Obviously not, or he would have done so.'

Forrix sighed and snapped, 'Perhaps that tainted blood of yours has made you as slow-witted as Dorn's lap-dogs from whence it comes! Think, Honsou. Had the Warsmith named you Borak's successor there and then, would any of his warriors have accepted you? No, of course not, and nor should they have, because to them you were just a despised half-breed.'

'Not a lot has changed, Forrix.'

'Then you are more foolish than I took you to be,' snarled Forrix, marching back along the trench to the supply depots and leaving Honsou confused and alone in the half-finished battery.

Five

THE MACHINE TEMPLE at the heart of the citadel pulsed with barely contained power as though the very walls themselves breathed with an inner life or sentience. Its structure was strangely organic, though the chamber was built in honour of exactly the opposite.

The mass of the chamber was filled with baroque machinery that infested the space like a gigantic coral reef, steadily growing and increasing its mass with every passing year. A sickly amber glow permeated the chamber, alongside a low, throbbing hum, just at the threshold of hearing.

Shaven-headed technicians and servitors in faded, yellow robes wandered like ghosts through the bewilderingly complex labyrinth of machines, their ministrations to the holy technologies ritualised over thousands of years to the point that any true purpose had long been forgotten.

Regardless of their function, the rituals and blessings applied to the machines served their purpose: keeping the chamber's sole inhabitant alive.

Arch Magos Caer Amaethon, Keeper of the Sacred Light, Master of Hydra Cordatus.

Lodged atop a tapered rhomboid at the chamber's centre, the flesh of the arch magos's face – all that remained of his organic body – was suspended in a gurgling vat of life-preserving fluids. Ribbed copper wiring trailed from behind the skin, twitching wires stimulated the atrophied muscles of his face. Clear tubing pumped oxygen-rich nutrients through his ravaged capillaries and the fragmentary scraps of cortex that were all that remained of his brain, the rest having been replaced and augmented with kilometres of twisting corridors of logic stacks.

Amaethon's features creased as twitching electrical impulses awoke him to the fact that he was being addressed.

'Arch Magos Amaethon?' repeated Magos Naicin, taking a draw on a smoking cheroot. The smoke gusted from his back, whipped away as the recyc-units cleared the arch magos's chambers of their pollutants.

'Naicin?' asked Amaethon hesitantly, the fleshy lips having difficulty in forming the words. 'Why do you disturb my communing with the holy Omnissiah?'

'I come to bring you news of the battle.'

'Battle?'

'Yes, master, the battle above on the surface.'

'Oh, yes, the battle,' stated the arch magos. Naicin ignored Amaethon's lapse in memory. For six centuries, Amaethon had been linked to the beating heart of the citadel, monitoring every facet of its operation and that of the cavernous laboratorium hidden beneath it. For the last century of that service, he had been unable to leave this sanctuary, steadily becoming more a part of the citadel as each portion of his body withered and died. Soon the old man would be gone completely, his bio-engrams broken down and reduced to nothing more than task instruction wafers to be fed into worker-servitors.

Naicin knew Amaethon's fragile grip on reality was slipping, and it was a rare moment when he was able to summon up enough memory to interact with others. The first flush of panic when the invaders had attacked had galvanised the arch magos into remarkable lucidity, but even that was beginning to fade.

'The battle,' repeated Amaethon, a fragment of his crystal memory reacting to the word. 'Yes, I remember now. They come for what we protect here. They must not have it, Naicin!'

'No, arch magos, they must not,' agreed Naicin.

'How could they even know of its existence?'

'I do not know, master. But they do, and we must make plans in case the citadel's defences do not hold the invaders at bay.'

The flesh of Amaethon's face bobbed in its amniotic suspension. 'But they must, Naicin, this citadel was built by the finest military architects of the day, there are none who can breach its fastness.'

'I am sure you are correct, arch magos, but nevertheless we should have a contingency plan. The Guard are but men. Flesh, blood and bone. Organic and therefore weak. They cannot be relied upon.'

'Yes, yes, you are right,' agreed Amaethon dreamily. 'The flesh is weak, Naicin. Only the machine is strong. We must not allow the laboratorium to fall into enemy hands.'

'As ever, your words are filled with wisdom, arch magos. But even as we speak the enemy drive towards the fastness of Tor Christo, and it is likely that it will fall within days.'

Amaethon's flaccid features twitched at this news, his eyes fluttering in sudden alarm.

'And the tunnel that links us to Tor Christo? Do the enemy know of it?'

'I do not believe so, arch magos, but should the Christo fall, it is inevitable that they will discover it.'

'They must not be allowed to make use of it!' trilled Amaethon.

'I agree, that is why I have armed the demolition charges that will destroy it.'

'Have you made Vauban aware of this?'

'No, arch magos.'

'Good. Vauban would not understand the necessity of such action. His compassion for his men would be our undoing.'

Amaethon seemed to sigh and was silent for some minutes before saying, 'I am... not as strong as once I was, Naicin. The burden I carry here is great.'

Magos Naicin bowed. 'Then allow me to bear some of that burden, arch magos. When the time comes that the enemy approach the inner walls of the citadel, you will be under immense strain to hold the energy shield in place as well as maintaining the citadel in working order. Allow some of that burden to fall upon my shoulders.'

Amaethon's skin mask nodded and with an abrupt change of subject the arch magos whispered, 'And what of the astropaths? Have you been able to isolate the contagion that afflicts them and renders their mind-voices mute?'

Momentarily taken aback, Naicin paused before answering. 'Ah, regrettably, no, but I am confident the answer lies within your logic stacks. It is just a matter of time before I am able to restore their abilities and once again send messages off-world.'

'Very good. It is imperative that we summon aid, Naicin. The magnitude of the consequences should we be defeated here is beyond imagination.'

'We shall not be defeated,' assured Magos Naicin with another bow.

ON THE MORNING of the eleventh day of the siege, Forrix's batteries were complete and the giant guns of the Iron Warriors were either dragged forwards by gangs of sweating slaves or rumbled along under their own diabolical power. Within minutes of the observers on the walls of Tor Christo spotting the movement of the giant artillery pieces, the Imperial Basilisks began firing, the endless barrage of shells turning the ground before the fortress into a hell of fire and shrapnel.

But the deepened and widened trenches were proof against all but direct hits, and only two machines were destroyed, their crews and those manhandling them shredded by lethal steel splinters. One massive gun, an ornate long-barrelled howitzer, was struck a glancing impact by a shell bursting directly overhead. Imbued with the bound energy of a daemon from the warp, the war machine screamed in lunatic fury, breaking free of its sorcerous bindings and running amok in the communication trench, crushing the four score slaves who pulled it and the guards who watched over it.

It took the combined efforts of Jharek Kelmaur, seven of his cabal sorcerers and the souls of a hundred slaves to placate the daemon, but soon, the gun was in its prepared position before the walls of Tor Christo.

The gunners on the walls attempted to shift their fire to the two batteries, realising that the chances of damaging the war machines traversing the trenches were slim, but Forrix had placed his batteries well and the Basilisks could not land their shells so close to the promontory.

It took another three deafening hours before Forrix was happy with the placement of his guns and the slaves shackled the daemonic war machines to the steel plates laid on the floor of the batteries.

At last, several hours after the sun had passed its zenith, Forrix gave the order to fire.

THE FIRST SHELLS smashed into the south-eastern face of Kane bastion, throwing the men stationed on its walls to the ground. The rockcrete cracked under the impact, fist-sized chunks of grey rubble blasted skyward in a cloud of choking dust. It was followed seconds later by a volley from the second battery, smashing into the opposite face of the bastion.

This second volley was aimed high, blasting the top of the firing step clear in a storm of stone fragments that scythed men down by the dozen.

Blood and screams filled the air. Medics rushed to the aid of the wounded as their comrades dragged screaming soldiers from the walls to the courtyard below. Barely a minute had passed when yet more shells slammed into the walls of the Kane bastion, shaking it to its very foundations.

The noise was unbelievable. Major Tedeski knew that he would never forget the sheer, skull-pounding volume of the enemy bombardment. Each battery took it in turns to fire, the massive guns hurling explosive projectiles at his walls with incredible force. The stocky major had changed from his normal dress uniform and simply wore the standard issue sky blue jacket of the regiment, the one empty sleeve tucked inside. A flinching Captain Poulsen stood behind Tedeski, his face twitching with every crack of shell on stone.

Tedeski watched the corner gun tower crumble from the walls, carrying a dozen men screaming to their deaths on the rocks below.

'Upon my soul, it's bad,' he muttered.

'Sir?' enquired Poulsen.

'Nothing,' said Tedeski, scanning the walls. 'I want those men off the walls. Leave platoons one and five on the parapet and order all the others to withdraw.'

Poulsen relayed his commanding officer's order, grateful to have something to distract him from the thunderous shelling. Tedeski watched as the command filtered through to the walls, seeing the relief on the faces of the men ordered to withdraw and the fear of those who remained. The ground shook again as more shells impacted and Tedeski swore as an entire section of the southern wall cracked and crumbled to the base. Though the firing step was taking a punishing barrage, it would be some time before the enemy guns had pounded enough of the walls to form a practicable breach and brought down enough rubble for attacking troops to climb.

Stone splinters ripped through the bodies of the men who remained on the walls, tearing them to bloody rags, but

Tedeski knew that he couldn't leave the walls totally unmanned for fear that an escalade was underway. There was every chance he was consigning these men to die, and the guilt of their deaths tasted like ashes in his mouth.

Suddenly, he set off towards the walls, climbing the dusty, fragment-strewn steps that led from the courtyard to the parapet.

'Sir?' shouted Poulsen, 'Where are you going?'

'To stand on the walls with my men,' snapped the irascible major.

Years of ingrained obedience kicked in and, without thinking, Poulsen trotted up the steps after Tedeski before his conscious brain truly understood what he was doing.

A ragged cheer greeted Tedeski's arrival as he marched to the head of the bastion, defiantly facing the enemy guns. The parapet here was cracked and sagging, several metres of rockcrete missing from its length, and Tedeski had a clear view of the scene below.

The two batteries were wreathed in clouds of thick grey smoke, which was periodically pierced by flashes of fire. Screaming projectiles slashed through the air as a soldier unnecessarily shouted, 'Incoming!'

The shells slammed into the base of the wall below Tedeski, blasting chunks of rock high into the air and enveloping him in a drifting bank of smoke. Tedeski didn't flinch and when the cloud cleared, merely dusted off his uniform jacket with his one hand.

As the noise of the explosion faded, Tedeski shouted, 'The enemy must have bad fevers. Do you hear them cough? Perhaps we should offer them some sweet wine!'

Laughter and cheering swelled from the throats of Battalion A of the Jouran Dragoons, their courage bolstered by their commander's words and bravery.

Another nerve-stretching hour of shelling followed which Major Gunnar Tedeski endured with his men in determined silence.

As dusk turned the sky the colour of congealed blood, Tedeski turned to Poulsen, and took his aide-de-camp's data-slate with a shaking hand.

With an effort of will to keep his voice from breaking, he said, 'Order the guns below to deploy and shell those batteries out of existence.'

FORRIX PICKED HIS way across the cratered plain as quickly as his bulky suit of Terminator armour would allow him, followed by thirty of his hand-picked warriors. Like him, they had dulled the lustre of their Terminator armour with red dust from the plains, and under the fury of the bombardment would hopefully escape detection by the soldiers above them.

He knew they did not have much time. The commander of the garrison above would know by now how devastating the artillery of the Iron Warriors was, and that unless he destroyed it quickly, his fortress was lost. It followed that he would now deploy his hidden guns and this was just what Forrix wanted. Honsou waited in the forward parallel with forty of his warriors and nearly six thousand human soldiers spread along the extent of the trench.

The timing would need to be precise. Too early and the Imperials would seal the tunnels leading to the guns; too late and his artillery would be bombed out of existence.

Forrix stalked through the cratered wasteland and secreted himself less than fifty metres from the entrance to the concealed artillery pits. His veteran warriors filed into position alongside him and waited, the noise of the shelling swallowing the thump of their heavy footfalls.

They did not have long to wait. A sliver of light and rumbling of heavy rolling stock grinding along rails announced that the guns were indeed moving into position.

'Honsou,' hissed Forrix, rising to his feet and charging towards the guns, 'go now!'

HONSOU SNARLED IN anticipation as he heard Forrix's words echo within his helm and kicked down the sandbagged barricade that led from the forward parallel onto the plain. He sprinted forward, the Iron Warriors fanning out behind him as they raced across the uneven ground towards the base of the steep, rocky slope. Behind him thousands of red-clad soldiers climbed from the trench and the guns continued to fire, pounding the walls to breach the central bastion.

The augmented fibre bundle muscles of their armour powered the Iron Warriors upwards, leaving the human soldiers floundering in their wake, stumbling around in the strobing, shell-lit twilight.

He and his warriors would be first to reach the fortress. This type of action had once been known as a Forlorn Hope, because the first men into the breach would invariably be the first men to die. It was the duty of the Hope to draw the enemy fire as the remainder of the force closed with the fortress. The men of the Hope would storm the breach and buy time with their lives for the following troops to push through. Hundreds of men might be sacrificed in this way simply to get a handful through the breach.

Storming a breach was always a bloody affair, because the enemy knew exactly where the attack would be coming from, though Honsou hoped the constant bombardment from the batteries would keep the Imperial defenders' heads down.

He clambered swiftly up the jagged rocks, each powerful thrust of his thighs pushing him closer to the top. As the noise of shell impacts intensified, he looked up into the darkening sky, seeing the broken top of the ramparts and a huge tear ripped in the side of the bastion. Tonnes of rubble spilled down its flanks and provided a ready-made ramp to the defenders above.

'Battery guns, cease fire,' ordered Honsou as he cleared the top of the slope.

Shouts of alarm echoed from the top of the walls and a handful of las-blasts stabbed towards him, but they were poorly aimed and flew high.

Honsou muttered the Iron Warriors' catechism of battle: 'Iron within, iron without,' as his men pulled themselves onto the ground before Tor Christo and charged with him towards the breach.

FORRIX SWEPT HIS power glove through the chest of a man wearing a gunner's reinforced flak vest, his upper body exploding in blood and bone. Roaring reaper cannon fire ripped through the Imperial gunners and soldiers, spraying the flanks of their artillery with blood.

'Protect the guns!' screamed a junior officer before Forrix tore his head off.

Fools. Did they really think the guns were their target; that the Iron Warriors did not already have a surfeit of guns?

Their attack had hit without warning and the first Imperial troops had died without knowing what had killed them. Their guards tried to fight back, but within seconds had realised the fight was hopeless and fled before Forrix and his Terminators. But the old veteran was not about to let his prey escape him so easily. Three of his warriors levelled their reaper cannons, the barrels studded with spikes, and unleashed a deadly hail of shots that felled men by the dozen.

Forrix lumbered forward, ignoring the Imperial guns and charging as fast as he could towards the wide doors in the mountainside. Already the alarm had been raised and they were rumbling closed, but too slowly. Forrix and his retinue burst through into the space beyond.

A volley of las-fire greeted them, hissing harmlessly from the thick armour of the Terminators. Scores of Guardsmen were spread through the cavernous chamber, but Forrix ignored the bright flashes of weapons fire as he searched for the door mechanism. Thick rails ran across the rockcrete floor from three enormous bays and ordnance magazines, each with cranes and pulley chains filling the space above them.

He could see stairs ahead leading upwards carved through the rock. The majority of the cavern's defenders were gathered at their base behind hurriedly constructed barricades of crates and barrels. Another group was clustered behind a pair of giant bulldozers, firing from behind their yellow bulk at the invaders. Guessing the controls for the door were housed here, Forrix charged forwards through the hail of shots, his armour easily deflecting the defenders' pitiful fire. He and his Terminators fired their combi-bolters across the flanks of the bulldozers, explosive shells killing a dozen soldiers and ricocheting from the dozers' flanks with flaring detonations.

More Terminators headed for the soldiers guarding the stairs as Forrix rounded the forward edge of the closest bulldozer and hosed the men there with bolter fire. Grenades burst harmlessly around the Terminators as one man dived aside and swung a heavy rifle with a ribbed barrel towards Forrix.

A white-hot beam of plasma energy slammed into his chest, instantly obliterating the blasted iconography there and searing through layers of ceramite armour. Forrix felt the heat of the plasma scorch his skin and he staggered under the force of the impact. His Terminator armour had been forged on the Anvil of Holades on Olympia itself and its ancient spirit was as corrupt as he, and not yet willing to fall. Forrix recovered his balance and punched his power fist through the plasma gunner's chest in a shower of bone splinters, lifting the impaled body from the ground and hurling it through the air in a bloody arc.

Bursts of bolter fire and disembowelling sweeps of lightning claws silenced the resistance. Forrix strode to the access door controls on the far wall and wrenched the release lever into the 'open' position. The doors screeched, the mechanisms protesting as their motors suddenly reversed and began to rumble open again. Forrix backed away and put three bolts through the control mechanism.

Satisfied the gun bay doors would not be closing any time soon, Forrix rounded the blood-splattered bulldozer, watching as his warriors with reaper cannons began slaughtering the remaining defenders of the cavern in controlled bursts of gunfire.

As the slaughter continued, the Guardsmen broke and ran for the steps. Those not quick enough to reach the cover of the stairs were shredded by the Iron Warriors' firepower, their screams drowned in the deafening roar of the cannons. Any not killed in the initial bursts were soon torn apart as the shells destroyed their barricade in an instant. Within seconds the entire defence was gone, only chewed up crates and mangled corpses remaining.

A single, terrified soldier suddenly broke from cover, sprinting for the stairs. Three cannons tracked him as he ran, but Forrix said, 'No, this one is mine.'

Forrix let the man get within a hair's breadth of safety before he fired his weapon.

Shells tore great chunks from the wall behind his victim, shattering several control panels.

As fast as the soldier had run, it was not fast enough. A single shell clipped his thigh as he twisted out of the line of fire, instantly shearing his leg from his body just below the hip.

He landed in a bloody bundle, shrieking in agony as he saw the ragged stump of his leg, its remains hanging by gory threads. Forrix smiled and marched across the rockcrete floor, stepping across the wide rail tracks to stand above the man. He was hyperventilating and staring in horror at his ruined leg.

'The hydraulic shock will drag the blood from your heart in a few seconds,' said Forrix, his voice distorted by his armour's vox-unit. The man glanced up, uncomprehending, his eyes glazing over as death drew near.

'You are lucky,' said Forrix. 'You will die before the War-smith ascends. Thank your Emperor for that.'

The sound of battle faded and the cavern was theirs. Terminators hurried past him, eager to continue the killing.

He opened a channel to the remainder of his company.

'The lower level of the fort is ours. Send the rest of the men.'

Forrix lifted his eyes from the dying soldier and climbed the stairs to where two Terminators were attacking a wide set of steel doors, driving their powerful chainsaw-equipped fists into the junction of the doors.

Molten sparks filled the tunnel, spilling down the steps onto the waiting Terminators.

HONSOU SCRAMBLED UP the jagged piles of debris and loose rubble cascading down the breach in his wake. Twisted reinforcement bars jutted from smashed blocks of rockcrete like tendons, and dust fogged the air. Bright stabs of las-fire from above pierced the smoke in huge numbers, melting rock and hissing against armour. A bolt stuck his shoulder guard, staggering him, but he pressed on. A grenade burst at his feet, deadly fragments ringing from his armour and embedding themselves in his leg greaves.

He could see the enemy had cast down a barrier of rusted abatis, sharpened iron girders, crudely welded together to form waist-high obstacles to their charge. Honsou knew that the longer they were under fire, the less likely they were to be able to scale the breach. This was the point at which many assaults came to end, broken by obstacles and shredded by the defenders' fire.

For this attack to have any chance of success at all they had to mount the breach in one leap to overwhelm the defenders lining the parapet. Honsou tripped as the rocks slid out from beneath his feet, narrowly avoiding being obliterated by a shot from a lascannon. He pushed himself angrily to his feet and cursed as he saw three black-steel tubes bound together with packing tape clatter down the slope of the breach.

Honsou threw himself flat onto the rocks as the demolition charge exploded. The shockwave dislodged whole swathes of rubble and he felt himself sliding back down the breach, his auto-senses kicking in to protect him from the deafening and blinding detonation. Two Iron Warriors were snatched away in the blast, their armour ripped open by the force of the demo charge. Honsou rolled upright, his armour smoking from the explosion and clawed his way back up the breach.

More shots riddled the shattered breach, vitrifying the rock and pitting the ground with bullet impacts. Honsou felt powerful impacts from a heavy bolter slam into his armour. Pain blossomed up his left arm as one shell found its mark in the gap between his vambrace and elbow guard. Fire from the bastion to the north delivered murderous flanking fire into his men. The sheer amount of enemy firepower was now telling. Honsou saw another Iron Warrior fall, his armour pierced by a smoking hole punched in his breastplate.

More grenades bounced down the breach. Honsou pushed upwards, reaching for the abatis and pulling himself forward. The grey flanks of the wall stretched high above him. The only way in was through this six metre wide breach the guns had blasted, and the sliver of red sky he could see through it was a beacon to him.

This was taking too damn long! Already the human Chaos soldiery were clambering over the lip of the rocks below and he hadn't even fought his way into the mouth of the breach yet. Honsou gripped the rusted girders of the abatis in both hands, roaring as he ripped them from their position, sending them tumbling to the base of the breach, crushing half a dozen soldiers as they fell.

Another Iron Warrior climbed up to join him and the two of them went forwards, firing their bolt pistols as they climbed. Through the dust and smoke, Honsou could see shadowy forms at the jagged top of the breach and could hear screaming voices yelling him onwards. He shot into the smoke, hearing screams of pain as his bolts hit home.

He pushed forwards, gripping the stonework as the slope grew steeper. A shot punched into his breastplate, another grazed his head. Shots filled the air, flashes of las-fire vaporising the smoke as they slashed past him. The one remaining tower at the head of the bastion sprayed bullets across the breach, kicking up spurts of rock dust while grenades wreathed them in ringing detonations and spinning fragments. The warrior beside him fell, his helmet a molten ruin, but Honsou pushed on through it all, oblivious to the screams of dying men around him and the battle cries of the hundreds of soldiers that now clambered up the rocky slopes behind him.

The top of the breach was close now; he could make out individual forms through the smoke. He saw a Guardsman rigging another demolition charge and waited until the man stood up, ready to heave the explosives over the lip of the breach, before shooting him in the head. Blood sprayed from the stump of his neck and the man tumbled backwards, the primed demo charge falling from his dead fingers.

Honsou dropped flat as the rocks above him were swept clear of defenders by the massive explosion. Screams and desperate orders sounded from above. He leapt to his feet, drawing his sword and sprinting for all he was worth towards the billowing pillar of black smoke that wreathed the crest of the breach.

He collided with a pair of figures dressed in sky blue uniforms, and swept his sword across their chests, dropping them screaming to the ground. He could see more soldiers rushing to plug the sudden gap in their defence and shouted, 'Iron Warriors, with me!'

But Honsou was alone. He turned to face the nearest Guardsmen as they charged him. He killed the first men easily, but soon more and more clustered around him, entangling his blade with their bodies and restricting his movements with their corpses. He kicked out, spinning in a bloody arc as he clove his sword through his enemies. Shots and blades rang against his armour.

Where were the rest of his men?

He glanced down the sloping face of the breach. Below was a hell of lasers and bullets, enfilading fire from the flanking bastion ripping great holes in the ranks of the human soldiers as they struggled up the rocks. Hundreds had fallen, their bodies shredded by automatic weapons or burned by las-fire. The northern bastion had escaped relatively unscathed thus far. A few shells burst overhead, but the main shelling had been directed against this bastion, and the men assaulting it were now paying the price for that decision.

More enemies closed in around him as he shot, cut, stabbed, kicked and punched a red ruin through the defenders, roaring in triumph as the warriors of his company climbed onto the walls, sweeping left and right along the ramparts. Bolters fired again and again and men died in droves as the Iron Warriors took the ramparts of Kane bastion in blood and steel.

Silhouetted in the flames of the defenders' rout, Honsou leapt for the courtyard below, the stonework cracking under his weight. Enemy soldiers streamed towards the narrow neck of the bastion, Iron Warriors in hot pursuit. The momentum of the charge must not be lost. Despite this success, there were sure to be thousands more soldiers in the bastions either side of this one.

Honsou ran through the confusion of the battle, firing as he ran and cutting down those soldiers not quick enough to escape. At the neck of the bastion he saw the Imperial troopers were heading for a wide trench, crossed by a narrow bridge. Troops bottlenecked on the crossing despite the desperate shouts of officers for them not to. As Honsou watched, the bridge collapsed into the trench, crushing those unfortunate to be trapped beneath it. Some soldiers dropped into the trench, turning to fire on the Iron Warriors, but many more were streaming in panic to the main esplanade where a squat, round tower crouched at the base of the steep escarpment.

Black coated officers in skull-embossed peaked caps bellowed orders for their men to stand firm, enforcing these orders with bullets. Honsou let them shoot their own men, blasting holes in those enemy soldiers who weren't running. A swelling roar of hate filled the night as the Iron Warriors' indentured soldiery swarmed over the walls, fanning out towards the stairs or simply jumping into the courtyard. The bastion was theirs, now they just had to break out of it.

Stuttering volleys of las-fire blasted from the trench, but it was too little, too late as Honsou dropped into the prepared position and killed with wanton abandon. His sword chopped through a terrified Guardsman, the reverse stroke disembowelling another. He worked his way down the trench, hacking a bloody path through the defenders who fell back in horror from his deadly blade. As Honsou killed the Guardsmen, he revelled in his superiority, and could well understand the attraction of Khorne's path.

The Iron Warriors swept over the trench killing everything in it with the fury of those who had fought their way through hell and lived to tell the tale, butchering anything that came within reach.

* * *

FROM INSIDE THE keep of Tor Christo, Major Gunnar Tedeski watched the slaughter with a desperate heart. His men were dying and there was nothing he could do to stop it. He'd gambled with the lower guns, trusting that they would be able to stop the relentless advance of the Iron Warriors, but they had second guessed him, and now the fortress was as good as theirs.

He had failed and while Tor Christo's fate had never really been in doubt, it was galling for it to have fallen so quickly. The attackers had not yet broken out of Kane bastion, but they would surely overrun the entrenchments behind the bastion soon. He knew the images he was seeing on the remote pict-viewers did not capture the horror and carnage taking place outside. Thousands of men were streaming over the walls and it would only be a matter of time until the Mars and Dragon bastions came under attack from their vulnerable rears. If he let them, the men there would fight bravely, but they would die, and Tedeski would have no more deaths on his conscience.

'Poulsen!' sighed Tedeski, wiping dust and sweat from his brow.

'Sir?'

'Send the "Heaven's Fall" signal to all company commanders and Castellan Vauban.'

'"Heaven's Fall", sir?' queried Poulsen.

'Yes, damn you!' snapped Tedeski. 'Quickly, man!'

'Y-yes, sir,' nodded Poulsen hurriedly and ran off to pass the evacuation code to the vox operators.

Tedeski turned from his aide-de-camp and straightened his duty uniform jacket before addressing the remaining men and officers standing with him in the Christo's command centre.

'Gentlemen, it is time you left this place. It grieves me to say that Tor Christo is about to fall. As the commanding officer, I am ordering you to lead as many men as you can into the tunnels and make your way to the citadel. Castellan Vauban will need every man on the walls in the coming days and I will not deny him those men by sacrificing them needlessly here.'

Silence greeted his words until a junior officer asked, 'Will you not accompany us, sir?'

'No. I will stay to overload the reactor and deny our foes this fortress.'

Tedeski raised his arm as objections were shouted. 'I have made up my mind and will not be argued with. Now go! Time is of the essence!'

'THE HEAVEN'S FALL signal has been sent from Tor Christo, arch magos,' reported Magos Naicin, staring at the encrypted vox-thief before him.

'So soon?' hissed Amaethon, and though his flesh had lost any true emotive qualities, Naicin saw a passable approximation of genuine alarm cross the face of the arch magos.

'It appears that the men of the Guard are weaker than even I feared,' said Naicin sadly.

'We must protect ourselves! The citadel must not fall!'

'It must not,' agreed Naicin. 'What would you have me do, arch magos?'

'Blow the tunnel, Naicin! Do it now!'

CAPTAIN POULSEN HURRIED down the carved steps, clutching bundles of paper folders and an armful of data-slates. The fear was unlike anything he had felt before. He'd never been on the front line before, his talents in organisation and logistics making him much more valuable to the command echelons behind the line.

But standing on the walls of the Kane bastion with shells exploding all around him, he'd felt the bowel-loosening terror of an artillery bombardment and was desperately grateful he had been spared the horror of combat. Hundreds of men thronged the tunnels beneath the keep, descending into the depths of the promontory and heading for the wide cavern-tunnel that led back to the citadel. Similar underground passageways allowed the men from the flanking bastions to escape, though it was too late for the men in Kane bastion.

It was inevitable that some men would have to die so that the others might live.

Weak illumination from the glow-globes strung from the ceiling cast a fitful light over the soldiers around him. Fearful and guilty expressions were writ large across his fellow officers' faces. Dust drifted from the ceiling and sputtering recyc-units struggled to keep the air moving in the hot, stagnant underground.

Eventually, the steps ended and the tunnel widened into a large, roughly circular cavern with passages leading off into the rock beneath Tor Christo. Men from the Dragon and Mars bastions were already streaming from these tunnels, yellow-coated provosts attempting to impose a semblance of order of the retreat with limited success. Major Tedeski's order to withdraw was being obeyed with speed. Four giant, blast-shielded elevator doors studded one wall and, ahead, the cavern narrowed to a well-lit underground highway, nearly twelve metres wide and seven high.

Normally this level of the fort was used to move artillery and ordnance between Tor Christo and the citadel, but it was equally well-suited for large scale movements of troops. Poulsen jostled alongside sweating troopers, the shouts of the provosts and soldiers almost deafening. The heaving mass of men moved towards the main tunnel and Poulsen felt himself being carried along with it. An elbow dug painfully into his side and he yelped, dropping the armful of data-slates to the painted floor.

The bureaucrat in him took over and he fell to his knees to gather up the fallen slates, cursing under his breath as a booted foot crunched the nearest one to splinters. A hand grabbed him and hauled him roughly upright.

'Leave them!' snarled a grim-faced provost. 'Keep moving.'

Poulsen was about to protest at this rough treatment, when the ground shook and cries of alarm echoed around the cavern. A rain of dust dropped from the roof and an eerie quiet descended upon the chamber.

'What was that?' breathed Poulsen. 'Artillery?'

'No,' hissed the provost. 'We wouldn't hear artillery down here. That was something else.'

'Then what?'

'I don't know, but I don't like the sound of it.'

Another louder vibration shook the cavern, then another. Shouts of alarm turned to cries of terror as Poulsen saw a hellish orange glow race towards them down the main tunnel, followed by a furious whooshing roar. Poulsen watched the approaching glow with incomprehension. What was happening?

His unasked question was suddenly answered as someone shouted, 'Emperor's Blood, they're blowing the tunnel!'

Blowing the tunnel? That was inconceivable! While there were men still here? Castellan Vauban would never give such an order. This couldn't be happening. Hundreds of soldiers turned in panic and attempted to race back into the tunnels they had recently fled, pushing their comrades aside in terror. Men fell and were trampled underfoot as the terrified men of the Jourans stampeded back from the collapsing tunnel.

Poulsen stumbled backwards, dropping the slates he had collected from the floor, all thoughts of their worth forgotten. Explosions of demolition charges marched their way along the tunnel, bringing down thousands of tonnes of rock upon the trapped men of the Guard within it.

He staggered back towards the clogged tunnel he had just come from, clawing at the men in front of him, desperate to escape.

The main tunnel suddenly exploded in fire and noise, rubble blasting from its mouth, crushing and burning hundreds of men in an instant. Poulsen wrenched a man from in front of him, and pushed his way forwards as he heard an ominous crack from the ceiling above him. A demolition charge set in the centre of the cavern's roof exploded, showering the soldiers below in chunks of rock and collapsing the entire cavern roof.

Poulsen screamed as falling rocks pummelled him to the ground, smashing his skull and crushing his body to a jellied pulp.

Nearly three thousand men joined him in death as the tunnel between the citadel and Tor Christo was sealed.

MAJOR TEDESKI SWIGGED from a bottle of amasec as he stared at the pict-viewer displaying the exterior of the keep, watching thousands of soldiers in red swamp the walls of his fortress. Mars and Dragon bastions were thronged with enemy soldiers, firing their weapons into the air and cheering at their victory. He'd watched in fury as his captured soldiers were lined up and shot against the bastion walls or herded into the trenches and set alight with flamers. Tedeski had never felt such a strong hatred before. A grim smile touched his lips as he pictured sending these bastards to hell.

He took another drink from the bottle and nodded slowly. The command centre was empty except for himself and Magos Yelede, who sat dejectedly in the corner. The machine priest had protested at being ordered to stay behind, but Tedeski had told him that he would either stay willingly or he would be shot.

Tedeski drained the last of the bottle and turned away from the sickening atrocities being committed within his walls. He gripped Magos Yelede's robes, hauling him to his feet.

'Come on, Yelede. Time to earn your keep.'

Tedeski dragged the reluctant magos from the control centre, through a maze of corridors and security sealed barriers before descending in a key-controlled elevator to the power chamber far below the keep. As the elevator rumbled downwards, a pounding vibration shook the elevator car, the lights flickering and metal squealing as it ground against the walls of the shaft.

'What the hell?' began Tedeski as the elevator began its downward journey again.

No sooner had the elevator doors opened than Tedeski pushed Magos Yelede out into the featureless grey corridor that led towards the reactor chamber. He tried to raise Captain Poulsen and the rest of his company commanders on the vox, but met with no success and his worry grew with each step.

The powerful shockwave had felt like some vast, underground detonation and as far as he knew there was only one way such a detonation could have occurred. But surely Castellan Vauban would never have allowed the Adeptus Mechanicus to destroy the tunnel and cut off thousands of men from their retreat? A terrible sinking feeling settled in his gut and he fervently hoped his suspicions were unfounded.

At last they arrived at the main doors to the reactor chamber and Tedeski stood aside to allow the machine priest to access the entry controls.

'Open the damn door!' snapped Tedeski when Yelede failed to move.

'I cannot, Major Tedeski.'

'What? Why the hell not?'

'I have been given instructions not to allow this facility to be destroyed.'

Tedeski slammed Yelede against the wall and drew his bolt pistol, shouting, 'If you don't open that door, I will shoot you in the head!'

'Anything you can threaten me with is irrelevant, major,' protested Yelede. 'I have been given a sacred order by my superiors and I cannot disobey it. Our word is iron.'

'And my bolt is 0.75 calibre, diamantine tipped with a depleted uranium core and if you don't open this bloody door right now, I will fire it through your poor excuse for a brain. Now open the damn door!'

'I cannot–' began Yelede as a roaring screech of tearing metal ripped along the corridor. The two men watched as an enormous, crackling fist tore open the elevator doors and a gigantic figure stepped through, filling the corridor with its bulk.

Almost three metres tall, the huge figure took a step into the light and Tedeski felt his heart hammer against his chest. The figure wore a bloodstained suit of iron-grey Terminator armour, slashed with diagonal chevrons of black and yellow stripes. The helmet was carved in the shape of a snarling jackal, and his molten chestplate bore the visored skull-mask of the Iron Warriors.

Yelede whimpered in fear and squirmed free of Tedeski's grasp, swiftly pressing his palm to the identification slate.

'Blessed Machine, I abjure thee to grant your unworthy servant entry to your holy sanctum, to your beating heart,' said Yelede, the words coming out in a desperate rush.

'Hurry up, for the Emperor's sake!' hissed Tedeski as the Terminator lumbered towards them. More enemy clambered from the wrecked elevator car, following their leader. Tedeski fired a short burst from his bolt pistol, but the heavy suits of armour were impervious.

The reactor room door slid smoothly open and Tedeski and Yelede gratefully ducked inside as it slammed shut behind them.

Tedeski pushed Yelede towards the centre of the chamber where a tall podium with a dozen thick brass rods set into grooves on the floor pulsed with energy.

Tedeski dragged the protesting magos towards this arrangement and pointed his pistol at his head.

'Give me any more trouble and I will kill you. Do you understand?'

Yelede nodded, what little flesh remained of his face twisted in fear. The magos jumped as thundering impacts slammed into the door and the inner face bulged inwards. Quickly, he ran to the brass columns and pressed his palm into the top of the first, twisting it and chanting a prayer of forgiveness to the Omnissiah. He climbed onto the central dais and rotated several cogged dials.

Tedeski fought for calm as the first brass column rose from the floor, steam hissing from the newly revealed metal. Warning klaxons blared and a stream of words, meaningless to Tedeski, issued from a pair of speakers mounted on the dais.

'Can't you do this any faster?' hissed Tedeski urgently as the door buckled inwards again.

'I am going as fast as I can. Without the proper ministrations to appease the machine spirits that invest the reactor, I will not be able to persuade them to aid us.'

'Then don't waste time talking to me,' snapped Tedeski as another hammer-blow slammed into the door.

FORRIX SMASHED HIS power fist into the door, feeling the layered metal starting to give. He knew he did not have much time. The Warsmith's captured magos had told them of the capacity of Tor Christo's commander to destroy the fortress and Forrix was under no illusions as to what the two men within this chamber were attempting to do.

His warriors gathered behind him, impatient to kill their prey and begin refortifying this place. He slammed his fist against the door again, feeling the metal crumple beneath his assault. He gripped the twisted metal and pulled, tearing the door from its mounting with a roar of triumph. Forrix pushed through the doorway to see a magos in white robes ministering to a machine in the centre of the chamber, and a one-armed Imperial Guard officer standing beside him. The man fired his bolt pistol and Forrix grinned as he felt the ringing impacts against his thick armour. He felt a sensation he had not known in many centuries, but recognised as pain.

He raised his own weapon and squeezed off a short burst, the shells taking the magos between the shoulders, disintegrating his torso and blasting him clear of the dais in a welter of blood and bone.

The Guard officer turned and leapt towards the dais, fumbling with the brass columns, vainly attempting to complete what the magos had begun. Forrix laughed at the man's efforts and shot him in the leg, toppling him to the floor with a scream of pain. He deactivated the energy field surrounding his power fist and lifted the howling officer from the ground, hurling him to a waiting Terminator.

Forrix mounted the dais and saw that they had cut it close, a few more minutes and Tor Christo would have been reduced to a useless molten ruin. He put a bolt through each of the wall-mounted speakers and the screaming klaxons were silenced.

'Replace the rods. It will prevent the reactor blowing,' he said to another of his Terminators and strode from the room.

Tor Christo had fallen.

THE SECOND PARALLEL

One

As Lieutenant Colonel Leonid entered the Sepulchre the flame at the end of the taper wavered in the draft that gusted in from the open door. Kneeling before a basalt statue of the Emperor in the chapel's ossuary, Castellan Vauban cupped the flame behind his hand, shielding it from the wind and lit a candle for the men of Battalion A, as he had done every day for the last six days since Tor Christo had fallen.

Leonid kept a respectful distance from his commanding officer, awaiting the completion of his ministrations to the dead, and Vauban was grateful for his officer's understanding.

The grim tower known as the Sepulchre stood on the north-western slopes of the mountains, high above the citadel. Constructed of smooth, black marble, veined with threads of gold, it was a tall, hollow tube, some thirty metres in diameter and a hundred high. Its inner walls were studded with hundreds of ossuaries containing the bleached bones of every man who had borne the title of castellan. It had been a great comfort to Vauban to imagine that one day he too would have a place of honour amongst the immortal dead, but he knew that was nothing but a dream. In all likelihood, he would end his days as a desiccated corpse somewhere below in the citadel, murdered by this infernal foe. The thought of his bones scoured clean by the dust storms of this planet filled him with great melancholy.

The entire floor was a polished disc of solid brass, its surface etched with intricate traceries and swirling lines that looped gracefully across its surface, weaving and intersecting in a beguiling dance. It looked like a puzzle where the solution, if there even was one, was forever elusive. Vauban knew it was possible to happily lose several hours trying to untangle the design with your eyes, but he had long ago decided that it was a mystery he would never solve.

He rose from his knees, wincing as his joints cracked painfully. War was a young man's game and he was too old to bear the horrors being placed before him. He bowed towards the Emperor's graven image and whispered, 'Lord Emperor, give me the strength to do your bidding. I am but a man, with a man's courage, and need your holy wisdom to guide me in this, our time of need.'

The statue remained silent and the commander of Hydra Cordatus turned on his heel, marching towards the door to the outer chambers of the Sepulchre.

Vauban thought he had known anguish as he had watched the scenes of destruction at Jericho Falls and on the plains when the Iron Warriors had tricked the gunners at Tor Christo into shelling their own men.

But with the fall of Tor Christo and the death of nearly seven thousand men, he knew the true depths of misery. So many dead, and the battle not yet over.

He nodded to Leonid as he passed, his second-in-command closing the door to the candlelit house of the dead. The outer chambers of the Sepulchre were light and airily constructed, as though the architects had understood that the human mind could absorb only so much grief, and that there were times when it was good to rejoice in the immortality of the spirit.

Bright glow-globes, set behind arched windows of stained glass, threw gold and azure light across the marble-flagged floor. Vauban paused to admire the handiwork of artists dead these last ten millennia. Scenes of battle were played out above him alongside images of the Emperor ascending to his throne and feats of bravery of long-dead Space Marine heroes.

'Beautiful, aren't they?' whispered Vauban.

'Yes, sir, they are,' affirmed Leonid.

'Sad then, that they will be destroyed.'

'Sir?'

Vauban returned his gaze to his second-in-command with a sad smile. 'I think our enemies would as soon see this place reduced to dust, don't you, Mikhail?'

'Possibly,' conceded Leonid, bitterly. 'But as long as we are not betrayed by one man's lust for glory, or another's cowardice, we shall make them pay for every metre they advance.'

Vauban could understand Leonid's venom. Princeps Fierach had doomed nearly two thousand men to death when his Titans had abandoned the Jourans to hunt the corrupted Imperator Titan. Those Titans that had survived the battle had wisely retreated to their armoured hangars for repairs, their crews confined to barracks while the Legio's judiciary sought to apportion blame for the debacle. Fierach's death made it that much easier for them, giving them a conveniently dead scapegoat. Princeps Daekian, commander of the Warlord Titan *Honoris Causa* had come before the senior officers of the Jouran Dragoons in full dress uniform, offering his sorrow and a formal apology on behalf of the Legio Ignatum.

For the sake of unity, Vauban had accepted the apology, but the words tasted bitter. Leonid had shown no such restraint, walking up and striking Daekian. Vauban had been ready for the worst kind of reaction, but Princeps Daekian had merely nodded and said, 'That is your right and privilege, Lieutenant Colonel Leonid, and I bear you no ill-will.'

Princeps Daekian had then drawn his curved sabre, stepping forward to offer it, hilt first, to Leonid.

'But know this: the Legio Ignatum stands ready to fight at your side and we will not fail you again. I swear by my blade that it shall be so.'

Vauban had been stunned. For an officer of the Legio to offer his sword to another was a declaration that should he fail in his sworn duty, he was willing to be killed by his own blade, and have the gods of battle mock him for all eternity.

Leonid had stared at the blade for several seconds. In such circumstances it was customary for an officer and a gentleman to refuse to accept the sword, indicating that the gesture was enough. But Leonid had taken the sword and thrust it through his officer's sash before returning to his seat. Vauban had been disappointed, but not surprised. Leonid's battalion had been badly mauled in the battle and he was determined to extract a blood price for his men's deaths.

Leonid wore the sword still, and Vauban knew that when word of this incident had reached the ears of the common soldiers, his popularity had soared within the ranks.

'I am proud of you, Mikhail,' said Vauban suddenly. 'You have a quality that I do not: you have the ability to empathise with the men in your command on every level. From the formality of the officers' mess to the gutter-talk of the barracks.'

'Thank you, sir,' beamed Leonid, pleased with his commander's sentiment.

'I am a competent and experienced leader,' continued Vauban, 'but I have never enjoyed the love of my soldiers. I have always told myself that it is not necessary for my men to love me, only that they obey. Your men love and respect you, and, better, they trust you not to lead them into harm's way without good reason.'

The two officers left the Sepulchre, pulling their uniform jackets tighter about themselves as they stepped into the whipping wind that blew stiffly across the high peaks of the mountains. A thousand steps led downhill between eroded statues of faded Imperial heroes, and an honour guard of fifteen soldiers awaited to escort them back to the citadel.

Both officers stared in trepidation at the blasted plain before the citadel, feeling a gut-twisting sense of despair at the sight that met their eyes. Pillars of smoke curled skyward from countless forges and campfires as the enemy soldiers broke their fast this morning. The plain was a mass of men and machines, supply depots and digging parties.

In the days after the fall of Tor Christo, the main east/west parallel had been extended westwards to the base of the rocky promontory, and two zigzagging saps were being driven towards the citadel. The first was aimed at the salient angle of the Primus Ravelin, while the second was on a course for Vincare bastion's left flank.

'We're not slowing them down enough,' said Vauban needlessly.

'No,' agreed Leonid, 'But we are slowing them.'

'Yes, but we need to stop them,' said Vauban, lifting his eyes to the blackened form of the Imperator Titan standing immobile at the foot of Tor Christo, still swarming with men attempting to buttress it firmly and allow it to fire without collapsing. Behind it, huge gangs, thousands strong, had spent the last six days heaving and sweating to carry massive siege mortars and howitzers up the rocky slopes to the forward edge of Tor Christo's promontory. From there they would be able to lob their shells with impunity within the walls of the Vincare bastion and place breaching batteries to shoot over the glacis, targeting the main curtain wall with direct fire.

They were still some days away from completion, but when they were ready the carnage they would inflict on the garrison was sure to be horrific.

'By the Emperor, Mikhail, it will go badly for us once those guns are brought to bear.'

Leonid followed Vauban's stare and said, 'Have you thought any more about my idea for Guardsman Hawke?'

Guardsman Hawke, still trapped in the mountains, was proving invaluable to the artillerymen of the citadel. His daily reports of where the main work parties were gathering had forced the invaders to dig extra approach trenches to ensure that they were able to reach the front line alive, slowing the advance. Vauban's admiration for this lowly soldier had grown daily, as he had reported the enemy's movements, dispositions and apparent numbers in minute detail, allowing them to get a clearer understanding of the enemy's capabilities and direct their artillery fire accordingly. If they lived through this, Vauban would ensure that Hawke received a commendation.

'I have, but such a plan would involve the Adeptus Mechanicus and I do not trust them any more.'

'Nor I, but we will need their help if it is to work.'

'That is for Arch Magos Amaethon to decide.'

'Sir, you know Amaethon is slipping and cannot be relied upon any more. He is a fool, and worse, he's dangerous. Just look at what he did to the tunnel!'

'Be careful, Mikhail. The Adeptus Mechanicus is an ancient and powerful body, and Amaethon is still senior to you and therefore deserving of your respect. Despite the truth of your words I will not have you utter them again. Understood?'

'Aye, sir. But we are supposed to be above this sort of thing!'

'We are above it, my friend, which is why you will say nothing more about it. If we are to triumph here, we need to keep the Adeptus Mechanicus on our side. It will achieve nothing if we alienate them.'

Leonid said nothing more, and Vauban both understood and agreed with Leonid's reticence concerning the priests of the Adeptus Mechanicus. Blowing the tunnel between the Christo and the citadel was an act of unforgivable callousness, and were Amaethon not already less than a man, he would have made him pay for his crime.

Magos Naicin had explained how he had pleaded with the arch magos not to destroy the tunnel, but the venerable Amaethon had not listened to reason. Vauban had also asked Naicin why, after the Heaven's Fall signal had been received, the Christo had not been destroyed.

'I do not know, Castellan Vauban,' had been Naicin's answer. 'Perhaps Major Tedeski's courage failed him at the last and he could not fulfil his duty.'

Vauban had come close to losing his temper then, remembering the horrific sight of a swaggering giant in Terminator armour hurling Tedeski to his death from the battlements of the Mars bastion at the battle's end.

Fighting to keep the fury from his voice, he said, 'Be that as it may, but in future there will be no action taken by the Adeptus Mechanicus without direct approval from myself or Lieutenant Colonel Leonid. Is that clear?'

'As crystal, Castellan. And let me say, that I agree with you wholeheartedly. I cannot bring myself to condone the death of the men you lost at Tor Christo, but the magos is old and does not have long left in this world. He will soon be with the Omnissiah, and, may the holy spirit of the Machine forgive me for saying so, perhaps it might be better for us all were he to be taken sooner rather than later...'

Vauban had not replied to Naicin's sentiment, but had immediately sensed the younger magos's desire to take over from Amaethon.

And, while he did not approve of such machinations, he gloomily realised that Naicin might well be correct.

GUARDSMAN HAWKE RAN a hand through his tousled hair and settled into a more comfortable position on the rocks, using his jacket as a rest for his elbows and training the magnoculars on the enemy camp below.

'Right, let's see what's going on now,' he muttered.

The dusky plain below was a patchwork of activity, with whole swathes of ground given over to weapon and tool manufacture, with thousands upon thousands of men milling about in regular patterns. It had taken him a few days to find this perch from which to observe the camp. It was far from comfortable, but it was probably as good as it got in these mountains. It was sheltered from the worst of the winds and there was a rocky overhang that allowed him to snatch some sleep when the noise from below wasn't too bad. He yawned, the mere thought of sleep making his body crave it all the more. Night was drawing in anyway and he wouldn't be able to see much more at the rate the daylight was fading.

He'd eaten and drunk only sparingly and his food and water supplies were still holding out, but he had long since run out of detox pills. However, worries that he would fall prey to the toxic atmosphere of Hydra Cordatus appeared to be unfounded. His health, aside from a few bruises and scrapes, was better than it had been since he'd ended up on this useless planet.

After the initial pain and stiffness had left his underused muscles, he had felt clearer and fitter than ever. The constant headaches had vanished like morning mist and the ashen taste that always caught in the back of his mouth had also disappeared. His skin was taking on a healthy glow; his natural paleness replaced by the beginnings of a tan.

Whatever the cause of his sudden good health, Hawke was grateful for it. Perhaps it was the feeling that he was now proving his worth to the regiment; that he was a good soldier and could hack it with the best of them. As he panned the magnoculars across the enemy camp, counting the number of work parties that made their way to the approach trenches, Hawke was forced to admit that, all things being equal, he was having the time of his life.

Two

THE BONE-BLADED knife scraped a clean furrow through the ingrained blood on the heavy vambrace, the dried crust gathering on the curved rear of the blade. Larana Utorian dipped the blade in the bucket of warm water beside her and returned to her task. Once again, Kroeger had returned to the dug-out with dried blood caked across his armour and without a word to her, had indicated that she should remove his armour and clean it for him.

Each piece was heavy, almost too heavy, and were it not for the wheezing mechanical arm Kroeger's butcher-surgeons had grafted to her shoulder she would have been unable to lift his armour clear. The black-steel metalwork of the mechanical arm was nauseating to look at and the feel of its corrupt bio-mechanical components worming their way through her body made her want to rip it from her shoulder. But the writhing black tendrils of synth-nerve had forged an unbreakable bond with her own flesh and she could no more remove it than she could stop her heart from beating.

A heavy steel frame carried the individual components of Kroeger's armour, each moulded breastplate, cuissart, greave, vambrace and gorget precisely arranged so that it resembled some gigantic, disassembled mechanical man. Virtually every surface was stained with gore and the stench of decaying matter made her want to gag every time she looked at the armour.

She bent to her task once more, scraping yet another clean furrow in Kroeger's armour. Tears ran down her cheeks as she cleaned the armour of a monster, knowing that tomorrow she would be performing the same task again.

Why Kroeger had not killed her was a mystery and every day she found herself almost wishing that he had.

And every day she found herself hating herself for wanting to live.

To toil in the service of such a beast was to play handmaiden to a daemon itself.

And this was a capricious daemon; there was no way she could predict its moods and behavioural mores, no way to know Kroeger's reaction to anything she did. She railed against him, beating her fists against his bloody armour and he laughed, throwing her aside. She acquiesced to his desires and found him surly and brooding, picking at old scars and licking his own blood from his hands – he refused to allow his wounds to clot – as he glared at her with contempt.

She hated him with a fiery passion, but so wanted to live. There was no way to know how to behave to stop Kroeger killing her. She scraped the last of the blood from the vambrace and put aside the bone knife, taking up an oily rag and polishing the silver of its surface until it shone. Satisfied that the heavy piece of armour was as clean as she could manage, she rose to her feet and hung it upon the armour frame.

As she hung the vambrace in place, she found her eyes drawn again to the sight and stench of the interior faces of Kroeger's armour. She polished and cleaned the exterior of his armour, but she would not touch its interior surfaces. Coated in a loathsome, creeping horror, these internal surfaces looked like flensed hunks of rotten meat, their putrid surfaces undulating as though imbued with some foul internal life. Yet for all its vile appearance, the armour exuded a hateful attraction, as though it called to her on some unknowable level.

She shivered as she removed the next piece of armour from the frame, the rounded elbow guard. This piece was not so heavily stained and would not take long to clean.

The blood I have worn will take more than your little knife to clean…

She picked up her knife again she glanced furtively to where Kroeger's weapons lay upright on an ebony and silver rack. A massive, toothed sword, its hilt carved in the shape of an eight-pointed star and quillons tipped with stabbing spikes. Beside that, an ornate pistol with a skull-mouthed barrel and bronze plated flanks. The magazine alone was bigger than her forearm.

Go on, touch them… feel their power…

She shook her head; Kroeger never allowed her to clean his weapons, and the one time she had offered had been her last. He had backhanded her lightly across the face, cracking her cheekbone and loosening teeth, saying, 'You will never touch these weapons, human.'

Bitterness rose with her tears and she cursed herself for wanting to live, for serving this creature of evil, but she could see no other way. She was powerless to do anything except play house-pet to a madman who bathed in gore and revelled in slaughter.

Is that so bad? To take pleasure from the death of another… is that not the highest honour you can pay another creature?

Her hate for Kroeger was a bright flame burning in her heart and she felt that if she did not let it out it would eventually consume her.

Yes, hate, little one, hate…

Her eyes were once again drawn to the armour and she swore she could almost hear distant laughter.

FIRST LIGHT WAS breaking across the mountains as Honsou watched the slave gangs haul the last components of an artillery piece's gun carriage over the lip of the promontory. He noted with satisfaction that there were a few slaves with the blue jackets of the enemy within their numbers. It seemed as though there were a few yet able to serve the Iron Warriors.

Forrix stood beside him, a head higher in his Terminator armour, surveying the slow progress below on the plain. Between the booming explosions of artillery fire from the two bastions and the central ravelin, the saps were advancing from the extended parallel, but they were doing so cautiously, moving forward under the protection of heavily armoured sap-rollers, low, wide-bodied behemoths crawling slowly forwards to shield the workers who dug the saps.

'The Warsmith is displeased,' said Forrix, sweeping his arms out to encompass the works below.

Honsou turned to face the pale veteran, his brow wrinkled in puzzlement. 'But we have proceeded with great speed, Forrix. In less than two weeks we have captured this outwork and our saps are almost close enough to the citadel that we can link them into a second parallel. Scarcely have I seen a siege progress with such haste.'

Forrix shook his head. 'There are matters afoot that require we make even better speed, Honsou. The Warsmith wishes us to be done with this place within ten days.'

'Impossible!' sputtered Honsou. 'With the second parallel not yet complete? The batteries here will take another four days at least to prepare, and it will probably take several days for them to effect a breach in the walls. And I do not believe we will be able to make a practicable breach without the establishment of a third parallel and bringing up our siege tanks. All this will take time, you know that better than anyone.'

'Nevertheless, it must be done.'

'How?'

'By any means necessary, Honsou. Time is a luxury we do not have.'

'Then what do you suggest?'

'That we push the saps forwards with greater speed, build more sap rollers, throw slaves and men at the digging, so that the mounds of corpses will shield the diggers from the Imperial artillery,' snapped Forrix suddenly.

'That will be difficult, Forrix,' said Honsou slowly. 'The Imperial gunners are proving to be uncannily accurate with their fire.'

'Indeed they are,' mused Forrix, staring at the mountains surrounding the plains. 'Almost too accurate, wouldn't you say?'

'What do you mean?'

'You are sure you killed everyone in the places you attacked before the invasion?'

'Aye,' snarled Honsou, 'We left nothing alive.'

Forrix returned his gaze to the mountains and sighed. 'I think you are mistaken, Honsou. I believe there is still someone out there.'

Honsou said nothing and Forrix continued. 'Send Goran Delau back to the places you attacked and if there are any signs of survivors, have them hunted down and killed. We cannot afford to be slowed further by your incompetence.'

Honsou bit back an angry retort and simply nodded stiffly before marching away.

THE HEART WAS a notoriously hard organ to burn, but the blue flames curling from its roasting muscle tissue were well worth the effort thought Jharek Kelmaur, sorcerer to the Warsmith and Wielder of the Seven Cryptical Magicks. The darkness of his tent was wreathed in ghostly shadows cast by the burning heart and moonlight pooling at its entrance. He rubbed his hands across his tattooed skull, spreading his arms before the blazing organ.

Though his eyes were sewn shut, he stared into the flames, seeing spectral images, beyond the ken of mortal sight. They flickered in and out of focus as his magicks sought to shape the power bestowed by this latest offering into a useable form. He opened his mind to the glory of the warp, feeling the rush of power and fulfilment that came each time he communed with the immaterium. As always he felt the scratching, insistent presence of innumerable astral beasts that clawed at any intrusion into their realm, their mindless thrashings drawn by his presence.

Such formless phantoms were of no consequence to him, it was the other, mightier creatures that lurked in the haunted depths of the warp that were of more concern.

He felt the warp-spawned energies flow through him, channelled and intensified by the carven sigils on his gold and silver armour. Symbols of ancient geomantic significance helped contain the powerful energies he drew within his flesh, and though his physique was enhanced, he knew that the power he was tapping could destroy him in an instant were he to lose control of it.

The power raced along his fragile nerve endings, dispersing throughout his body and a luminescent green fire built behind his eyes, spilling out from beneath the stitching, and gathering like emerald tears on his cheeks before billowing out in a noxious cloud of glittering fog. The fog twisted and spiralled, though no wind disturbed it, coiling from his mouth and eyes before slipping around his shoulders like a snake.

Questing tendrils of green light slithered from the sorcerer and waved through the air to reach into the flames of the burning heart, the flames hissing and sputtering with greater ferocity as they consumed it.

Fleeting images flashed before Kelmaur's eyes: the rock of Tor Christo, a hidden chamber in its depths, a disc of bronze that shone like the sun and, enfolding it all, a slowly spinning cog wheel, its surface cracked and blemished. As Kelmaur watched, the cog suddenly erupted with brown, necrotic threads of rust, each one spreading rapidly through its structure until it crumbled to dust.

As quickly as the vision had appeared, it vanished, to be replaced with one of a spear of white light arcing through the darkness, its brilliance fading as it travelled before it was in turn replaced by a warrior in yellow power armour, his weapons trained directly at Kelmaur. As he watched, the warrior turned his weapon towards the sorcerer and pulled the trigger, the barrel exploding in brilliant light.

Jharek Kelmaur screamed and collapsed to the floor of his tent, blood leaking from every orifice in his head, and pounding pain thundering against the innards of his skull.

He groggily pushed himself to his feet, steadying himself against the iron tent pole.

He moved unsteadily to a long, cot bed and sat on its edge, rubbing the heels of his palms against his inked temples and taking deep breaths. It was the same as before, but with each passing vision, the intensity grew stronger and he knew a crucial time of confluence was approaching.

He had to divine the meaning of the visions, though he feared he knew the answer to the second apparition. As the Iron Warriors had attacked the spaceport, he had sensed a psychic signal reach out from the planet, too quick for him to block, yet surely too weak to be received by its intended recipients. But Kelmaur was afraid that others may have heard it, and if they grasped its significance, might already be on their way to this planet now. He had not told the Warsmith, and trusted that his master's war-captains would be able to complete the destruction of the citadel before whatever aid was coming to Hydra Cordatus arrived. He had despatched the battle barge *Stonebreaker* to the system's distant jump point to lie in wait for any would-be-rescuers, but, consumed by the nagging suspicion he was already too late, he had since recalled it.

His cabal of acolytes had spoken of mind whispers on the planet that were not theirs, and how this could be was a mystery to Kelmaur. It would take great cunning to have evaded detection by the *Stonebreaker*, but then it wasn't here, was it…? The vast cargo ships that orbited this planet were not equipped with mystical surveyors that would allow them to detect any approaching enemies. Had something slipped past while the *Stonebreaker* had been away?

And if so, where had it gone and what had it done in the intervening time?

Paranoia, his constant companion, held him tight in its grip and his mind was alive with all manner of fearsome possibilities. Should he tell the Warsmith of his suspicions? Should he deal with it on his own? Should he feign ignorance?

None of the options were particularly appealing and Kelmaur was filled with a dreadful foreboding. As to the first vision... well, that he was more sure of. He turned as a low moan sounded behind him.

He smiled grimly, staring into the face of Adept Cycerin.

The former priest of the Adeptus Mechanicus that Kroeger had almost killed in the attack on the spaceport was chained, naked, to an angled trestle, part surgical table and part engineers' workbench. His missing hand had been replaced with an augmented bionic gauntlet, its pulsating black surface daubed with ancient symbols of power. Encircling the wrist was a broad, spiked bracelet with curved talons embedded deep in the flesh above the gauntlet. A modified form of the Obliterators' techno-virus seeped from the talons, slowly working its way around Cycerin's body. Eruptions of mecha-organic components appeared all over his flesh, their form fluid, yet angular. His flesh seethed with the workings of the virus as they integrated themselves with his organic matter.

Jharek Kelmaur smiled humourlessly and rose to go to the twitching priest of the Machine God.

The changes wracking his body must have been painful, but the adept's face gave no sign of it. Instead his features were twisted in rapture and obscene pleasure.

'Yes,' whispered Kelmaur. 'Feel the power of the new machine fill your flesh. You have great work ahead of you.'

Cycerin opened his eye, the pupil a dilated black, its internal surfaces alive with crawling, newly-birthed circuitry. He smiled and nodded towards the pulsing gauntlet.

'More,' he hissed. 'Give me more...'

Three

ON THE TWENTIETH day of the siege the two saps driven forward from the first parallel were linked by a second parallel, some six hundred metres from the edge of the ditch protecting the walls of the frontal bastions. This was well within the range of the unerringly accurate Imperial gunners and thousands of lives had been expended to complete the second parallel, but the Iron Warriors were heedless of the human cost of such endeavours. All that mattered was that the Warsmith's orders were obeyed.

The second parallel stretched from the ground in front of the Vincare bastion's salient to that before the tip of Mori bastion. The second parallel's northern face was piled high with rammed earth and revetted with iron hoardings to ensure that it could withstand artillery impacts. A well laid out battery was constructed at either end, their firing embrasures placed perpendicular to each bastion's flank.

Already, markers had been laid for yet another approach sap, this time aimed at the head of the Primus Ravelin, but until the batteries had had a chance to open fire and dismount most of the citadel's wall guns, work could not yet begin. This was siegework at its most brutal and obvious. There would be no methodical approach to flank each of the bastions in turn, but a full frontal advance on the works, with batteries to pound the walls to oblivion before a devastating assault was unleashed.

With the establishment of the batteries, the trenches behind were widened and deepened to allow the daemonic war machines to move safely to the front line. Lessons had been learnt following the destruction unleashed by the rampaging war machine in the trenches approaching Tor Christo, and those charged with keeping the monstrous daemon engines in check were taking no chances.

The following morning, the guns placed in the batteries of the second parallel opened fire in conjunction with those situated on the northern slopes of Tor Christo's promontory. The guns in the batteries were not yet close enough to fire over the lip of the glacis – the raised area of ground before the ditch that prevented enemy artillery from striking the vulnerable base of the walls – but they could hammer the ramparts and make the firing step untenable for the defenders. And this they did with remarkable efficiency, smashing the wall head with solid projectiles and reducing the thick ramparts to jagged piles of rubble. Counterbattery fire from the citadel was desultory and shots that did strike home were either deflected by the reinforced earthworks or, in the case of the guns on Tor Christo, found to be out of range.

Hundreds of men died in the first minutes of the bombardment, before the order was given to fall back within the bastions' enclosures. For the men of Mori bastion this was a life saving order, but for many of those in Vincare it proved to be a death sentence.

Howitzers from the promontory now fired explosive shells on high trajectories, landing their bombs within the walls of Vincare bastion and shredding the men gathered within its walls. Scores of men died with each shrieking explosion, the airbursting shells taking a fearsome toll, razor fragments ripping flesh and bone apart with ease. Officers rallied their men, shouting at them to take cover within the wall bunkers.

As their targets took shelter, the guns on the promontory shifted their fire to the interior of the citadel, their increased elevation giving them the range to drop shells inside the perimeter of the inner curtain wall. Three large barrack buildings were gutted by fire and a handful of others reduced to rubble before Arch Magos Amaethon was able to raise the energy shield that protected the inner citadel.

The shelling continued throughout the day, ripping apart the tops of the two bastions and the ravelin, dismounting a huge number of guns and rendering much of their frontal sections wide open.

As night fell and the guns continued to pound the citadel, hundreds of slaves trudged through the approach trenches from their corpse-infested dug-outs and began digging the approach sap forward.

Four

VAUBAN CIRCLED THE briefing table and poured each of his weary officers a glass of amasec, searching their faces for signs of resignation. Pleased to find none, he returned to his seat at the head of the table, poured another glass and set it before Gunnar Tedeski's empty seat.

All the officers appeared to have aged, their features lined with fatigue and numb with the unceasing, grinding nature of the siege.

Morgan Kristan looked the worst, his arm in a bloody sling and a wide bandage wrapped around his midriff where fragments from an exploding shell had torn into him. His men in the Vincare bastion had taken a battering and he had been there with them during it.

All his officers had been blooded now and he was fiercely proud of them.

'Gentlemen,' began Vauban, raising his glass. 'To you all.'

His officers raised their glasses and drained their amasec as one. Vauban set down his glass and poured himself another. None of the men gathered around the table said anything as the castellan of Hydra Cordatus sipped his drink.

Leonid consulted a featureless gold box before nodding slowly to Vauban.

Eventually Vauban broke the silence, saying, 'We are in a perilous position, gentlemen. The enemy is at the gates and if the estimates of our engineers are correct, we have days at best before they breach our walls and enter the citadel.'

'I pledge that my men will fight to the last,' vowed Morgan Kristan, slamming the table with his one good hand.

'As will those of Battalion C,' echoed Piet Anders.

Vauban suppressed a sly smile and said, 'Hopefully that will not be necessary. There have been some… unexpected developments in the last few hours and Lieutenant Colonel Leonid has a plan that may buy us some more time. The enemy artillery, especially that on the promontory, is killing us. To have any chance of survival we must knock it out, and that will not be easy. Mikhail?'

Leonid stood and checked the gold box again to make sure that the vox-scrambler was functioning properly before handing out data-slates to the senior officers of the Jourans. Leonid and Vauban watched as each man scanned the contents of the slate, their expressions changing from weariness to sudden hope.

'Is it really true?' asked Major Anders.

'It is, Piet,' confirmed Leonid. 'I have seen them.'

'An entire company?' breathed Kristan. 'How?'

Vauban raised his hand, halting further questions and said, 'The files you are holding in your hands are to be considered the most sacred thing in your possession, gentlemen. Follow the orders within them. Do so with care and resolution, and tell no one outside this room what we are about. Be ready to move on this plan the instant I give the order, for if you are not, then we truly are lost.'

Morgan Kristan scanned further down the slate and grunted as he saw a familiar name.

'Is there a problem, Major Kristan?' asked Leonid.

'There may be,' nodded Kristan. 'Any plan that involves – relies even – on Hawke, scares me to the soles of my boots.'

'Do not concern yourself with Hawke's involvement in this,' soothed Vauban. 'I have faith in him, and Lieutenant Colonel Leonid will handle that part of the plan.'

Piet Anders lifted his eyes from his slate and asked, 'And who will lead us?'

'I will,' replied Vauban.

THE RUINS OF listening post Sigma IV had long ceased smouldering as Goran Delau squatted by its entrance, his servo-arm sifting through the wreckage.

He and ten soldiers clad in red overalls had searched the mountains these last few days without finding another living soul and Delau was beginning to believe that Honsou had sent them on a fool's errand. A body without a face lay beside the buckled doorway, its bones gleaming through the torn fabric of its uniform and Delau kicked it aside as he ducked inside the listening post, remembering the battle they had fought to take this place, the roar of assault cannon fire and the storm of shells as it tore through them.

Inside, all was darkness, but Delau's enhanced vision easily pierced the gloom. Shattered equipment and blackened metal lay strewn about, the walls peppered with grenade fragments. A body lay against one wall, the little flesh that remained on its skeleton was scorched and black. This body's face was blown away, and Delau remembered the two shots Honsou had fired to kill these men.

Where then was the body of the third?

As he scanned the deserted listening post, he saw the open footlocker and the discarded items that lay strewn about it. He fell to his knees, examining them all in turn. All were useless trinkets and, to a man trapped on the mountain, worthless.

So, one soldier had somehow survived and salvaged everything of value from the bunker.

Where had he gone?

Delau marched from the listening post and examined the dusty ground outside. The corpse on the ground had no rifle and Delau guessed that the survivor had taken it before moving on.

Delau sniffed the air and knelt beside the decaying corpse, noting a patch of discoloured rock beside its feet. Without needing to taste it, he knew it was blood and, from its patterning, that it had not come from the corpse's wound.

So Forrix was correct. There was someone still alive on the mountains. A resourceful man as well, if Delau's reasoning was correct.

Scanning the surrounding environment, he knew there was only one way a man determined to strike back at the Iron Warriors would have gone: north-west across the knifeback ridge to a position of observation.

Swiftly he gathered the indentured soldiery to him and set off up the mountainside.

Goran Delau grinned within his helmet at the thought of facing this worthy foe.

HAWKE SCRAMBLED ACROSS a jagged outcrop of rock, breathing heavily as he traversed the steep slopes of the mountain. He had travelled three kilometres across exceptionally difficult terrain and had another two kilometres to go before nightfall, but he was determined to make it.

Despite the weary exhaustion filling his limbs, he was filled with real purpose. He pulled himself onto a relatively flat slab of rock and took a moment to get his breath back. He checked his location on the direction finder, knowing where he had been ordered to go, but not knowing exactly what he would find when he got there. Lieutenant Colonel Leonid himself had given him his mission on the vox earlier that day and Hawke had assured him that he would not let them down.

'You cannot,' Leonid had said, 'all our hopes rest upon you.'

Hawke had felt that was kind of melodramatic, but hadn't said so. He was too pleased by the fact that he was being trusted with something so important.

'Well, Hawke,' he chuckled to himself, 'It's a commission for you when you get back home.'

He mopped his brow with his sleeve and unwrapped one of his last ration packs, chewing on the remains of a high-energy bar. Hawke groaned as he pushed himself to his feet. He was amazed at how good he felt, despite not having taken any detox pills for over two weeks. He had become lean and his muscles, especially in his legs, had become well-defined. He smiled as he realised he was in better shape than he had been for years. His spreading midriff was gone and his lungs felt clearer than ever.

True, his food and water supplies were all but exhausted, but Lieutenant Colonel Leonid had assured him that they were working on that even now. He wolfed down the last of the food bar and tossed the wrapping aside as he squinted into the afternoon sun.

'Well, you ain't gonna get there just by standing here, Hawke,' he said, climbing further along the rockface.

Hawke set off again through the afternoon's heat.

VAUBAN AND LEONID stood watching the rainbow flares of energy rippling above their heads, as enemy shell impacts slammed into the invisible energy field that protected the areas within the curtain wall.

Observers in the blockhouse on the northern slopes scanned the shield for breaches, as some shells were slipping through where coverage was incomplete, and detonating within the citadel's supposed safe areas. The warning they could give was probably too short to do any real good, but it was better than nothing and, once again, Vauban felt his anger mount towards Arch Magos Amaethon.

When the shells had first breached the shield he had spent an infuriating hour waiting to be hooked up with the Machine Temple on the holo-link. He knew he would be wasting his time attempting to see the arch magos in person.

'Why is the shield not holding?' he had demanded.

'It is... arduous work to maintain such a... a prodigious energy barrier,' explained the arch magos in stuttering, halting speech. 'To maintain all other systems at peak efficiency as well as the shield... requires great strength.'

'Then let the other systems go to hell,' raged Vauban. 'If you allow the shield to falter, then very soon there will be no other systems to maintain!'

'That cannot be,' snapped Amaethon as he shut off the link, and no matter how desperately Vauban petitioned the arch magos, he would not re-establish it.

Perhaps Naicin was right; perhaps it would be better for them all if Amaethon were to be got rid of. Indeed, Naicin had contacted him personally not long after his brief conversation with Amaethon and had insinuated that such an event might not be too hard to contrive.

Vauban pushed his thoughts of the damned arch magos and his scheming underlings from his mind, forcing himself to concentrate on the job in hand.

'Have you heard from Kristan and Anders yet?' he asked Leonid.

Leonid nodded. 'So far everything is proceeding as planned. Weapons, ammunition and demolition charges have been distributed to the soldiers taking part in the mission and the storming parties are gathering at the rally points.'

Vauban looked up into the crimson sky just as the day slipped from afternoon's warmth into evening's twilight. 'I wish it was already dark. I can't abide this waiting.'

'They say the waiting is the hardest part, sir.'

'And are they right, Mikhail?'

'No,' chuckled Leonid. 'Not by a long shot. Give me the waiting any day.'

Vauban checked his pocket chronometer and frowned. 'Any word from Hawke?'

'Not yet, sir, no, but we should give him time to get there.'

'He'd better get there soon or that magos you sequestered will be missed by his brethren and spill his guts. I'm keen to avoid that, at least until it is too late for them to interfere, Mikhail.'

'We should give Hawke a little more time, it's a tough journey,' pointed out Leonid.

'Do you think he can do it even if he does get there?'

'Yes, I think he can. His profile has him as above average intelligence, and he's come a long way from the disgrace of a man we once knew as Guardsman Hawke. He's a soldier now.'

'Any idea why he's not coughed up his lungs yet? He claims to have run out of detox pills over a week ago.'

'Not yet, sir. I asked the Magos Biologis how long we could expect Hawke to keep going, but he was pretty vague, and claimed it wasn't possible to predict exactly.'

Vauban shook his head. 'Emperor preserve us from the meddling of the Adeptus Mechanicus.'

'Amen to that, sir,' agreed Leonid. 'What of our new arrivals? Are they in agreement with our plan?'

Vauban smiled, though there was no warmth in his expression. 'Oh yes, they are wholeheartedly with us.'

Leonid nodded, but said nothing, noting the way the castellan gripped the hilt of his power sword. Both officers were arrayed for battle and had taken pains to appear so for their men. Vauban had put on his dress uniform jacket and wore his silver breastplate over it, the bronze eagle at its centre polished to a brilliant sheen. Leonid's breastplate was bronze, but also gleaming. The dent in its centre where he had been shot had been repaired and the armour was as good as new.

'How long now?' asked Vauban.

Leonid looked at the darkening sky and said, 'Not long.'

GORAN DELAU TURNED the drained vox-battery and ration pack in his hands as though trying to gain some deeper understanding of his prey by touch alone. His early admiration for this man had diminished as they had closed in and discovered the detritus of his passing. The man had not even bothered to cover his tracks, leaving his waste in the open where any half-competent tracker would easily discover it.

He guessed that his prey could not be more than an hour or so ahead of him and Delau was irritated by his foe's lack of savvy. The challenge of the hunt had now been reduced to reeling in the man and then killing him.

The men who followed him now only numbered six. One had fallen to his death down a wide ravine they had been forced to leap; the other three Delau had killed himself because of their lack of skill and stamina. They were irrelevant and he knew he could kill this man on his own anyway.

Wherever this man was going, he seemed to be making his way there with real purpose, since his course had kept true this last few hours. Whatever lay at the end of this chase, Delau was certain of one thing.

It would end in the prey's death.

HAWKE CHECKED THE direction finder to check he was in the right place, unable to see anything much in the encroaching darkness. He stood on a flat plateau, in part of the highest reaches of the mountains, the constant thunder of the invaders' artillery nothing more than a distant rumble from here. His breath caught in his throat and he wiped sweat from his brow. He was exhausted, but pleased to have arrived here – wherever here was – before darkness had fallen.

There wasn't much to see, just a spill of rocks lying against a flat, vertical slice of the mountainside, though the ground looked pretty churned up, as though someone had set off a bunch of explosives. He shucked off his pack and pulled out the portable vox, cursing as he saw he was down to his last battery.

He slotted the battery home and pressed the activation rune, breathing a sigh of relief as the front panel lit up with a reassuring glow. He lifted the handset, spun the dial to the correct frequency and thumbed the talk button.

'Bastion, this is Hawke, do you copy?'

The vox crackled for a second before a voice came on the line. 'Receiving you loud and clear, Hawke. This is Magos Beauvais, are you at the specified co-ordinates?'

'Yeah, but aside from the view I don't see anything that makes the climb worthwhile.'

'Describe what you can see,' ordered Beauvais.

'Not a hell of a lot. It's pretty damn flat here, aside from a pile of rocks, but not much else.'

'Go over to the pile of rocks and tell me what's there.'

'Ok,' said Hawke, lugging his pack and the vox over to the rocks and peering through the gloom. He stepped forwards and brushed away a thick coating of dust.

'There's a door behind here! The rock fall's covered most of it, but there's definitely a door.'

'Is there a panel with a keypad visible to the side of the door?'

'Yeah, it's a bit dusty, but looks alright.'

'Good, here's what you have to do,' explained Beauvais. 'Using the keypad, enter the following code: tertius-three-alpha-epsilon-nine.'

Wedging the handset between his shoulder and ear, Hawke punched in the code and stepped back as the door juddered open on buckled rollers. A faint wind brushed past him, like the exhalation of a dead thing and he shivered.

'Ok, door's open. I guess I'm going in,' said Hawke.

'Yes, go inside,' confirmed Beauvais. 'And follow my directions. Do not deviate from them at all.'

'What the hell do you think I'm going to do, go on a tour?'

He ducked his head below the rocks and entered a gloomy corridor. He stepped forward, stumbling as his foot met resistance then tripped as he trod on something soft. He swore as he hit the ground and rolled onto the floor of the corridor, finding himself face to face with a corpse, its mouth twisted in a rictus mask of death. He yelped and pushed himself back towards the dim light at the door where he saw another three bodies slumped on the ground.

Their fists were covered with dried blood. Looking at the door, Hawke saw bloody handprints smeared over its inside surface.

'Imperator! There's dead bodies here!' shouted Hawke.

'Yes, the orbital bombardment was slightly off-course, and hit the mountains instead of the facility. We believe the explosions threw enough debris up to cover the oxy-recyc units and the men within choked to death.'

'Choked to death? Then why are their hands covered in blood?'

'It is logical that the men stationed here would have tried to exit the facility when they realised their air supply was cut off,' said Beauvais, his voice devoid of any compassion for the dead.

'But why couldn't they get out?' wheezed Hawke as his breathing returned to normal.

'Facility staff do not have access to the codes that allow the exterior doors to open. It would constitute a security risk were one to be compromised.'

'And for that, they died. You cold bastards!'

'A necessary precaution and one all staff are aware of when stationed in these facilities. Now, if we may continue? The facility commander should have a bronze key around his neck? Take it.'

Forcing down his repugnance, Hawke checked the bodies, finding the key on the third body. He vowed that if he got out of this alive, he was going to find Beauvais and punch his face in. He stepped over the bodies and made his way down the corridor, tucking the key into his pocket. The air felt stagnant and he soon found himself wheezing.

'I can hardly breathe in here,' he complained.

'Do you have a respirator to use until the outside air filters in?'

'Yeah, I got one,' snapped Hawke. He fumbled in the pack for the clumsy breathing apparatus and dragged it over his head, flicking on the illuminator above the faceplate.

A featureless corridor stretched off into the darkness, and he started his descent. Following Beauvais's instructions, he passed several iron doors sealed with keypads which were unmarked save for the cog symbol of the Adeptus Mechanicus. His breathing sounded loud in his ears and the click of his worn-down boot heels and the tinny voice of Beauvais echoed from the walls, the torch-lit darkness seeming to magnify the sounds. Despite himself, Hawke felt his trepidation growing the further he descended into the mountain.

At last, Beauvais's directions led him to an unremarkable door, stencilled with wording he couldn't read, but a symbol that was clearly a warning. He raised the handset to his mouth.

'Right, I'm here, now what?'

'Use the key you took from the facility commander to unlock the door.'

Hawke dug the key from his pocket and did as instructed, standing back as the door clicked open and a gust of oil and incense-scented air rushed to meet him. Inside was darkness and he stepped through the door, panning the light from his respirator around him.

The room appeared to be circular, its blank walls running around a gigantic white pillar at its centre that took up most of the space. A metal-runged ladder set into the rockcrete wall ascended into the darkness beside him, and he stared in puzzlement at the massive object before him.

Hawke put his hand out and touched it. It was warm to the touch and felt as though there was a quiver of movement within, but perhaps that was just his imagination. The base of the column sat in a sunken pit and as he leaned over to get a better look, he saw what appeared to be vast nozzles, like the ones he'd seen on the end of one of the heavy weapon team's missiles, but bigger.

Bigger...

Realisation sank in as Hawke craned his neck in an attempt to see how high this chamber was.

'Is this what I think it is?' he asked Beauvais.

'That depends on what you think it is, but I can tell you that it is a Glaive class, ground-launched orbital torpedo.'

'And what in the name of the High Lord's balls do you expect me to do with it?' spluttered Hawke.

'We want you to fire it, Guardsman Hawke,' explained Magos Beauvais.

Five

FOLLOWED BY NEARLY two thousand men, Castellan Prestre Vauban clambered over the lip of the citadel's ditch and sprinted towards the Iron Warriors' raised earthworks. There was no battle cry, no shout of rage, only the silence of soldiers who knew their only chance of survival was stealth.

The men's faces were smeared with soot and their sky blue uniform had been left in the barracks in favour of plain black flak jackets.

Leonid's storming parties spread out from the ditch, clustered around the demolition teams and Vauban knew that this attack was a desperate gamble indeed. But as his second-in-command had pointed out, they had no choice but to attempt to destroy the enemy guns. To not try would be to allow the Iron Warriors to pound them into dust.

A thrill of fear and exultation coursed through his veins at the prospect of battle; it had been too long since he had led men into combat.

He clutched his bolt pistol close to his chest, running crouched over, the breath heaving in his lungs. The traitor line was still a few hundred metres away. His breathing sounded hellishly loud and the thump of boots on the dusty earth was like the thunder of a Titan's tread, but so far the alarm had not been raised. Perhaps there was a chance this reckless attack might just succeed.

Even in the dim light, Vauban could see a head raised above the level of the ramparts of the enemy earthworks and counted down the seconds until the attack hit home.

All they needed was a little more time.

URAJA KLANE PULLED himself up to the ramparts of the earthworks and peered into the darkness, resting his rifle on the rough, earthen parapet. There was something happening in front of the works, but he couldn't quite see what. Lord Kroeger had charged them with the protection of these guns and he knew better than to disappoint his master. But the flickering lights and noise from the sprawling campsite made it difficult to make out anything.

Behind him, several hundred soldiers slept on the firing step or drank distilled spirits from tin mugs in their muddy dug-outs.

He glanced down and kicked Yosha awake. He had a pair of battered field glasses that could see in the dark, didn't he?

'Hey, Yosha, wake up, you useless piece of...' hissed Klane.

Yosha mumbled something foul and unintelligible, then rolled over. Klane kicked him again.

'Yosha, wake up, damn you. Gimme your goggles!'

'What?' slurred Yosha. 'My goggles?'

'Yeah, I think there's something out there.'

Yosha grumbled, but dragged himself to his feet, rubbing his eyes with filthy hands and yawning hugely. He peered out into the darkness.

'There's nothing out there,' he declared sleepily.

'Use your damn goggles, you idiot.'

Casting a scathing look at his comrade, Yosha pulled out a set of blackened and ancient field goggles. A bizarre protuberance slotted over the eyepiece and Yosha pulled it over his shaven head. He rested his chin on his hands and trained his gaze over the parapet.

'Well,' pressed Klane. 'You see anything?'

'Yeah,' whispered Yosha. 'There's something coming. Looks like—'

'Like what?'

'Like—'

Klane never got the chance to find out. A sharp, buzzing crack whipped by him and blasted the back of Yosha's head open in an explosion of blood and brains. Yosha crumpled slowly and toppled from the rampart.

'Khorne's teeth!' swore Klane, jerking back and switching his gaze from the headless corpse to the ground before the earthworks.

The whipping noise slashed past him again and a puff of earth exploded next to him.

Sniper!

Klane ducked down behind the parapet and cocked his rifle, his head working left and right to see other sentries dropping, no doubt picked off by Imperial snipers on the walls of the ravelin. He swore again. There must be an attack coming in!

He crawled along the firing step, clambering over sleeping bodies towards the alarm siren, and pulled himself up the timber spar where the flared bullhorn was bolted. He grabbed the cranking handle.

Klane heard booted steps approaching the parapet and realised he didn't have much time. He turned the squealing handle, the wailing cry from the bullhorn growing in volume as he spun it faster and faster. A shot blasted the timber beside him, showering him with splinters and he flinched, releasing the handle and taking up his rifle.

Thudding footsteps hit the soil of the earthworks below. Damned Imperials! He snarled, pleased to have this chance to kill. Scrabbling hands sounded on the far side of the parapet.

No bastard Guardsman was going to get past Uraja Klane!

He roared in hatred and rose to his feet, swinging his rifle around to find himself facing a giant warrior in yellow power armour with a crackling sword and scarlet Imperial eagle on his breastplate.

'What the f—' was all he had time to say before the Imperial Fists Space Marine clove him in two with his power sword.

SIRENS SCREAMED, PIERCING the night with their cries and Vauban knew that with the element of surprise lost they had only a limited time to achieve their objective before they would have to fall back. He climbed the steep exterior slope of the earthworks, using the butt of his pistol for purchase. His soldiers scrambled over the parapet with a roar of released fury.

A grenade detonated nearby, showering him with earth and he slipped, feet scrabbling for grip.

A gauntleted hand reached down and closed on his wrist, lifting him easily across the parapet in a single motion. He was deposited on the firing step beside a broken corpse, and swiftly drew his power sword. The Space Marine who had hauled him over the parapet turned and began firing a bolt-gun into a mass of enemy soldiers in red overalls. His brethren were pushing further into the entrenchments as the Imperial Guard scrambled over the parapet and into the battery.

'Thank you, Brother-Captain Eshara,' said Vauban breathlessly.

The Imperial Fists captain nodded, slammed a fresh magazine into his bolter and said, 'Thank me later. We have work to do,' before turning and charging from the firing step.

Gunfire and explosions lit the trenches and dug-outs of the battery with strobing light, screaming soldiers and wounded men providing a cacophonous backdrop to the attack. Hundreds of Jourans poured over the earthwork, killing anything in their path. The Chaos soldiery had been caught largely unawares, and the Imperial troops offered no quarter to the unready foe. Storming parties slaughtered the enemy soldiers, shooting them where they lay or stabbing them with bayonets as they scrambled for weapons.

Fifteen gigantic war machines were situated here, enormous howitzers and long cannons with barrels so wide a man could stand upright inside. Bronze plates embossed with skulls and unholy icons were fixed on each machine's flank, and thick chains looped around giant rings were securely bolted to their track units. There was a terrible sense of menace surrounding the siege engines and Vauban had a gnawing sense of wrongness in his gut. He knew without doubt that such blasphemous creations should never have been allowed to come into existence.

The Imperial Fists swept efficiently through the battery, securing its perimeters and killing the war machines' gunners. They established themselves in strong positions around the approach trenches and parallel, ready to hold off the inevitable counterattack.

Vauban dropped from the firing step and shouted, 'Alpha demo team, with me! Bravo team with Colonel Leonid!'

Two dozen men followed him towards the machines and, even over the crack of small-arms fire, Vauban shivered as he felt the pulse of monstrous, daemonic breath grating along his spine just below the threshold of hearing. He stepped across scores of corpses, making his way quickly towards the daemon engines. As he and his men drew near, the sense of wrongness grew stronger and stronger. As he set foot on the metal decking where the machines were chained, agonising pain ripped into him and he felt his guts cramp and his knees buckle. Terror seized him as his mind was filled with the unshakable belief that to touch these unholy monsters was to die.

He could see he was not alone in this hideous sensation. Soldiers were dropping to their knees, some vomiting blood as the daemonic aura of the nightmare machines washed over them. Chains rattled and metal groaned beneath them as the war machines supped on the red liquid, a bass thrumming building from the line of daemon engines.

The sounds of bolter fire intensified from the edges of the battery, and Vauban knew the Iron Warriors must be counterattacking, fearful of losing their hellish artillery.

They couldn't fail! Not now they had come so close.

Vauban pushed himself to his feet, gritting his teeth against the waves of sickness that wracked him and dragged the soldier nearest to him to his feet.

'Come on, damn you!' he yelled. 'On your feet, soldier!'

The man grabbed his satchel charges and stumbled after Vauban, his face contorted in terror and agony. The two men lurched towards the nearest machine, its chains jangling furiously and geysers of steam venting from corroded grilles. A furious static descended upon his vision, like looking through a faulty holo. A bitter, metallic taste flooded Vauban's mouth as he bit the flesh of his lip to keep from screaming.

Then, as suddenly as it had begun, the pain and terror vanished like the light from a snuffed candle. Vauban felt a huge, pressing weight lift from his mind. His lungs heaved and he spat blood, spinning as he heard a booming chant from behind him.

One of the Imperial Fists, his yellow armour decorated with numerous purity seals and one shoulder guard painted blue, strode towards the daemon engines, his proud voice clear and true. He carried a carved staff of ebony, coils of blue light coruscating along its length.

Vauban did not know the warrior's name, but knew by his words that their saviour was a psyker, one of the Chapter's Librarians. Somehow, he was fighting against the corrupting power of the daemon engines and protecting them from its malign influence.

Ghostly streamers of insubstantial energy flared from the icons and markings on the armoured flanks of the war machines.

Vauban could see by the sweat pouring in runnels from the Librarian's face and the pulsing vein in his temple that the effort of holding their daemonic essence at bay was stretching him to the limit.

The Librarian had bought them a chance, but they would need to be quick.

'Quickly!' he bellowed over the bark of gunfire and explosions. 'Demo teams, plant your charges and let's get the hell out of here!'

The men with demolition charges picked themselves up from the steel decking of the battery and, under the direction of Vauban's best ordnance officers, began placing the explosive charges at vital points on each daemon engine. The vast machines strained at their bindings, thrashing in fury at these mortals who dared to defile them.

As the men moved on to the next machine the vox-bead in Vauban's ear clicked and Captain Eshara's voice filled his skull. 'Castellan Vauban, we must leave! The enemy are coming in overwhelming numbers with heavy support and I do not believe we can hold them.'

'Not yet!' yelled Vauban. 'Give us enough time to set the explosives then fall back! We need you alive!'

'How long do you need?' asked Eshara, his voice muffled by nearby shots and detonations.

Vauban looked along the line of bucking war machines and said, 'Give us four minutes!'

'We'll try! But be ready to move when you see us falling back!'

'HOLD ON A minute!' snapped Hawke. 'Attach the bronze cable with the sacred halo symbol to the two pins with the what?'

Even over the vox-link, Hawke detected more than a trace of impatience in the magos's voice as he answered.

'The bronze cable attaches to the pins with the demi-cog symbol. Just like I said before. Once you have–'

'Hold on, hold on…' grumbled Hawke, fiddling with the cable clips as he fought to find the correct pins and hold the wire steady over the exposed circuitry. The illuminator on his respirator was growing dim and he had to squint to see the symbols Beauvais was talking about. There! He reached in and snapped the clips over the pins, flinching and almost losing his balance when they sparked violently and burnt his fingertips.

He grabbed onto the steel gantry he was lying on and tried not to think of how high above the floor he was. The gantry was solidly constructed, one of several bolted to the wall at various points around the room, presumably for technicians to carry out routine maintenance to the torpedo. He seriously doubted it was used for people trying to hotwire the device. Behind him, a mesh grille in the wall led off into darkness. It had taken him a frustrating twenty minutes to climb the ladder, find the correct access panel in the side of the giant torpedo and use Hitch's knife to undo the sacred bolts that held it in place.

And over the past hour, he'd been mildly electrocuted twice, burnt his fingers three times and almost fallen thirty metres to the solid rockcrete floor. Hawke was not a happy man. He steadied his breathing and spoke into the vox.

'You might have bloody warned me!' he complained.

'Is it done?'

'Yes, it's done.'

'Very good, you have now armed the torpedo.'

Hawke pushed himself back along the gantry, suddenly very alarmed at the prospect of this armed behemoth being less than a metre from his head. 'It's armed. What next?'

'Now we have to inform the war-spirit within the torpedo the whereabouts of its victim.'

'Uh-huh…' shrugged Hawke. 'And how exactly do I do that?'

'You don't. I will perform that sacred task. Now, I need you to remove a red and gold cable embossed with the rune of telemetry, then–'

'The what? Just tell me what the damn thing looks like.'

Beauvais sighed. 'It resembles a winged triangle with a cog at its centre. It is connected to the war-spirit's seeker chamber. That's the gold box at the top of the panel. Once you have the cable, plug it into the vox-unit's remote triangulation output socket and wait. Once the lights on the vox stop flashing, reattach the cable to the war-spirit's seeker chamber.'

Hawke found the plug and pulled it from the panel. He swore as he saw it would only extend some fifteen centimetres from the torpedo. He lifted the vox unit to the edge of the gantry, propping it against one of the uprights. He slotted the cable home, watching as the front panel of the vox unit faded and the lights arranged around the dial flickered in strange patterns. As the sequence continued he propped himself up on one elbow, looking up at the top of the giant torpedo.

The top of the giant missile was rounded and strangely irregular. There was a serrated, spiral groove cut in the warhead and Hawke guessed that this was to help it burrow through the thick hull of a starship before detonating deep inside.

He waited for several minutes before the clicking sequence of lights finally stopped, then unplugged the cable and reconnected it to the torpedo. He thought he heard a noise below and glanced over the gantry. Dismissing it, he returned his attention to the torpedo as Beauvais came back on the vox.

'The war-spirit now knows its prey, Hawke. Now you must speak the Chant of Awakening to set it on the hunt.'

'Ok, Chant of Awakening... right. And after that, then what?'

'Simply strike the rune of firing upon the–'

Beauvais never finished his sentence as a hail of bolter fire ripped through the vox and blasted it to fragments. Hawke jumped in shock, grabbing onto the upright, very nearly going over the edge of the gantry.

'Emperor's holy blood!' he swore, grabbing his rifle and pressing his back against the cold metal grille in the wall behind him. His breath pounded in his throat and his heart beat wildly against his chest. What the hell was going on?

He risked a glance over the gantry and saw a giant in iron-grey power armour with a smoking gun and a mechanised claw snaking over his shoulder. Men in red uniforms clustered around the warrior, all carrying rifles aimed upwards.

A deep voice, rich and full of threat drifted up to him.

'You are going to die, little man. You have led us a merry dance, but now it is over.'

Hawke shut his eyes tight and whispered, 'Oh damn, oh damn, oh damn…'

INCANDESCENT FIRE ERUPTED from the first demolition charges, vaporising the chains and bindings holding the first daemon engine in place. Painstakingly wrought symbols of arcane protection were incinerated and the mechanical components of the war machine ran molten under the volcanic heat of the explosion. The scream of the daemon engine's death whiplashed around the battery as the terrifying creature bound within its infernal mechanisms was freed by the blast.

Those closest, even though well clear of the explosives' blast radius, were swatted to the floor of the battery by its shriek of release. A swirling hurricane of etheric energy, insane geometries warping through its daemonic form, tore through the Jourans with the power of the immaterium, turning men inside out and exploding others from within as it shrieked in the throes of its dissolution.

HONSOU HEARD THE screech of one of the creatures of the damned and cursed Kroeger again. Where were the men from his company tasked with guarding these precious beasts? Creatures that had required countless thousands of lives and diabolical pacts to conjure into being. The answer came easily enough; drunk on slaughter somewhere, slaking their thirst for blood in an orgy of butchery.

He ducked as a hail of bullets stitched the trench wall before him and a clutch of human soldiers fell, their bodies blown apart by the burst. He racked the slide on his own weapon, then paused as he realised the shots he'd heard were fired from a bolter. Honsou stepped over their bleeding corpses and jerked his head around the bend in the trench. He was stunned to see a Space Marine in yellow power armour firing down the trench. The length of the narrow earthen corridor was choked with bodies and there was no way through.

Hundreds of human soldiers gathered behind him, fearfully clutching their primitive rifles as they crouched in the shelter of this trench. They looked to him for guidance and Honsou snarled as he reached back and grabbed one by the neck, tossing him into the approach trench. The man landed hard and, as he rose to his feet, bolter fire shredded him.

Before the body had even hit the ground, Honsou spun low around the corner of the trench, firing controlled bursts at the Space Marine. His victim crumpled, his armour breached by his shots. Honsou's jaw hardened as he saw the clenched, black fist icon on the warrior's left shoulder guard.

Imperial Fists! The ancient enemy, source of his polluted blood and cause of millennia of misery at the hands of those who were not fit even to serve beside him.

Blind rage took Honsou and he roared in hate, charging through the body-filled trench, the desperate need to kill Imperial Fists driving him onwards. Another yellow-armoured warrior appeared at the entrance to the battery and levelled his bolter, but Honsou was quicker, pulling the trigger and emptying his weapon's magazine at the hated foe.

Sparks and earth flew as his shots ricocheted from the Space Marine's armour.

Honsou screamed in fury, throwing aside his bolter when the hammer slammed down empty, and drew his sword as the warrior before him dropped to one knee and took careful aim.

He felt impacts slam into his chest, but nothing, not even death itself would prevent him from reaching his enemy. Pain ripped through him, but he ignored it, hammering his boot into the Space Marine's breastplate. He reversed his grip on his sword hilt and drove it downwards through the chest of the fallen warrior, hate-fuelled strength driving it hilt-deep into his victim.

Blood splashed him as a flaring explosion thundered through the battery and another daemon engine vanished in a sheet of flames, its shriek momentarily drowning out the noise of the blast. Psychic shockwaves buffeted Honsou and he felt the ancient malice of a being that was ancient before mankind was born roar through him. He rejoiced in its hate, feeling it consume him, pouring fresh vigour through his body as it took his unworthy flesh for its own. He spread wide his arms, actinic bolts of black lightning arcing from his hands.

Destruction ripped through the battery as the bolts lashed out, indiscriminately ripping apart banks of soil, machinery and groups of soldiers – both enemy and allied.

Honsou revelled in such carnage, though he knew that it was but borrowed power. Flaring purple afterimages seared across his retinas, but he laughed, hurling spears of warp energy into the confused mass of men and machines. His body swelled as daemonic power poured in. His armour buckled and he screamed as joints and sinews stretched, bones cracked and his jaw stretched wide in a soundless cry of agony.

More thunderous detonations rocked the battery and Honsou felt yet another daemonic presence explode from within its iron machine-prison. He dropped to his knees as the daemon within him suddenly withdrew, feeling its hatred of the newly-birthed entity. As the power drained from him, he watched the two daemonic creatures spiralling heavenward, locked in battle and fading from his vision even as he watched. He ached for such power again, even though he knew it would destroy him.

He groaned in pain as the terrible damage done to him by the daemon's brief occupancy surged through his nerve endings. He pushed himself to his feet as the human soldiers swarmed around him, shooting into the mass of Guardsmen and Space Marines.

A mad shrieking filled the battery as more explosions lit up the night. A daemon engine, its bindings cracked and flailing, howled as it fought to finally sever the magicks that bound it to the war machine. Men were crushed beneath its bronze treads, and Honsou watched as its mighty gun swung ponderously around and fired repeatedly. The screaming projectiles sailed over his head, exploding somewhere deep in the Iron Warriors' camp, and a string of secondary detonations swiftly followed.

Honsou dragged his sword from the body beside him, wincing as his tortured muscles protested. There were still Imperial Fists to slay and he set off into the fiery hell of the battery to find them.

BOLTER IMPACTS RANG from the walls, almost deafening, and Hawke felt the impact of countless bullets hitting the underside of the gantry. Desperately he hammered his elbow against the grille behind him, firing the lasgun blindly over the edge.

Sparking ricochets spanged from the torpedo and Hawke filled the air with a constant stream of expletives, expecting the damn thing to blow with every impact. He could hear the metallic thunk, thunk, of boots on the ladder beside him, and rolled over in time to see a grizzled face atop a red collar appear at the edge of the gantry.

He lashed out, his elbow smashing the man's nose across his face in a spray of blood. The man's hands flew to his face. He screamed as he fell from the ladder.

Hawke yelled, 'And stay down!' before glancing over the edge of the gantry to watch him fall. A bullet streaked past him, grazing his temple and he yelped in pain, blood washing down his face from the cut. He rolled back as another man clambered up the ladder.

A bolter shell plucked at his sleeve and blood streamed from his bicep. His hand spasmed and he dropped the lasgun. It rolled to the edge of the gantry and he lunged for the rifle, just stopping it from falling. Something heavy landed on him.

A fist cracked against his jaw, but he rolled with the blow, twisting his head aside as the man on top of him repeatedly punched him.

Hawke drove his knee into the man's groin and delivered a thunderous head-butt as his opponent's shoulders dropped. He hammered the heel of his hand into the man's neck and gripped his red overalls. Hawke slammed his head into the metalwork of the railings before heaving him over the edge.

Another enemy soldier stood in front of him, aiming a rifle.

Hawke kicked out hard, cracking his boots against the man's legs and shattering his kneecaps. The man shrieked and dropped to the floor of the gantry.

Hawke fired a hail of las-bolts, ripping the man's chest to bloody ruin and blasting clear the wall-mounted grille behind him. More bullet impacts raked the wall around him and he rolled away from the gantry's edge, finding himself looking into the depths of the torpedo's access panel.

How the hell did he fire this bloody thing?

He couldn't remember.

He heard more people climbing and cursed as he saw the charge indicator on the rifle flash red. Almost empty. He could see another soldier had reached the top of the ladder. He snatched the late Guardsman Hitch's pride and joy from his belt and rammed the full length of the Jouran fighting-knife into the man's neck. Bright arterial blood spurted from the wound, drenching Hawke. He frantically wiped his eyes clear, scrambling back towards the torpedo and ramming the knife back in its scabbard.

Gunfire sounded from below, but none of the shots seemed to be directed at him. He risked another furtive glance over the gantry and saw that the armoured giant had killed his remaining soldiers. Perhaps they hadn't been keen to meet the same fate as their comrades.

Hawke grinned suddenly. He didn't blame them.

'You are braver than I took you for, little man,' said the Chaos Marine, mounting the iron ladder. 'I will honour you with the most brutal death.'

'If it's all the same to you, I'll pass on that,' shouted Hawke, firing his lasgun, but the weapon was useless, his shots bouncing from the warrior's burnished armour. He searched desperately for something to use as a weapon, his gaze finally falling on the one thing he knew would finish this bastard off.

But how to use it? What had Beauvais said?

Strike the rune of firing upon the…

The what?

He bit his lip as he heard the warrior climbing.

'To hell with it,' he said and closed his eyes, reaching inside the access panel and hammering his open palm against the exposed runes, switches and buttons.

Nothing happened.

'Emperor damn you!' Hawke screamed in frustration. 'You useless pile of worthless junk! Fire, damn you! Fire you bastard! Fire!'

As the last word left his mouth, a rumbling tremor filled the chamber, klaxons blared and a series of lights began flashing at the chamber's top. Hawke opened his eyes and laughed hysterically. Of course! The Chant of Awakening!

Sudden heat filled the chamber and steam flashed up the walls as powerful rocket engines began igniting sequentially. He'd only gone and bloody done it, hadn't he?

As the heat in the torpedo room suddenly leapt upwards he realised his danger. The ladder was sure as hell not an option and he cried in relief as he saw the duct exposed by the shattered grille. He didn't know where it led, but was sure it had to be better than here.

'Well, Hawke, my lad,' he whispered, 'time to get going.'

Swiftly he crawled towards the duct, pushing his lasgun ahead of him. It was easily wide enough to accommodate him and he slithered inside.

Something tugged at his fatigues. He turned and cried out as he saw the Chaos warrior's loathsome, mechanised claw snap shut on his ankle.

The giant was too large to enter the duct, but the claw would soon pull him out.

'If we are to die, we will die together, little man,' promised the warrior.

'Guess again,' snapped Hawke as he drew his knife and sawed through the throbbing power cables that ran from the claw. Black oil and hydraulic fluid spurted out, and the claw jerked spastically.

Its iron grip slackened and he kicked it clear, powering along the smooth metal duct. With every passing second he expected a bullet in the back, but none came. Vibrations rumbled along the duct and he pushed his muscles harder than he would have believed possible.

Hot steam billowed after him. Sweat poured from his brow as the rumbling of rocket engines grew behind him and the ductwork creaked as it expanded in the burgeoning heat.

Suddenly there was space above him. He pulled himself from the duct and slung his rifle over his shoulder as he found himself in what looked like a vent chamber. Other ducts fed into the chamber and another ladder ascended to a circle of reddish sky high above him. He leapt onto the ladder, climbing as fast as he could, hearing the rumble behind him build to a full-throated bellow, like a mighty dragon waking from its slumbers.

He climbed and climbed as the roar built below him.

Geysers of scalding steam flashed past him.

The heat was intolerable and he gritted his teeth. His skin blistered, but he shut out the pain, putting one hand above the other and pulling himself onwards.

Hawke reached the top of the ladder and moaned in fear as he felt a blaze of heat rush towards him and searing orange light flare around him. He shouted with one last herculean effort, hurling himself over the lip of the vent and rolling aside as a fountain of fiery exhaust gasses exploded behind him.

Hawke squeezed his eyes shut, and rolled away from the heat until he was sure he was safe. He gasped for air and pushed himself into a sitting position, opening his eyes in time to see the torpedo roaring through the sky on a pillar of fire.

Guardsman Julius Hawke knew he'd never seen a more beautiful sight.

THE GLAIVE CLASS ground-launched orbital torpedo climbed rapidly through the red sky of Hydra Cordatus on a blazing tail plume, lighting the battlefield below with its brilliant glare. It soon became nothing more than a flickering point of light in the sky, climbing to an altitude where the air was thinner and its speed could increase. As it reached a height of nearly one hundred kilometres, the first stage of the torpedo separated and stage two ignited, increasing its velocity still further as the war-spirit caged within the warhead calculated the time, distance and vector to its target.

The torpedo nosed over, travelling at almost fourteen thousand kilometres per hour, and began hunting for its prey. The Adeptus Mechanicus had cursed its target and that curse now passed to the war-spirit. As the torpedo angled itself back towards the planet, the warhead identified its target.

With its target locked in its sights, the war-spirit vectored the nozzles on the second stage to fire a corrective burn that altered its flight path and sent the torpedo plummeting back to Hydra Cordatus.

FORRIX STOOD AT the edge of the promontory watching the battle raging below with impotent frustration. The batteries were being attacked by the Imperials and he could do nothing about it. Who would have believed the curs of the corpse-god could be so bold? His hands bunched into fists and he vowed that someone would pay for this.

Flashes and rippling explosions lit up the night and his enhanced sight could follow individual acts of bravery and heroism in the battle. Not only that, but he could clearly see the yellow armour of the Imperial Fists in the flickering light. To have the ancient foe here was as close to perfect synchronicity as he could have wished. He remembered fighting Dorn's warriors on the walls of the Eternity Gate on Terra, ten thousand years ago. Then they had been warriors to walk the road to hell with, but now…?

He would soon find out. An inferno of hate burned within his heart with a passion he had all but forgotten.

He'd watched the spear of light roar from the mountains to the east of the citadel and had experienced a moment's unease as he watched the orbital torpedo climb higher and higher.

How had it been fired and where was it bound? But these questions seemed largely irrelevant now, as it had streaked into the heavens then vanished through the clouds.

Forrix returned his attention to the battle below, sneering in contempt as he saw the Imperials begin to pull back under the fury of the Iron Warriors' counterattack. He saw Honsou leading a rabble of soldiers through the battery, killing those not quick enough to make their escape, and smiled grimly.

Honsou was becoming a fearsome war-leader and Forrix knew that, given the chance, he could be amongst the greatest Warsmiths the Legion had ever seen.

The battle below was as good as over. Forrix turned away, marching past the huge number of artillery pieces he had assembled on the promontory and over the breach Honsou had fought his way across. Tomorrow they would begin firing again and the walls of the citadel would crumble.

He crossed the entrenchment on long, flat sheets of metal, stopping as a sudden premonition sent a shiver along his spine. He craned his neck upwards.

The sky was, as usual, the colour of blood, lit by reflected flashes of explosions from below.

What had made him look up?

Then he saw it.

A burning dot of light high in the sky, arcing down towards the planet at fantastic speed. Forrix's jaw hung slack as he realised the ultimate destination of the torpedo. Hot anger flooded his body as he watched molten streamers of light flare from the torpedo as it entered the lower atmosphere.

He bolted for the keep, shouting a voxed warning to the warriors inside.

'By all that is unholy, raise the keep's void shield!'

He lumbered towards the sunken blast doors that led within, casting a hurried glance over his shoulder. The burning corona of fire that surrounded the torpedo appeared to him like a baleful eye in the heavens, aimed straight for his heart.

Forrix entered the keep, hammering his fist across the door-closing mechanism and set off towards its command centre. He heard the pervasive hum of the void shield generator buried beneath the tower powering up and fervently hoped that it would raise in time.

For if it did not, he and everyone in the keep were as good as dead.

THE TORPEDO IMPACTED almost exactly in the centre of the Kane bastion of Tor Christo where its triple stage warhead detonated with devastating results. The lead element of the warhead was designed to crater an opening through the thick hull of a starship, while the tail element would explode simultaneously, acting as a propellant and hurling the middle charge deep within its target,

But instead of the metres-thick, reinforced adamantium bulkhead of a starship, the torpedo slammed into the ground of the Kane bastion, travelling at over a thousand kilometres an hour. The first stage of the torpedo exploded with phenomenal power, flattening everything within three hundred metres and blasting a crater fifty metres deep. The tail section blew and thrust the torpedo deeper into the rock of the promontory where the more powerful centre charge detonated with the power of a sun, ripping the rock of Tor Christo apart.

Night became day as blinding light fountained from the impact. Tank-sized chunks of stone were hurled through the air like pebbles as an expanding wave of blinding smoke and dust filled the valley. The thunderclap of detonation was like the hammer of the gods, come to smite the surface of the planet, and a surging mushroom cloud billowed a thousand metres into the sky, hurling ash and burning rock in all directions.

The ramparts of the bastions either side of the torpedo's impact sagged and cracked, their rockcrete walls splitting under forces they were never designed to endure. The crater in the centre of the promontory expanded with terrifying rapidity, tonnes of rubble and artillery pieces collapsing into the fiery pit.

With a tortured groan, millions of tonnes of stone cracked and rumbled, sliding free of the slopes of the promontory, crashing down in a rocky tidal wave of destruction. The western end of the first parallel was buried beneath the avalanche of rock, and the zigzag approach saps leading to the second parallel filled and collapsed. Thousands died screaming as they were crushed beneath the sweeping tide of earth.

The battery constructed before the walls of the Vincare bastion vanished in a torrential downpour of earth and rock, the guns buried forever beneath thousands of tonnes of debris.

Hundreds of secondary explosions were touched off as burning shards of wreckage dropped into the Iron Warriors' camp, detonating ammo dumps and fuel bladders, and setting light to hundreds of tents. Anarchy filled the camp as men attempted to fight the blazes, but they were as ants fighting a forest fire; nothing could halt the spread of the voracious flames.

The blast wave buffeted the towering form of the *Dies Irae*, but the workers had done their job well and the towering buttresses and scaffolding held, keeping the monstrous leviathan from toppling. The massive Titan shook, its joints groaning and squealing as its external gyros fought for balance, but the shockwave passed over it and left it intact. Several other Titans were not so fortunate and three Warlords of the Legio Mortis were brought down by massive hunks of rock or collapsed by the force of the blast.

The death toll had reached nearly ten thousand by the time the final echoes of the blast had died away and the blinding light of the torpedo's detonation had faded. All that remained of Tor Christo was the void-shielded keep, perched precariously on a splintered corbel of rock.

In a single stroke, Guardsman Hawke had suddenly tilted the balance of power on Hydra Cordatus.

CASTELLAN VAUBAN PUSHED himself up out of the dust and earth and shook his head clear of the ringing din that filled his skull. Bright light filled the valley and he laughed in triumph as he saw the enormous mushroom cloud wreathing Tor Christo in smoke and flames.

He and Leonid had seen the torpedo launch, but they had been too busy rallying the men to fall back towards the Primus Ravelin to follow its course. The chaos of the attack on the battery had consumed him and the first he'd known of the torpedo's impact was when he'd seen his shadow suddenly thrown out before him and an enormous force smashed him to the ground. Fleeting impressions of flashing light, thunderous detonations and pain as rocks and earth came hammering down around him.

Dizzily he pushed himself to his feet, casting his gaze through the grey smoke, attempting to see the extent of the damage, but it was futile. He couldn't see more than a dozen metres; the dust and smoke was too thick. He could see shapes picking themselves slowly from the ground, but whether they were friend or foe was impossible to tell.

Muffled rallying cries of sergeants pierced the gloomy, dust-filled air and he thought he heard Leonid's voice calling his name, but it was hard to tell. He tried to shout a reply, but his mouth was dry with ash and all he could manage was a hoarse croak. He spat, wiping his face clear of dirt and futilely dusting down his jacket and breastplate.

It was time to impose some order. He stumbled towards where he thought he'd heard Leonid's voice. He turned blindly, all sense of direction lost in the haze.

Vauban froze as he heard a voice in the smoke and an enormous figure in burnished, dust and blood stained armour wearily emerged from the swirling clouds before him.

The warrior was helmetless, his close-cropped black hair tight against his skull and his eyes burning with a hate that chilled Vauban to his very soul.

The two faced one another in silence until Vauban drew his power sword and assumed a relaxed fighting stance, though fear of this warrior pulsed along every nerve of his body.

In a calm voice he said, 'I am Castellan Prestre de Roche Vauban the sixth, heir to the lands of Burgovah on the planet Joura, scion of the House of Vauban. Cross blades with me if you wish to die, foul daemon.'

The warrior smiled. 'I have no such impressive titles, human. I am called Honsou. Half-breed, mongrel, filth, scum. I will cross blades with you.'

Vauban activated the blade of his sword and dropped into a fighting crouch as Honsou approached. The battery fell silent as the two combatants circled one another, searching for a weakness in the other's defence.

Vauban raised his sword in salute and, without warning, leapt towards Honsou, thrusting with his energised blade.

Honsou swayed aside and swept his sword round, slashing the blade towards Vauban. He ducked and spun away, slashing high with his sword.

Honsou deflected the sweep and stepped back, his sword raised before him. Vauban recovered his balance and advanced towards Honsou. He lunged again and Honsou expertly blocked the thrust, rolling his wrists and slashing at Vauban's head. But he had read the move in Honsou's eyes and the castellan dodged the blow.

Wary now, the pair again circled each other, their defences alert for any sudden moves.

Honsou attacked, a flashing whirlwind of steel, forcing Vauban backwards step by step. Vauban parried a vicious slash aimed at his chest, launching a lightning riposte at his foe. The blade scraped a deep furrow in Honsou's armour, but slid clear before drawing blood.

Honsou retreated and Vauban followed with a grin of anticipation, launching himself at Honsou with fresh vigour. Honsou was a powerful warrior, but Prestre Vauban had been a student of swordplay his entire life and each attack drew fresh blood from his adversary.

He hammered his enemy's defences again and again, forcing him slowly backwards until Honsou stumbled and lost his footing.

Vauban spun left and struck out at Honsou's sword arm. Honsou was quick, bringing his block up just in time to intercept the blow, and their weapons met in a coruscating halo of sparks. Vauban roared as Honsou's blade snapped and his own smashed home. The Iron Warrior grunted in pain as his arm was severed just above the elbow.

Honsou retreated, stumbling as blood sprayed from the stump of his arm.

Seizing the opportunity, Vauban leapt in to deliver the deathblow, but, at the last second, realised that Honsou had lured him into the attack.

Honsou roared and stepped to meet Vauban, slamming inside his guard and hammering the snapped length of his sword blade through his silver breastplate and into his heart.

White-hot pain flooded Vauban as Honsou twisted the blade, bright blood pouring down his chest and darkness veiling his sight. Had he heard someone crying his name?

He felt his lifeblood pouring from him and looked into the eyes of his killer.

'Damn you...' he whispered.

'That happened a long time ago, human,' hissed Honsou, but Vauban was already dead.

Six

DAWN BROKE ACROSS the valley, scarlet beams of light throwing its unforgiving glare over a scene of utter devastation. A pall of grey dust hung heavy in the air and smothered all sounds in an unnatural silence.

The Warsmith surveyed the destruction before him with an impassive eye. The swirling metamorphic shadows that wreathed his features were a clue to his fury, and none of his war-captains dared approach their master for fear of his rage. The writhings in his armour spun faster, their agonised mewling becoming more desperate.

Two batteries all but destroyed, the guns on Tor Christo gone and almost every daemon engine shattered. Millions of rounds of artillery had been blown to pieces, thousands were dead and weeks of work had been buried under the rubble of a destroyed mountain.

The Warsmith turned to face his captains and not one was spared a moment of utter terror as he advanced towards them. Each of them could see that the forces of change at work within the Warsmith's body were increasing at a furious rate and the force of his presence was almost overpowering.

'You disappoint me,' he said simply.

Each captain felt the horrendous changes working in the Warsmith's body wash over them. He leaned close to his first captain.

'Forrix, I trusted you to have our siegeworks at the walls by now. They are not.'

He moved on. 'Kroeger, I trusted you to protect my war-engines. You did not.'

The Warsmith faced his last war-captain, his voice dangerously soft and controlled.

'Honsou, you have been blessed by the touch of a creature of Chaos. You are now one of us. You have done well and I shall not forget this service you have done me.'

Honsou nodded his thanks, flexing the freshly-grafted mechanical arm the Warsmith's personal Chirumek had gifted him with at the conclusion of last night's battle.

The Warsmith stepped back, his monstrous form swelling and the darkness of his face parting for the briefest moment to reveal the roiling chaos beneath.

He roared, his voice like the bellow of an angry god, 'I do not have time to be thwarted in my ascension by your incompetence. Go now! Get out of my sight and break open that citadel!'

THE THIRD PARALLEL

One

IT WAS FITTING that the interment of Castellan Prestre Vauban took place under overcast skies. Colonel Leonid – Castellan Leonid now – thought it would have been inappropriate for the sun to be out on this sombre day.

It had been two days since the torpedo had struck Tor Christo, but thick clouds of ash still hung low in the blood-red sky, plunging the valley into perpetual twilight and dropping the temperature to almost freezing. Leonid shivered as he made his way up the thousand steps on the northern flank of the valley towards the Sepulchre. He was one of the four pallbearers carrying their dead leader to his final resting place.

A final honour guard of two thousand men lined the last route of their commander, one on each side of every wide step, and Leonid felt tears gather in the corners of his eyes at this spontaneous tribute.

Vauban had said that he believed his men did not love him.

Now Leonid knew he had been wrong.

Between them, Morgan Kristan, Piet Anders and Brother-Captain Alaric Eshara of the Imperial Fists carried a bier of dark Jouran oak upon which lay a simple ebony casket. Inside lay the mortal remains of Castellan Vauban, his bones prepared by the Magos Biologis to take their place in the Sepulchre's ossuary. The day was deathly silent, as though even the enemy paid tribute to the brave warrior who was laid to rest.

Thinking of the enemy sent fresh tears spilling from Leonid's eyes.

He had watched the Iron Warrior drive his sword through Castellan Vauban's chest, as he screamed a denial and dropped to his knees in the rubble-filled battery. Captain Eshara and Librarian Corwin had driven the foe away from the castellan's body, and the soldiers of the 383rd Jouran Dragoons had borne their commander-in-chief back to the citadel.

He hoped that Vauban had died knowing how successful his daring raid into the enemy's camp had been. Virtually every war machine in the battery had been destroyed, either by Jouran bombs or the cataclysmic detonation of the orbital torpedo. Emperor alone knew how much collateral damage had been caused by the fallout from the explosion.

Leonid again offered his thanks to the almighty God-Emperor that He had seen fit to deliver the Imperial Fists to them. Not only had their arrival caused the morale of the garrison to soar, but the news they brought had made Leonid believe that there was real hope.

News of their arrival had reached him just before he was due to present his plan of attack to Castellan Vauban. At first he had not believed it, thinking it to be some cruel hoax, but as he sprinted from his chambers and saw them, ash-stained and weary, he'd raised his eyes to the heavens and blessed the name of Rogal Dorn.

He'd run to the Imperial Fists, but all he could think to say was, 'How?'

The leader of the Space Marines said, 'Brother-Captain Eshara. Are you the commanding officer here?'

'Uh, no...' he'd managed. 'Castellan Vauban commands the citadel. I am Lieutenant Colonel Leonid, his second-in-command. Where did you come from?'

'The *Justitia Fides*, our strike cruiser, was about to make the jump into the Empyrean when the astropaths reported a faint distress signal emanating from this planet,' explained Captain Eshara. 'The prefix on the signal was of sufficient urgency that I immediately ordered them to pass it on to the naval base at Hydraphur before turning the ship back to Hydra Cordatus.'

'But what about the enemy vessels in orbit?'

'We narrowly avoided detection by a Chaos warship near the jump point, but once we were clear, I ordered best speed to the source of the distress signal. It was a relatively simple matter to evade detection by the cargo hulks in orbit, but to avoid being spotted by enemy ground troops we flew the Thunderhawks to the mountains some hundred kilometres north of this fastness. After that, we simply crossed the mountains on foot to reach you.'

Leonid still marvelled at Eshara's casual description of his men's incredible journey across the mountains. Two days to cross some of the most inhospitable terrain Leonid had ever seen. It had taken Guardsman Hawke almost a full day to cross eight kilometres, never mind a hundred.

Not only that, but less than five hours later, the Space Marines had fought a major battle and emerged triumphant. The Battle of the Battery was as much their victory as the Jourans'.

Leonid shivered as he looked up at the grim, black tower before them, hating its bleak austerity and wishing that they did not have to perform this solemn duty. But perform it they must. He lowered his eyes as they approached the doors to the Sepulchre.

Tonsured priests stood at the open portal with their heads bowed. Smoking censers hung from hooks beside the door, giving off the heady aroma of Jouran incense.

As the pallbearers entered the Sepulchre, a lone voice sounded from the ranks of the assembled soldiers, '383rd, present arms!'

The sound of two thousand men slamming their heels down on the steps echoed from the mountainsides and the valley resounded to the deafening salute of rifles firing in perfect unison.

THE BRIEFING CHAMBER was hot, despite the chill of the day, as the citadel's commanding officers filed into the room. Even though he was now in command of the Jouran Dragoons, Leonid was not sitting at the head of the meeting table, but in his usual seat to the right of Vauban's chair.

He watched as the officers of his regiment – his regiment now, the thought had not yet sunk in – entered the briefing chamber, saluting before they took their seats. They looked to him for leadership now, and he just hoped he could provide it.

Vauban had been a natural leader who made command look effortless, but the last two days had shown Leonid how difficult it truly was. Every day, a hundred decisions had to be made and each one had potentially life-threatening consequences. Could he really take charge of the regiment and command the citadel's defences? He didn't know.

Morgan Kristan and Piet Anders took their usual seats. Opposite them sat the two leaders of the Imperial Fists detachment: Brother-Captain Eshara and Librarian Corwin, their polished armour a brilliant yellow. Leonid felt grateful for their support and knew he would need to rely on them more than ever over the coming days now that Vauban was gone. Princeps Daekian and Magos Naicin were also present, but their placement further down the table was indicative of their status as pariahs to the Jourans.

Major Kristan lifted the bottle of amasec from the tray at the table's centre with his good arm and poured a glass for himself, Leonid and Anders before also filling the glasses at the empty seats of Vauban and Tedeski. He offered the two Space Marines a drink, but both politely refused. Pointedly, he did not offer a drink to the new commanding officer of the Legio Ignatum or the representative of the Adeptus Mechanicus. Piet Anders took out a bundle of thin, twine-bound cheroots, the kind Vauban had enjoyed, from inside his uniform jacket and offered them around the table. All the Jouran officers took one in honour of their former leader, but again the Space Marines declined.

Once the drinks were poured and the cigars lit, Leonid raised his glass, sweeping his eyes around the regimental colours and shields mounted on the wall. So many men had garrisoned this place, so many forgotten heroes. He promised himself that Prestre Vauban would not go unremembered.

'To Castellan Prestre Vauban,' toasted Leonid, raising his glass.

'Castellan Vauban,' repeated the officers, draining their amasec in a single gulp.

Leonid took a draw on the cheroot, coughing as the acrid smoke caught in his throat. A few chuckles greeted his discomfort. They all knew he disapproved of such vices.

'Gentlemen,' began Leonid, grimacing in distaste at the smoking cheroot. 'It has been over three weeks since this siege began, and though it has been hard and we have seen good friends fall, we've given these Chaos scum a bloody nose they'll not forget. Regardless of the eventual outcome of this battle, I want you all to know that you have done all that honour demands and I am proud to have fought beside you.'

Indicating the Space Marine on his immediate left, Leonid continued. 'Captain Eshara informs me that the Imperium is now aware of our plight, and that relief is en route to us even as we speak. Captain Eshara expects aid to arrive within–'

'Fifteen to twenty days at the most,' said Eshara, his voice clipped and regal. 'Fortunately, there is an Adeptus Mechanicus astrotelepath way-station less than twenty light years from where we picked up your distress call and naval vessels are within easy reach. The alert code we encrypted in the communiqué will ensure swift reaction.'

Smiles broke out across the table and hands were shaken in congratulation as Leonid pressed on. 'Aid is on its way, but in order to maintain discipline I do not want that fact to become common knowledge. When the soldiers ask, tell them only that we are expecting to be relieved, but not when. Make no mistake, the enemy will now be more determined than ever to avenge their defeat in the battery.'

'Your castellan is correct,' said Librarian Corwin, leaning forward and steepling his fingers before him. His face was still drawn and pale from the effort of shielding the Jourans from the Chaotic energies of the war machines.

'The guns you destroyed in the battery were more than simple weapons of war, they were imbued with terrifying daemonic entities, conjured into the machines with the blood of innocents and diabolical pacts made with the Ruinous Powers. The destruction unleashed in the battery will have caused many of those pacts to be broken and the Iron Warriors will need blood to restore them. Our blood.'

'You know a great deal about the Iron Warriors, sir. Is there anything you can tell us that will help us fight them?' asked Piet Anders.

Corwin nodded, saying, 'The Iron Warriors are amongst the most terrible foes the Imperium has ever seen. Once, ten thousand years ago, they were counted amongst the Emperor's most favoured sons, his best and bravest fighters, but they became bitter and twisted as the long wars of the Great Crusade continued, their own desires taking precedence over their duty to the Emperor. When the Great Betrayer, whose cursed name I will not speak, rebelled against our lord and master, the Iron Warriors renounced their oaths of loyalty and joined him in war against the Emperor. Much of the truth of these days has been lost, but what is true is that the Iron Warriors desecrated the holy soil of Terra, using skills honed by constant warfare to breach the walls designed by our holy Primarch, Rogal Dorn.

'The biggest mistake you can make is to underestimate the Iron Warriors. Yes, they have suffered a grievous blow with the loss of their daemon engines, but they will find other ways of striking back at us. And we must be ready for them.'

'Librarian Corwin is correct,' stated Leonid. 'We must do everything we can to be ready for when they come at us again.' He pushed back his chair and stubbed out the cheroot, rising to circle the table with long paces.

'We need to get the parapets repaired so we can put men behind them again. We need to remount the guns on the walls as I have no doubt that they are digging fresh trenches towards us even now and I want them hammered every second of every day and every night.'

'I am not sure if we have the ammunition stockpiles to maintain such levels of expenditure, Colonel Leonid,' pointed out Magos Naicin.

Leonid didn't bother to mask his contempt for the magos. 'Naicin, when I want your input I shall ask for it. Understand this: the more powder we burn now, the less blood my men will shed when the final assault comes.'

Turning from the magos, he said, 'I want the platoons in each battalion divided into shifts, six hours on the walls, six hours off. The men are exhausted and I want the soldiers manning the ramparts to be at their best. But drill them hard in manning the walls. When an alert signal is given, I want every soldier on the walls in an instant.'

Anders and Kristan nodded, taking notes on their personal data-slates. Princeps Daekian scribbled one last note before asking, 'What can the Legio do to help?'

Leonid glanced down the table.

'I don't know. What *can* the Legio do?' he growled.

Daekian stood stiffly, clasping his hands behind his back.

'Until the enemy cross the outer walls, not a great deal,' he admitted.

'Then what use are you to me?' snapped Leonid.

Daekian continued smoothly, as though Leonid had not spoken. 'But if the enemy do carry the walls, we can cover your retreat to the inner curtain wall more efficiently.'

Seeing Leonid's sceptical look, Daekian smiled grimly, 'Wall-mounted guns can be quickly bracketed and destroyed, believe me. I have two Warhounds left that will not prove so static. Warhounds are not tall enough to be targeted from beyond the walls and will provide the best fire support. The Reavers and the *Honoris Causa* will need to remain behind the curtain wall or they will be destroyed before battle is joined, but they give you a powerful reserve for a counterattack.'

Daekian paused before continuing. 'You are a proud man, Castellan Leonid, but I know you are wise enough to see the truth of this. Do not let your anger towards the Legio blind you to the sense of my words.'

The muscles bunched in Leonid's jaw and the colour rose in his cheeks.

Captain Eshara rose to his full height and stepped between the two officers.

'Castellan Leonid, might I interrupt here?'

Leonid nodded and returned to his seat, lacing his hands before him as Eshara circled the meeting table, collecting each officer's marching cane. Each thin, silver-topped cane was a purely ceremonial affectation, carried tight under the left arm by the officers of the regiment during marching drill.

When he had gathered enough of the canes, he returned to stand beside Leonid's chair, handing him one.

'Break it,' he said.

'Why?'

'Indulge me.'

Leonid easily snapped the cane in two, placing the splintered wood on the table.

The Space Marine captain handed him another. 'Again.'

'I don't see what this has–'

'Do it,' commanded Eshara. Leonid shrugged and snapped the second cane as easily as the first, laying the pieces next to the others. A third cane was broken before Eshara picked up the six pieces lying before the commander of the Jourans. He gathered them in a bundle, bound them together with the twine from the cheroots and handed them to Leonid.

'Now try to break them,' he ordered.

'As you wish,' sighed Leonid, gripping the thick bundle and twisting. He grimaced with the strain as he tried to break the pieces, but without success. Eventually he was forced to give up and tossed the unbroken bundle onto the table.

'I cannot,' he admitted.

'No, you cannot,' agreed Eshara, picking up the bundle and placing his hand upon Leonid's shoulders.

'When I look around this room, I see men of courage standing firm in the face of the most dreaded of foes and it fills me with pride. I have fought for longer than any of you have been alive. I have faced enemies of all kinds and fought beside some truly great warriors. I have never been beaten, so listen well. To do battle in the service of the Emperor you must understand that you are part of an unimaginably larger war and that you cannot fight for yourself. That way lies damnation and ruin.

'Together you are stronger than adamantium, but if you do not stand as one, you will all be broken like these canes. Castellan Vauban knew this. He may have been angry with certain decisions that were made in the past, but he knew not to put his own feelings before the welfare of his command.'

Eshara marched to the Jouran regimental flag and lifted it, tracing his finger along the hand-stitched lettering of the embroidered scroll at its base.

'Your regimental motto, Castellan Leonid: *Fortis cadere, cadere non protest*. Tell me what it means.'

'It means, "the brave man may fall, but will never yield".'

'Exactly,' said Eshara, pointing down the table. 'And Magos Naicin, is "Strength through Unity" not one of your order's aphorisms?'

'One of many,' conceded Naicin.

Eshara nodded towards Princeps Daekian. 'Princeps? Your Legio's motto if you please.'

'*Inveniam viam aut faciam*. It means, "I will either find a way, or I shall make one".'

'Very good,' nodded Eshara returning to his seat. 'Do you all understand? I have been here but a short time, but already I see division amongst you. Such petty squabbling must be put aside. There can be no other way.'

Leonid looked at the unbroken bundle of canes before him and rubbed his hand across his unshaven jaw before rising to address his men.

'Captain Eshara speaks with a truth and clarity we have lost. Gentlemen, from this moment on, we are a brotherhood united in our holy cause, and I will have words with any man who dares put that brotherhood asunder.'

Leonid marched towards the end of the table to stand before Princeps Daekian, who rose from his seat. The Castellan of Hydra Cordatus drew the sword Daekian had given him and bowed as he presented it to its rightful owner.

'I believe this belongs to you,' he said.

Daekian nodded, proffering his hand to Leonid. 'You keep it, Castellan Leonid. It looks better on you. I have another.'

'As you wish,' smiled Leonid, scabbarding the sword and accepting Daekian's grip.

The two men shook hands then Leonid rounded the table to face Magos Naicin.

'Magos. Any help you could give us would be gratefully received.'

Naicin stood and bowed. 'I am your servant, colonel.'

Leonid shook Naicin's gloved hand and nodded his thanks to Captain Eshara.

Perhaps he could hold this brotherhood together after all.

Two

HONSOU KICKED OVER a blasted chunk of rubble. Squatting on his haunches, he picked up a handful of rock dust and let it spill through his mechanical fingers. The new arm pleased him mightily, it was stronger and more robust than his own had been. It had originally belonged to Kortrish, the Warsmith's former champion, and was a physical indication of his master's favour. Honsou was surprised by the Warsmith's sudden favour, since he had equalled, if not exceeded his deeds in the battery many times before.

He was also sure that Forrix must have told the Warsmith how Honsou had failed to kill everyone in his initial attacks and thus was responsible for the destruction unleashed by the torpedo. Since that time Honsou had been unable to make contact with Goran Delau, and was forced to assume that his second-in-command had failed.

But if that were the case, why then did the Warsmith honour him so?

Perhaps in part it was due to the cleansing presence of the daemon that had briefly possessed his unworthy flesh. Had it stripped away the polluted gene-seed within him in the searing fire of its occupancy, to make him pure? The magnitude of the power he had felt in those fleeting moments had been intoxicating and though he knew it would mean oblivion, he longed for its touch once again. His body was still healing after the daemon's blissful violation and, though he was unsure, he believed he could feel some lingering remnants of its presence within him.

Had the Warsmith also sensed it, recognising a kindred power within him?

Kroeger had been livid and Forrix dangerously quiet following their admonishment by the Warsmith, and Honsou had stayed clear of both captains since then. Kroeger had, unsurprisingly, chosen to vent his frustrations on prisoners, slaking his anger in their bloody entrails. Honsou wondered how long it would be before Kroeger irretrievably descended into madness to become just another faceless berserker.

The Warsmith had then charged Forrix and his warriors with the thankless task of constructing and advancing the final sap. Honsou smiled to himself at the thought of Forrix, commander of the First grand company, labouring in the trenches, a task that had surely been earmarked for Honsou and his impure company.

The trenches were still knee deep in ash, despite the hundreds of slaves working constantly to clear them. Looking around him, he knew there was no way that the siegeworks were going to be at the walls within the ten days the Warsmith had demanded.

The final sap was pushing forward to the head of the central ravelin, but its progress was maddeningly slow. This close to the citadel, the angle of each zigzag arm of the sap had to be dug in increasingly shallower angles as they came within range of the weapons carried by the soldiers on the walls. Whereas the saps dug forward from the first and second parallels were constructed by piling excavated earth onto the forward edge of the trench, this sap had, by necessity, to be advanced with much more care and sophistication. Most of the surviving slaves (and there were precious few left, thanks to the Imperial torpedo) were digging out what materials and supplies had survived the destruction of Tor Christo back in the campsite, while the Iron Warriors themselves prepared this last sap.

Teams of Iron Warriors inched forwards on their hands and knees under cover of the lumbering sap-rollers, laboriously ramming the excavated earth on the trench's outer face then dragging forward iron palisades to strengthen it. Gangs of specially picked slaves followed behind, deepening the trench and readying the sap for the storming squads. Constructing such a sap was dangerous and tedious work, requiring a great deal of skill and teamwork, since the workers were under constant fire from the citadel's defenders. If the trench had advanced ten metres by nightfall, it was counted a good day's work.

Work parties from Kroeger's company were even now cannibalising every non-essential vehicle for parts to construct more sap-rollers, for the Imperial forces had managed to remount many of their parapet weapons following the attack on the battery. The Imperial guns would hammer each sap-roller with devastating barrages, blowing them apart within hours, and the Iron Warriors had little with which to reply.

The *Dies Irae* pounded the citadel, but its remaining guns were at their maximum range and unless the mighty warengine could be made mobile again, its usefulness was limited. The remaining two Titans of the Legio Mortis were being kept in reserve until the final assault, though Honsou wondered if the grievous wounding of the *Dies Irae* had broken the nerve of the Legio's warriors.

Even from here, Honsou could see that the ramparts were being quickly repaired, no doubt under the direction of the reviled Imperial Fists. Much as he hated to admit it, the ancient enemy were competent siege engineers and would make their job all the harder.

Honsou eagerly awaited the final attack. The need to kill Imperial Fists was now his only imperative, and he chafed at the slow speed at which the sap advanced.

Slow though their progress was, Honsou calculated that within three days the sap would be almost at the lip of the citadel's huge ditch, in a position where it could be branched left and right to form the third parallel. Under normal circumstances, a trench cavalier would be built along the parallel's length, a solid earthwork some three metres high with a parapet that would allow troops manning its firing step to obtain plunging fire into ramparts of the ravelin. This, combined with fire from Vindicator siege tanks and the spider-legged Defilers, should compel the defenders to abandon the ravelin, allowing the attackers to assault the breaches.

But these were not normal circumstances and the unexpected destruction of their siege batteries meant there were no breaches in the walls.

They would need some other way of bringing down the walls if they were to take this citadel. As he turned back towards the camp, it came to him how such a feat could be achieved.

CROUCHED IN A dark part of Kroeger's dugout, Larana Utorian rocked back and forth, her knees tucked up under her chin, her hands clasped over her ears. A red line dribbled down her chin where she had chewed her lip and her thin, wasted frame was malnourished to the point of starvation. Her features were gaunt and sallow and her ribs pushed against her filthy skin beneath the threadbare remains of her uniform jacket.

Kroeger's armour once more hung on its frame, its surfaces slathered in gore.

On the ground before her lay the armoured gauntlet, the fingers curled in a fist, the knuckles caked with pounded-in blood. Her bone knife rested against it, its edge nicked and bloody.

Larana's breathing came in short, hiked gasps. The voice had come again.

'Who are you?' she asked, the sound no more than a hoarse whisper. There was no answer and for the briefest second she wondered if she had imagined the hissing voice that had spoken to her.

A nervous laugh built in her throat, but died as the voice came again.

I am all that you want, little one. I feel your hate and it is exquisite.

The voice slithered around her head, seeming to come from all around her, sounding more dead than alive. The horrific voice was composed of many, each overlaying the other, monstrously intertwined with sussurating hoarseness.

Larana whimpered in fear. Looking up at Kroeger's armour she saw a pale nimbus of light building up behind the visor of the helmet. The eyes seemed to be looking straight through her, through her skin, past her bones and organs and into her very soul.

The sense of violation was horrific.

She screwed her eyes shut and wept as the sensation crawled around her mind, teasing open every dark and secret place of her soul.

Then, as suddenly as it had begun, the loathsome exploration was done.

Oh yes, you are ripe, little Larana. You have a fecund and inventive hate. You shall be my greatest work...

'Stop speaking to me!' wailed Larana, beating her fists against her head. 'What do you want?'

I want to take away your pain if you will but let me. I can make you strong again.

Larana opened her eyes, hope and fear shining in equal measure.

'How? Why?'

I am done with Kroeger. He has descended to the point where his petty slaughters no longer amuse me. But you, oh you have such hate within you! It smoulders, but I see in you the seeds of an inferno. It will be an age before I tire of you, Larana.

Almost against her will, her eyes were drawn towards the gauntlet lying on the dusty floor of the dugout. As if sensing her gaze, the fingers of the gauntlet slowly uncurled so that it lay palm up before her.

Go on! I can feel hate oozing from every pore of your flesh. We shall strike back! He is a butcher of men and deserves to die, does he not? I can help you kill him. Is that not what you desire above all else?

'Yes!' snarled Larana, picking up the heavy gauntlet and slipping her hand inside.

CASTELLAN LEONID RESTED his elbows on the parapet of the curtain wall and stifled an exhausted yawn as he watched the men on the walls of the two forward bastions with pride. Under the direction of the Imperial Fists, the ramparts had been rebuilt, fresh entrenchments dug at the necks of the bastions and bomb shelters constructed at the base of the walls. The sense of optimism amongst the soldiers was palpable.

He and Captain Eshara stood on the walls beside the towers flanking the Destiny Gate, looking out over the blasted expanse of the plain before the citadel. Craters and thousands of metres of trenches covered the ground, with bodies and wrecked machines left to rot and rust where they lay. Smoke rose in a constant pall from the camp at the end of the valley and seeing the might of the Iron Warriors like this, Leonid wished he shared his soldiers' optimism.

Despite a fearful hammering from the remounted wall guns, the sap driven forward from the partially collapsed second parallel had come to within fifteen metres of the edge of the ditch. A fresh scar on the landscape stretched before them, a third parallel running from the flank of Vincare bastion to that of Mori bastion.

'It will not be long, will it?' asked Leonid.

'No, not long,' replied Eshara.

'When do you think they will attack?'

'It is difficult to say,' answered Eshara. 'The Iron Warriors never begin an attack until every detail of the assault is in place. There will be a bombardment, feint attacks, diversionary tactics and frontal escalades. Everything will be designed to keep us off balance.'

'I will need you with me when the assault comes, captain.'

'I shall be honoured to fight alongside you.'

'How will they come at us, do you think?'

Eshara considered the question for a moment before replying.

'Without their batteries, it is unlikely that they will try and blast a breach in the walls. All the signs suggest that they will attempt to undermine the walls.'

'They do?'

'Yes. Your forward observers have not reported the construction of batteries, but this parallel is close enough for siege tanks to be deployed behind the earthwork.'

'So why does that suggest the Iron Warriors will be constructing a mine?'

Eshara pointed towards the sap that ran from the second parallel to the third. Plumes of exhaust wreathed the trench in clouds of blue oilsmoke.

'There is an almost constant stream of vehicles travelling back and forth from the forward trench. The trench here is not being widened or extended, yet the earthen rampart they build before it continues to grow. That would suggest that there are mining works being carried out below.'

Leonid swore. He should have noticed that himself. He cursed himself for a fool for not thinking of such a possibility.

'What can we do to stop it?'

'I have begun a series of countermines. One from within a derelict building behind the inner wall and another from within the Primus Ravelin. When they are complete I will fill them with assault troops equipped with auspexes. The troops also have charges for blowing any tunnels they discover and the Adeptus Mechanicus have provided me with an unpleasant surprise for anyone within those tunnels. However, countermining is not an exact science, and we will need to be ready should the Iron Warriors manage to bring down a significant portion of the wall.'

Leonid nodded, watching the activity on the plain with fresh eyes, picturing how the enemy would come at them, and devising counters to meet them.

The citadel's first line of defence was the ditch, six metres deep and thirty wide, in which sat the Primus Ravelin. After crossing the ditch and ravelin, all the while under constant fire from the ramparts, the attackers would have still have to fight their way across the walls.

And if the enemy did manage to carry the walls, then every building within the perimeter of the citadel was a fortress in its own right. From the stores of the Commissariat to the field hospital, each building was equipped with looped windows, armoured entrances, and was capable of offering fire support to those nearby.

But many buildings had taken severe damage already and were continuing to suffer as Arch Magos Amaethon's ability to maintain the shield grew weaker with every passing day.

All the defences needed strengthening, and the men of the Jouran Dragoons worked hand-in-hand with the warriors of the Imperial Fists to make the citadel as impregnable as possible. Eshara and Leonid watched the labours of the soldiers below and were heartened by the sense of shared purpose and camaraderie they saw.

'My compliments, Castellan Leonid, your men do you proud,' observed Eshara, following Leonid's gaze.

'Thank you, captain, we have made fine fellows out of them.'

'Yes, it is a pity that war brings out both the best and worst in men,' sighed Eshara.

'What do you mean?'

'You have seen combat, Castellan Leonid, you know full well the barbarity soldiers are capable of in the fire of battle. But look around you: the bond of brotherhood that has formed here is something that only soldiers facing death can truly know. Every man and woman here understands that they may be dead soon, and yet they are in fine spirits. They have seen the sun rise, but none know whether they will live to see it set. To know that and make peace with it is a rare gift.'

'I don't know that many soldiers would appreciate that.'

'Probably not on a conscious level, no,' agreed Eshara, 'but on a level they may not even be aware of, they do. They fear death, but only by facing it can they truly find their courage.'

Leonid smiled. 'You are a remarkable man, Captain Eshara.'

'No,' said Eshara, without hint of false modesty. 'I am a Space Marine. I have trained my whole life to fight the

Emperor's enemies. I have the finest weapons, armour and faith in the galaxy. It is of no matter to me who I fight; I know I shall be triumphant. I say this without arrogance, but there are few foes in this galaxy that can stand before the might of the Adeptus Astartes.'

In any other person, Leonid would have said Eshara's words were arrogant, but he had seen him fight in the battery and knew that the Space Marine captain spoke the truth.

'I know I can defeat any foe,' continued Eshara, 'but your soldiers have no such knowledge, yet still they stand, knowing the enemy is superior to them. They are true heroes and will not fail you.'

'I know that,' said Leonid.

'Speaking of which, have you been able to raise your man Hawke yet?' asked Eshara, looking towards the mountains.

Leonid frowned and shook his head. 'No, not yet. Magos Beauvais lost contact with Hawke just before the torpedo launched. Once the Adeptus Mechanicus got over their pique at having been kept out of the loop on that one, they went over the recordings and filtered the last few seconds through their cogitators. It seems that there was gunfire just before the signal was lost.'

'So you think Hawke is dead?'

'Yes, I believe he is,' nodded Leonid. 'Even if his attackers didn't kill him, the torpedo's engines would have.'

'A shame,' noted Eshara. 'I think I would have liked to meet Guardsman Hawke. He sounds like a most heroic individual.'

Leonid smiled. 'Had anyone used the words "Hawke" and "heroic" in the same sentence a month ago, I would have laughed at them.'

'An unlikely hero then?'

'The unlikeliest,' agreed Leonid.

FORRIX SWEATED INSIDE his armour, the heat and choking air of these tunnels an anathema to him after the planet's surface. The floor of the tunnel sloped down at a steep angle, roughhewn steps leading into the sweltering depths of the mine. The red rock of this planet held the day's heat in a miser's grip, releasing it as night fell in baking waves. Scores of slaves had died of heat exhaustion already, but the tunnel was making swift progress.

Galleries already branched to either side of the main tunnel. Lined with explosives to blow the lip of the ditch, they would allow the attackers to descend into it. Beyond these branches, the tunnel dipped more steeply in order to pass under the ditch, where the drilling rigs pushed towards the main curtain wall. Once this tunnel was complete, further galleries would be constructed beneath a sizeable length of the wall's foundations and a vast quantity of explosives detonated to bring it crashing down.

Like the construction of the third parallel, it was dirty, thankless work and brought little glory to its builders. Forrix knew he was being punished, and the knowledge that his punishment was unjustified was a twisting knife in his gut. He had watched Honsou strutting around with the bionic arm that had once belonged to Kortrish, swaggering in his new-found favour. Did he not realise that it had been him, Forrix, who had nurtured his ambition, kept him hungry to prove himself? And this was how he was repaid, forced to toil like a slave, a beast. He, the captain of the First grand company, labouring in the depths of a mine!

How could things have reversed so suddenly? Less than a week ago, he had been pre-eminent in the Warsmith's eyes; credited with the swift capture of Tor Christo and honoured with the direction of the advancing saps and parallels. No matter that Kroeger had allowed the daemon engines to be destroyed! No matter that Honsou's incompetence had allowed the Imperials to launch an orbital torpedo at them.

With the Warsmith on the brink of greatness, being stuck down here was the very last place he needed to be.

Jharek Kelmaur had confessed the truth of the matter after the debacle in the battery. Forrix had gone to the sorcerer's tent with murder in his heart and stormed in, his power fist sheathed in lethal energies. He had lifted the shocked magicker from his feet and thrown him across his alchemist's table, where a bound figure writhed in gurgling pleasure.

'You knew!' stormed Forrix. 'You knew the Imperial Fists would come to this place. You knew and you did not tell us.'

Kelmaur picked himself up and rounded on Forrix, his hands spreading with the beginnings of a sorcererous incantation. Forrix smashed his fist into Kelmaur's belly, doubling him up, and lifted him from his feet.

'Do not waste your cantrips on me, sorcerer,' sneered Forrix, hurling Kelmaur to the ground and squatting beside him. He wrapped his gauntlet around Kelmaur's neck and bunched his power fist above the sorcerer's head, poised to pound his skull to destruction.

'You knew the Imperial Fists would come, did you not?'

'No! I swear!'

'You are lying to me, Kelmaur,' snapped Forrix. 'I saw the look on your face when you told the Warsmith that the defenders had not managed to send a warning. You lied to him, didn't you? There was a warning given, wasn't there?'

'No!' wailed Kelmaur. Forrix slammed his power fist into Kelmaur's face, deactivating the energy field at the last second. Kelmaur's nose broke and he spat bloody teeth.

'Do not lie to me again or I will keep the fist active next time,' warned Forrix.

'I did not... know exactly, but I feared there had been a signal sent. It was so weak I knew it could not have left the system and believed that no one would hear it.'

'But someone did, didn't they?'

'So it seems, but I took steps to try and prevent any intervention.'

'What steps?'

'I despatched the *Stonebreaker* to the system jump point to intercept any reinforcements.'

Forrix groaned at Kelmaur's foolishness. 'And it never occurred to you that this might well have allowed them to approach the planet in the first place? Your stupidity is galling.'

Forrix released the sorcerer and shook his head. 'Answer me this then, Kelmaur. Why are we here? Why does the Warsmith bid us attack this place? What drives us towards this citadel with such haste and, more importantly, what is happening to the Warsmith?'

The sorcerer did not answer immediately and Forrix reactivated his power fist. Kelmaur squirmed away, but not quickly enough. The Iron Warrior gripped his robes and dragged him to his feet.

'Speak!'

'I dare not!'

'You will tell me or you will die. Decide now,' snarled Forrix, drawing back his fist.

'Gene-seed!' wailed Kelmaur, the words tumbling from his lips in a desperate rush. 'This citadel is a secret bastion of the Adeptus Mechanicus. They store and monitor the purity of the Adeptus Astartes' gene-seed here. There is a laboratorium hidden beneath the citadel with enough genetic material to create legions of Space Marines! The Despoiler had given the task of its capture to the Warsmith in return for his ascension. If we are successful, the Warsmith ascends to daemonhood! If we fail, he will be destroyed, reduced to the mindless horror of spawndom, cursed to live forever as a writhing, mutated monstrosity.'

Forrix lowered Kelmaur as the implications of such a prize sank in.

Gene-seed. The most precious resource in the galaxy. With such a prize, there would be no limit to the Despoiler's power and his Black Crusades would carve a new empire from the ashes of the Imperium. The scale of such a vision astounded even Forrix's jaded senses.

Daemonhood! To become a creature of almost limitless potential, with the power of the warp to call your own; to be able to mould reality to your own ends and become master of a million souls. Such a prize was worth any cost and Forrix now understood the Warsmith's all-consuming need to break into the citadel. And if that meant sacrificing every warrior here to achieve those ends, then that was a small price to pay for immortality.

Such a prize would be worth risking everything for. To travel in realms beyond the ken of mortal men, where nothing was denied and every possibility could be played out was a dream Forrix could well understand. His flinty gaze locked with Kelmaur's.

'Tell no one what you have told me, or the Warsmith shall hear of your folly.'

'He would not believe you,' whined Kelmaur.

'That is irrelevant. If the Warsmith even suspects you have deceived him, he will kill you. You know this to be true,' promised Forrix, stalking from the tent.

Now, deep in the dim tunnels below the planet's surface, Forrix watched as a gang of emaciated slaves dragged back another load of excavated soil. The tunnel was advancing and soon the Iron Warriors would be inside the citadel.

Forrix smiled, picturing the limitless possibilities ahead of him.

LARANA UTORIAN WATCHED as Kroeger placed his helmet on the iron frame and stood naked before her. His body was a mass of scar tissue, his slab-like muscles powerful and well-defined. But she had a sense of diminishment, a sense that without his armour he was somehow less terrifying.

His voice was dull and lethargic, and as always after his slaughters, his movements were sluggish, as though bloated with the blood he had consumed in his butcheries.

She kept her hand tucked within her jacket, its flesh pink and raw where she had worn the gauntlet. The skin still burned with the sensations that had wracked her body as renewing fire seared her from the inside out. Already, she felt her strength returning.

New flesh filled her, monstrous vitality pulsing through every fibre of her being, strength coursing along every artery and vein. Her heart pumped with power and she saw with a clarity she had never experienced before.

The sense of impending revenge was intoxicating and she had to keep the excitement from her face as Kroeger sullenly bade her once more clean his armour. He stumbled towards a corner of the dugout and collapsed into blood-gorged unconsciousness.

Larana calmly approached the corrupted armour, feeling its soundless call. She smiled as she felt its silent approval and removed the gauntlet she had first worn; lifting it to her lips and sucking on the fingers, tasting the blood and feeling its power suffuse her.

Yes, the blood is the power, it fills you, drives you. It carries your passions, your lusts, your hate and your future. Only the blood can save you.

Larana nodded, the words making complete sense to her. She could see clearly now. To survive, she must look to whatever power offered her a chance to exact her revenge.

She thrust her hand into the gauntlet, throwing her head back in rapture as power flooded her limbs, hot and urgent. The skin of her arm stretched as muscle tissue grew and swelled, layering upon her bones with grotesque speed.

Yes! Yes! Now the rest and our bargain will be sealed…

Piece by piece, Larana removed Kroeger's armour from its frame, donning each piece without conscious thought. Though designed for a warrior far larger than her, each portion fitted her exactly. Strength poured through her and Larana laughed as her body swelled with terrible power.

As each piece adhered to her body, she felt the armour become more and more part of her, its undulating inner surfaces moulding to her own body, dark tendrils of energy pushing inside her.

Deep within Larana, a tiny voice screamed in warning, but it was lost in the howling gale of powerful change that remoulded her. It shrieked to her of the price to be paid for such abominable gifts, but consumed with hate, Larana pushed it aside.

One last step, Larana. One last bargain to be made. You must give me all, hold nothing back. Your soul must be mine and then we shall be one. We shall become the Avatar of Khorne!

Larana lifted the grinning, skull-masked helm and slowly lowered it over her head.

'Yes,' she hissed. 'Take it all. I am yours…'

And the warning voice within Larana was pushed to the lid of her creaking skull as the Armour of Khorne claimed her.

Her last act as a human being was to scream as for one terrifying instant she realised the scale of the mistake she had just made.

KROEGER WOKE SUDDENLY, a scream dying on his lips as he rose from a dreamless void, terrifying in the oblivion it promised. His breath came in short, dry heaves and it took long seconds before he could remember where he was. Dim light filtered into the dugout from the doorway, and Kroeger was suddenly struck by a sense of something deeply wrong.

He pushed himself to his feet and padded through to the entrance of his dugout. Shadows coiled and his belief that there was something amiss grew to a raging certainty. He reached for his sword, his fury growing as he saw that it was missing. Had the little human bitch taken it? She would pay for such a transgression with her life.

Suddenly Kroeger became aware that he was not alone in the dugout and he turned around slowly. There was a gloom here that was not wholly natural and he squinted, trying to make sense out of what he saw before him. His armour stood where he had left it, but there was something different... It took him several seconds before he realised what.

There was someone wearing it. And they carried his sword.

'Whoever you are, you are dead,' promised Kroeger.

The intruder shook its head. 'No, Kroeger, you are. We grow weary of you, and have no more need of you.'

Kroeger started as he recognised the voice. But it was impossible. It could not be her, not that weak snivelling human.

She would pay for such impudence. He launched himself forward, club-like fists raised to strike her down. The woman swayed aside, slashing the sword across his flank, the blade biting a hand's-breadth into his flesh. Kroeger roared, blood washing in a crimson flood from his body.

Before he could recover, the sword struck again, ripping through his belly and spilling his looping guts to the earthen floor of the dugout. Kroeger dropped to his knees, a pleading look in his eyes. The sword came at him again and he vainly raised his hands to ward off the blows.

The armoured warrior spared him no mercy, hacking him into pieces. First came his hands, then his arms. Kroeger flopped onto his back, amidst his severed limbs and pooling blood as the woman knelt astride him and cast aside the sword.

With deliberate slowness, the warrior removed the helmet and Kroeger coughed thick gobbets of blood as he saw the reborn face of Larana Utorian.

Gone was the terrified woman he had tortured these long weeks, and in its place was a twisted face, devoid of pity or mercy. A face so full of hate that it chilled him to the very core of his being.

She raised her arms high above her head, a dulled bone knife gripped in both hands.

The thing that had once been Larana Utorian plunged the knife through Kroeger's eye socket and into his brain, stabbing again and again until there was nothing left of her tormentor's skull but a pulverised mass of shattered bone and matter.

FORRIX CONSULTED A dust-covered data-slate, checking on the position of the mine, content it was following the correct path. The tunnel had traversed beneath the ditch and he expected to be under the walls within the hour. He stepped over the corpse of a slave and watched the activity on the rockface before him. The drilling rigs could not work this close to the wall for fear of Imperial detection and so gangs of slaves worked with cloth-wrapped picks and shovels to extend the tunnel.

Human soldiers guarded the slaves with barbed cudgels and electro-prods. It was a pleasing irony that these fools were precipitating their own species' downfall.

Satisfied that all was proceeding as planned, Forrix made his way back along the hot tunnel, pushing past teams of cowering slaves. He passed various galleries and blind passages designed to disguise the true direction of their attack from the Imperial sappers.

Iron props supported the roof of the tunnel and sound absorbent mats were laid along its length. Forrix was taking no chances that this tunnel might be discovered, though he knew that the enemy must be aware of the tunnelling operation. There was always the chance the Imperials might discover it through blind luck.

Forrix had prayed they would not and that his successful demolition of a portion of the curtain wall would restore his master's favour.

He had not seen the Warsmith since the destruction of the batteries. The lord of the Iron Warriors had retreated within his pavilion and had allowed only Jharek Kelmaur into his presence. He didn't know whether the Warsmith was aware of Kelmaur's folly, but he fully intended that he would learn of it. The idea of the sorcerer's downfall was only marginally more appealing to him than Honsou's. Why the Warsmith had allowed the half-breed to live after Forrix had told him that it was Honsou's failure that had cost them the guns on Tor Christo was a mystery to him.

Thinking of Honsou brought his anger to the fore again, and he vowed the ungrateful half-breed would pay in blood for his usurping of Forrix in the Warsmith's favour.

Consumed with resentment, Forrix almost didn't hear the noises from the rockface until it was too late. Screams and the crash of stone startled him from his bitter reverie and he threw aside the data-slate as he realised what was happening.

He grabbed the nearest soldier, shouting, 'Go to the surface and send warning. The tunnel is under attack!'

Forrix dropped the terrified soldier, who scrambled away from the giant Terminator and sprinted back along the tunnel in panic. Forrix heard the crack of gunfire and screams echoing through the mine and activated his power fist, the crackling blue arcs of energy throwing the darkness of the tunnel into stark relief.

The rapid firing of automatic weapons grew louder as he strode through the tunnel, combi-bolter at the ready. A group of human soldiers ran towards him, dropping their electro-prods and clubs as they ran in terror from the rockface. Throngs of slaves fled alongside them. Forrix shot them down in a hail of bolts, stepping over their shredded bodies as he fought his way forward.

Ahead, he saw five figures in yellow power armour beneath a hole blasted in the cavern roof, standing in a ring of dead bodies. Two Space Marines were advancing towards him, while the others prepared explosives to bring down the tunnel before it could reach the citadel's wall. Forrix opened fire before they saw him, the sound of his weapon deafening in such a confined space. One Imperial Fist dropped, a series of red craters torn in his breastplate.

Ricochets blew out the glow-globes, sputtering light casting lunatic shadows over the tunnel walls. The second Space Marine dropped into a crouch and returned fire with his bolt pistol. The impacts hammered against Forrix's breastplate, but Terminator armour had been designed for just this kind of close-quarters fighting and not a single bolt could penetrate the thick armour.

Forrix shot again, swinging his power fist. The warrior ducked and rolled aside, Forrix's blow smashing apart an iron prop and pulverising a huge section of wall. Rock and dust filled the air as he rounded on his opponent. The Imperial Fist drew a sword, its blade wreathed in amber fire, but the tunnel was too cramped to wield it effectively.

Forrix batted aside the blade and pistoned his fist through the warrior's chest, smashing his ribcage and ripping out his heart and lungs. He pushed aside the bloody corpse, stepping into the main gallery and spraying the Imperial Fists with bolter fire. One man dropped, blood washing down his thigh as the others dived for cover. Bolter fire blasted the rock around him and pounded his armour.

Somehow a bolt found its way through his shoulder guard and blood started to pour from a wound in his arm. He roared in anger and emptied the remainder of his bolter's magazine into the nearest Imperial Fist, the snap of the hammer dropping on an empty chamber shockingly loud in the cramped tunnel.

Behind him, Forrix could hear the shouts of approaching soldiers. His bolter empty, he pulled back the arming slide on his combi-weapon's other armament fixture.

The last Space Marine rose from his cover and opened fire, hosing Forrix with bullets. Forrix rocked under the impacts, bringing his weapon to bear and fired the underslung melta gun. The white-hot blast of superheated air punched into the Imperial Fist, incinerating his torso with a hissing detonation, the oxygen-rich blood in his body flashing to a stinking red steam.

A pile of armoured limbs and a head – all that remained of the Space Marine – clattered to the floor, the gory stumps cauterised and molten. Forrix dropped his weapon and swept up a fallen bolter as red-clad human soldiers raced to join him from the surface.

Suddenly, Forrix caught the stench of something vile from the opening in the cavern roof and realised he had to get out of here. He turned from the rockface and ran past the startled soldiers without a word. He ran as fast as he could back towards the surface, but as he heard the roaring thunder behind him, he realised he wouldn't make it in time.

Forrix lurched left into one of the deception tunnels. He heard screams from behind him and knew that every soldier down here was a dead man. The roaring grew louder, magnified by the closeness of the walls.

Forrix continued down the side tunnel, ducking round a bend as the first rush of chemicals swept towards him.

A tidal wave of poisoned chemical waste thundered through the tunnels, diverted from every culvert, septic tank, latrine and night-soil pipe in the citadel. Forrix had smelled the reek of the waste and the acrid tang of the bio-toxins. He clung onto the rough walls as the foul, liquid effluent roared through the tunnels, sweeping all before it.

Men were crushed to death against the rocky walls as the vile solution pummelled them, filling the tunnels with excremental fluids. Those not killed by the first tidal wave were drowned or poisoned in the toxic waste as it rose to the ceiling, shorting out the remaining glow-globes and snuffing them out one by one.

Sheltered from the worst of the flood in the side tunnel, Forrix hung on as the grey-brown sludge sloshed around him, rising higher with each second until he was immersed in the thick tide. He knew he was in no danger, his armour was proof against the hard vacuum of space and it had suffered worse fates than this in its long life.

How far up the tunnel the flood of liquid would reach, Forrix had no idea, but guessed it could not be too far. To effectively flood the tunnels, this amount of waste would have had to have been diluted with much of the garrison's drinking water. Perhaps, believing their salvation had arrived in the shape of the Imperial Fists, the defenders thought they could afford to be cavalier with their water supplies.

A few minutes passed before the tunnel began to drain. The Imperials' plan had failed. Forrix had built scores of such mines and had had more lethal substances than toxic waste flooded through many of them. Drainage channels diverted much of the water into specially constructed flood chambers and the natural dryness of the soil absorbed a great deal of moisture. The tunnel would survive, but there would need to be additional props installed to keep it from subsequently collapsing. Such work would need to be carried out by the Iron Warriors, since these toxins would remain lethal for many hundreds of years. But to warriors in power armour, they were irrelevant.

Forrix shook his helmet clear of thick sludgy deposits and waded back through the waste-filled darkness to the main tunnel, knowing what must happen next. Bones crunched beneath his heavy tread as he stepped on drowned corpses. The toxic waste was draining rapidly. As he made his way back to the rockface he checked the action of the bolter, clearing it of obstructions.

Up ahead he could see beams of light stabbing down into the cavern from the hole in the roof and heard the first splash of something heavy drop from above. The darkness of the tunnel was no impairment to Forrix, and he saw an Imperial Fist rise to his feet. The Space Marine moved swiftly through the knee-deep sludge towards the tunnel mouth.

Forrix shot him in the head as more Imperial Fists dropped to the cavern floor, spreading out as the echo of his shot faded. Bullets hammered the rock around him and ricocheted from his armour. He raised the bolter and swept its fire around the cavern, gunning down Space Marines as he backed into the relative safety of the tunnel where the enemy could not bring their superior numbers to bear. If they wanted to kill him, they were going to have to come and dig him out.

Shapes darted across the opening and he fired at each one as it presented itself. Forrix laughed as he killed, spraying the tunnel mouth with bolter fire. Muzzle flashes lit up the stygian darkness as gunfire blasted from the walls of the tunnel. He felt sharp pain in his side and shoulder as more bolts impacted on his armour. As mighty as Terminator armour was, it could still be brought down by sheer volume of fire.

The bolter he carried clicked empty and he dropped it into the effluent, reactivating his power fist as two Imperial Fists rushed him. He killed the first with a mighty punch to the head, and the second with a reverse stroke that tore out his throat.

Another two warriors charged. Forrix roared in battle fury as he felt the blade of a crackling sword rip through his armour, between his ribs and into his primary heart. Angrily he slammed his fist down across the blade, wrenching it from the Space Marine's grip before removing his arm with a backhanded blow. He shoulder charged the other warrior, crushing his helmet against the tunnel wall before disembowelling the armed Space Marine with his power fist.

Gunfire hammered him and he felt the bone shield within his chest cavity crack as a bolter shell exploded within the ceramite plates of his armour. He dropped to his knees as the Imperial Fist closed the gap, firing as he advanced. Forrix tore out the sword protruding from his chest and hacked the warrior's legs out from under him, pitching him face-first into the waste matter.

He pulled himself to his feet as more bullets hammered him. A grenade splashed next to him and he hurled himself back as it detonated. Muffled by the water, the blast threw up a spray of liquid and debris, but its lethal force was spent and he was unharmed.

He rose to his knees as another Imperial Fist charged him. A bolt took Forrix high on the temple, blasting a portion of his helmet clear and blood streamed down his face. Something slammed into his visor, ripping the helmet from his head. He felt his jawbone shatter. Bright lights burst before his eyes and he splashed backwards into the water, gagging as the liquid waste poured into his nose and open mouth.

The toxins seared his eyes and blistered his skin in seconds. He lashed out with his fist, feeling it connect with something solid, and scrambled back, lifting his head from the slime. He spat a froth of viscous matter, retching as his body fought against the toxins he had ingested.

He blinked through the searing pain in his eyes, battling to focus as something came towards him. He punched out blindly, but missed and bellowed in pain as he felt the wide blade of another sword pierce his chest, tear through his lungs and burst through the backplate of his armour.

He gripped the sword blade and kicked out, hearing something splinter and a cry of pain. Blindly, he groped in the swirling, bloody water, feeling something thrashing in front of him. Forrix roared and smashed his power fist down upon the shape, breaking it apart in a flurry of crushing blows. His chest burned with hot agony as his secondary heart and multi-lung fought to keep him alive despite the massive traumas his body had suffered.

He heard more shouts behind him, but he had lost all sense of direction in his blindness. Rescuers or killers?

'Iron within!' he bellowed, raising his power fist, the pain in his chest more intense now.

'Iron without!' came the answering shout and Forrix lowered his arm as the warriors of his company swept past him. He heard echoes of bolter fire and roars of hatred, but they seemed to be growing more and more distant with each passing second.

Forrix tried to climb to his feet, but his strength was gone and he could not move.

A tremendous, deafening explosion shook the tunnel. Rocks fell from above him and orange flames briefly lit up the battle-scarred tunnel walls.

He sagged forward, supporting his broken body on shaking arms.

He heard the victory chant of the Iron Warriors coming from somewhere that seemed impossibly far away.

Only then did Forrix allow his elbows to buckle, collapsing him to the tunnel's floor.

IN THE DAYS following the abortive attack on the Iron Warriors' tunnel system, the morale of the citadel's garrison slumped as it became obvious that nothing they could do would prevent the mine from reaching the walls. Another assault was mounted through the countermine in the Primus Ravelin, but it was repulsed with heavy losses by a strong tunnel guard that never left the mine workings.

Forrix was carried back to his dugout, where he was attended by the Warsmith's Chirumeks. The master of the Iron Warriors made it very clear that their survival was directly linked to that of his war-captain.

While Forrix healed, Honsou volunteered to take over supervision of the mining operations. Kroeger had not emerged from his dugout for days and Honsou wondered what new blood-madness now possessed him. The Imperial Fists had explosively sealed their countermines when it had become obvious that their attacks could not succeed. Once the damage done by the sally had been repaired, the undermining works progressed once more.

Siege tanks now moved up through the saps towards the third parallel, taking their positions in the heavily fortified earthwork. Day and night, trucks laden with shells for these iron behemoths would make the dangerous trip from the campsite, depositing the ordnance in newly constructed and heavily armoured magazines.

Observers watched as embrasures were cut in the earthworks, the soil left in place until such time as the tanks were ready to unleash their firepower against the defenders.

Fresh trenches were dug backwards from the third parallel, equipped with smaller parallels where huge numbers of soldiers could muster, ready to hurl themselves at the walls.

A sense of dread began to permeate the garrison, despite the officers' attempts to raise spirits and boost morale. The sheer scale of the assault soon to be unleashed upon them preyed upon the minds of even the most determined Imperial defenders.

Three days after the attack on the tunnels a terrible rumbling rocked the walls of the citadel, like the beginnings of an earthquake. The ground beneath the fortress heaved upwards and cracks split the roadways throughout the inner walls.

Along the edge of the ditch, a huge wall of fire and smoke leapt upwards as explosives planted there blasted its crest apart, scattering rubble into the ditch and providing a means for infantry to descend into it.

But barely had the dust settled when an explosion of far greater magnitude shook the ground. Wide galleries that ran underneath the curtain wall linking the Destiny Gate and the right flank of the Mori bastion collapsed as vast quantities of ordnance detonated and vaporised huge swathes of the wall's foundations.

The centre section of the great wall groaned as it sagged, the noise swelling as a giant crack split the curtain wall, the sound like a deafening gunshot. Officers shouted at their men to clear the walls, but for many it was already too late as the sixty-metre high wall slid ponderously into the ground, huge chunks of rockcrete shearing away and tumbling into the ditch. Hundreds of men were carried to their deaths and vast clouds of dust billowed skywards.

As more of the wall fell, the speed of its collapse increased exponentially, whole sections of the ramparts toppling into the ditch. The scale of the destruction was incredible and it seemed inconceivable that such a mighty edifice could be so thoroughly annihilated.

By the time the collapse had ceased, almost the entire centre of the wall had been brought down. A great breach some thirty metres wide had been torn in the curtain wall, the rubble from the wall's destruction forming a debris slope that ran from the floor of the ditch to the crest of the breach.

The Iron Warriors had broken open the citadel.

STORM OF IRON

One

As THE GREAT wall came crashing down into the ditch, a swelling roar burst from the thousands of Iron Warriors' human soldiers who went over the top of their trenches and charged the citadel. Despite the pleas from his officers, Leonid stood on the rubble at the crest of the breach, his power sword and bolt pistol drawn. His bronze breastplate shone like new and his uniform was freshly pressed and immaculate. Brother-Captain Eshara stood alongside him, twin swords gripped tightly in his gauntlets.

Leonid felt the fury of the enemy soldiers strike him like a blow and its intensity stunned him.

'They hate us so,' he whispered to himself. 'Why?'

'They are heretics and hate all that is good,' stated Eshara in a voice that brooked no argument. The Space Marine captain swung his arms, loosening his shoulder muscles and rotating his neck.

The guns of Mori bastion opened fire and a second later were joined by those in the Primus Ravelin. Hundreds of soldiers were scythed down in the murderous crossfire, their bodies torn apart in a hail of shells and lasers.

The first wave was almost completely annihilated, but thousands more followed, spilling down into the ditch and swarming across the rubble-strewn ground.

The floor of the ditch heaved upwards, obscuring the attackers in fire and shrapnel, as anti-personnel mines exploded and gouged bloody holes in the charging horde. The ditch became a blood-soaked killing ground as soldiers died in their hundreds, blown apart by mines or shot from the walls. A few hardy souls managed to climb to the top of the ravelin where they were brutally hacked down by Guardsmen with long-bladed poleaxes. The noise of gunfire, screams and the clash of steel on steel echoed from the valley sides as the slaughter continued.

More mines exploded. As some bloodied survivors managed to push themselves through to the rubble slopes of the breach, they found themselves facing a barbed and spiked barricade of twisted girders hurled from above.

The attack floundered at the base of the breach, the ditch carpeted with bodies and blood. In the re-entrant angle of the Mori bastion, where the arrowhead shape of the bastion narrowed before rejoining the main wall, Leonid had placed cannons armed with shells filled with ballbearings, bolts and metal fragments. The first cannon fired, the shell bursting apart as it left the muzzle and spraying lethal fragments in an expanding cone. The remaining cannons fired seconds later and the attackers at the base of the breach were snatched away in the bloody storm, torn to ribbons by the guns' discharge.

Leonid shouted a warning to Major Anders in the Primus Ravelin, as the sheer volume of soldiers flooding the ditch finally managed to sweep around the flanks of the V-shaped outwork. But Piet Anders was ready for them, leading his warriors in a furious counter-charge. Battle was joined within the ravelin as the men of the Jouran Dragoons crashed into the disordered mob of soldiers, chopping them down with swords and bludgeoning them with rifle butts. Major Anders hacked a bloody path through the attackers with his blade, the ensigns bearing his colours fighting to keep up with the officer, killing anyone who came near.

The battle for the walls of the ravelin became fiercer as a giant of a man with a huge axe gained its ramparts. Huge and fat, his reach was long and he killed anyone that stood against him. Enemy soldiers bunched around the man, beginning to fan out along the ramparts in a fighting wedge that would allow yet more warriors to climb to the ramparts.

Leonid watched in desperation as the giant slaughtered the ravelin's defenders until a squad of Imperial Fists on the eastern wall counterattacked. A volley of grenades blasted a hole in the wedge and the squad's sergeant shot the axe-wielding giant dead, blasting his head from his shoulders with his plasma pistol. The defenders rallied and pushed the last of the enemy from the walls. Leonid let out the breath he hadn't realised he was holding.

The carnage below was terrible. The scale of such killing in so short a time was incredible. But despite the death-toll, the soldiers in red kept coming at the walls until every square metre of the ditch was covered in blood or bodies.

'They are brave, I'll give them that,' said Leonid, watching as another enemy soldier was shot dead as he clambered across the barricades below.

'No,' snapped Eshara, raising his voice to be heard over the din of battle. 'They are not brave. Do not ever give voice to such thoughts, Castellan. These traitors are heretics and know nothing of notions such as bravery and honour. They keep coming at our walls to die because they fear the wrath of their masters more than us. Push such thoughts from your mind. You must not allow yourself to identify with this scum in any way, lest you find pity staying your hand and pay with your life for that moment of laxity.'

Leonid nodded and returned his gaze to the massacre below. 'What purpose is served here?' he asked. 'They will never gain a foothold on the walls like this. It is madness.'

'They gain a clearer understanding of our defences, explode our minefields and clog the walls with dead.'

'Why don't the Iron Warriors come, damn them?'

'Do not worry, Castellan, you will get your chance to fight the Iron Warriors, but you may soon regret that wish.'

'Perhaps,' said Leonid, watching as a dozen soldiers managed to survive long enough to traverse the barricades below and begin scrambling up the breach. To either side of him, his platoon waited, rifles aimed in a line down the breach. Leonid swept down his sword and shouted, 'Fire!'

Thirty rifles fired in a perfect volley and the enemy were blasted backwards, flopping like boneless puppets as they cartwheeled down the breach.

For a further three bloody hours the enemy threw themselves at the wall before pulling back at some unheard signal, leaving over two and a half thousand men dead in the ditch. Not a single traitor had managed to climb the breach.

A hoarse cheer followed the traitors back to their lines as the weary Guardsmen hurled enemy corpses from the walls of the ravelin, and orderlies rushed from posterns in the Destiny Gate to carry back the wounded.

'Well, we survived,' said Leonid.

'That was just the beginning,' promised Eshara.

CAPTAIN ESHARA'S WORDS were to prove prophetic, as the soldiers of the Iron Warriors launched another two assaults on the walls. Thousands more died in the nightmare hell of the ditch, shelled to bloody rags, shot or blown apart by mines. On three occasions, the Primus Ravelin almost fell, but Piet Anders and the Space Marines managed to rally the defenders every time and take back the walls just when everything seemed lost.

Flanking fire from the face of the Mori bastion swept the face of the ravelin clear of attackers and as night fell on the first day of the escalade, Leonid guessed that some five thousand enemy soldiers lay dead in the citadel's ditch. The preliminary butcher's bill amongst his own men for today's fighting was estimated to be a hundred and eighty dead, with perhaps twice that seriously wounded. Of these wounded, perhaps a third would not fight again.

The Iron Warriors could afford to suffer such horrendous loss of life without fear, but Leonid could not.

Even if the Jourans could keep up such an impressive kill-ratio, the Iron Warriors would inevitably wear them down. Leonid knew he could not allow this battle to become one of attrition.

Under cover of darkness, he and Eshara descended from the walls, leaving the citadel through the Destiny Gate's postern and making their way to the Primus ravelin. Here they found Major Anders, his face blood and sweat stained, sitting with his men drinking a mug of caffeine.

'You've done well, men,' called Leonid. 'Damn well.'

The soldiers beamed with pride at their commander's words.

'But tomorrow will be just as hard, and I'll need your very best.'

'We won't let you down, sir,' said a soldier from the ramparts above.

Leonid raised his voice and said, 'I know you won't, son. You're doing fine here, and I'm damn proud of you. You've shown these curs what it means to take on the 383rd!'

The soldiers cheered as Leonid turned to Piet Anders and shook his hand.

'Nice work, Piet, but watch your left flank,' he cautioned. 'With the breach on that side, we can't bring enough guns to bear and more of the enemy are getting around it.'

Anders saluted. 'Aye, sir, I'll keep an eye out.'

Leonid nodded, confident in his officer's ability to hold the ravelin. He returned Anders' salute before he and Eshara returned to the citadel.

They visited Vincare bastion, the curtain wall, the breach and Mori bastion, heaping praise on the soldiers and exhorting them with tales of valour from the other sections of the citadel. Each body of men vowed to outdo the others, and by the time Leonid returned to his temporary billet in the gate towers he was exhausted and a little light headed from the amount of amasec his men had forced upon him.

He lay down on his simple pallet bed and fell into a dreamless sleep.

* * *

Two

JHAREK KELMAUR CLIMBED the blasted mountain of Tor Christo, picking his way confidently across the rubble, despite the darkness. His head scanned from side to side, as though searching for something, while a red-robed figure followed behind him, hands clasped beneath its robes and head bowed. The robed figure's physique was swollen and disproportionate, with broad shoulders, grossly misshapen arms and a barrel chest.

The sorcerer crested a ridge of jagged rock and scanned the ground before him. His tattooed skull bobbed as he hunted for something within the wreckage of the mountain. Something that, for now, eluded him.

'It should be here,' he muttered to himself, withdrawing a tattered scroll, its gold lettering faded and almost illegible. His frustration was growing and he knew he did not have much time left. His vision had promised him a hidden chamber beneath the rock of Tor Christo, so where was it? He descended into a huge crater of loose stone and scarred rock, his footing sure even through the black night and rough ground.

His silent companion dutifully followed him, its footsteps surprisingly heavy for a being of such mass.

The moonlight pooled around the curious pair, bathing them in vermilion light. Kelmaur circled the crater with increasing desperation. Behind him, the robed figure stopped abruptly and lifted its head to stare directly towards a huge slab of rock, toppled from the mountain and lying flush with the blasted rockface.

Without any word to Kelmaur, the figure strode across the crater towards the rock, halting ten metres from the slab.

Jharek Kelmaur smiled.

'You sense it, don't you?' he whispered and watched as the figure unclasped its arms and extended them towards the slab. The fabric of its robe rippled, as though some monstrous motion disturbed it, and something black and glossy extended from the ends of the sleeves.

The crater was suddenly bathed in light as twin beams of incandescent fire shot from the figure's arms and the rock exploded into fragments. As the dust dissipated, Kelmaur rejoiced at the sight of an ancient, verdigris-stained bronze gate. Again the searing beams stabbed out and the gate exploded into molten chunks, revealing a darkened passageway that led deep into the mountain.

Kelmaur felt his heart race in excitement. Here, he would walk passages that had not known the tread of man for ten thousand years. The robed figure clasped its arms once more and set off towards the revealed passage. Kelmaur followed and the pair made their way through the remains of the gate and into the mountain.

Neither Kelmaur nor his fellow traveller required light to see. The sorcerer marvelled at the precise, geomantic precision of the tunnel as it descended for hundreds of metres into the rock of Tor Christo.

Eventually, the tunnel emerged into a wide, domed chamber, lit by a diffuse glow that radiated from the walls. The floor was a broad disc of solid bronze, almost thirty metres in diameter, with an intricately designed pattern etched onto it. It was familiar to Kelmaur, but he could not remember why. Reluctantly, he tore his senses away from its beguiling pattern.

His wordless companion moved to the chamber's centre, reaching up with glistening, black hands that seemed just a little too large, and pulled back the hood of its robes.

Beneath was a face that had once been human, but was now disfigured beyond all recognition. Adept Etolph Cycerin's face was alive with crawling bio-organic circuitry. Even the augmentations grafted on by the Adeptus Mechanicus had transformed, their mechanical structure hideously altered by the techno-virus. Cycerin turned expectantly to face Kelmaur and raised his other arm, the flesh of the limb running, liquefying and transforming from the shape of a weapon into a hand. The hand pointed at Kelmaur and the sorcerer frowned at such impatience.

Had the transformation obliterated any sense of awe or reverence Cycerin once had?

Kelmaur removed the tattered scroll once more and unravelled it, clearing his throat before chanting a series of guttural and clicking harmonics in a language that had not been spoken in ten millennia. The chant consisted of syllables no human mouth was ever meant to give voice to, sliding between the air, pulling its fragile structure further and further apart.

Whipcord arcs of purple lightning flickered around the circumference of the bronze disc, growing in brightness as Kelmaur's chant continued. The air in the chamber grew dense, like the heavy overpressure before a thunderstorm, and the actinic tang of ozone set his teeth on edge.

The chant neared its end, the lightning arcs whipping upwards and joining in a tensing web of magenta that spun faster and faster around the disc's perimeter.

As the last syllable passed Kelmaur's lips, crackling, whirling lightning exploded, flaring outwards with a powerful coronal discharge. The sorcerer was hurled from his feet and slammed into the cavern wall, slumping to the floor in a bruised pile.

Dazed and in great pain, Kelmaur raised his head and smiled.

The creature he had created from Adept Cycerin had vanished.

A BLAZE OF light flared in the centre of the glowing disc, a dancing crackle of energy swirling around the chamber as the pulsing afterimages slowly faded. Adept Cycerin turned his head left and right, orientating himself with the location he had been transported to. The scent of Jouran incense filled the air, and his altered eyes precisely mapped out the exact trigonometric properties of the chamber he found himself in.

He wondered if he had set foot here in his previous life, but could not remember. He could only remember the imperatives that thundered in his brain, firing along strange, new inorganic dendrites infesting his skull.

The chamber stretched high above him, black and studded with reliquaries. He stood on a floor of bronze, on a disc identical to the one he had just left. Two tonsured priests hurried towards him, their faces lined with frantic worry.

The priests stopped at the edge of the disc and shouted at him, the words were unintelligible; part of his previous existence. He could only converse in the machine language of the techno-virus now and the priests' banal, limited form of verbal communication was utterly inimical to him.

He raised his arms, the black surface of his limbs writhing as the virus within him moulded his machine-flesh into a new form. Metallic barrels and hissing muzzles formed from the engorged substance of his arms and Cycerin opened fire with his biomechanical weaponry, blasting the two priests from their feet in a storm of shells.

Dozens of urns in the lower levels of the Ossuary shattered, spreading the bones of former castellans across the floor. Skulls grinned up at Cycerin as he passed, making his way to the Sepulchre's exit.

At the door to the outer chambers, he stopped, lowered his arms and waited.

JHAREK KELMAUR PICKED his way painfully down the rocky slopes, pleased that he had answered the potential of his vision. He did not know what part Adept Cycerin had yet to play in the unfolding drama on Hydra Cordatus, but was satisfied that he had been instrumental in its fulfilment.

As soon as Cycerin had vanished, the pattern etched in the bronze disc in the floor had begun to fade along with the glow in the walls, until any hint that either had existed was gone. The scroll had crumbled to dust and, with it, any means of using the ancient device again. Kelmaur knew it didn't matter: Cycerin was where he needed to be and his involvement with him was over.

He groaned. The expenditure of so much power had left him drained and his bones hurt where Cycerin's explosive teleportation had thrown him against the chamber wall. His 'near-sense' was weakened and he stumbled several times, losing his footing on the slippery rocks and loose rubble.

As he reached the bottom of the slope he straightened his cloak and set off towards his tent, his strides becoming more confident as he found himself among more familiar surroundings.

Acolytes bowed as he passed, but he ignored them, too intent on rest and recuperation. As he ducked below the low entrance to his abode, painful cramps seized his stomach. Immediately he sensed the Warsmith's presence.

'You were successful,' said the Warsmith. It was a statement, not a question.

Kelmaur bowed extravagantly.

'Yes, my lord. The servant of the machine with but one hand has gone. The secret chamber was below the mountain, just as I had foreseen.'

'Good,' hissed the Warsmith, raising himself up to tower over Kelmaur. The sorcerer turned his head away, unable to look directly at the roiling metamorphosis of the Warsmith's face. The lord of the Iron Warriors reached up and cupped Kelmaur's chin in one massive gauntlet.

Kelmaur gasped in pain at the Warsmith's searing touch, squirming against his grip as black discolouration spread from where his master held him. The tattoos on his skull danced as Kelmaur cried out, his face contorted in agony.

'Now, Jharek, is there anything you wish to tell me? Anything you have kept from your Warsmith?'

Kelmaur shook his head. 'No, my lord!' he wheezed. 'I swear I have told you true every vision I have had.'

'Is that true?' asked the Warsmith, his disbelief plain. No answer was forthcoming and he sighed in feigned regret.

The Warsmith said, 'You achieve nothing by lying to me, Jharek,' and reached out his hand, pressing a burning palm against the sorcerer's temple.

Kelmaur screamed in agony as his flesh hissed and melted, filling the tent with the sickening stench of burned meat.

'You have one chance to live, Jharek,' promised the Warsmith. 'Tell me anything else you have kept from me and I will not kill you.'

'Nothing!' gasped Kelmaur. 'I have kept nothing from you, my lord, I swear! I see nothing more than that which I have told you!'

The Warsmith said, 'Then you are of no more use to me,' and exhaled a foetid breath of dazzling orange and green.

Kelmaur, already hyperventilating in fear, took a huge breath of the Warsmith's corrupt substance and began convulsing.

Kelmaur burned with horrific change and his screams were music to the Warsmith's ears. Evolutionary anarchy ripped through the sorcerer's frame. Kelmaur's body spasmed, grotesque changes warping through his flesh in a tornado of mutation. Tentacles, pincers, wings and other more unnameable organs burst from every part of his rebellious anatomy; his body now unrecognisable as human in the soup of aberrant growths.

Within seconds, all that remained of the sorcerer was a seething pile of pulped meat and bone, too grossly misshapen to survive.

'I promised I would not kill you, did I not?' sneered the Warsmith, turning and leaving the hideously mutated body of Jharek Kelmaur hissing in mindless torpor on the floor of his tent.

Amongst the gibbering ruin of distorted flesh, a single unblinking human eye stared out in horror and incipient madness.

Three

THE ATTACKS ON the walls continued for another three days, with thousands of men throwing themselves at the citadel and dying in droves. Casualties amongst the Jourans were lighter than on the first day, the weakest men having fallen in the early assaults.

On the third day, at the height of the attack, the embrasures were removed from the earthwork that ran the length of the third parallel and in a jet of exhaust fumes one hundred and thirteen Vindicator siege tanks moved into position and opened fire with an ear-splitting crack.

The walls of the citadel and bastions disappeared in a rolling bank of grey smoke and fire. Before the echoes had begun to fade, a second volley of shots battered the walls. Soldiers from both forces were pulverised in the massive barrage as shell after shell hammered the walls and breach.

Whole swathes of unstable structure tore free from the breach, hundreds of tonnes of rubble crashing downwards, carrying scores of men to their deaths and burying yet more beneath the falling blocks.

The bombardment continued for two punishing hours, undoing the repair work undertaken by the Imperial Fists and the Jourans to the ramparts. Hundreds died before they were able to take shelter in the bombproof shelters and the screams of the wounded carried as far back as the statue-lined road that led towards the Sepulchre. The face of the Mori bastion crumbled under the onslaught, tonnes of shat-tered masonry crashing into the ditch and forming a steep, but practicable breach. But by this time, there was no one left alive in the ditch to exploit it.

Broken by the twin blows of the stubborn defence of the Jourans and the betrayal of their masters, the Iron Warriors' soldiery turned and fell back from the walls in disarray.

As the bloodied survivors of the attack stumbled away from the citadel, shell-shocked and insane with terror, they broke and swirled around a giant figure in iron-black armour. A clear space surrounded the giant, who stood as still as a statue amongst the fleeing soldiers of his army.

The Warsmith marched through the mob, the soldiers parting before the bow-wave of corruption that travelled before him. He carried an arrow-headed icon bearing the skull-masked symbol of the Iron Warriors, which he planted in the blood-soaked earth at the edge of the ditch.

Leonid lowered his bloody power sword and watched the giant figure with a terrible sense of foreboding. Who this warrior was, he had no idea, but, instinctively, he feared him.

He turned to Corwin. The Space Marine Librarian's armour was scored with dozens of lasblasts, and blood ran from a gash torn in his upper arm.

'He is their Warsmith, the leader of this army,' said Corwin.

The Warsmith was well within weapons range, yet not one amongst the garrison could raise his gun to open fire.

They watched as the Warsmith pointed to the icon and then towards the fortress. Then he lifted an enormous axe from a shoulder scabbard and, in a rasping voice that carried the weight of ages said, 'You have until tomorrow morning to satisfy your honour and fall upon your swords. After that, your souls belong to me and I promise I will send every man alive within these walls to hell.'

The enemy commander's voice should not have been able to carry across the walls, but every soldier of the Jourans felt the terror of the Warsmith's words lodge like a splinter in his heart.

Leonid watched the Chaos warlord turn and march back through the earthworks, the lingering nausea in his gut fading to a dull ache as the Warsmith vanished from sight.

NIGHT WAS FALLING as the Warsmith's champions gathered beneath his intricate pavilion. They knelt before the master of the Iron Warriors, in awe at the changes rippling through his form. Honsou watched as a darkening shadow ghosted behind the Warsmith's body, rippling the air with its passing, like mighty wings beating the air, or at least the *suggestion* of wings. The roiling souls spinning within his armour were silent, their cries drowned out by the unheard crescendo of change writhing within the Warsmith.

'A time of great moment is upon us, my champions,' began the Warsmith.

He turned his gaze towards the hazily lit silhouette of the citadel, barely visible over the lip of the earthwork. Flashes of artillery fire lit the sky as Imperial mortars dropped shells on the Iron Warriors' camp, but it was undirected; and the vehicles and troops were protected from all but direct hits in their reinforced bunkers.

'The future is becoming less tangled now, its paths unravelling and revealing their ultimate destinations to me. It is a wonderful thing to see and to know that Perturabo chose the right path. To see the enemy's palaces in ruins, to see his warriors hung, broken and defeated from stakes lining the roadways from here to the gates of Terra vindicates everything we have done. I have seen this and more, victories and slaughters magnificent in their scale. It is pleasing, and the poor fools we must destroy will not accept this. Like most mortals, the true majesty of Chaos turns them into frightened children. Such limited understanding and vision is to blame for what their Emperor has brought them to.'

Honsou felt his pulse rising in time with the cadence of the Warsmith's voice. Each word dripped with potential. The battle here was almost at an end and the Warsmith was promising them victory. The human soldiers had fulfilled their appointed task and now the honour of taking the citadel would fall to the Iron Warriors. It would be soon; the Warsmith would not, could not, wait any longer.

Any fool could see that.

Even the faintly disturbing presence of Kroeger beside him could not dampen his enthusiasm for the coming fight. Kroeger had not spoken a single word to anyone for several days and while normally Honsou would have been grateful for such a reprieve, his suspicions were aroused. Though he could not see his face beneath his helmet, Honsou's warrior's eye could tell that there was something different about Kroeger. He moved with a confident, easy grace, rather than the bullish swagger he usually affected, more like a fighter than of a simple butcher and Honsou did not like the change one bit.

He glanced over at Forrix, the ancient veteran shifting painfully under the weight of his new bionics. The Chirumeks had worked wonders to reconstruct his body in so short a time, and daemonic sorceries had brought his life back from the brink of the void.

The Warsmith approached them again and Honsou steeled himself for the aching cramps and nausea.

'I now know the truth of the universe,' began the Warsmith. 'Only Chaos endures. The web of action and reaction, cause and effect that has brought us to Hydra Cordatus began many thousands of years ago, though in this universe nothing ever really begins or ends.'

The Warsmith turned and spread his arms before him, encompassing the extent of the citadel.

'Towards the end of the Great Crusade I helped build this citadel, working shoulder to shoulder with the great Perturabo himself. We raised its magnificence towards the heavens for the glory of the Emperor. But Perturabo knew, even then, that the Emperor would one day betray us, and fashioned it with great cunning. What I created, you will now put asunder.'

Honsou was amazed. The Warsmith had built the citadel? Now he began to understand the true genius behind its construction. Had this been any other fortress, it would have fallen much sooner. The finest siege engineers of the day had built it and it would take the finest warriors to tear it down.

'Billions upon billions of potential consequences spread out from the here and the now and each is capable of being massively shaped by the tiniest action,' continued the Warsmith. 'Each of you will play a part in that future and you will not fail me. You will not fail me or you will die, by my hand or the enemy's, it matters not. Some of you will die, and some of you have died already.'

Honsou's brow wrinkled as he pondered the Warsmith's words. Was he going to tell them the outcome of tomorrow's battle? As though hearing his thoughts the Warsmith answered Honsou directly.

'Only the Great Conspirator himself knows the infinite possibilities the future can bring, but I have seen tantalising glimpses of the shape of things to come. The myriad complexities of alternate histories yet to be written lie open to my sight.'

The Warsmith stood before each of his champions and bade them stand with a curt gesture.

'Honsou, you have proven yourself to be a worthy leader and though your blood is polluted beyond redemption with the seed of the very enemy we face, you are a true son of Chaos and I see worlds that will yet burn in your name. Your life hangs by the most slender of threads and it is probable you will die tomorrow. If it is to be so, die well.

'Forrix, I have fought beside you many times and we have shed the blood of millions together. Whole sectors cursed our names, and legions of the dead await to walk with you on the road to hell. You will be a legend amongst the Iron Warriors.

'Kroeger... Kroeger, for you I see nothing beyond the slaughter of these walls. You will go places I shall never see, but I do not know whose is the greater loss.'

Honsou could not understand all the Warsmith's words, but knew there was great significance in every one. He had barely heard the words directed at the other captains, so intent was he on fathoming the meaning of those directed at him. Was he to die tomorrow? Would he yet live to make more worlds of the False Emperor bleed?

Such concerns were beyond his ability to comprehend; yet he felt a terrible vindication as he received the Warsmith's acceptance.

HIS FOOTSTEPS WERE loud against the smooth stone steps, but Magos Naicin knew there was no one to hear them. Even had there been, he could easily have explained away his presence here.

The dark tower was a black spear against a garnet sky and Naicin rubbed a gloved hand against the metal of his bronze mask, feeling its edge chafe against the tissue beneath. It would be pleasing to finally be rid of the augmentations enforced by his role and feel air against his true flesh again.

Naicin felt a thrill of anticipation course through his body at the thought of the task before him. Until now his greatest challenge had been to mislead and confuse an already disorientated, barely-human machine priest who grew easier to influence with each passing day. Since the day he had replaced the real Naicin, nearly a century ago on Nixaur Secundus, the threat of discovery had been negligible, and it was a testament to how blindly the dogmatic machine priests could be manipulated and fooled.

All it required was the correct symbols, a few ritualistic lines of doggerel and they would believe you were one of their own. It was galling to think that an organisation that could be so easily deceived was one of the foundations the cursed Imperium rested upon. The sooner his master destroyed it the better. United under the yoke of Chaos, humanity would be the stronger for its absence.

Naicin reached the top of the slope and looked back upon the wasteland of Hydra Cordatus. The Iron Warriors' attack would come with the dawn, and a storm of iron would engulf the citadel, against whose wrath none could stand. The men struggling on the walls below were fighting bravely, but he wondered if they would fight as hard knowing the truth of what had happened to this world, why it was such a desolate wilderness. Or, indeed, what was happening to their own bodies even now.

He raised his eyes to the opposite flank of the valley, wondering again where the body of that troublesome soldier Hawke lay. His survival had almost alerted Leonid to the truth of how the Adeptus Mechanicus had deceived them all, but Naicin had briefed his underlings well and the colonel had emerged from the Biologis infirmary none the wiser.

He strode towards the doors of the Sepulchre, sputtering torches guttering in their sconces either side of the portal, and pulled them open, smelling the distinctive tang of blood and death the instant he opened the door. This place was a tomb, and thus he was not surprised at the latter stench, but the former was a newcomer to the Sepulchre.

Naicin stepped into the well-lit outer chambers, marvelling at the images on the stained glass windows above him.

Depicting anonymous Space Marines in battle, the utter ruthlessness they displayed was out of all proportion to their enemies; the savagery frightening in its intensity. No loyalist Space Marines these, but a tangible warning of how easy it was for even those raised above all others to fall from grace.

The irony of the windows' subject matter was not lost on Naicin, given that he knew the truth of this place and the true identity of its architects, but he was not here to admire the aesthetics of the Sepulchre, he had a more vital errand.

Thin slivers of red light were making their way across the floor as night released its grip on the valley and the dawn of the Iron Warriors began. It was time.

Gripping the handles of the Ossuary's door, Naicin took a moment to savour the significance of this moment, etching the sensations of each second on his memory before pulling wide the inner doors.

A tall, weirdly baroque leviathan stood on the other side, thick, cable-like arms hanging by its side and clad in robes that rippled with barely concealed motion. Naicin could see the face of the corrupted Adept Cycerin below its hood, the skin of his face alive with writhing mecha-organic circuitry as it wove into new and more evolved patterns in his subcutaneous layer. The colour had drained from Cycerin's face and his skin was a flat, metallic white with crawling mercurial veins. A terrible power radiated from the former machine priest and Naicin felt a suffocating fear rise in his chest at the monstrous creature before him. He stepped back in awe.

Cycerin's arms raised, fluidly morphing into wide barrelled, biomechanical weapons as his eyes tracked Naicin's movements. For a second, Naicin was sure Cycerin was about to destroy him, but some unknown algorithm in the adept's altered brain must have identified that he was not a threat, and the weapon arms lowered.

Naicin gulped away his fear and indicated the doors that led down the mountainside towards the citadel.

He said, 'Adept Cycerin, I have come to take you home.'

Four

DAWN WAS AN hour old as Honsou watched spears of light break over the top of the earthworks. His sense of urgency mounted with the sun as the red sunlight spilled over the valley, throwing the shadow of the citadel out across the ditch and making his gunmetal armour shine like bloodstained silver. An artillery duel was underway between the Imperial gunners and the siege tanks of the Iron Warriors, throwing up plumes of earth and smoke. It was an unequal struggle as the siege tanks methodically dismounted the citadel's guns one by one.

Honsou crouched with his warriors behind the siege tanks. The noise was phenomenal and the ground shook with the violence of their firing. In moments he would unleash his warriors over the earthworks and attack the Primus Ravelin, capturing the outwork and preventing its guns from flanking warriors from Forrix and Kroeger's companies to his right. Forrix had been granted the honour of attacking the breach in the curtain wall, while Kroeger and his berserkers were poised to storm the tear blasted in the Mori bastion. But both attacks would surely founder without the fall of the ravelin.

Once the ravelin had fallen, he was to lead his men across the ditch and follow Forrix through the breach. After that, any strategy or plan was irrelevant as the soldiers who had fought through the hell of a storming would be so blood-maddened that almost nothing could stop a rampage of colossal proportions. Honsou looked forward to it.

Forrix and his men gathered in the approach trench that zigzagged its way back from the third parallel, and Honsou could see the veteran captain was becoming more used to his mechanised body with each step. At the far end of the parallel, Kroeger stood motionless before the firing step of the earthwork, staring intently towards the breach he would soon be attacking. Normally Kroeger would be strutting up and down the length of the parallel, boasting of his prowess and heaping scorn upon Honsou, but there was nothing now, merely a sinister silence.

Honsou had approached Kroeger as dawn had broken, sensing the change that had overtaken his nemesis more clearly than ever.

'The Warsmith honours you, Kroeger,' he had said, but Kroeger had not answered him, nor even acknowledged his presence.

'Kroeger?' repeated Honsou, reaching up to grip the edge of Kroeger's shoulder guard.

As soon as Honsou's hand touched the metal of the armour, Kroeger's hand shot up and gripped his wrist, wrenching it away and pushing him back. Honsou snarled, drawing his sword partway from its scabbard, but Kroeger turned, and Honsou was seized by a dire premonition that to attack Kroeger would be to die. A pale nimbus of light played around Kroeger's helmet and, though he couldn't be sure, Honsou thought he could see that same light seeping through the visor of Kroeger's helm. The light carried hints of an ancient malevolence and Honsou had slowly sheathed his sword, turning on his heel and returning to his company.

He shook his head free of the memory, shifting his weight from foot to foot, impatient for the attack to begin. The boom of the Vindicators suddenly ceased and, with a huge revving roar, the siege tanks pulled back from the earthworks. This was the signal he had been waiting for. Honsou rose to his feet, raising his pistol and sword high above him.

'Death to the False Emperor!' he roared and sprinted through the embrasure in the earthwork. He scrambled down its blasted front, his warriors following him through this and other gaps fashioned in the earthwork.

The rubble slope of the ditch was less than ten metres away and Honsou ran towards it as the crack of small arms fire snapped from the crumbling ramparts of the curtain wall and the flanks of both bastions. Shots slashed through the air beside him, bright streamers of las-fire plucking at his armour or vaporising nearby patches of earth. A roar of hate built in Honsou's throat as he slid down the rocky slope into the ditch.

A sea of red bodies, already beginning to rot in the heat, carpeted the trench. He charged across the multitude of corpses, crushing bones and pulverising soft, decaying tissue underfoot as yet more fire was directed at them. The soldiers on the Primus Ravelin had fought hard these last few days, but they had faced only the chaff of the Iron Warriors' army. Now they would fight the best.

Heavier blasts of las-fire speared from the ramparts, blasting craters in the floor of the ditch and tossing severed limbs and gas-bloated corpses high into the air. But Honsou could see the inferior quality of the Imperial soldiers was telling now as the majority of their shots flew high. Without a huge mass of targets to aim at, their shooting was woefully inaccurate and barely a handful of Iron Warriors had fallen.

Honsou reached the blasted foot of the ravelin, its once-smooth face now cracked, broken and easily climbed. He fired at the top of the ravelin and began scrambling his way up the slope. A shot struck the top of his shoulder guard, but he ignored the impact and kept climbing.

Withering hails of bullets and las-bolts from the flank of the Mori bastion hammered the walls of the ravelin. He heard a roar of warriors unleashed far to his right and knew that Forrix and Kroeger were beginning their attack.

Dozens of warriors were clambering up the slopes of the ravelin amid the explosion of grenades and constant snap of lasgun fire. The Iron Warrior beside him lost his grip as a shell burst above him, tearing his head off in a fountain of blood. His heavy corpse smashed half a dozen warriors from the wall as he fell.

Honsou shook his helmet clear of blood, punching his fist deep into the wall and gripping onto a reinforcement bar as he saw a cluster of grenades slither down the wall towards him. He pressed his body flat against the wall as they detonated, blowing clear a chunk of grey rockcrete. Torn ligaments in his arms shrieked as the force of the blast lifted him from the wall, but his grip on the rebar held him firm.

Red runes winked into life on his visor, and he felt blood flowing along his limbs, but he pushed upwards, dragging himself up the wall.

The slope grew less steep as he climbed, reaching the broken sections of the wall pulverised by the siege tanks. Gunfire from below slackened as the Iron Warriors firing at the parapet now holstered their weapons and began climbing.

A face appeared above Honsou. He put a bolt through it and carried on upwards. He risked a glance behind him. Perhaps a dozen Iron Warriors were dead and they had yet to clear the ramparts. Honsou turned in time to see an Imperial Fist swing the crackling edge of a power sword towards his head. He threw himself flat against the wall, feeling the sword blade hack a portion of his shoulder guard away. He rolled as the sword swung again, cutting through the rockcrete and sliding free in a shower of orange sparks as it struck an embedded reinforcement bar.

Honsou dragged his own sword from its scabbard and rolled as he saw the Imperial Fist on the rampart draw back his sword for another strike. Honsou lunged, spearing his foe through the chest with his sword. He hurled himself over the parapet, barrelling into a group of Guardsmen rushing to plug the gap in the walls and landing in a tangle of limbs.

Honsou battered his elbows downward, hearing screams, feeling bones break and skulls cracking open.

He rolled to his knees, slashing low with his sword at a charging Imperial Fist, hacking his legs out from under him. Honsou reversed the grip on his sword and hammered the blade through the Space Marine's helm, dragging it free in time to block the swing of another sword, this time swung by an Imperial officer with a major's star on his chest.

Honsou blocked a clumsy thrust and kicked the man in the groin, shattering his pelvis and dropping him screaming to the ground.

'Iron Warriors to me!' he bellowed, clearing a space around him with wide sweeps of his sword. Bullets and las-bolts ricocheted from his armour.

Another two Iron Warriors climbed over the lip of the parapet, forming a wedge with Honsou at its point. Together, the Iron Warriors hacked a path through the Imperial Guardsmen, splashing their silver armour with blood.

An Imperial Fist sergeant saw the danger and charged towards Honsou, firing his plasma pistol as he ran. Honsou swayed aside, the beam streaking past him and punching through the helmet of an Iron Warrior as he pulled himself over the parapet.

Honsou gripped his sword two-handed and charged to meet the Space Marine, diving forward and rolling beneath the swing of his opponent's blade. He rose to his feet and cut high, decapitating the Space Marine in a single blow.

Perhaps a dozen Iron Warriors had gained the ramparts and more were flooding the walls as Honsou's wedge pushed further into the ravelin, pushing the enemy back before them. Honsou yelled in triumph as his men spread out along the walls, killing everything in their path. The Guardsmen fell back in the face of such savagery and the ramparts were his. The enemy retreat was practically a rout, a few Imperial Fists all that held it from collapsing completely.

Honsou leapt from the ramparts as he saw a reserve of Guardsmen with heavy weapons, commanded by a junior officer, lying in wait in the centre of the ravelin. He hit the ground and rolled, watching the officer gauging the correct moment to fire.

The officer's sword swept down and heavy weapon fire raked the inner faces of the ravelin, pitching four Iron Warriors from the walls. Bolter fire answered them and a handful of men fell, clutching gaping wounds in their bodies.

The crescendo of guns and screaming soldiers was powerful in its intensity as battle was joined across the walls and bastions. Smoke billowed from fires set by shell impacts and gunfire that had ignited the uniforms of the fallen.

More bolter shots tore amongst the Guardsmen as the officer swept his sword down again, but it was too late. Honsou was amongst them, hacking and killing with frenzied abandon. Blood spurted, limbs were severed and entrails spilled as he tore the beating heart from the defence.

Dozens more Iron Warriors were spilling into the ravelin itself. Yellow armoured Space Marines were like tiny islands of stubborn resistance, but Honsou could see they would soon be overwhelmed.

Ahead he could see the massive golden gate of the citadel, flanked by two high towers and topped with battered gun turrets. Without siege tanks it was inviolable, but to the right of the gate was the great breach and Honsou could see fierce fighting raging at its top.

'Iron Warriors, rally to me!' roared Honsou, bellowing to be heard over the din of battle. Raising his bloody sword, he set off at a run towards the breach.

The Primus Ravelin had fallen.

'FORWARD!' SCREAMED FORRIX from below the crest of the breach, his power glove crackling with deadly power. They were so close he could taste victory. His armour was dented and torn open, but he felt nothing, the arcane mechanics of his newly augmented body impervious to pain. He felt another impact against his chest and laughed insanely as the bolt exploded against his breastplate, the shell fragments scoring shallow gashes in his helmet.

The breach was wreathed in the smoke and confusion of battle. Bodies lay strewn about, both friends and foes. Three times they had taken the crest of the breach and three times they had been hurled back by Dorn's lapdogs.

He clambered up, pulling himself forward in great powered strides.

Then he was hurled backwards as a buried mine exploded beneath him, the ground rearing upwards in a pillar of smoke and fire. A chunk of rock smashed into his newly repaired helmet and shattered the visor, cracking it too badly to see through. Forrix rolled a few metres down the breach, before sliding to a halt in the loose rock.

Angrily, he pushed himself to his feet and wrenched off his ruined helmet, hurling it into the smoke above him. He could see dim shapes ahead and opened up with his combibolter, spraying the breach with fire. One figure dropped, but the others swung their weapons to bear at him.

A blast of gunfire ripped into the hazy figures, deadly fire from a reaper autocannon that swept them away in a hail of shells. Forrix glanced around him, seeing that his company had suffered fearsome losses to get this far. It would all be for nothing if they should fail now. Iron Warriors climbed past him towards the top of the breach.

He heard a great roar of victory from below and knew that the half-breed had succeeded in capturing the ravelin. But how Kroeger's attack on the eastern bastion was faring, he had no idea. He snarled and resumed his climb, shooting blindly into the smoke above him. Nearly twenty Iron Warriors in Terminator armour climbed with him, firing their weapons into the breach.

Las-bolts and bullets spat from the nubs of wall to either side of him, but Forrix ignored them. The breach was all that mattered.

His powerful strides had almost taken him to the top of the breach when a deafening roar erupted from beyond the crest and the rocks before him exploded, huge chunks of rockcrete blasted to powder by shell impacts. Six Iron Warriors were obliterated in a single, devastating volley as a searing energy beam vaporised another's upper body, leaving his legs standing for a second before they toppled back down the rubble slope. Forrix dropped and crawled towards the edge of the breach, lifting his helmetless head over the rocks.

The beast of legend was before him, not just one, but two of the agile Scout Titans darted back and forth in the gap between the citadel's inner and outer walls. Constantly in motion, the Warhounds loped back and forth like caged beasts, pausing every now and again to spray the breach with murderous fire from their Vulcan bolters.

Forrix's heart sank.

While the Warhounds covered the breach, there was almost no way they could cross it.

THE THING THAT had once been a determined lieutenant in the Jouran 383rd, but was now something infinitely older and more malevolent, pushed its way forwards over the jagged steel and rockcrete of the Mori bastion's breach. The Avatar of Khorne roared in primal lust as it drank deep from the well of hatred supplied by Larana Utorian.

Hatred of the Guard for shelling her.

Hatred of Kroeger for driving her to this.

Hatred of the Emperor for allowing this to happen.

Larana Utorian now had hatred carved upon her heart.

The warriors of Kroeger's company followed the thing they believed to be their leader, fighting their way through the hell of gunfire and explosions, in awe of the ferocity and sheer good fortune he displayed.

Bullets seemed to float around him, lasers passed through him and explosions that should have ripped him in two pattered like rain against his pristine armour. Where they struggled up the steep slope, their leader ascended as effortlessly as if he walked on level ground. The distance between the Avatar and the Iron Warriors widened as it powered ahead to the top in easy, loping strides.

As the Avatar leapt to the top of the breach, its sword sang out in dizzyingly beautiful traceries, and wherever it struck, an enemy died. The Iron Warriors were still some distance behind, and soon Imperial Fists surrounded the Avatar, their swords bright and deadly.

The Avatar cared not. It welcomed this. It needed it. It vaulted over the heads of the lead warriors, decapitating two before it landed behind the others. It kicked out, snapping a warrior's spine and clove another in half with a two-handed sweep. Imperial Fists and Guardsmen clamoured around it, but none could land a blow.

The Avatar pistoned its fist through the skull of a screaming soldier, gripping his uniform jacket and hauling him upwards to allow the jetting spray of blood to drench its gleaming armour. The blood hissed as it landed, seeping within the armour with a monstrous suckling noise.

Yet more foes closed in, and each died at the hands of the Blood God's Avatar.

A rippling haze formed around the Avatar, its form bulging as though unable to contain its sheer vitality. A booming laugh, redolent with the malice of ages echoed across the Mori bastion, and the Imperial defenders quailed before such evil.

The Iron Warriors finally clambered over the lip of the breach, spreading out from behind the Avatar, drawing their weapons and hurling themselves into the fight.

The Avatar watched it all, feeling the waves of hatred and aggression washing through it like a tonic, nourishing its new host with pain and death.

A sharp jolt of cold pain startled the Avatar from its reverie of carnage and the white glare behind its helmet burned with the fire of a sun as it sought out its attacker.

A Space Marine in the spartanly embellished armour of an Imperial Fists Librarian advanced towards it. He carried a crackling force staff and the Avatar laughed as it recognised the power of a psyker. Here was a death worth inflicting.

Glittering haloes of psychic energy flared from the Librarian's helmet, engraved with hexagrammic sigils of great potency and scrimshawed purity seals.

'Abomination!' hissed Librarian Corwin. 'I shall send you back to the hell from which you crawled!'

A beam of coruscating light lanced from the Librarian's force staff and struck the Avatar in the centre of its chest. The Avatar staggered, dropping to its knees as it was bathed in flickering balefires. It bellowed in pain, suddenly thrusting with its sword and impaling an Iron Warrior on its blade.

Blood sprayed along the weapon and the Avatar roared as it fed, rising to its feet as the drained Iron Warrior collapsed to the ground.

Flaring washes of energy erupted from the Avatar's body as the power earthed through its armour. The Avatar laughed again.

'You are deluded,' grated the altered voice of Larana Utorian. 'Do you not realise that Khorne is the bane of psykers?'

The Librarian braced himself against the rocks as the desperate struggle at the top of the breach swirled around them. Neither side was willing to intervene in this battle that was fought in the realm of the spirit.

'The power of the Emperor commands you!' bellowed Corwin, striking the Avatar with another blast of light and driving it to the ground once more. 'Begone, foul daemon!'

Again and again he fired searing bolts of psychic power at the figure of the Avatar, sagging against the side of the breach as his reserves of energy dwindled.

His very soul was being drained as he fought to destroy this monster.

The Avatar spread its arms and gave vent to a shout of hatred that shook the very walls of the bastion with its fury. A rippling whirlwind of raw, red hunger swept from the Avatar's armour, spreading throughout the breach like the pressure wave of an explosion and scything through every warrior within a hundred paces. A lashing storm of hate-fuelled energy whipped around the interior walls of the Mori bastion, and every man touched burst apart in an explosion of red, his blood swept up in the etheric whirlwind as it howled back to the Avatar at its epicentre.

The Avatar swelled to monstrous proportions, its armour creaking and groaning as it sought to master the energies ripped from the deaths it had just caused.

Dry, fleshless husks surrounded it, Iron Warriors, Jourans and Imperial Fists, their vital fluid drained to feed the monster that had killed them. The Avatar rose to its full height, towering in the breach, its armour and weapons blazing with barely-contained power.

Only one figure remained standing: Librarian Corwin, his knees buckled and the sacred sigils on his armour little but faded scorch marks. He supported himself on his staff, swaying unsteadily as the Avatar's pounding footsteps crashed towards him across the breach.

'Not dead yet, psyker?' roared the Avatar, raising its sword. 'Soon you will wish you were.'

Corwin looked up into the blazing eyes of the Avatar and saw death.

The Avatar swung its sword, the passage of the iridescent blade cutting through the fragile veil of reality with a dreadful ripping sound, like tearing meat.

A black gouge torn in the walls separating realities opened, filling the air with sickening static, as though a million noxious flies had flown through from some vile, plague dimension.

Librarian Corwin closed his eyes and died without a sound as the Avatar's blade split him in two, both halves of his body sucked into the black tear opened in space and time.

The Avatar feasted on the slaughter it had caused, sensing the oceans of blood yet to be shed through the gateway its sword, bloated with death, had torn in the world. Galaxies of billions upon billions of souls awaited harvest and feeding to the Blood God. There were realms where the time it had wasted here was but the blink of an eye, where there were slaughters that would perhaps one day assuage Khorne's hunger.

The Avatar laughed, knowing that such a thing could not come to pass: the Blood God's hunger was a depthless ocean and would never be sated. New life and new purpose thundered through the bulging fabric of its armour as the pull of fresh souls suffused it.

Larana Utorian continued to scream inside her mind as she saw the eternity of slaughter that lay before her, and all the deaths to come.

She screamed because she realised that some vile part of her soul desired this.

Without a backward glance, the Avatar abandoned Hydra Cordatus to its fate, stepping through the dark portal to a time and place beyond mortal understanding.

An age of battle awaited, and it had time without end to be part of it.

HONSOU SCRAMBLED UP the slopes of the breach, his blood afire with killing. Iron Warriors gathered at the crest of the breach, the rocks there enveloped in clouds of explosions pierced with stabs of flame from some unseen weapon. Already he could tell that the gunfire had to be coming from a Titan.

Forrix saw him coming and waved him forward, shouting over the din of the sawing fire of the Warhounds' Vulcan bolters.

'We cannot go further!'

'But the guns of the bastion will cut us to pieces if we stay here!' retorted Honsou. 'We must carry the breach!'

Forrix pointed through the smoke to the shadowy outline of the Mori bastion and Honsou suddenly noticed the complete absence of any sounds of battle. No gunshots, no screams of wounded men and no clash of steel on steel. Only then did he notice the slowly shrinking wound torn in the air that hung in the breach, a veil of stars glittering from beyond.

'What in the name of Chaos is that?'

'I do not know, half-breed, but it is where Kroeger has gone.'

'I don't understand,' said Honsou as the shimmering vision faded to nothingness.

'Nor I, but the whereabouts of Kroeger is the least of our worries. We need something to shift these thrice-damned Warhounds.'

As if in response to Forrix's demand, the thunder of something impossibly vast slamming against the earth shook the ground, loosening giant rocks from the breach. The massive vibration hammered through the ground again and Honsou turned as he felt the presence of something ancient and fearsome approaching.

More rocks tumbled downwards from the breach as the tempo of the thunderous impacts grew.

The smoke parted and the *Dies Irae* limped from the smoke and strode towards the citadel.

HIGH IN THE command bridge of the Warlord Titan, *Honoris Causa*, Princeps Daekian heard the excitement in Princeps Carlsen's voice even over the vox, and smiled with grim resignation.

'It's the *Dies Irae*, it's mobile again. Emperor knows how, but it's coming straight for Vincare bastion, princeps!'

Carlsen's warning was unnecessary; Daekian's forward observers had already reported the appearance of the corrupted Emperor Titan. He could sense the unspoken desire of Carlsen to come and join the fight against the *Dies Irae*, but even a cursory glance at the tactical plot told Daekian that Carlsen's Warhounds were best employed covering the breach.

'Hold fast, Princeps Carlsen. Stay where you are,' he ordered.

'Aye, princeps,' replied Carlsen, his disappointment plain.

Daekian expertly walked his Warlord through the gateway of the inner wall, ducking the Titan's massive head to avoid losing its carapace weapons. The two Reavers that followed him, the *Armis Juvat* and the *Pax Imperator*, were smaller and passed below the gate without trouble. All three Titans had undergone hurried repairs after their first engagement, but none was yet fully operational.

Daekian had faith in his crews and the fighting spirit of the *Honoris Causa*, but he had made his peace with the Emperor before climbing to the bridge of his Titan. He had long known that it would come to this and though he was sure it would mean his death, he was honoured that it would fall to him to avenge Princeps Fierach.

Already he could see the effect the *Dies Irae* was having on the battle. Imperial troops were streaming back in terror from the gargantuan apparition that had emerged from the smoke. The Imperial Fists fell back in good order, even the Space Marines realising the futility of standing before this beast. Their ramparts were no protection against such a towering monster, able to cross the bastion with a single step, able to obliterate the walls with a shot.

Daekian cursed as the troops fled beneath him, unable to step forward for fear of crushing whole platoons beneath his tread. The *Dies Irae* had reached the third parallel and was barely seconds away from reaching the walls.

'Moderati Issar, take down that abomination's shields!' he yelled, raising the massive foot of his Titan and praying that the men below would get out of his way.

'Engineering deck, give me slow striding speed.'

He watched as flaming traceries of staccato gunfire pumped from his carapace-mounted Gatling blaster, the high velocity shells ripping across the body of the *Dies Irae*. Bright pulses flared as void shields collapsed, but Daekian knew that it would take more than the gatling blaster to finish this beast off.

The *Armis Juvat* and *Pax Imperator* spread out to his flanks, firing as they went, as he gracefully manoeuvred the *Honoris Causa* through the mass of fleeing troops. A massive explosion threw up chunks of rockcrete as the enemy Titan's plasma annihilator opened fire and vaporised a corner gun tower on Vincare bastion, melting the rockcrete of the walls and causing them to sag under the intolerable heat.

Daekian grunted as he felt shields collapsing under the weight of fire from the *Dies Irae*, cursing as he swung his Titan left into the bastion, stepping over the lines of entrenchments.

His monstrous foe was before him, and a cold, lead weight settled in the pit of his stomach as he clearly saw the terrifying form of the *Dies Irae* over the jagged top of the broken ramparts. Its body was blackened and scorched by fire and its head was a molten, dented mass, green fire blazing from behind its single remaining eye. Gunfire blazed from its weapon mounts, sawing through the ramparts and hammering the Titans of his battle group.

The *Armis Juvat* staggered, a round from the enemy Titan's hellstorm cannon defeating its shields and clipping the knee joint of its left leg.

'*Armis Juvat* and *Pax Imperator*, brace for firing!' shouted Daekian as he increased speed and thundered towards the bastion's flank.

The princeps of the Reavers planted their Titans' feet squarely on the ground and unleashed a deadly volley of fire at the *Dies Irae*. The enemy Titan returned fire as it continued to advance. Daekian initialised the linear accelerators that powered the Volcano cannon and took command of the weapon himself. Not that he did not trust and respect the Moderati who controlled the weapon, but if there was to be a kill shot, he would be the one to make it.

Another shot from the *Dies Irae's* plasma annihilator blew apart a further section of the wall as it stepped down into the ditch, crushing hundreds of corpses with every ponderous tread. He flinched as a flare of bright light to his side briefly illuminated the bridge and he craned his neck to see what had exploded.

The *Armis Juvat* toppled backwards, the top half of its upper body blown away. Geysers of plasma fire spilled from the ruptured reactor as the slain Reaver crashed to the ground. The *Pax Imperator* was suffering under the barrage of fire from the daemon Titan, but was still fighting.

'Void shields failing, princeps!' shouted Moderati Issar as a volley of shells struck the *Honoris Causa*.

'Full speed! We must close with the monster before we suffer a similar fate!' replied Daekian.

Less than a hundred metres separated them now and Daekian could make out the terrible damage Princeps Fierach had managed to inflict on this warp-spawned beast before being dragged to his death. Huge steel plates were crudely welded across the *Dies Irae's* midsection and all manner of auxiliary mechanisms had been grafted to its legs to allow it to move.

Fire from the gatling blaster blasted off more of its void shields and as Daekian saw a single shell explode against its upper bastions, he knew that the beast was stripped of its infernal protection.

He pushed the *Honoris Causa* forward and raised the volcano cannon.

'This is for Princeps Fierach,' he snarled and fired.

He watched the searing beam of unimaginably powerful energy streak towards the *Dies Irae's* head, knowing, even as he fired, that the shot was true.

His triumph turned to disbelief as the beam struck on a void shield, repaired at the last second before impact. The *Dies Irae* ground its torso towards him, the white-hot barrel of its plasma weapon aimed directly at him.

'Evasive manoeuvres!' he bellowed, even as he knew it would be too late.

The *Honoris Causa* lurched sideways as the plasma bolt fired.

Princeps Daekian was almost quick enough. Almost.

The shot impacted on the Warlord's volcano cannon, instantaneously vaporising the weapon in a seething ball of plasma. The explosion ripped up the Titan's arm, the adamantium structure flashing molten in a heartbeat.

Daekian screamed in agony, convulsing as the flashback from his arm's destruction flared along the mind impulse link. Blood streamed from his nose and ears, but he kept true to his course, striding towards the hazy outline of the *Dies Irae* through the smoke filling the command bridge.

He reached the walls at the same instant as the *Dies Irae,* the raised ground inside Vincare bastion bringing him level with his foe's head. The *Pax Imperator* circled around to his right, its carapace running with plasma fire and limping as its leg joints trailed streamers of white sparks.

Daekian lashed out with the *Honoris Causa's* one remaining arm, his battle claw slamming against the *Dies Irae's* chest. The massive Titan rocked back under the powerful blow, swinging its arm against the lip of the bastion and smashing through the rockcrete and hammering into the *Honoris Causa's* upper leg.

Daekian felt the leg crack and heard the screams over the vox from the engineering decks. He had moments at best.

He swiped again at his gigantic foe, ripping the armour plating away from the *Dies Irae's* belly as it pummelled his wounded flank with its arms. It lurched backwards, attempting to protect its now vulnerable reactor.

The horrendously damaged *Pax Imperator* charged into the fight, its chain fist ripping through the upper bastions of the *Dies Irae*, its blade shrieking as it tore downwards towards the war machine's bridge.

The *Dies Irae's* barbed tail swung and pulverised the knee joint of the *Pax Imperator*, shaking loose its chain fist and staggering the mighty god-machine.

Daekian watched the *Dies Irae* turn and hammer the barrel of its plasma annihilator into the bridge of the *Pax Imperator* and fire at point-blank range.

The upper half of the Reaver vanished in a searing blast, enveloping the two battling Titans with liquid fire. The remains of the *Pax Imperator* crashed over the walls of the bastion into the ditch, huge plumes of black smoke trailing from its burning hulk.

But its death had given Daekian the opening he needed.

He rammed his battle claw against the heat-softened midsection of the *Dies Irae's* reactor chamber, through the wound first opened by Princeps Fierach. He roared as he punched through into his foe's guts, gripping its nuclear heart in his iron grip and crushing it with all his might.

HONSOU WATCHED THE battle between the enormous war machines through the drifting haze of smoke, willing the majestic form of the *Dies Irae* to smash its inferior foes to scrap metal. He sheltered in the lee of the breach, his armour dusty and bloodstained.

His frustration grew with every explosion above him. They could not force the breach like this.

He watched as the leviathans struggled on the far bastion, their battle shaking the ground as though a powerful earthquake gripped the world. 'Forrix!' he yelled over the din of shells exploding at the crest of the breach. 'One way or another, this battle will soon be over. It is time to withdraw!'

Forrix shook his head, sneering. 'I should have known your cowardice would finally come to the fore! We stay and take this breach.'

Honsou felt his anger flare and gripped Forrix's armour, shouting. 'We have to go! The attack has lost its momentum and the enemy will be regrouping behind the walls. We only reinforce failure if we stay. There will be another time!'

For a second, Honsou thought Forrix was about to rebuke him again, but the fury drained from his eyes and he nodded, turning without a word and scrambling down the breach.

Honsou followed him and the Iron Warriors retreated from the walls, falling back to the ditch in disciplined groups. As he clambered over an iron-bar-studded chunk of rockcrete, the day was lit by a terrible brightness. The sky was bleached of colour and everything before him was bathed in the blinding light of a star.

The *Dies Irae* was enveloped in a dazzling ball of incandescent fire, huge sprays of plasma gouting from its belly. The enemy Titan with the burning white eyes had its fist buried in its guts, tearing and destroying the magnificent daemon machine. Locked together, the two Titans wrestled to escape each other's grip, the ground heaving with their battle.

As Honsou watched, a terrible groaning rent the air as the two machines rocked past their combined centre of gravity and slowly began to fall towards them into the ditch.

'Run!' he shouted, all thought of a disciplined retreat forgotten in the face of this new danger. He sprinted past the ravelin and leapt up the rubble slopes of the ditch as the two war machines slammed into the outer face of the curtain wall between Vincare bastion and the gate. Their massive bodies scraped down its face, trailing flaming sheets of burning plasma and ripping another great tear in the walls.

Honsou scrambled over the lip of the ditch, desperate to reach the safety of the earthworks. Forrix ran alongside him, his new bionics enhancing his speed, despite the Terminator armour he wore.

The two Titans slammed into the ground, the impact throwing Honsou from his feet and hurling him forward. He smashed into the top of the earthwork, rolling over its top as a river of plasma spilled from the ruptured reactors of the Titans.

Burning plasma flooded the ditch, incinerating the corpses that filled it in an instant. The Primus Ravelin was destroyed, crushed beneath thousands of tonnes of armaplas and ceramite. Huge flames and geysers of magma-hot steam ripped along the ditch, vitrifying the rocks throughout its length.

Razor sharp chunks of white-hot debris rained down inside the citadel, one shard from the *Honoris Causa's* bridge section hammering through a section of ramparts less than five metres from Castellan Leonid.

Both war machines thrashed weakly in the molten soup that filled the ditch, grappling to the last as the searing fires consumed them.

The first attack had failed.

Five

CASTELLAN LEONID POURED himself a glass of amasec and drained his glass in a single swallow. He set down the glass on his desk and sat on the edge of his bed, his entire body aching. He winced as stitches from a dozen shallow cuts pulled tight across his arms and legs, rubbing his temples in an attempt to ease the pain of the last few days.

Such a miracle was beyond his powers. He poured himself another glass, looking through the armoured loophole in the tower's wall. A dim glow still radiated from the dying plasma fires in the ditch where the two Titans had fallen and he raised his glass to the light. 'Here's to you, Princeps Daekian. May the Emperor watch over your soul.'

He drank the fiery spirit and briefly considered pouring another. He decided against it, knowing he had much to organise before morning. He rubbed a calloused hand through his hair when a knock came at his door.

'Come in.'

Brother-Captain Eshara ducked his head as he entered the room, pulling up a sturdy chair from beside Leonid's desk and sitting opposite the citadel's castellan.

The pair sat in a companionable silence before Eshara said, 'Your men fought bravely today. They are a credit to Joura, and your kin would be proud of you all.'

Seeing Leonid's sadness, he added, 'I was grieved to hear of Major Anders's death.'

Leonid nodded, remembering the awful sight of an Iron Warrior casually butchering his brave friend in the Primus Ravelin.

'As did yours, captain. We all feel Brother Corwin's loss.'

Eshara's face was lined with sorrow, 'I do not pretend to understand what happened in that bastion, but I believe he gave his life to save us all.'

'As do I,' replied Leonid.

Reports of the battle in the Mori bastion were confused to say the least. The infirmary building was awash with soldier's ravings, telling of a giant warrior killing everything in the bastion by his voice alone and a whirlwind that fed on blood. Luckily, Leonid had been able to scotch these wild tales before they had reached the remainder of the garrison.

'Tomorrow will be the last day will it not?' asked Leonid.

Eshara didn't answer and Leonid thought he was avoiding the question, but the Space Marine had merely been considering his answer.

'If we do not pull back to the citadel's inner wall, then, yes, it will be. We have less than four thousand men, virtually no heavy guns and three breaches. The wall is too long and we cannot hold everywhere at once. We will make it a thankless, bloody battle for our enemies, but, ultimately, the citadel will fall.'

'Then we will give up the outer wall and fall back to the inner citadel. The wall there is unbroken and, despite its irregular coverage, we still have the protection of the energy shield.'

Eshara nodded. 'Aye. The sacrifice made by Princeps Daekian has bought us some time to regroup, and it would be best if we begin now.'

'I will issue the orders immediately,' stated Leonid pouring himself a last glass of amasec and taking out his vial of detox pills.

He swallowed one and shook his head at the dreadful taste, placing the vial on the desk.

'I have observed your men taking these pills as well,' noted Eshara. 'Might I enquire as to what they are?'

'What, the detox pills? Oh, of course, you do not need these do you? Well, I don't suppose any of us will need them any more really.'

Eshara looked puzzled and said, 'Need them for what?'

'Well, it's the air here,' explained Leonid, waving his hand around him, 'It's poisonous. The Magos Biologis of the Adeptus Mechanicus provide these pills to keep the men from getting sick from the toxins in the air.'

Eshara leaned closer and lifted the vial. He shook out a handful of pills and took what seemed, to Leonid, an unnecessarily deep breath.

'Castellan Leonid, are you aware of an organ unique to the physiology of the Space Marines known as the neuroglottis?'

Leonid shook his head as Eshara continued. 'It is situated at the back of the throat and is capable of analysing the chemical content of anything we ingest or breathe. If need be, it can shift the pattern of my breathing to divert my trachea to a genetically altered lung better able to process the toxins in any given atmosphere.'

Eshara replaced the vial on Leonid's desk and said, 'I am afraid you have been misled, my friend, because I can assure you that the air on this planet is quite harmless. Unpleasant to breathe, yes, but poisonous? Most definitely not.'

LEONID FELT HIS anger grow with each step that took him towards the Machine Temple, situated deep beneath the citadel. He clutched the vial of detox pills in his left hand, his laspistol in his right, as he made his way along the antiseptic corridors that led to the lair of Arch Magos Amaethon. Captain Eshara was beside him and his honour guard of carapace-armoured Guardsmen marched in step behind him.

Now he knew why Hawke had not sickened and died on the mountains. Now he knew why the men stationed here were afflicted with headaches and constant nausea.

Now he knew why there were so many flags and regimental plaques around the briefing chamber. With these 'detox' pills, it was only a matter of time until the citadel would need another garrison.

Eshara had sampled one of the pills, allowing the chemicals to swill around his mouth before spitting them into an empty water jug.

'Poison,' he declared at last. 'Slow-acting to be sure, and subtle in its effects, but poison nonetheless. There are many chemicals present in this tablet I know to be highly carcinogenic. It is my guess that after a few years of taking these, the victim would be suffering from one or more highly virulent cancers.'

Leonid was horrified and stared in revulsion at the vial of pills before the cold realisation of how long he had been taking them struck him. 'How virulent?' he whispered.

Eshara frowned. 'Debilitating after maybe six or seven years and fatal soon after that.'

Leonid was speechless with rage. The magnitude of the betrayal was unbelievable. That the Adeptus Mechanicus could have perpetuated such a lie upon their own people was staggering. Thinking of the hundreds of regimental flags in the briefing chamber, he tried to calculate how many men the Adeptus Mechanicus had murdered, but gave up, appalled, as the numbers spiralled into the millions.

'Why would they do such a thing?'

'I do not know. What is it that this citadel defends? Is it so valuable that not even its defenders can be allowed to tell what they know?'

Leonid shook his head. 'No, well, maybe, I don't know for sure. As far as I know, this place is some sort of way-station for xeno artefacts discovered in the sector. I was told that the facility was built upon a ruin from the Dark Age of Technology.'

'Again, I feel you have been misled. I do not believe the Adeptus Mechanicus would stoop to such base behaviour simply to protect recovered xeno artefacts. There is a secret hidden within this citadel that is worth the life of every man who serves here.'

Leonid vowed he would find out what that secret was, even if he had to wring Naicin's neck or threaten to put a las-bolt through whatever machine kept the remains of Amaethon alive. It might already be too late for the 383rd

Jouran Dragoons, but Leonid would make damn sure the
Adeptus Mechanicus were made to pay for their crimes.

Several corridors branched off the main one, but Leonid
unerringly followed the path towards the Machine Temple.

'Someone is ahead of us,' whispered Eshara, drawing and
cocking his bolt pistol.

Leonid followed suit as his honour guard raised their rifles
and moved to surround him.

The armed party rounded a bend in the corridor as it
widened into a vaulted chamber, with latticed iron girders
lacing above them to form a web-like dome. Glow-globes
floated in suspensor fields, the walls were inscribed with cog
symbols and all manner of metal crates and bulky machines
lay scattered around the room. Worker servitors and indentured labourers moved mechanically around the wide room,
oblivious to the goings on around them.

At the far end of the chamber, a wide, semicircular cog-
toothed door sat half open, a small group of people
clustered around it.

Leonid immediately recognised Magos Naicin and the
ungainly form of two Praetorian battle-servitors. Servitors
were surgically altered slaves utilised by the Adeptus
Mechanicus for a variety of manual tasks. Praetorians fulfilled the adepts need for heavy defence, featuring an
augmented slave body atop a mechanised track unit, with a
variety of lethal weapon combinations implanted in the
servitors' arms.

The last figure was unknown to Leonid, but he was aston-
ished at the hideous bulk of the man that not even his
shapeless robes could conceal. His skin was the colour of
black steel, his face more dead than alive.

Naicin saw them coming and darted through the door,
dragging the enormous robed figure after him.

Leonid growled in anger and set off towards the closing
door as the two battle-servitors rumbled forwards. Leonid
was too intent on the door to pay them any heed. Nothing
would prevent him from reaching Naicin and killing him.

The first Praetorian raised its weapon arms as Leonid's
honour guard rushed after him, realising his danger. The

fastest man of the team dived for his commander, knocking him to the ground as the Praetorian opened fire, the rhythmic thumping of a massive bolter filling the chamber as it hosed the chamber with shells.

The shells passed over Leonid, but the men behind were not so lucky. Three were thrown back, huge holes blasted in their chests. Leonid and his rescuer rolled into the cover offered by a huge tracked drilling rig as more shots filled the chamber, heavier auto cannon shells blasting metal chunks from the machine.

A flurry of las-blasts struck the Praetorian, which rocked back, bloody craters torn across its body. The battle-servitor didn't slow, it merely adjusted its aim and ripped apart yet more of Leonid's guard with deadly accurate gunfire, bullets spewing from the gun at a furious rate.

The man who'd saved Leonid's life spun from the cover of the drilling rig, taking careful aim at the Praetorian's head. He dropped as he was struck in the head and chest, blown apart by the mass reactive bolter shells as they detonated within his flesh.

Leonid scrambled away as the heavy bolter and auto cannon began tearing up the chamber. Glass, plastic and blood erupted all around, showering them with sparks as soldiers and worker-servitors went down, panels and glow-globes shattering.

The lobotomised worker-servitors were not programmed to react to such external stimuli and continued working at their posts. They died silently as the Praetorians walked the shells into them, raking their fire left and right, servo assisted muscles easily absorbing their guns' huge recoil.

Emergency lights flickered on as fluorescent panels were shot out and Leonid slithered towards Eshara, who had drawn his crackling power sword.

Human workers scrambled to disconnect themselves from their stations and seek shelter as the battle-servitors slowly advanced towards them. One dropped to his knees, begging for mercy.

The Praetorian shot him in the face.

The rest died in three controlled bursts of fire.

Leonid surged from behind the drilling rig as the wounded Praetorian finished the slaughter of the technicians. He squeezed off two rounds and the servitor staggered, two massive holes blasted in its skull. It raised the heavy bolter and fired as Leonid's third shot took it in the throat, blowing its head clean off.

It fell backwards, firing the gun as it toppled, stitching a line of bullets towards Leonid and clipping his shoulder. He yelled in pain, the impact spinning him to the floor.

The second Praetorian trained its auto cannons on Leonid, the firing mechanisms whining as they built up speed to fire.

Before it could shoot, Eshara leapt from the cover of the crate and slashed his sword through the barrels in a bright explosion of sparks. He spun on his heel, hammering his elbow into the battle-servitor's face and smashing its skull from its shoulders in a welter of blood. His reverse stroke hacked the organic top half of the Praetorian's body from the track unit. The whine of its weapons motor sputtered and died.

Leonid picked himself up from the ground, clutching his wounded shoulder, and nodded his thanks to Eshara before turning the closed door behind which Naicin and his unknown accomplice had vanished.

'Damn!' he swore. 'How in the name of Joura are we going to get through that?'

Eshara looked over Leonid's shoulder and indicated something behind him.

Leonid frowned and turned to see what the Space Marine was pointing at. And grinned.

THE DOOR TO the Machine Temple was thirty centimetres thick and composed of solid steel, but it crumpled like tinfoil when the eighty-tonne drilling rig slammed into it. The roof section was torn free by the low clearance of the door as it came screeching through, spewing torn scraps of steel and sparks all across the inner sanctum of the Machine Temple.

The giant tracked machine slewed around as Eshara lost control for a second, the enormous rig smashing into a bank of monitors and control panels. The amber-lit chamber was filled with pulsating machinery and barely had the drilling rig skidded to a squealing halt than Leonid, Eshara and the four surviving members of his honour guard leapt from the rumbling machine.

Leonid grunted in pain as he landed, trying to make sense of the scene before him.

Magos Naicin stood with his head bowed beside a squat, rhomboid structure topped with a shattered vat of draining fluid. In one gloved hand he held his bronze facemask and, in the other, what looked like a glistening slab of wet meat. He tossed it aside and Leonid was horrified to see the slack features of Arch Magos Amaethon staring up at him from the floor. After centuries of service, the organic remains of the arch magos were finally dead.

The bulky figure that had accompanied Naicin stood atop the rhomboid, its wide, misshapen arms spread wide. Bulging motion undulated beneath its robes as though a collection of snakes writhed beneath them. Even as he watched, the robes split and fell from its body, revealing a massive, iron-black musculature that rippled in a horrific amalgamation of organic and biomechanical components. Was this creature machine or man, or some horrific symbiosis of the two?

'Naicin!' shouted Leonid. 'What have you done?'

The magos lifted his face and Leonid gasped in horror as he saw Naicin's true features, a swirling mass of thin, worm-like tentacles that glistened and writhed together to form the mass of his head. A cluster of milky and distended eyes bulged in the centre of his features, above a sphincter-like mouth, ringed with needle teeth.

'Mutant,' spat Eshara, raising his pistol.

The four Guardsmen were transfixed in horrified wonder at the bizarre sight before them. And their perverse fascination killed them.

The figure atop the rhomboid raised its arms, its flesh writhing as they transformed into two massive-barrelled weapons. A roaring crescendo of fire erupted from the weapons, blasting through Leonid's honour guard and disintegrating them in a heartbeat. Leonid once more dived for cover behind the drilling rig as Eshara charged towards the giant figure at the chamber's centre.

Magos Naicin hissed and leapt to intercept him, moving with inhuman speed, his arms whipping out and toothed proboscis erupting from his fingertips to smash Eshara from his feet. Hissing ichor splashed Eshara's shoulder guard, the ceramite plates of his armour rapidly dissolving beneath it. The Space Marine captain rolled beneath the questing mouths as Naicin came at him again, hissing acids spraying from his lashing, whip-like hands.

Leonid took advantage of the distraction to rest his pistol against the track guard of the drilling rig and take aim at the monstrous figure that had killed his men.

The gun arms had changed again, morphing into long, ribbed cables that waved like serpents. As he squinted down the barrel, the figure's ribs cracked wide open, spreading apart like some ancient moss-covered gateway. A dozen grooved tentacles of dripping green metal snaked from his chest cavity and spiralled through the air as though searching for something.

Leonid squeezed the trigger, the las-blast striking the figure in the head.

But a blaze of green light flared and Leonid saw his target was unharmed.

Leonid fired again and again, but his shots were wasted. The thing on the platform was invulnerable. The metallic tentacles continued to lengthen, hooking into the banks of machines around the chamber's centre. More tentacles sprouted from the writhing mass of biomechanical intestines, slipping through the air like branches of a tree and attaching themselves to the life-preserving mechanics of the Machine Temple and the regulatory systems of the citadel.

Alarm bells chimed and warning lights flashed around the chamber's circumference.

Leonid knew he could do nothing to stop the vile creature without Eshara and rushed towards the Space Marine, who was fighting the abhorrent mutant.

Eshara swung his sword at Naicin, but the thing moved with blinding speed, its dripping proboscises swaying aside from his every blow. The captain's bolt pistol was a molten pile on the floor and Leonid could see Eshara's armour was pierced by several smoking round holes where Naicin's corrosive proboscis had struck. He raised his pistol.

'Step back, Brother-Captain,' ordered Leonid.

Eshara dodged a blow aimed at his heart and rapidly backed away from the disgusting mutant. Naicin drew back to the base of the rhomboid platform as the chamber's omnipresent amber light dimmed, changing to a sickly green. Leonid drew a bead on the mutant's head.

Naicin chuckled, the sound somewhere between slurping and gurgling. 'Fools! You cannot win. You can kill me, but my masters will trample your bones within the day.'

'Why, Naicin?' asked Leonid.

'I could ask you the same question,' spat Naicin. 'You do not even know what you fight to protect.'

'We fight to protect a world of the Emperor, mutant,' snapped Eshara.

Naicin laughed, a horrible retching noise. 'You think your Emperor cares about this world? Look around you, it is a wasteland! A wasteland created by human hands. This was once a fertile and bountiful world until the Adeptus Mechanicus sought to make it their own. Virus bombs killed every living thing on the surface of this world and rendered it uninhabitable for centuries.'

'You lie. Why should the Adeptus Mechanicus do such a thing?'

'They wanted to make sure no one ever desired this world. So that when they built their geno-labs here, they would be undisturbed and forgotten. You stand in one of the most hallowed places of the Adeptus Mechanicus and you don't even know it. The gene-seed you prize so highly, the future of the Space Marines... this is one of only two places in the galaxy where it is created and stored.'

Seeing the look of horrified shock on Eshara's face, Naicin laughed. 'Yes, captain, when the Warsmith and the

Despoiler have your gene-seed they will use it to create Legions of Space Marines loyal to the glory of Chaos!'

'But you won't be around to see it,' snarled Eshara plucking the pistol from Leonid's hand and pulling the trigger.

Naicin's head exploded, showering the platform with stinking yellow fluid and scraps of rubbery, tentacled flesh. The corpse slumped to the ground as Eshara pumped another four shots into the body.

Eshara wordlessly handed the pistol back to Leonid as alarms began shrieking throughout the chamber. Both men looked up as the figure on the platform was lifted from its feet, its arms spreading wide in a cruciform pattern. More and more cabled tentacles sprouted from its body, the green haze that filled the chamber pulsing from deep within its chest.

Explosions of jade sparks burst from the edges of the room, flickering lines of lethal electricity arcing from machine to machine as the corruption of the techno-virus spread to every system of the citadel.

A lashing tongue of electrical discharge licked the ground beside Leonid and Eshara, and the two warriors stumbled away from the monster in front of them. Explosions filled the chamber and a crackling storm of lightning blazed through the Machine Temple. Eshara gathered Leonid into the shelter of his body as he sprinted for the ragged hole of the door. Spears of emerald lightning flashed around the chamber. A bolt struck Eshara's back and he grunted in pain, diving through the doorway as forks of green fire blasted behind him.

Eshara rolled aside as the unnatural lightning danced across the door to the Machine Temple, forming a crackling electrical web that completely blocked the entrance.

The two scrambled away from the pulsing green light, breathless and groaning in pain.

Eshara pushed himself to his feet and offered his hand to Leonid, who gripped his wounded shoulder and pulled himself upright. Before either man could speak, the vox-bead in Eshara's helmet crackled and the captain listened intently to the message he was receiving.

Leonid could tell the news was not good.

'Well?' he asked, expecting the worst.

'It has begun. The shield has gone down and the enemy are attacking once more.'

Leonid nodded and looked back into the sealed green hell of the Machine Temple.

'Then our place is on the walls,' he said grimly.

THE REMAINING TWO Titans of the Legio Mortis advanced on the citadel accompanied by a wave of Vindicator tanks and forty-two screaming Dreadnoughts. Nearly six thousand battered soldiers in red uniforms sprinted amongst this armoured thrust and dropped into the ditch, its surfaces smooth and vitrified by the plasma fire from the downed Titans.

Sunfire shells streaked into the darkness as alarms rang from the citadel and scattered shots lanced out to the charging horde.

Honsou watched from the bastions mounted atop the shoulders of the *Pater Mortis*, nearly thirty metres above the ground. He saw the Vindicators pull into their firing revetments along the third parallel and pound the weakened walls of the citadel, bringing down vast quantities of masonry as the Dreadnoughts made for the ditch. He gripped the edge of the bastion's iron pallisading as the Titan stepped down into the ditch, the rubble claws fitted over its massive feet keeping its stride sure.

Sixty-two Iron Warriors, all that remained of his company, filled the bastions either side of the Titan's head, ready to be unleashed upon the ramparts of the inner wall of the citadel. The Imperial defenders had abandoned the outer wall and the shield was down. They would never get a better chance than this.

The fire against the bastions and curtain wall slackened as the Titans closed with the walls, now little more than shattered piles of rubble. Honsou raised his sword in salute to the *Dies Irae* as they passed over its molten remains.

Honsou glanced to his right, making out the shadow of the Legio's other remaining Titan, its bastions crammed with Forrix's warriors. This was the last assault and it could not afford to fail. He braced himself as the mighty war machine battered its way through the breach torn by the death of the *Dies Irae* and felt the rumbling roar of fury build from within the daemon Titan. Powerful blasts of gunfire ripped from both war machines, blowing great chunks from the inner wall and demolishing whole sections of rampart.

The gap between the inner and outer wall was empty of foes; the Warhounds that had frustrated the first assault wisely having withdrawn behind the inner wall. Soldiers on the wall opened fire, but the Titans' shields were proof against such pinpricks. Flickering green fires played around the wall-mounted guns. Honsou could not understand why they were not firing, but gave thanks to the dark gods for their silence.

As the two Titans thundered forwards, the Vindicators churned over the breaches in the outer wall. The walls shook with thunderous impacts from the siege tanks, the inner gate pounded by shell after shell. The Dreadnoughts added their own weight of fire to the barrage. Three of the insane war machines, gripped in the frenzy of battle, lumbered forward to attack the gate with their massive hammer arms, only to be caught in the Vindicators' fire and blown apart.

The gap closed with every step of the *Pater Mortis*, and Honsou could clearly see the faces of the men lining the walls. Las-fire slashed towards him, but he laughed, feeling utterly invincible. He swayed forward as the Titan's arms pistoned into the walls, bracing hooks punching deep within the rockcrete.

Seconds later, the battle drawbridges slammed down from the shoulder bastions, crushing the rampart beneath them as they dropped.

Honsou raised his sword and charged onto the walls, shouting, 'This place is ours! Show no mercy!'

He jumped onto the rampart, hacking a trio of Guardsmen to death with one blow and firing his bolt pistol down the line of the walls. Hundreds of warriors were arrayed against them, but Honsou faced them all without fear, killing with preternatural skill.

Iron Warriors fanned out from the Titan's shoulder bastions, slaughtering the defenders and hurling them back. The noise was tremendous as the ramparts became slick with blood and entrails. Each time the Iron Warriors came close to breaking through the defenders' lines, the Imperial Fists would lead a desperate counterattack and push them back and hold the line together. Honsou killed another Guardsman and risked a glance to where Forrix led his warriors. Here too, the Iron Warriors were confronted with the incredible tenacity and stubborn defiance of the citadel's defenders.

They were holding, but only just, and Honsou saw they were close to breaking.

Honsou blocked a blow aimed at his neck and disembowelled his attacker as a monstrous, black shadow, darker than the blackest night fell across the walls. For the briefest second, the fighting slowed as heads craned upwards to see what new devilment had been unleashed.

With a thunder that cracked the walls, the Warsmith crashed down on the rampart, the newborn darkness of powerful wings spread behind him. Guardsmen around him dropped, vomiting blood and convulsing. His arms swept out, his taloned hand and mighty axe killing everything within reach. The darkness enfolding the Warsmith's head billowed and spat bolts of dark light that dissolved everything it struck.

Screams of terror spread along the walls and horrified soldiers turned and fled before this diabolical apparition. The Warsmith reared up to his full height, his armour stretching and swelling, the keening faces bound within his armour straining and wailing a banshee's choir.

Shaking off his amazement, Honsou bellowed, 'We have them now!'

He charged after the fleeing mass of soldiers, hacking them down with his sword. The Imperial front line collapsed and not even the Imperial Fists could halt the rout.

He could see Forrix slaughtering fleeing Guardsmen by the dozen. A terrific crash echoed from below, and Honsou knew the citadel's inner gate had fallen. The Warsmith took to the air once more as the carnage on the walls continued, casting his pall of corruption and change throughout the ramparts.

Honsou kicked down the iron door to one of the giant towers that flanked the gate and dived through, firing as he rolled. The soldiers within the tower screamed in terror as he rose to his feet. They were no threat, but he killed them anyway.

He swiftly made his way down the stairs, his blood afire and singing with the promise of victory.

'Iron Warriors! With me! The citadel is ours!'

FORRIX THUNDERED DOWN the stairs of the tower, firing as he went. The stair spiralled downwards to the left, bolter shells whining and ricocheting from the walls. On two levels there were defensible landings, but the furious assault of the Iron Warriors could not be stopped. Forrix and his Terminators smashed each one aside with ease.

Even as he killed, he marvelled at the appearance of the Warsmith. Their leader stood at the very cusp of daemon-hood, the changes wracking his body becoming more manifest. Surely his final ascension was at hand? Forrix had sensed a terrible urgency to the Warsmith, and knew that he was fighting to hold his form coherent. One wrong move now and the Warsmith could just as easily explode into the thrashing riot of anatomies of a Chaos spawn, doomed for an eternal life of mindless mutation.

The base of the tower levelled into a wide killing zone, but it had been designed to defend against attacks from outside, not inside, and the defenders had nothing to shelter behind. Las-fire raked the walls beside Forrix. He swept his combi-bolter around the room, slaughtering Guardsmen with every pull of the trigger.

Terminators spilled down after him, their horned helmets carved in the masks of snarling beasts of prey. The image was not inappropriate, thought Forrix. Narrow doors led from the tower, too small to allow a Terminator through, but Forrix slammed his power fist into the stonework, shattering the lintel and punching his way through. The Terminators followed him outside into the citadel's interior.

Forrix grinned as he watched the Warsmith swooping high above the battlefield. The wings at his back were becoming more substantial and his form rippled and blurred, as though in a constant state of flux. Across the ruined gateway, he could see Honsou leading his warriors from the opposite tower, hacking down a mob of fleeing Guardsmen.

Ahead, across a wide cobbled esplanade, he could make out a cluster of ruined buildings, their windows gaping like blackened, empty eyesockets. Human soldiers, Vindicators, Dreadnoughts and Defilers poured through the blazing remains of the gate, gunning their engines as they spread out to avoid the return fire coming from the ruins.

Amidst the flames, sporadic volleys of las-fire pierced the night, but it was disorganised and undirected. Smoke billowed in thick, black plumes from the ruins and Forrix heard the crash of massive power claws tearing at the curtain wall behind him as the two Titans of the Legio Mortis ripped it down, eager to be part of the slaughter.

The smoke parted and the high-pitched blasts of Vulcan bolter fire ripped up the esplanade in a line towards the gate. Three Vindicators exploded and a Dreadnought toppled, thrashing its arms in frenzy as it tried to right itself.

Forrix charged across the courtyard as he caught sight of the Warhound he had marked for himself earlier. The beast darted through the smoke, pausing only long enough to draw a bead on the charging Iron Warriors. But in the open, its gunfire was nowhere near as effective as it had been in the breach.

'Spread out!' yelled Forrix as he gathered his Terminators to him and set off towards the Warhounds.

'You escaped me once, beast, but this time I have you,' he promised his prey.

'MARK YOUR TARGETS!' yelled Leonid as volleys of las-fire lashed the Iron Warriors charging from burning building to burning building. Smoke filled every street. None of their attackers were falling, and Leonid knew they must make

every shot count. The Warhound *Defensor Fidei* walked backwards behind his men as they fell back from this assault,
firing into the mass of the enemy as they pursued the
Jourans.

Through gaps in the smoke pouring from shelled buildings, he could see massive chunks of rockcrete being torn
from the wall by the Titan siege towers, and knew they had
only minutes until these gargantuan war machines joined
the battle. Tanks and grotesque, multi-limbed constructs,
with turrets adorned with hateful runes, poured through the
smashed gate, and fear was visible in every bloodied face.

Brother-Captain Eshara had regrouped the survivors of his
company, thirty Space Marines, and fought alongside him,
firing his bolter with every grudging step backwards.

Suddenly, a dozen of the Iron Warriors' damnable red clad
soldiery charged through the smoke to their side. Shots from
crude rifles felled five of his men before they could react.
Leonid knelt, jamming his rifle to his shoulder and opening
up on full auto, spraying the smoke-filled street with bright
lasbolts. Three enemy soldiers dropped and Eshara killed
another four with deadly accurate bolter fire. The remainder
drew a bead on Leonid, but before they could shoot, the
ground rocked and a massive adamantium foot slammed
down, crushing them to death.

The *Jure Divinu* sprayed the building across from Leonid
with turbo laser fire and he saw six enemy soldiers tumble
from it, burning debris crashing down as its already unstable structure finally gave way.

From the smoke, Leonid saw a warrior in Terminator
armour charging straight for the *Jure Divinu*, bright hunger
etched on his face. His dead features spoke of ancient malice and bitter hatred.

Leonid had no time to think. Eshara grabbed his arm and
hustled him back through the burning ruins towards the
northern wall of the citadel. Space Marines ran alongside
them, the men of the Guard having already passed through
the Valedictor Gate and descended into the caverns.

Built flush against the flank of the mountain with two
armoured blockhouses to either side of it, the Valedictor

Gate was intended to bar the route into the underground caverns, but with Naicin's betrayal in the Machine Temple, it remained treacherously open.

Explosions ripped through the buildings behind Leonid and smashed him to the ground.

Eshara dragged him to his feet as the thirty Imperial Fists formed a semi-circle around the Valedictor Gate, facing outwards.

The Space Marine captain lowered his dented and blackened helm level with Leonid's and said, 'Castellan, you must get below and destroy the gene-seed.'

'How?' gasped Leonid breathlessly. 'The Machine Temple's gone, there's no way to do it.'

Eshara gripped his arm tighter. 'Do what you must, find flamer units, plasma gunners, anything, but do not let even a scrap of gene-seed fall into the enemy's hands. It is better that it all be destroyed than have the foe claim it. Do you understand?'

'We will need time to destroy it all, my friend. Can you hold them here for long enough?' asked Leonid, fully aware of the price that time would be bought with.

The two warriors locked eyes then shook hands in the warrior's grip, wrist to wrist.

'We will hold them for long enough,' nodded Eshara as he dropped his empty bolter and drew both his power swords.

Leonid said, 'Good luck, Brother-Captain Eshara.'

'And to you, Castellan Leonid.'

Without another word, Leonid turned and sprinted through the Valedictor Gate.

FORRIX WATCHED THE beast stagger as a shell from a Vindicator burst against its leg. The Warhound lurched, its weapon mount shearing off as it slammed into a ruined building. They had it now, backed into a corner and stripped of its protection.

There was another Warhound nearby, but the billowing smoke and thump of explosions obscured its whereabouts.

'It is time for a reckoning, beast!' he yelled as he crashed forward. More gunfire hammered the armoured carapace of the Warhound, its legs buckling under the weight of fire. The pilot's compartment swung low to the ground, the green of its eyes locking with Forrix and he laughed, knowing that the beast's life was forfeit. He had it now.

He and his Terminators closed on the struggling machine, power fists raised to deliver the killing blow. Forrix clambered onto its massive foot and hammered his power fist into the ankle joint of the Warhound's leg again and again.

The war machine lifted its leg, realising the danger and stepped backwards, swaying drunkenly and smashing into the building across the street, causing it to collapse.

Forrix held on for dear life as the Warhound sought to dislodge him, hammering his fist against its ankle. The Titan's leg swept round, slamming down on a jagged section of rubble. Forrix was thrown clear as the full weight of the Warhound came down awkwardly on its pulverised ankle.

The joint sheared off in an explosion of flame and the Warhound toppled, smashing backwards through the burning building and slamming into the ground in a cascade of rockcrete blocks. The pilot's compartment cracked open under the impact and Forrix scrambled across the flaming wreckage to finish the beast.

Shadowed forms struggled weakly within as Forrix emptied his combi-bolter into the Warhound's bridge, slaughtering its crew in a storm of bolts.

Forrix laughed as he slew the crew of the *Jure Divinu*, racking the arming slide of his underslung melta gun.

The wall behind the slain beast collapsed, showering him with rock and smoke, momentarily obscuring his vision.

As it cleared he felt his pleasure at the kill drain from him as he found himself staring into the baleful eyes of the second Warhound.

'No!' hissed Forrix.

Its weapons whined, building power to fire.

Forrix raised his weapon and pulled the trigger as both the turbo lasers and Vulcan bolters fired.

Forrix had the briefest sensation of pain and frustration before the *Defensor Fidei's* guns utterly destroyed him.

* * *

HONSOU JOGGED THROUGH the fallen citadel, elated beyond words at the slaughter around him. The warriors of both his and Forrix's company followed him through the streets of their enemy's fastness, cheering his name to the dark gods.

Loud gunfire roared from somewhere to his left and he angled his advance towards it, rounding a corner in time to see a wrecked Warhound topple to the ground and Forrix charging towards the war machine's head.

Honsou saw the wall before Forrix collapse and the furious form of the Warhound's twin emerge from the smoke. He saw it raise its weapons and blast Forrix from the ruins in an explosion of blood and mechanised body parts.

As he watched Forrix die, Honsou felt nothing but triumph. Kroeger had vanished and Forrix was dead; truly the gods of Chaos favoured him this night.

The Warhound's victory was short-lived as the might of the *Pater Mortis*, its crashing footsteps collapsing buildings all around them, emerged from behind Honsou and fired its weapons. The Scout Titan vanished in a flurry of bright explosions, its few void shields and light armour no match for the power of the Warlord Titan.

It reeled under the impacts and, for an incredible moment, Honsou believed it had survived, but a massive explosion engulfed its head and the Warhound fell, its crew compartment a blazing ruin.

Honsou snarled in satisfaction and set off once more.

Everywhere the enemy was defeated, broken and fleeing before them.

He emerged into a wide square, at the far end of which he saw a pitiful ring of the Imperial Fists. They stood, swords bared at the entrance to caverns gouged into the mountains, their faces proud and defiant.

Honsou laughed as he marched at the head of his company, the Warsmith descending from the hot darkness above him. The master of the Iron Warriors landed hard, the cobbles hissing molten with his step, as though the ground itself rebelled against the chaos writhing within him. His body rippled with change, as though a million forms sought to be birthed from his unquiet anatomy. The black wings at his back quivered and his armour was becoming glossier, more organic looking, like the carapace of an insect.

The Warsmith nodded to Honsou, a gesture of respect between warriors.

'It is time we finished this,' rasped the Warsmith, his voice thickened and coarse.

'Aye,' agreed Honsou, marching towards the Imperial Fists as the Iron Warriors spread out to surround them, weapons raised.

A stillness fell as the ancient foes faced one another in the glare of the burning citadel and a massive shadow fell across the square as the *Pater Mortis* strode from the ruins.

A warrior stepped from the ring of Space Marines and removed his helmet. Honsou could feel the hatred this warrior had for him as he spat, 'I am Brother-Captain Eshara of the Imperial Fists, proud son of Rogal Dorn, soldier of the Emperor and scourge of deviants. Face me and die, traitor.'

The Warsmith faced Eshara and Honsou grinned as he saw the effect his presence had upon the Space Marine. As the captain's face twisted in sudden pain, the Warsmith leapt forward, his mighty axe sweeping down to cleave Eshara in two.

Eshara crossed his swords above his head, blocking the blow, the impact driving him to his knees. He grunted and spun low, slashing a blade across the Warsmith's flank. Black blood gouted from the wound. The Warsmith smashed his fist against Eshara's chest, cracking his breastplate open.

As Eshara fell, the Imperial Fists charged, the name of Rogal Dorn on their lips.

Gunfire erupted from the Iron Warriors, cutting them down as battle was joined.

But it was an unequal struggle and though the Imperial Fists fought hard, the outcome was never in doubt.

Honsou drove his sword through an Imperial Fist, watching in amazement as Eshara groggily rose to his feet, coughing thick wads of blood. The Warsmith roared and hammered his axe down upon Eshara's shoulder guard, cleaving him from collarbone to pelvis, the blade shearing through his armour like paper.

Eshara crumpled, but weakly raised his head as the Warsmith sheathed his massive axe and stooped to lift him from the ground.

'Know this, son of Dorn,' hissed the Warsmith. 'I will gorge myself on your gene-seed and I shall make you and all your kind extinct.'

The Warsmith lifted Eshara's dying body to his head where there was a monstrous cracking, sucking noise. Blood splashed the steaming ground at the Warsmith's feet and he bellowed in orgiastic pleasure, dropping Eshara's mutilated corpse.

Even Honsou was shocked as he saw the Space Marine's entire chest cavity had been bitten through, the organs within sucked from his body and devoured by the Warsmith.

Honsou dismissed the incident from his mind and set off after the Warsmith as he charged through the gateway that led into the mountains and their ultimate goal.

LEONID HAMMERED HIS rifle butt through the glass of an incubation tank and stood back as the amniotic fluid spilled out along with its foetal cargo. He used brute force because his lasgun's power cell had long since drained. He moved onto the next capsule, staring in awed wonder at the sheer scale of the cavern stretching before him. Its end was lost in shadows, the vastness broken up by wide avenues of incubation capsules. Thousands of tanks ran in ordered lines into the darkness, their clear surfaces frosted and cold to the touch.

Now Leonid understood the danger inherent in this place. If what Naicin had told them was even partly true, there was enough genetic material stored here to create untold thousands of twisted warriors of Chaos. The very thought of such creations being birthed from here was truly horrifying.

Worker-servitors with shoulder-mounted illuminators were spots of light in the darkness, moving silently through the echoing cavern as they tended to their biological charges. Hundreds of his soldiers rampaged through the cavern, shooting, burning and smashing everything they could. But Leonid knew it was a hopeless task, the sheer scale of the facility here would defeat them. There was no way they could destroy it all before the Iron Warriors came to kill them.

But they would try. It was all they had left.

HONSOU AND THE Iron Warriors followed the Warsmith as he sped down through the corridors beneath the mountains. There was a desperate hunger to the Warsmith now, like a fleshhound with the scent of blood in its jaws. His body pulsed like a heart in the throes of a massive seizure, as though containing a whirlwind of potentiality that strained to be born.

Ahead, Honsou heard sounds of destruction and knew they were approaching the prize the citadel had jealously guarded. As the passageway widened and levelled out, he saw a massive set of gold doors, green lightning dancing across their surfaces, and a cavern beyond.

Shouts and the sound of shattering glass quickly turned to cries of alarm as the humans saw the charging Iron Warriors. A few brave souls attempted to stand before the Warsmith, but quickly crumpled as he neared them, screaming and spasming in agony.

The Iron Warriors plunged into the cavern, gunfire echoing from the walls as they slaughtered the last defenders of the citadel.

The Warsmith halted beside a shattered incubation capsule and dragged out a limp rag of pink flesh, sodden and only vaguely humanoid. The Warsmith feasted upon the genetic host matter, feeding on the soft, boneless tissue and Honsou felt his skin crawl as though a powerful electric charge was building.

The Warsmith moved to the next capsule and fed once more. He turned to Honsou and rasped, 'Finish them all.'

LEONID WORKED HIS way back to the cavern's entrance, his power sword gripped tightly and his face set with grim resolve. There was no more they could do here to make a difference and he felt their failure as a bitter weight in the pit of his stomach. If this was to be their end, they would meet it head on, not hiding. His men had no ammunition left and the sounds of battle around him were brutal and short lived.

He and perhaps fifty soldiers followed a revolting sucking, guzzling noise, determined to sell their lives as dearly as possible now that the end was inevitable.

Leonid rounded a corner of dripping capsules and recoiled at the sight before him.

THE WARSMITH CAST his arms to the cavern roof as he felt the power of the gene-seed coursing through him, though he realised that its power was largely symbolic. He had succeeded and the power of the dark gods poured into their chosen vessel, ripping him from his mortal flesh and gifting him with the boon of immortality.

His armour sloughed from his body, its material form no longer appropriate for such a magnificent creature of Chaos. A spiralling vortex of dark energy surrounded him, cracks exploding in the rockcrete floor as power flared from his limbs.

As the psychic energy built up, the Warsmith swelled, roaring as he felt his power magnifying.

His chest hiked convulsively as the might of Chaos poured through him. He was aware of his warriors and the Imperial soldiers, but he needed all his concentration to direct the incomprehensible energies that remoulded his new daemonic flesh.

The Warsmith roared in ecstasy and agony as unprecedented power engulfed him. His body swelled hugely, bloated by the maelstrom of energy that cycloned within.

A ridged horn burst from his forehead in a welter of blood and tissue. The mottled spike writhed like a living thing, swelling and wrapping itself around his head. His skin darkened, taking on a loathsome scaled texture. His spine cracked and he screamed as it elongated and thickened, roaring as the shadows at his back solidified and the dark wings spread wide and flapped powerfully.

The newly elevated Daemon Prince was lifted from the ground, hanging suspended before the horrified witnesses

to its birth as the last of the psychic energy drained from its
body in an explosive wash of power.

THOUGH HE KNEW it meant death, Leonid raced towards the
floating daemon, his sword raised to strike it down.

The winged daemon turned its gaze upon him and he
dropped to his knees as the sickening aura of the creature
overcame him. Its monstrous form was utterly black, the
nightmare depths of its form glittering with far-off galaxies
and stars. He felt revolted just looking at the beast and
rolled onto his side as debilitating cramps seized him.

He vomited, feeling his guts contract again and dry-
heaved, having nothing more to expel. He vainly tried to
push himself to his feet, but the pain was too great, like a
red-hot knife twisting in his belly. His men were also on the
floor, their bodily functions rebelling in the presence of such
horrific power.

Leonid wept in pain, hearing the terrible, booming laughter of the daemon prince above him, the discordant noise
sending jagged bolts of pain down his spine.

He felt unconsciousness rising to claim him and tried to
fight it.

But he could not resist its balm and slipped into darkness.

THE FIRES STILL burned throughout the citadel as the first rays
of morning crested the mountains and columns of tracked
tankers rumbled through the molten remains of the Destiny
Gate. Each tanker had been specially built for this moment,
insulated and rigged with blast freezing mechanisms to preserve the precious gene-seed on its journey through the
immaterium towards the Eye of Terror and Abaddon the
Despoiler.

The fallen Iron Warriors were already aboard the ships in
orbit, the Chirumeks dissecting them even now to harvest
their organs for implantation into the next generation of
Iron Warriors.

There had not been enough of Forrix to bring back and
while stripping down the siege works, a party of slaves had
found a rotting corpse in Kroeger's dugout. It was clearly

that of an Iron Warrior, but if the body was Kroeger's, who had led the assault on the eastern bastion?

It was a mystery that Honsou guessed he would never know the answer to, though in that, he was very wrong.

Honsou watched the tankers as they made the slow journey through the blasted landscape of the plain before the citadel. The satisfaction of victory was tempered with a hollow emptiness from knowing that the foe was defeated and there were no more battles to be fought here.

When the Warsmith had ascended to daemonhood, Honsou had prostrated himself before the daemon prince, prayers of devotion spilling from his lips.

'Stand, Honsou,' commanded the daemon.

Hurriedly Honsou obeyed as the daemon continued, 'You have pleased me mightily these last centuries, my son. I have groomed your hatred well and you have the seed of greatness within you.'

'I live only to serve, my master,' stammered Honsou.

'I know you do. But I know of your hunger to lead, to tread the path I have taken. It is clear to me now the course the future must take.'

The daemon Warsmith drifted towards Honsou, its massive form towering above the Iron Warrior.

'You shall be my successor, Honsou. Only you hold true to the vision of Chaos, of the final destruction of the false Imperium. Forrix had lost that vision of our ultimate destiny and Kroeger, well, he cast it aside long ago. I shall not name you captain, I shall name you Warsmith.'

Before Honsou could answer, the Warsmith folded his midnight wings around his body, his form a sliver of impenetrable darkness.

'The power of the warp calls me, Honsou, and it is a call I cannot refuse. Where I go, you cannot follow... yet.'

The Warsmith's outline shimmered as he faded from the material realm into places beyond Honsou's understanding.

He still couldn't believe it. Honsou the half-breed. Now Honsou the Warsmith.

He turned from the wreckage of the citadel and made his way back towards the ridge that led down to the spaceport, passing a wretched column of blue-coated prisoners marching towards the prison hulks and a life of slavery. Honsou caught sight of a prisoner in a bronze breastplate with the shoulder boards of a lieutenant colonel, his battered features cast down in crushed resignation, and laughed.

He quickly outpaced the prisoners, marching through the masterful contravallations Forrix had constructed around the spaceport, past the heavy, transport shuttles that were returning the surviving tanks and artillery pieces to the cargo hulks.

The landing platforms were awash with men and machines preparing to depart Hydra Cordatus.

He crossed the runways towards a shuttle idling on a far landing platform.

An honour guard of Iron Warriors stood before the cavernous entrance to the vessel.

'Your shuttle is ready, Warsmith,' said a bowing Iron Warrior.

Honsou smiled and stepped aboard the shuttle without a backward glance.

EPILOGUE

THE ADEPTUS MECHANICUS vessel *Mordekai's Light* drifted in geo-stationary orbit above Hydra Cordatus, its smooth black surfaces dull and non-reflective. Its kilometre-long hull was sleek and quite unlike the ungainly vessels of the Imperial Navy.

This vessel was designed for speed and stealth.

Dark robed adepts of the Machine God ghosted through the incense-scented air of the command bridge, reverently tending to the arcane technologies of the massive starship.

Standing behind the command altar at the end of a wide, veneered nave, High Magos Kuzela Matrada stared at the smouldering ruin of the citadel projected on the forward viewing bay. The great fortress was no more, its mighty bastions cast down, its walls reduced to rubble and, more importantly, its precious gene-seed stolen.

The scale of this disaster did not bear thinking about and the repercussions would reach to the very highest and mightiest on Mars and Terra.

A light flashed on the pict-tablet before him and he swept his bronze hand across the runes beside it. An interference filled image swam into focus on the tablet, the hooded face of Magos Sarfian, staring up at him from the surface of the planet below.

'Well?' demanded Matrada.

'You were correct, high magos. The laboratorium is empty and the gene-seed gone.'

'All of it?'

'All of it,' confirmed Sarfian.

'Have you found any survivors?'

'No, my lord, only corpses. From the wreckage and sheer level of destruction we have discovered, it is evident that the battle was fierce indeed.'

'Have you removed all evidence of our blessed order?'

Sarfian nodded. 'The cavern has been purified with fire and melta charges set.'

'Very well, return to the ship and we will cleanse the entire site from orbit.'

'Yes, my lord,' said Sarfian.

Matrada shut off the link and opened a channel to his ordnance officer. Yes, this was a disaster, but he would ensure that no one would ever find out about it.

'Lock in co-ordinates and prepare to fire on my order.'

GUARDSMAN HAWKE STUMBLED down the rocky slopes of the mountains, dehydrated, malnourished and suffering from second-degree burns. He'd watched as the enemy had seized the citadel, butchering the last remnants of his regiment, helpless as the battle raged in the darkness. With the citadel's fall, the enemy had pulled back from the valley and left Hydra Cordatus with the same speed and efficiency with which they had arrived.

Never in his whole life had Hawke felt quite so alone. With the departure of the enemy forces, the silence was unnerving. The constant rumble of artillery and explosions was gone, as was the distant screaming of men in battle. Only now, with it absent did Hawke realise how omnipresent it had been.

Not a soul moved on the plain below and he decided that enough was enough. He scavenged a few unspoiled ration packs from the torpedo facility's crew quarters as well as some hydration tablets and, thankfully, some detox pills.

With the battle over, he began the long trek to the valley floor, a skinny shambling wreck, covered in dust and blood. Quite what he intended to do when he got there, he didn't know, but knew that it sure beat staying in the mountains.

It was on his third day's travel, as he rested in the shadow of a tall boulder, that he saw the ship. It roared low along the valley before vanishing to land beyond the smashed walls of the citadel.

Though he knew he was too far away to be heard, he shouted himself hoarse, scrambling downhill at a furious rate. The fact that he was almost a day's journey from the citadel didn't occur to him, and soon he was breathless and exhausted, his head pounding in pain.

When he recovered, he set off once more, filled with fresh determination. He travelled for another five hours across the treacherous terrain of the mountains, when he heard the whine of the ship's engines once more.

Hawke watched the ponderous craft rise up from the distant citadel and angle itself towards the crimson sky.

'Oh, no,' he moaned. 'No, no, no… come back! Come back you bastards! Come back!'

But the crew of the ship ignored his pleading and the craft shot upwards on a burning tail plume. Hawke dropped to his knees as the craft vanished from sight, weeping and cursing its crew.

He was scanning the sky, desperately hoping the ship would return, when the first orbital lance strike lit up the sky with unbearable brightness and streaked through the atmosphere to impact on the citadel.

He sat bolt upright as a massive explosion mushroomed from the citadel, scrambling backwards as a cascade of light fell from the sky, enveloping the citadel in blinding explosions.

Hawke watched, horrified as the barrage continued for another three hours. By the time it was complete, there was nothing left to indicate that the citadel had existed at all.

He slumped onto his side, closing his eyes as the weight of the last few weeks crashed down upon him and he realised he was trapped on Hydra Cordatus. He squeezed shut his eyes and rolled onto his back as exhaustion finally claimed him.

ROUGH HANDS SHOOK him awake and he grunted in pain as he felt himself being dragged to his feet. He tried to open his eyes, but they were gummed with dust. All he could make out were blurred, yellow forms and shouted questions. Shapes either side of him held him upright as an insistent voice nagged at him.

'What...?' he slurred.

'What is your name?' repeated the voice.

'Hawke,' he managed, 'Guardsman Hawke, serial number 25031971, who the hell are you?'

'Sergeant Vermaas of the Imperial Fists strike cruiser *Justitia Fides,*' said a voice in front of him.

He felt hands lifting his dog-tags from beneath his uniform jacket.

Hawke blinked his eyes and turned his head, seeing two giants in yellow power armour either side of him, a third standing before him without his helmet. Even in his exhausted state, Hawke recognised Space Marines and wept in relief when he saw the boxy shape of a Thunderhawk gunship sitting on the plain behind them.

'Where is Captain Eshara?' demanded Vermaas.

'Who?'

'Brother-Captain Alaric Eshara, commander of the Imperial Fists Third Company.'

'Never heard of him,' said Hawke.

Vermaas nodded to the Imperial Fists either side of him and Hawke was marched roughly towards the gunship as the Space Marines boarded ahead of him.

'Where are you taking me?' he asked.

'We're taking you home, soldier,' said Sergeant Vermaas.

Hawke smiled and stepped aboard the Thunderhawk.

ABOUT THE AUTHOR

This regular Inferno! author hails from Scotland
and narrowly escaped a career in surveying to work
for the Overfiend, Andy Chambers, as one of Games
Workshop's Warhammer 40,000 development team,
working on such projects as Codex: Tau and Codex:
Necrons. When not at work, he can often be found
mumbling about home cinema and mucking about
with cables while deafening his flatmates with the
latest addition to his DVD collection.

More Warhammer 40,000 from the Black Library

NIGHTBRINGER
An Ultramarines novel
by Graham McNeill

URIEL HIT THE deck of the alien vessel and rolled aside as the next Ultramarine warrior slammed down behind him. He sprang to his feet and drew his power sword and bolt pistol in one fluid motion.

He thumbed the activation rune on the hilt of his sword and the blade leapt with eldritch fire as a pair of crimson-armoured warriors charged through an oval shaped doorway. Their armour was smooth and gleaming, adorned with glittering blades, and they carried long rifles with jagged bayonets.

'Courage and honour!' screamed Uriel, launching himself at the eldar warriors.

NEWLY PROMOTED *Ultramarines Captain Uriel Ventris is assigned to investigate Pavonis, an Imperial planet plagued by civil disorder and renegade eldar raiders. But nothing is as straightforward as it appears, and wheels are turning within wheels. Uriel and his allies are forced into a deadly race against time to destroy their shadowy enemy – or the whole planet must be sacrificed for the good of humanity.*